S

BROTHER

Obsessed

Devon Hartford

COPYRIGHT NOTICE

Want to get an email when Devon's next book is released and receive a FREE Bonus Story?

Sign up here: **http://eepurl.com/B7crf**

or go to **devonhartford.com**

and **click** the **blue SIGN UP button**

DEDICATION

To Amy Cossio for rocking the Awesome Saucio

STEPBROTHER

Obsessed

REMEMBER THAT HOT OLDER GUY YOU DREAMED OF HOOKING UP WITH IN HIGH SCHOOL, BUT NEVER GOT TO?

NOW YOU CAN.

Skye Albright is starting her senior year. Her biggest focus in life is doing well on the SAT so she can get into a good college.

Her sexy stepbrother Dante Lord is a high school dropout turned world traveler. He hasn't been on U.S. soil since he was 14.

Skye and Dante have never met face to face. That all changes when Dante finally comes home for a surprise visit.

From the moment Skye and Dante meet, the sparks fly. Their mutual attraction is a scorching hot bomb ready to go off. The last thing on their minds is the trouble their attraction will cause for their family.

It doesn't help matters that Skye and Dante are sleeping under the same roof.

When word of Skye and Dante's illicit affair gets out, everything blows up. Skye's life spins out of control. Their parents freak out. But Skye and Dante can't stop themselves. Their mutual desire is too strong.

Friendships will be shattered.

Lives will be ruined.

A family will be broken.

Hearts will be torn apart.

THIS IS A STANDALONE NOVEL. NO CLIFFHANGER!!

WARNING: Due to strong language and sexual situations, this book is intended for mature readers ages 18+

Chapter 1

The summer before my senior year in high school ends with a glorious bang.

Does the banging involve a ridiculously hot swoon-worthy guy, you ask?

Of course it does.

Sadly, most of my summer leading up to the glorious bang is spent studying for the SAT (a.k.a. the Stress.A.T.), not engaged in glorious banging. What a way to spend your summer, right? Tell me about it.

I'll get to the juicy stuff in a second. So hold your panties. I promise, they'll be dropping as quickly as mine did.

See, I only did okay when I took the SAT for the first time at the end of junior year. My dad insisted I take the test early, in case I needed to improve my score by taking it again senior year. I'm one of those students who has to work their butt off to get good grades. I'm also one of those students whose parents expect good grades whether I want to work my butt off or not. My dad is an overbearing ladyball buster. Luckily my stepmom Catarina is more laid back.

I did take Advanced Placement English Language & Composition last year and will take AP English Literature & Comp senior year (English is my best subject), but I'm not even close to being on the math or science fast track. I don't know how those kids do it. Between my decent grades and not so decent SAT score, my college career at an upper tier university is still in question. My dad is none too happy about that. If I don't get into a top ranked school, he will take it as a personal offense to our family name: Albright. Funny, huh? You know how parents always talk about "bright" kids? The smart ones? Yeah, I'm not one of those. I'm more of a street smarts girl.

Why don't they have an SAT subject test for street smarts? I'd ace that.

Anyway, at the beginning of summer, Dad decreed that I would spend it enrolled in an SAT prep course. Yay. Not. He said I could quit the prep course early if I could consistently score 2,000 on the practice tests. 2,000?! Yes, my dad is a tyrant. Never happened. Half way through summer, he hired a math tutor to help out. Was it a sexy stud college guy math tutor? Was *he* my glorious bang? No. My tutor was this 14 year old home-schooled math genius named Marvin who looks 11. No banging involved. Ew. He was nice enough. Maybe a bit too impatient for my tastes. But there's something about having some kid who's way younger than you making you feel sucky at math that is *not* fun. So much for my summer vacation. The good news is I'm pretty confident when I retake the SAT this October, I'll do much better, especially in math. Fingers crossed.

Okay, boring stuff out of the way.

Now that summer is almost over, I'm ready for a study break in a big bad way. I have to beg my dad to let me have the last week of summer vacation to myself. I remind him that even he gets *three* weeks of vacation every year, which is three times more than I'm asking for. Of course, he usually doesn't take any time off. Yes, my dad is a workaholic. But with the help of Catarina, we convince Dad to let me out of SAT jail for a week.

Catarina is awesome, btw. Unlike my real long-gone mom, but that's another story I'd rather not talk about. Sigh.

Okay, perk up! Big smiles!!

Aaaaaand… that leads me back to the glorious bang that happens at the tail end of my summer vacation. And it *totally* involves a smokin' hot guy, not a nerdy math genius.

Ready for some steam?

Here's how the banging starts.

First, picture the hottest surfer stud ever: tall, tan, bleach blond hair, broad muscled shoulders, rippling abs, slim hips.

Second, add tattoos.

Third, imagine yourself in his arms.

Got it?

Okay, go!

His hot body presses against mine in the cool water of the huge wave pool at Blazing Waters, the best water slide park in Los Angeles. My head spins from the most luscious, mind-altering kiss I've ever had. We're still kissing and I never want to stop. His hard muscled arms envelop my waist in a hot embrace. I'm surprised the water isn't boiling and steaming around us from our heat.

Hundreds of people frolic in the aqua blue water surrounding the two of us; laughing, hollering, and having a blast under the bright sun while waiting for the next wave to hit.

I don't notice the crowd.

I only notice him.

He and I may as well be floating in a tropical blue ocean in the middle of a quiet paradise. There is only me, Mother Nature, and...

Him.

The most amazing boy, I mean *man*, I've ever kissed.

I've kissed a few guys in my time. Some cute, some not so cute. But compared to Him, every one of those guys was a boy.

The naked muscles of his hard chest press against my breasts. I'm practically naked in my hot pink bikini. When it comes to bathing suits, I prefer minimalism. I may not have a fitness model body, but it's good enough for a bikini, and I'm proud of it. I work hard to stay in shape.

Speaking of hard, *He* is hard.

He may be wearing board shorts, but with my legs wrapped around his waist, I feel every inch of his personal surfboard pressing against me. His rigid heat throbs and pulsates against my soft and yielding core. I want this man more than I've ever wanted any male of the species ever.

I squeeze my thighs tighter, grinding myself against him.

He responds by thrusting his pelvis against my softness.

It feels so damn good.

Pleasure sizzles up from between my legs.

If it wasn't for the water being up to our chests, I think we'd get arrested for public lewdness.

Nobody around us seems to notice.

So we continue to kiss.

His tongue is forceful and plows through my mouth with hot need. His rigid abs press against my stomach like he can't get enough of me. I can't get enough of Him. His scruffy stubble scrapes against my skin, tingling in a good way. This is how it feels to kiss a *man*. Sure, I've kissed boys. But it was never like this. Never so... *addictive*. I quiver all over as every inch of me flows into this kiss. He is putting everything he has into me too. Every inch. I can feel it. His naked need feeds mine. I am more turned on than I've ever been in my entire life. I'm crazy with lust and I love it.

Because we're in the pool, I can't tell how wet I am. But I know I'm soaked.

"Get a room!!" some random girl yells nearby.

"Can you taste her tonsils?!" a random guy cackles.

"What did she eat for breakfast?!" someone else yells.

Obviously, people are noticing our kiss. Like a bunch of starving dogs, they just *have* to ruin our moment. I can't help it if we have what they don't.

"Pervert!" Yet another jealous jerk.

Screw them. This moment is all mine.

His tongue slides slowly out of my mouth.

Hey, wait! I want his tongue to stay!

"Slut," some girl hisses.

I throw a scowl in her general direction.

People are assholes. I suddenly feel shy. Reluctantly, I end our kiss. But he's still holding me and I'm holding him.

I never want to let go.

Ever.

We touch foreheads.

My arms are wrapped around his strong neck. "Ohhh…" I moan, "That was incredible."

He chuckles confidently with that deep voice of his, "Of course it was."

"You're sure cocky," I giggle.

"You noticed?" He does a slow thrust against my folds that sends another pre-orgasmic wave up my spine.

My eyelids flutter as more pleasure blooms in my belly. Oh, gawd. I can only imagine what it would feel like if he was inside me right now. I release a spasming moan in his ear.

"You like that, don't you?" He massages my ass with powerful hands and grinds against me.

This is too much. I can't take any more. I'm going to come. It doesn't matter if there's a crowd around us. Although my brain says stop, my mouth can only moan, and my body responds to his languid thrusts. My pelvis tips forward, causing my buzzing clit to brush against his rigid length. Another freezing hot wave of pleasure erupts in my belly. "Oh, god," I shiver and whisper, "I'm coming."

"Yeah you are," he grunts.

My entire core clenches hard and my thighs shake around his waist.

"Come for me, babe. Come right now," he hisses, maintaining his rhythmic thrusting.

I obey.

As the orgasm quakes through my body, I bite my lip to stifle my scream. I clamp my eyes shut to block out everything except the hardness of this amazing man and the hammering pleasure that shakes every bone in my body.

I'm breathless as I come down from the sexual high.

"It was good, wasn't it?" He chuckles softly, his lips feathering my ear.

I'm too overwhelmed to respond. All I can do is pant. My arms are limp and float freely in the waving water of the pool. My head tips back, facing the sky.

He holds on, his powerful arms now wrapped loosely around my waist.

The bright sun glows red through my closed eyes, warming my face. "Oh my god," I whisper, "That was… that was—"

"The best orgasm you've ever had," he states with finality.

Yes. But I'm not telling him that. Eyes still closed, I repress a grin. "You're so full of yourself," I giggle.

"I'm full of something," he snickers.

Yeah, way too cocky for his own good.

I laugh and push away from him, floating into deeper water. "I hope you like blue balls, cause that's all you're getting from me."

He shakes his head, grinning that killer dimpled grin of his. The grin that slayed me the second I saw it earlier today. He knows he's hot.

I met this guy only a few hours ago. I shouldn't be this into him already. But I am.

He strokes toward me through the water like a hungry shark. He smirks, "If we weren't in a crowded wave pool, I'd be inside you right now and you know it."

"You wish," I laugh and splash water in his face. He's right. He is *totally* right.

He surges toward me and laces his arms around my waist, pulling me into him.

I let him. Then I slide my arms around his neck. I don't wrap my legs around him because I'm afraid of what I'll do when I feel his cock press into me again. *Oh, shiver…*

Looking for a distraction, I push his longish surfer-blond hair out of his eyes. It's thick and I love running my fingers through it. I keep using the word love a lot. I can't help it.

More importantly, now that we've kissed and he made me come, I feel like I should at least know his real name. When we exchanged names earlier in the day, I said my name was Angelina and he said his was Brad. We both knew we were giving each other fake names. It was a fun joke. I sigh, "Hey, um, can I ask you a question?"

"Anything, Angelina." He winks and grins his rakish grin. His emerald eyes flash back the sun rays that reflect off the water.

I wrinkle my nose and giggle girlishly, "Is your name really Brad?"

"What do you think, *Angelina*?" He winks.

"Duh." I roll my eyes and caress the bronze skin of his cheek. "So, um, *Brad*, what's your *real* name?"

His full lips spread over his perfect teeth. His smile glows, "Dante.

My name's Dante."

Sudden anxiety seizes me and pops the balloon of happy contentment that was floating in my chest a second ago. It has to be a coincidence. Lots of guys are named Dante.

"What?" he asks, slightly confused.

"Um, it's just…" I wrinkle my nose and shake my head for a second, then tilt it to the side. I frown, "What's your last name?"

"Does it matter?" he chuckles.

"Please," I beg, "just tell me your last name."

He frowns, "Are you gonna tell me to put a ring on it next?" He sounds defensive.

I feel a pin prick of disappointment when he says that. We all know that men like Brad, a.k.a. Dante, do not like to be tied down. But I'm not even thinking that far ahead. "No, it's not that. Believe me. But please, tell me your last name."

"Lord. My name is Dante Lord."

My heart stops, stabbed by a million pins all at once. My arms wither and slide off his neck.

He releases me. It's symbolic, but he doesn't realize it yet.

I drift away from him in the cold water. Now would be a good time to drown. All I have to do is let myself sink and let fate take me.

"What's wrong?" he laughs nervously. "Do we know each other or something?"

We don't know each other. But that's not the problem here. I'm afraid we have a *much* bigger issue. Tears well in my eyes. I want to sob, but not here, not surrounded by a crowd of people playing in a gigantic wave pool.

"Have we hooked up before?" he asks guiltily.

"Ugh," I groan, disgusted. Don't people usually remember things like that?

His face softens. His voice becomes delicate, "Hey, I have no idea what's going on here. Are you okay?" He clasps my hand gently under the water. The concern on his face spears my heart.

I've never seen a teenage boy look at me like Dante is looking at me right now. Like he actually cares. It seems like every guy I ever hooked up with always had the same look on their faces: Do we get to have sex this time? I got really tired of that look. Dante's look is entirely different. It's filled with compassion and caring. It's the look of love.

But it's the wrong kind of love.

The love on his face right now is a cruel hoax. A scam. A trick.

Part of me doesn't want to believe it. That part is holding on to hope like a life preserver. I want to believe that Dante and I have a chance, that there are other Dante Lords in the world besides this one. I have to make sure. In a weak voice I ask, "Is your mom's name Catarina?"

He frowns, "How do you know my mom's name?"

"No, no, no…" I mutter. Why me? Why now? Why like this?

"Hey," Dante says softly, "what's wrong? You look all messed up. Tell me what's bothering you. Please." He sounds so earnest. So loving.

This. Is. Killing me.

I'm about to lose it and start bawling, right in the crowded wave pool at Blazing Waters. I sniffle, "I'm your stepsister, Skye Albright."

"Skye who?"

"Skye Albright."

"Nice name. But I've never heard it before. I'd remember a name like that."

Dante has been estranged from his mom Catarina, my stepmom, since he moved to Baja California to live with his dad at age 14. According to Catarina, she and Dante had a huge falling out and haven't spoken since. That was seven years ago. Dante doesn't know the first thing about me, not even my name.

Dante frowns. "What? No way."

"Yes. Your mom married my dad this past June."

Dante's eyes volleyball in their sockets. "My mom got married?"

"To my dad."

"And you're my stepsister?"

I nod morosely.

His brows knit with dark humor. "No way. You're totally bullshitting me, right?" Hope shines in his emerald eyes. He doesn't want to believe it's true.

That breaks my heart more than anything else. "Is your mom Catarina a real estate agent?"

"What the…" His eyes pop. "No way. No fucking way! How did you know?"

My stomach knots. "Because I'm your stepsister."

"Really?" His disappointment is obvious.

"Yeah," I sigh.

His face sags with sadness. "I'm so sorry," he says softly.

Me too.

Between his gorgeous good looks, his cocky sense of humor, his arrogant attitude, and his surprise compassionate side, my stepbrother is the grandest prize among men that a woman could ever hope to catch. I've never met a boy or a guy or a man like him, and I don't know if I ever will again. I may still be in high school, but seriously, when you know, you know. Your heart never lies, and the truth is, my stepbrother is the most desirable man on the planet.

And he's totally off limits.

The artificial wave machine clunks and makes a fake wave that kicks out across the huge pool. The people closest to it cheer and scream with glee while my heart sinks.

When the wave reaches me, it slams into me and tears me away from Dante, knocking me underwater. I don't bother to fight it. The blue doom washes over me like a cold suffocating blanket. I let it overtake me because I suddenly feel dead inside.

I hope I drown.

After tumbling under the wave for awhile, and despite my morbid desire, my head bobs up above the surface, and the last thing I hear is Dante shouting:

"Skye!" Panic and concern strain his voice.

I may be ready to give up, but with that one word, that one syllable that is my name, I know that Dante Lord is going to fight for me, no matter what happens.

I just hope I can be as strong as him...

oOoOoOo + O+O+O+O

Okay, okay.

Right now, you're all asking yourselves, "How the heck can you NOT know he's your stepbrother?" Some of you are saying, "How dumb are you, Skye Albright?"

I'm no genius, but I'm not dumb.

It all makes sense. I promise.

Before our kiss at Blazing Waters, Dante and I had never met face to face. Well, not before that morning. I'll get to our first meeting in a moment.

Here's the deal. Catarina rarely talks about Dante. When she does, she always cries. And the oldest pictures I've seen of Dante were from when he was a skinny 14 year-old skater punk with a spiky dyed-black mohawk. In my mind, that's Dante Lord. He doesn't have wavy beach blond hair or five day's worth of facial hair. Nor does he have flames tattooed on both forearms. Or muscles. *Lots* of muscles.

Little Dante Lord is not the model of manhood I kissed today.

On top of that, he never told anyone he was coming to town. His visit was a total surprise for everyone. How was I supposed to know that the tan man I was all over at Blazing Waters was the boy in the photos?

I wasn't.

As for him not recognizing me, Dante didn't know I existed.

So we didn't recognize each other. It's that simple. Maybe if we had, things would've played out differently. But they didn't. They only got worse.

You know what they say: You can't decide who you fall in love with. Your heart decides for you. No matter how much of a mess it makes.

So, how did Dante and I go from zero to kissing without exchanging our real names?

It all started that morning, long before the kiss in the wave pool.

oOoOoOo + O+O+O+O

FIVE HOURS BEFORE THE KISS

My best friend Roxanne Slaughter and I are standing in line at 7-Eleven, waiting to pay for our stuff. I'm holding my breakfast: a bottle of chilled water and a bag of Peanut Butter M&Ms. Roxanne is holding a steaming cup of coffee and a doughnut.

I ask, "Don't you think it's a bit hot for coffee?"

"I run cool," she says seriously.

We both have flip-flops on our feet and are wearing bikinis under our T-shirts and shorts. She doesn't look cold to me.

"It's not like you're a reptile," I say sarcastically. "And it's already like eighty five degrees outside and it's not even nine a.m." Me and Rox live in The Valley, as in, The San Fernando Valley, and it's summer and it's going to be super hot today. It was 95 yesterday and it's supposed to be hotter today. I smirk, "Do you realize you're perspiring?" I reach out to touch the beads of sweat on her forehead.

She waves my hand away and backs up. "I want coffee. Shut it."

"Shouldn't you be getting an iced coffee or something?"

"An iced coffee would totally give me hypothermia," she growls impatiently.

"You might get heat stroke drinking all that hot coffee," I joke.

She glares at me, "I am not hot, okay?"

"How about coffee ice cream?" Now I'm just pestering her for fun. We've known each other since second grade, so this is usual for us. "Or a coffee Slurpee?"

She rolls her eyes, "They don't even make coffee Slurpees. And coffee ice cream has like zero caffeine."

"You need to seriously consider a twelve-step program. Caffeine is highly addictive."

"I'm not *addicted* to caffeine, Skye."

I snicker, "That's what addicts always say. You know the community center across from the library hosts twelve step meetings all the time. You should totally check them out."

She glares at me, "They don't have twelve steps for caffeine addicts."

"I'm pretty sure they do," I tease.

She opens her mouth to respond but shuts it just as quick. Her eyes flash and she whispers, "Hottie alert!"

I hear the door chime as someone comes into the 7-Eleven. At the moment, my back is to the door. Rox and I are both totally boy crazy, so I turn to look.

She yanks my wrist and hisses, "Don't look! He'll see!"

I hiss back, "Then why did you call hottie alert if you don't want me to look?"

"Wait till he's not looking right at you." Her eyes follow the mystery man behind me. "God damn it, he's hot," she moans.

Now I really want to look.

Rox yanks my arm again. A few seconds later, she mutters, "Okay, it's safe to look."

I turn slightly and glance over my shoulder. The first thing I see are the aisles bristling with candy, potato chips, pretzels, and sundry junk food. Past all of that, standing in front of the wall of refrigerators, I spot the towering broad shoulders and shaggy hair of the hottest guy I've ever seen in my life.

I am not exaggerating.

Wow.

It's like this guy sucked all the beauty out of the room when he walked in. He inhaled all of it in a three mile radius. Wherever he goes, he is the hottest thing there. The sun doesn't stand a chance against this guy.

In other words, he is miraculously hot. It's the only way I can describe him. Yes, I notice specific details like his perfect nose, lush lips, perfectly manly beard stubble, and his longish surf-blond hair. I have a thing for surfers, it's one of the reasons I'm applying to San Diego University, a.k.a SDU, which is walking distance from the beach. SDU isn't my dad's first choice, but he can suck it. Luckily, there's no way I'll get into USC or UCLA like he hopes.

Back to Mr. Miracle.

I can't see Mr. Miracle's eyes because they're hidden by black wraparound shades, but the shape of his cheek bones and his jaw are just... perfect.

To make matters worse, or should I say more perfect, Mr. Miracle is wearing a worn out leather motorcycle jacket. Wanna bet he has tattoos under that jacket? And, did you know it's a federal law that a guy as hot as him has to ride a motorcycle? I have no doubt he has his federally mandated motorcycle parked outside. I wouldn't be surprised if there's an entire gang of bikers waiting for him, like he's their king or leader or whatever.

With chins hanging against our chests, Roxanne and I gawk in awe as Mr. Miracle opens one of the fridge doors and pulls out a sixer of Heineken. Rox and I both openly stare, but the second he turns toward the register, we spin our backs to him. Not that I want to. Somehow, it makes me anxious to *not* look at him. Not because I'm afraid or anything, but because I just *have* to look at him.

Boots clack the linoleum behind us as Mr. Miracle gets in line. I literally feel his presence wash over me as he closes the distance. It's that sixth sense thing where you know someone is behind you, but in a good way and on steroids. My entire back vibrates. My body screams at me to turn around and throw myself at Mr. Miracle.

Roxanne starts to snicker like an imbecile.

Without a thought, I slap her stomach with the back of my hand.

She snickers more.

My cheeks burn with embarrassment. He *must* know Rox is snickering about him. Hot guys always do. I desperately want to turn around and apologize for our bad behavior. But I can't. Because I know if I do, I will make an ass of myself. Not that it matters. Guys this hot don't notice girls like me. They usually hang around Victoria's Secret photo shoots. You know the ones: the "Angels" photo shoots where every girl in it is a Perfect Eleven? Yeah, those women. That's who a guy like Mr. Miracle goes for. Don't get me wrong. I'm no troll, but Mr. Miracle is in a league of his own.

"Next!" the uniformed clerk says from behind the register. He looks bored. Obviously, he isn't gay, or he would be drooling at the sight of Mr. Miracle like we are. He arches his jungle-thick unibrow at us.

Neither Rox nor I can move or speak.

"Next," the clerk asks impatiently.

We still can't move.

"Ladies?" It's Mr. Miracle. His voice is music. It should win a Grammy for best male voice ever. It is low and gravelly and more manly than Superman. Or Bigfoot. Or if Superman and Bigfoot had a love child. I don't know. But I can literally feel that one word—*Ladies?*

—hum through my body, hypnotizing every inch of me with poetry and passion.

I am frozen in place.

I swear, this has never happened to me before. Yes, I've gone guy crazy a million times in the past. But I've never lost the ability to control my own limbs.

I. Can't. Move.

Neither can Rox, apparently.

The clerk glances between me and Mr. Miracle. Then he glares at me. "If you aren't going to pay, you need to get out of the line. Other customers are waiting."

"Uhh…"

Suddenly I'm flung forward because Roxanne shoved me into the counter. My water bottle skids across the top and clatters to the floor behind it, along with my bag of Peanut Butter M&Ms.

The clerk sighs like I'm an idiot while he bends down to pick up my food.

Not only does he have that over-pronounced unibrow that no caveman would be caught dead with, but he also has one of those curly hipster mustaches, which makes him an idiot, so I don't feel so bad. But I'm still totally embarrassed.

Roxanne nervously sets her coffee and doughnut down next to my stuff.

The clerk rings in everything.

Rox pulls her debit card out of her wallet and pays.

I don't know how she can remember how to use her fingers to punch in her password when I can't remember how to bend my knees or lift my feet off the ground to walk. Can you blame me? I'm still trapped in the cocoon of sweet confusion caused by Mr. Miracle. I don't *want* to move. I want to be as near to Mr. Miracle as I can. That's all that matters to me in this moment.

Is that weird?

It doesn't feel weird.

It feels entirely and unequivocally (that's an SAT word I learned the other day)… right. Like this feeling is more important than a high score on the SATs or getting a 3.75 GPA (as if). Right now, all I need is this man. I imagine that if he were to look me in the eyes and smile at *me*, then my life would be complete. It's stupid, but at the moment it makes perfect sense.

And yet, I can't turn around to look. I'm a swooning statue.

The clerk hands a receipt to Rox.

She fumbles with her wallet. "Take your stuff," she barks at me. "I can't carry everything." She jams the cold water bottle into my stomach.

That breaks the spell. The bottle bobbles in my fingers and I almost drop it on the floor when Rox hip bumps me toward the front door. I lunge for my M&Ms and swipe them off the counter. Can't start my day without breakfast.

Rox grabs my elbow and leads me out, causing me to drop my M&Ms. I lean down to pick them up and nearly trip all over myself.

We're such an embarrassment.

I can't imagine what Mr. Miracle is thinking, and I can't get out of here soon enough.

The door chimes as we push outside into the heat.

"That was humiliating," Rox groans as she strides up to the driver door of her mom's old Toyota.

"You think?" I bark. "You made me fall all over myself like a total spaz!"

She rolls her eyes. "Get in. Let's go before he sees us."

"Wait, I…" I don't know what, but I'm not ready to leave. I stop and look around.

A somewhat old racing motorcycle is parked two spaces over from Rox's Toyota. Told ya. It's the only other vehicle in the parking lot. It's definitely Mr. Miracle's. No motorcycle gang waiting for him, but with his rough and ready good looks and leather jacket, he's more than enough man for ten women.

"Come on, Skye. We can't hang around after that. We look like idiots."

Roxanne isn't normally this anxious about guys. We've made fools of ourselves in front of guys plenty of times. We have a blast at the mall stalking cute older guys from store to store. Then again, the guys at the mall are never this hot. And we never look this foolish.

"Skye! Let's go!!"

My mind is still too jumbled to make a coherent argument about why we should stay. All I can manage to mumble is, "But…"

"Skye!!"

I glance back at the doors of the 7-Eleven. With all the bright sunlight reflecting off the glass, I can't see inside. For whatever reason, every fiber of my being is telling me I *have* to have one last look at Mr. Miracle before we go. Even though I'll probably never see him again, something deep in my body is pulling me toward him. I can't help myself.

"Get in the car already!" Roxanne barks. She leans over in her seat and flicks the passenger door open. "Skye!"

Her anger is making me angry. I almost blurt, "What's your deal, dude?" But instead I whine, "I can't!"

I don't know why seeing Mr. Miracle one last time is such a big deal, but it is. I turn and take a step toward 7-Eleven. I don't know what I'm going to do. I don't know if I'm going to do anything. Maybe I'll just stare openly at him when he walks outside and hope he stops to talk. Or not. Maybe he'll ignore me and climb on his black motorcycle and ride off into the sunset. Either way, I can't leave without finding out. If Rox and I go now, I'll never forgive myself.

"Skye! I'm going!" Rox closes the driver door and starts the Toyota's engine. She wouldn't leave me here, would she?

Panic sets in.

At the same moment, the 7-Eleven door chimes for the third time this morning.

I whip around to face the double doors.

Mr. Miracle walks out and straight over to his motorcycle.

Damn. He didn't even notice me. He probably thought Rox and I were a bunch of clumsy kids. Not the women he's used to. The Perfect Elevens, which I'm totally not.

Sigh.

Wait a second.

He isn't riding off into the sunset.

Hope soothes my sense of defeat.

There's a backpack tied down to the back of his bike with a little red net. The backpack looks like the traveling kind, not a school knapsack.

Mr. Miracle busies himself unstrapping the net and the backpack. Then he starts stuffing cans of Heineken into the pack. The first four cans go in easy. The last two won't fit. It's obvious there's no more room in the already bulging backpack. Frustrated, he glances around, noticing me and Roxanne. He considers us for a moment.

Heat waves shimmer up from the asphalt between us. Or maybe they're coming off my body. I can't tell for sure. But it sure is hot. I mean, I went past simmering and came to a boil the moment I laid eyes on Mr. Miracle inside the store. Now it's worse. I'm dying in my T-shirt and shorts. Something inside me tells me this would be a good time for me to strip down to my pink bikini. No reason. Just cause it's hot.

It would also be a good time for Mr. Miracle to pull off his leather jacket. And everything else.

No reason. Just cause *he's* hot.

None of that happens.

Instead, Mr. Miracle heaves a sigh and looks at the two extra beer cans he's holding. He looks up and grins at me, flashing the most perfect teeth I've ever seen. His wide mouth is sumptuous and delectably—two more of my SAT vocab words—kissable.

He holds up a can of beer and says, "Want one?"

Is he talking to me? He can't be talking to me.

He arches an eyebrow over the frames of his black shades. It's the most perfect sculpted eyebrow I've ever seen, and it doesn't even look tweezed. Just ruggedly perfect and swoon-worthy in every way possible.

He motions with the beer can.

I still can't see his eyes through his shades, but my heart is hammering. I choke out the words, "Um... I'm only 18."

He grins, "So?"

"You know the legal drinking age is twenty-one, right?" I hate to be the adult here, but I should at least point it out.

"In the Netherlands the legal drinking age is zero."

"No it's not," I blurt.

"Have you ever been there?" he smirks confidently.

"No."

"Then how do you know?"

I don't know one way or the other. I hate to look ignorant, so I smirk, "Last time I checked, this is the U.S. Won't you get in trouble for giving alcohol to a minor?"

"Do you want the beer or not?"

Roxanne says, "I'll take it." Somehow she snuck up beside me without me noticing. I guess she's not in a hurry to leave all of a sudden?

He tosses it toward her.

Roxanne catches it and grins, "Thanks." Roxanne has always been more of a risk taker than me.

"*De nada.*" He smiles at me. "Here, you take one." Before I can object, he tosses the beer at me.

Surprised, I drop my water bottle and Peanut Butter M&Ms, which are probably mush by now, and grab for the beer like a first class spaz. I almost drop the can, but manage to hold on, preventing a frothy beer suds explosion.

"Easy," he chuckles.

Now I feel stupid. I squat down and pick up my water and M&Ms. I'm not normally this much of a spaz. I was on JV Volleyball until my dad made me load up on AP classes junior year. He also expected me to keep my grades up. Between that and never getting the growth spurt I was hoping for, I quit the team. Anyway, I have good hands and I'm not a spaz. So I blame Mr. Miracle for throwing me off my game today.

"You guys wanna help me drink them?" Mr. Miracle asks casually.

"Here?" I snap.

"Naw. Some place nice. Are there any good parks around here? Or maybe some trails? Some place with a good view where we can relax?"

Why does it sound like he's trying to get us alone and get us drunk so he can molest us? Not that I would mind. But a six pack isn't going to get all of us stupid drunk. Rox and I are both good for two beers without losing our good sense. And Mr. Miracle is way too hot to be a molester, but this still seems weird.

I glance at Rox for support.

She's looking all over the place. She does that when she's nervous.

I don't know what to do.

Sure, I'm tempted to jump into Mr. Miracle's arms and tell him he can take me anywhere he wants, do anything with me he can dream of (as long as it involves orgasms and not murder), thereby fulfilling my wildest teenage dreams. But I'm also very aware that Roxanne is with me, which nixes the wildest dreams part. I'm not into three-ways, at least I think I'm not. And let's be real. I don't know this guy. He just offered beer to a couple of high school girls.

That's bad, right?

No matter how hot the guy is?

Especially if somehow the cops get involved. That never looks good on your college transcript. Did I mention that I've been dreaming of going to SDU when I graduate, for like, ever? I really don't want to screw up my chances of getting in by doing something stupid.

A wicked smile lights up Rox's face, "I have an idea!" She always does. "Do you want to go to Blazing Waters with us? Over in San Dimas? It's a water slide park."

Mr. Miracle grins, "What... now?"

"Yeah." Roxanne tends to take the reins when it comes to adventuring. "Do you have a swimsuit?"

He nods. "In my bag."

"You can follow us there."

His cheek dimples, "I could do a water park."

He could do me, I think but don't say.

"Really?" Roxanne beams.

"Yeah." He straps his backpack to his motorcycle with the red net.

"You want to follow us?" Rox suggests, already climbing back into the Toyota. She isn't wasting any time.

Mr. Miracle swings a leg over his seat. "Yeah."

My heart is jumping all over the place as Rox drives the Toyota out of the parking lot. All I can think about is what lies beneath Mr.

Miracle's clothes.

I'm going to see him in his bathing suit.

The inside of my thighs are literally quivering with anticipation.

Why, you ask?

HALF-NAKED HOT MANSICLE!!!!

Duh.

oOoOoOo + O+O+O+O

"OMG, Skye! Biker Boy is way too hot for his own good," Roxanne marvels. "I'm having heart palpitations." She squeezes her hand to her chest and giggles.

"I call dibs!" I bark as we drive away from 7-Eleven. I watch Mr. Miracle in the side mirror. He's following behind on his motorcycle.

"No way!" Rox shouts. "I saw him first!"

"No you didn't!"

"Did too! When he walked into 7-Eleven! You were lecturing me about my caffeine addiction or some nonsense. He is *so* mine!"

Roxanne and I have never had a serious fight over a boy before. But this is a man. And there's a first time for everything. I just hope it isn't today. Rox seems really into him.

I sigh, "Rox, there's no way I'm letting a guy come between us. If you really want him, he's yours." I can't believe I'm saying it, but when the words come out of my mouth, I know I mean them.

I think.

"You mean that?" she asks shrewdly.

"Of course. Guys like him are everywhere."

She grins, "You are such a liar. Guys like him are nowhere. They don't exist."

I laugh, "Then can I have him?"

She chuckles, "You do want him, don't you?"

I sigh heavily. "Who wouldn't."

"Thought so. I have an idea," she says, eyes on the road.

"When don't you?" I giggle.

"That's why you love me. Cause I'm so much fun."

"So, what's your idea?"

"How about we let him pick."

"What do you mean?"

"We both know we're going to be flirting with him like crazy at the water park all day, right?"

"Yeah," I grin. Although we're both notorious flirts, usually the flirting is just for fun. This feels like it's for real.

She drums her fingers on the steering wheel. "The rule is, neither of us makes a move. Let him make the first move. Whoever he goes for first gets him."

"What if he doesn't make any moves?"

"Oh, he will. He already gave us these beers and invited us to go someplace secluded. This guy is a total player."

"What if he wants a threesome?" I gasp.

"What if he does?" she giggles.

"Rox!"

She laughs. "I'd totally toss your salad, Skye."

"ROX!!!" This is news to me. We've never dabbled in diddling each other, but we *are* BFSFs. Best Friends Since Forever. Who am I kidding? I barely have any experience with *guys*. I'm not jumping into a threesome with my bestie. It sounds WAY too complicated.

"Okay, no menage-a-twat," she snickers. "Whoever he goes after first gets him. Can you handle that?"

"I can if you can." I say confidently. I don't feel confident, but I play confident on TV. JK.

"I know it's going to be hard for you to keep your hands off him, but I promise I won't do anything if you won't. Deal?"

I glance over at my best friend.

A thick spray of dark curls spills out of her ponytail. When her hair is down, it's this living thing with a mind of its own that guys love. They also love her delicate features and flawless skin. I don't know how the hell she never has any zits, but she doesn't. And her blue eyes are incredible. They're so blue they are *actually* blue. Not muted, not pastel, but sky blue. I've never seen anyone with eyes like hers. You'd think with a name like Skye, I'd be the one with the sky blue eyes, but somehow Rox got them. Mine are just gray. Maybe we were switched at birth. I don't know. Also, my hair is nowhere near as luxurious as hers. Right now it's in a boring ponytail. My blonde hair is only shoulder length because it's very fine, so it doesn't grow much longer without breaking. I do have a wispy shag cut with long bangs, which looks good on me, but it doesn't scream SEX!!! like Rox's hair. Plus, mine takes way more work than hers if I want to wear it down.

Anyway, between her looks, her outgoing personality and her body —it's a work of art, believe me—she's the shoe-in with Mr. Miracle. I'm not ugly by any stretch, but if you were to put Roxanne and me head to head in a beauty contest, I think most guys would prefer her. In a wet T-shirt contest, she would win every time. I've seen her boobs. She will never need to get implants. Me on the other hand...you never know.

I sigh and gaze out the front window at the sun drenched foothills to the north. Twin Peaks and Mount Baldy are up there somewhere. Twin Peaks is also sitting right next to me. Groan. And Mount Baldy, because one time Rox gave herself a Brazilian wax job, but that's a whole nother story.

"What?" Rox asks thoughtfully.

"Nothing," I lie and sigh. "We could turn around and go home, you know."

She cocks her head, "Do you really want to do that? Don't you want to find out if he's into you?"

"What if he's into *you*?"

"Only one way to know for sure," she says with a huge smile on her face.

The one thing I know for sure is, if he's *not* into Rox, she'll be onto the next guy before the sun goes down. With any luck, she'll find some hot guy at Blazing Waters first thing, then she'll wander off with him. Here's to luck.

"Remember," I smile back half-heartedly, "no matter who he picks, no hate from the other person." I feel like I'm saying it to remind myself more than anything.

"That's totally fine because he's going to pick me," she giggles. "So don't be jealous." She giggles again, a bit more nervously than before. "Neither of us makes the first move, right?"

"Pinky swear?" I hold up my finger.

She hooks hers around mine. "Pinky swear," she says with finality.

As we drive east along the 210 freeway toward San Dimas and Blazing Waters, I feel electric anticipation crackling between us. Rox and I have had some squabbles over the years. No friendship is perfect. Luckily, our problems were never anything we couldn't get over, even when it involved boy drama. I would never want to lose my best friend over a stupid guy.

Roxanne is way too important to me.

But Mr. Miracle is hot in a way that literally makes me crazy.

Maybe this was a bad idea...

Chapter 2

"Do you mind if I leave my stuff in your trunk?" Mr. Miracle asks after we park in the crowded lot at Blazing Waters.

He can leave anything of his anywhere he wants, but this is Roxanne's mom's car, so it's her call.

"Sure," Roxanne says, opening the trunk.

Mr. Miracle unstraps his backpack from his dusty black motorcycle and sets it in the trunk.

I like the idea of Mr. Miracle leaving his stuff with us. It connects him to us. I don't want him getting away. No matter who he picks. Especially if it's me.

He removes his shades and takes off his helmet, which he sets next to his bag. He runs his hand through his golden hair, pushing it out of his face.

Oh my glob.

His eyes are literally sparkling like gemstones. Maybe it's the bright California sun, but I swear, if his emerald green eyes were set into gold bands, they'd make a fab pair of wedding rings.

Did I say wedding?

I'm getting way ahead of myself.

Or not.

Because Mr. Miracle is grinning at me like he's the bashful one. Does this mean he's picking me? I steal a glance at Rox, partially because that grin of his is making me squirm, and partially because I want to see what Rox is thinking.

She's watching his eyes closely and chewing her lower lip hungrily.

My eyes are magnetically pulled back to Mr. Miracle as he stretches out of his leather jacket. The material of his T-shirt stretches over his muscles and lifts to give a glimpse of his rippled and tan stomach. The lines of his abs angle toward his jeans.

Is he wearing underwear? I'm going with no, because I can see happy trail.

Rox and I are both transfixed. It's like a striptease and he's not even undressing.

He drops his jacket in the trunk. His tight T-shirt hugs his built body. Broad shoulders. Defined chest. Muscled arms. Both forearms are covered in tattooed flames that climb up to his elbows.

Wow.

"Gotta get my swimsuit," Mr. Miracle says and leans into the trunk to fish through his bag. The flames on his forearms flicker as his fingers work through his backpack. His shirt inches up his sculpted back, which is defined with hard muscles. A minute later, he tugs out board shorts. "You mind if I change now?"

"Yes," I moan, not even sure what I'm saying. I'm fully prepared to answer every question he asks me with "Yes, yes," and more "Yes!" You know what I mean.

His brows knit together.

"She means no," Roxanne adds.

He grins and nods. Without a second thought, he peels his T-shirt over his head.

Oh. My. Abs.

All eight of them writhe.

I am hypnotized.

Rox grabs my wrist and squeezes it.

Yeah, we're both freaking out.

Normally, Rox and I would take off our shirts and shorts and drop them into the trunk before going into the park without a second thought. But I suddenly feel nervous about doing it in front of The Bod God.

The Bod God, a.k.a. Mr. Miracle, a.k.a. Every Woman's Flesh Fantasy, tosses his T-shirt on top of his bag in the trunk.

I want to lunge for that shirt, bunch it up in my face, and inhale deeply. I want to take it home and stuff it in my pillow and cuddle with it every night from here until eternity.

From the look on Rox's face, she's thinking the same thing.

The Bod God sits on the back bumper of the Toyota and slides his boots off. Then his socks.

Gawd, even his tan feet are sexy.

I'm about to pass out.

He stands up and reaches down to unbutton his jeans.

CLANK! BONG!

That's the sound of my and Rox's jaws hitting the ground.

The Bod God narrows his eyes. It is the sexiest look I've ever seen on a male member—I said *member*... giggle—of the species. His face makes that cocky dimple again. *Cock!*

I am melting.

I think Rox is having a stroke.

"Aren't you guys gonna change?" The Bod God asks.

Rox and I respond by drooling.

"I'll change over here," he says with a hint of bashfulness. He grabs his board shorts out of the trunk and walks around the side of the Toyota. Although there's a big SUV parked next to it, and more cars all around, it's not exactly a changing room at Target. Privacy is an afterthought.

Rox and I stare at each other.

I glance around the parking lot. Thousands of cars glint diamonds of sunlight in every direction. People walk from their cars toward the main entrance. Fortunately, no one notices us.

But we are wide out in the open.

"You can't change out here!" I bark, leaning around Rox's Toyota. "Everyone will see you!"

He smirks, "You gonna stop me?" His pants are now officially unbuttoned and he's about to push them down his thighs.

"Uh..." Gulp!

He arches an eyebrow. "Better stop me before I'm totally naked. People might freak out," he quips.

I'm too stunned to do anything.

He teases his jeans down an inch.

Root! I can see root! Oh, holy hand job—I mean, I don't know what I mean!

I glance around frantically. He can NOT be pulling his pants off in the middle of a crowded parking lot! There are kids around! This is wrong! And yet so unbelievably right. I know, because Rox is hovering behind me, trying to get a better look, breathing heavily against the back of my neck.

He grins, "Are you both gonna stand there and watch, or is one of you gonna help?"

We are both speechless and paralyzed with naked desire.

He chuckles, "Fine, I'll do it myself."

I can't take it. I forcefully spin myself and Rox around so our backs are to The Bod God.

"You're missing out," he quips.

Wow, could he be any more cocky? I hear his jeans flapping as he kicks them off.

Something overtakes me. The overwhelming desire to peek. I can't help it. In order to peek, I need to twist my head and neck around to get a good view. So I twist. I twist with purpose, I twist with conviction, I twist with everything I've got. Now I can peek.

Flexing arms. Oh, those arms. A naked knee rises in the air and steps into the board shorts. The knee descends and—

COCK!

I see it!

Just the profile, but I! SEE! IT!

IT!!!!!

And it's beautiful. And yes, he's even more cocky than I ever would've guessed.

When he lifts his other knee, his manhood shifts and turns in my direction.

FULL FRONTAL!!!!!

My breath catches in my throat. I'm choking on oxygen. My eyes attempt to jump out of my skull to get a better view.

But in a flash, it's gone, covered by swim trunks. He bends over to pick up his jeans. Any second, he's going to look up and see us staring.

The only problem is that Rox and I have both twisted around so far to blatantly voyeurize The Bod God, we're both off balance. When I lurch forward, trying to straighten up, I bump right into Rox. She makes a choked "GLURP!" sound and I nearly knock her over. Somehow, we manage to regain our balance, but not without stumbling over each other like circus clowns.

The Bod God snickers behind us.

I want to shout, "WE DIDN'T SEE ANYTHING!!" But that would be a dead giveaway. The only thing I can think to do to hide my guilt is tear my T-shirt over my head like I was changing the whole time. Not peeping.

Rox follows suit, hastily unbuttoning her shorts.

The Bod God swaggers around the Toyota and sets his folded jeans on top of his backpack. "Enjoy the show?" he says casually without looking at us.

Rox and I bust into a giggle fit. We try to hide it by making a big production of stripping down to our swim suits. It doesn't work.

I toss my T-shirt into the trunk and it lands in a heap, hanging half off The Bod God's jeans.

Rox shoots me a goofy dagger look.

I didn't mean to do that! I'm not laying claim to his jeans or anything else!

She steps out of her flip flops and pushes her shorts off. While staring at me, she picks up my T-shirt and cattily tosses it into the corner of the trunk where it lands in a tangled heap. Then she sets her shorts on top of his jeans. Her lips curl into a fleeting snarl.

She's mad.

I don't blame her.

We both saw The Bod God's rod.

It's only natural for us to fight over him.

I glance at the man of the hour. His muscled arms are folded across his chest and he's watching us with amusement.

If Rox and I suddenly decide to claw each other's eyes out, I hope he'll intervene and save us from ourselves.

Who am I kidding? I can't fight with Rox. I step out of my own shorts and set them on the far side of the trunk, as far from The Bod God's bag and jeans as possible. Truce.

Rox makes a pouty face, but she peels her T-shirt off and sets it with my shorts as an apology.

I breathe a sigh of relief.

Her shoulders slump and she sighs too before closing the trunk of the car. It thunks shut.

Now it's me in my electric pink bikini and Rox in her white one. The Bod God's eyes flash and his face shines with naked admiration. If he was less hot, the look would be pervy. On him, with his billion dollar body and trillion dollar smile, the look is priceless.

I just hope he's admiring me as much as Rox. Well, maybe one percent more. But only one percent.

"We ready?" he asks casually.

"Yeah," Rox mutters nervously.

I can't speak.

"Let's go get wet," The Bod God winks and grins.

I already am.

oOoOoOo + O+O+O+O

The three of us walk toward the main entrance and the ticket booths. The booths are little grass huts. Colorful surfboards hang everywhere or stick out of the ground. A ton of people are in line, so we have to wait.

I can't stop thinking about The Bod God's Rod.

Can you blame me?

Of course not.

I'm gonna have a really hard—HARD!!—time not making a move on Mr. Miracle once we get inside Blazing Waters. But I can't. I pinky swore with Rox. She would never forgive me and I would never forgive me. I'll just have to woman up and do it for the sake of our friendship.

No first moves.

The Bod God will have to do it for us.

I can do that, right?

While we're waiting in line, The Bod God says, "What's your guys' names, by the way?" he asks.

There's a tense moment between me and Rox. We really don't do things *this* crazy with strange guys very often. I mean, The Bod God may be a total hot rod, but we don't know him or what school he goes to or even what college. He could be a criminal drifter for all we know. Yum! I mean, *Down, girl!*

He arches an expectant eyebrow, waiting.

"Angelina," I blurt nervously. Whenever Rox and I flirt with strange guys, we always give them fake names, just in case. I always use Angelina, as in, Jolie.

"Jennifer," Rox says, as in, Aniston. It's easy for us to remember.

Mr. Miracle's eyes dance between us. "Really?" It's obvious he doesn't believe us.

What can I say? We've always been Angelina and Jennifer and it's never been a problem in the past. Then again, high school boys are easy to fool. Hoping to distract, I ask him, "What's your name?"

He grins a super cocky grin, "Brad."

Yeah, he knows. I repress a snicker. There's no way his name is Brad.

I'm not holding it against him.

When we buy tickets, Brad The Bod God pays for all three of us. It's $125 for three tickets, but he refuses to let us pay. Such a gentleman. Inside the park, we find a rental locker and stash our keys and wallets and flip flops in it. Brad The Bod God offers to pin the locker key to his board shorts since we're in bikinis. Rox insists on holding the key. It's probably a good idea. It's not like I think he's going to sneak off with our wallets and steal Rox's mom's Toyota. His motorcycle is here. But it's the smart thing to do. I just hope I don't somehow piss off Rox and she leaves *me* here. Then again, that would mean I would have to ride home on the back of The Bod God's motorcycle. There's worse things.

But seriously, I'm not going to break my agreement with Rox.

No first moves.

Blazing Waters is filled with people. The sun is bright in the sky, the day is hot, and the wet water slides are the perfect cure for the San Fernando desert heat. I can't wait to get wet, because seriously, I am wet downstairs. I can't stop staring at The Bod God and thinking about what I know is hiding in his board shorts. My nipples tickle against the inside of my pink bikini top. I'm convinced that everyone in the water park knows I'm turned on.

It's only marginally embarrassing. By marginal, I mean just this side of extremely.

I try to think about SAT vocab words and reading comprehension. When that doesn't work, I run the quadratic equation through my head and think about polynomials.

That doesn't work either.

What *does* work is noticing all the women here at the water park who are openly staring at The Bod God. As we walk through the park, past the changing rooms and gift shops and concession stands, heads turn to stare at him. And by stare I mean gawk. I can easily tell which women have fillings or have had their tonsils removed from all the dropped jaws. Some of the women are very attractive, which makes me squirm with jealousy. Even Rox notices them. She acts like she doesn't care, but I can tell she does.

It's not like we can be mad at The Bod God. He's not even doing anything. Well, maybe he's smiling too much for his own good. He really needs to work on that. Less smiling. Smiling is bad. I learned that in Sociology class or something. Smiling starts wars. It's a proven fact.

Rather than do what I want, which is grab The Bod God by the arm, stand on tiptoes and scream in his ear, "STOP SMILING AT ALL THESE WOMEN!!!!", I turn to Rox and mutter, "What if he doesn't pick either one of us? What if he picks one of these sluts, I mean, fine young ladies?"

"He'll pick one of us," she says with forced confidence.

I wish I was as self-assured as Rox is pretending to be.

oOoOoOo + O+O+O+O

The first slide we ride is Tower Falls. The sign says you can reach speeds up to 35 miles an hour. They aren't lying. Going over a couple of the bumps, I feel like I'm going to fly out of the slide and plummet six stories to my death. Fortunately, I don't. When I splash into the pool at the bottom of the slide, my entire body is shaking with adrenalin.

When he and Rox splash down, the three of us run rampant through the water park, going from slide to slide. Blazing Waters has tons of different rides. It is so much fun. Roxanne and I always love it here. With The Bod God by our side, it's ten times better.

I keep waiting for him to touch one of our elbows unnecessarily, or hover closer to one of us over the other, or ask one of us to share a two-person raft on one of the raft rides, but he never does. He is such a gentleman. Still, I secretly hope he picks me over Rox. I know, I'm a terrible friend.

Eventually, my anxiety melts in the heat and is washed away by all the fun we're having.

Rox and I are both super flirty with him all morning. He takes it in stride, constantly joking with both of us. It turns out he's not just good looks, he's a totally cool guy.

After running from slide to slide for over two hours, I suggest that we relax and take a ride on Snake River. It's a mellow ride with no age restriction. All you do is sit in a transparent inflatable ring and bob along the water. There's lots of little kids with their parents. There's even a few babies cradled in parental arms. But there's also a group of rowdy boys floating near us, splashing and hollering. They look maybe 11 or 12. Old enough to behave like goblins.

One of the goblins splashes his buddy. His buddy responds by grabbing the raft of the first goblin and turning it. As the first goblin starts to spin around, a third goblin helps out. They spin the first goblin faster and faster. It would be no big deal because the water makes it hard to spin him too fast, but his legs are up in the air and he's whirling around like a human windmill. Or should I say goblin windmill.

"Hey!" I holler. "Watch it you guys!"

They laugh but ignore me.

"Animals," I say to Rox.

Eventually the goblins drift away from us, but end up next to a young mom with a baby in her lap. The baby is wearing the cutest little white sun hat and baby wet suit with little short sleeves.

When one goblin boy gets too close, the mom blurts, "Guys! Would you please be more careful! I have a baby here!"

The goblin boy doesn't care. He's whooping and spinning again and totally oblivious. So are his friends who decide now is a good time to tip over their friend. Rox and I watch all this in disgust. When the other boys push the first goblin's ring over, he spills into the water and nearly lands on the mom and her baby. She twists and holds her baby high to keep it out of harm's way, but this causes her to spill sideways off the raft. She and the baby splash below the surface of the water.

I gasp.

Without a thought, Brad The Bod God slides into the water.

The mom breaks the surface screaming, "My baby!"

My stomach clenches with fear. I roll out of my ring, wanting to help somehow, but I'm not sure where the baby went. The chlorine stings my eyes. All I see under water is a blurry sea of legs and butts hanging down from bobbing inflatable rings. The Bod God missiles past me, breast stroking in the general direction of where the mom was. I stick my head out of the water to see what's going on and take another breath.

"My baby!!" The mom screams, wiping wet hair out of her eyes. She twists around in the water frantically. She's lost her baby.

A wave of panic explodes out from her and smacks everyone nearby into nervous alertness. People start climbing out of their rings to help. Before anyone can do anything, The Bod God surfaces behind the mom, holding her wet and wailing baby over his head in both hands like an offering.

She spins around and sees them, "Oh my god! Megan! Is she okay?!" She lifts the child out of The Bod God's hands. "Oh my god, thank you so much." She cradles her baby, eyes intent, making sure the child is breathing. Little Megan's wails are proof that everything is going to be all right. The mom wades to the side of the artificial river, seeking safety.

The three goblins watch all of this with shocked faces. They realize what they've done.

A lifeguard whistle blows. A female lifeguard in red shorts strides toward the scene of the crime. She bends down and chats with the mother. I can't hear what they're saying, but they're glaring at the three goblins.

The goblins don't notice because The Bod God is talking to all of them in a serious tone. He says, "You guys know that was totally uncool, right? "

They look at him with a mixture of awe and fear.

He continues, "That baby could've been hurt bad. What if I hadn't been here? What if that baby inhaled water and needed CPR?" His tone isn't angry or frightening, but it is commanding. His deep voice makes everything sound important.

The goblins don't answer.

"Do any of you guys know CPR? Or how to clear water from someone's lungs?" He looks at each one of the kids in turn. "Do you know what to do if someone's drowning?"

The goblins are scared and humiliated, and The Bod God hasn't said anything insulting. He's just overwhelming them with the cold hard facts of what they've done.

A moment later, the lifeguard waves the goblins over to the side of the river and makes them climb out while she lectures them further.

The Bod God wades over to us and grabs his inflatable ring. Water droplets dazzle like diamonds on his tan chest and shoulders. "That was close," he says casually as he climbs onto his raft.

Roxanne is literally holding her hand over her heart, speechless.

"You saved that little girl," I marvel.

He smirks, "Nah. She was fine. Just went for a little swim."

He's acting like he isn't the hero of the day.

Wow. Just wow.

Did I mention he's perfect?

oOoOoOo + O+O+O+O

"I need a pee break," Rox says after we climb out at the end of Snake River.

The three of us stroll to the restrooms.

"I'll wait for you guys," Brad The Bod says.

Rox pauses at the entrance of the women's room and says to me, "Are you coming?"

"I don't have to go," I shrug.

"What, did you pee in the pool?"

"No!" I blurt. "I don't have to go. I swear."

She flashes me a look before going inside.

I smile at The Bod God, who is looking sexy as hell.

"Hey, Nightlight!" somebody yells at my back.

I recognize the voice.

It isn't Roxanne.

I twist around and see Ashley Masters in a racy black bikini. With her luxurious blonde hair and bronze skin, which *has* to be a spray tan because it's too perfect, she looks amazing. As in, effortlessly gorgeous. I don't know how she does it. She goes to North Valley High School with me and Roxanne. Ashley is a total bitch. I hate it when she calls me "Nightlight." It makes me sound like I'm still a baby who sleeps with a nightlight and a security blankie or something.

"Hey, Ashley," I groan.

"Is this your boyfriend?" she sneers as she stops in front of us.

Mr. Miracle cocks his head at Ashley, "'Sup."

"My mistake," Ashley says as she gets a good look at Brad The Bod, "he's too handsome to be dating the likes of you. Are you paying him to stand near you?"

Bitch! I wish I'd sharpened my claws when I got out of bed this morning. I need to take lessons from that Wolverine guy that Hugh Jackman plays in the X-Men movies. Since I don't have switchclaws, I'll have to do my cutting with clever and incisive words. "Uhhh..." What can I say? I'm never good in a showdown when it involves Ashley Masters. I hate her.

"Since this hunk couldn't *possibly* be your boyfriend," Ashley gloats, "maybe he'd like to ride a raft through the Tunnel Of Love with me?"

OMG. Really? She can't be serious. I didn't think she was *this* bold.

I glance nervously at Mr. Miracle.

Is he eyeing Ashley like the prize that she is? Is he going to drop me like an ugly rock, you know, the kind that's the opposite of hot? Will he forget about me completely and walk off into the sunset with Ashley Masters instead of me? Or is he trying to think of something cutting he can say, so that he and Ashley can double-team diss me when I'm down?

He opens his mouth to speak.

I wince in anticipation of the diss and my heart's demise.

"I paid her to stand next to me," he winks at me.

That'll work.

"Well," Ashley snivels, "whatever she paid, I'll pay triple." Everybody in school knows that Ashely's parents are loaded. "How about that ride on the Tunnel Of Love?"

"Naw," The Bod God dismisses her with a chuckle. "Me and her are together."

Together? Me and him? As in boyfriend-girlfriend? Am I reading too much into this?

Ashley scowls at me, "There's no way this hunk is with junk like you."

The Bod God drapes his arm around my shoulder and smirks at Ashley, "One woman's trash is another man's treasure."

Wait, was that him making a move? Or is he just doing it to annoy Ashley? I don't know. I'm not in his head. It doesn't matter because the disgusted sneer darkening Ashley's face is the most wonderful thing I've seen all day. I couldn't be happier. The thrill that shoots through my heart elevates my mood into a verified flight of fancy. All of my attention is riveted to where his skin kisses mine. Did I say kiss? I meant touch. His muscled arm feels pleasantly warm against my shoulders. Or is that just me heating up? It's impossible to tell. With all this skin-to-skin contact, I can't help but wonder what would it be like to be Mr. Miracle's girlfriend? A miracle? Obvi. I hope he keeps his arm around me for at least the next five hours.

A couple of girls walk up behind Ashley.

Monica Webb and Brittany Price. Both will be seniors at North Valley this fall, just like me and Ashley. They also wear bikinis, but neither look as good as Ashley.

"Hey, Monica," I say softly. "Hey, Brittany."

They both gawk at Mr. Miracle and say "Hey," like they're hypnotized by his hotness, which they obviously are.

Ashley glares at them. "We were leaving," she commands.

Monica and Brittany both look unsure of themselves, but neither are in a hurry to go anywhere.

"Let's go," Ashley barks and storms off.

Monica and Brittany stumble after her, but they both glance back at Mr. Miracle longingly.

Suck it, bitches!! His arm is around me!!

And now it's not. It slides away like treasure slipping through my fingers. Dang it.

"That chick was a piece of work," The Bod God chuckles.

A moment later, Rox walks out of the restroom. "Did I miss anything?"

"Only an appearance by Ashley Masters," I groan.

Rox grimaces and rolls her eyes. "*She's* here? I hate that bitch. Let's go before she comes back and ruins our fun."

I couldn't agree more.

oOoOoOo + O+O+O+O

We end up at the wave pool.

As you will remember, the wave pool is where I kiss Brad The Bod God, a.k.a Mr. Miracle, and find out he's my stepbrother. But as of now, I still don't know it. All I know is that he's shaping up to be the most incredible man known to woman.

The wave pool has fake rock walls on three sides and a fake beach on the fourth. Rox and I wade into the water. Brad climbs up on one of the fake rock walls and hops from stone to stone. The stones are uneven and the tops of them are about ten feet above the water. Brad keeps his balance without even trying. I doubt I could make it look so easy.

A shirtless lifeguard wearing red shorts and holding a red Baywatch-style torpedo float spots him and blows a whistle. "Sir! Get off the rocks! Sir!"

Brad isn't paying attention. He continues toward the back wall of the wave pool where the deep water is.

The whistle blows again. "Sir!" the lifeguard shouts.

Right at that moment, Brad leaps into the air and does a forward flip in a perfect pike position before extending his long body into a precise dive. He cuts a clean line into the deep water with grace and style. He must've had diving training to be able to do a move like that. When he surfaces, he whips his golden hair out of his face with a toss of his head like it's all no big deal.

"Such a bad boy," Rox jokes as we wade into waist deep water.

"I know, right?" I'm not complaining. A little bad is always good.

The lifeguard jams his hands on his hips and barks at Brad, "Sir, you can't jump off the rocks. Don't do that again, or you'll be ejected from the park."

"Sure buddy," Brad says casually.

"I'm serious," the guard says with obvious irritation. He motions with his red Baywatch float for effect.

"I heard ya. But tell me, what would you rate my front flip?" Brad grins big.

"What?"

"You know, if you were judging it at the Olympics? That was a pretty sweet one-and-a-half pike I pulled off." Brad The Bod grins with overwhelming charm.

The lifeguard's irritation melts into amusement. "If I give you a perfect ten, promise me you won't do any more dives to impress the ladies?"

Brad chuckles with good humor. "All right, all right. No more diving."

"Have fun," the lifeguard smiles at Brad. "Oh, and I'd give it a nine."

"Whaaaaat?!" Brad sings.

"Your knees were bent," the lifeguard laughs.

Brad shakes his head and rolls his eyes while swimming toward us, still grinning.

Rox mutters, "Such a charmer."

He sure is. Swoon.

Once we start riding the waves, it doesn't take long for the three of us to get separated. Each time the wave machine thunks, a huge swell travels the length of the pool, scattering the body surfers in every direction.

After a particularly fun ride, Rox insists we try to get as close to the wave machine as the lifeguards will let us, to get the maximum ride time.

The water this far out is up to my neck, so I tread casually instead of trying to keep my toes on the ground.

"You ready?" Rox asks, excited.

"Totes," I grin.

"How about you, Laird Hamilton?" she says to The Bod God.

"Yup."

Now that Rox mentions it, he does bear a passing resemblance to good old Laird, who is still hunky gorgeous at 50. Not only was Laird a champion surfer in his prime, he was also a model. It's a good comparison.

The Bod God grins at me, "What're you thinking about?"

"Nothing," I blush. Yeah, he could totally pass for a young Laird.

CLUNK!

That's the sound of the wave coming.

"Start swimming!" Rox hollers as she glances back at the wave. She's facing forward, poised to ride it.

A bunch of people are swept up by the huge swell. Some of them slide over it as it passes, others paddle and try to catch it. As it nears us, Rox starts to freestyle, kicking white water up behind her as her arms dig in.

I dip forward and throw my shoulder out in front of me.

A hand wraps around my waist.

The Bod God.

"Wait," he mutters.

Okay, that was officially a move.

I melt into his arm.

I'm pressed against him as the huge wave lifts us up. Kids barrel past on both sides, shouting gleefully.

After the water wave passes, a guilt wave hits. I've been having a wonderful time all day. With The Bod God *and* Rox. We have been a happy threesome the whole time. My fear that Rox and I would fight over him faded away at least an hour ago. But now it's back full force. I don't want to hurt Rox's feelings. It's obvious she likes The Bod God too. After the day we've spent together, *any* woman would like him. Even lesbians. Because he's super sweet *and* manly. He's everything. He's perfect. I mean literally perfect.

I'm shaking as The Bod God pulls me into his arms.

"What?" he asks softly. His emerald eyes glow from within his dark wet lashes.

He is so frickin' gorgeous it hurts.

I want to kiss him. But I won't. He has to do it. But it's not right. I keep thinking about Rox.

"It's just that—" I stop myself, catching my words in my throat.

"Sorry." He curls a half-hearted grin. "I kind of got the vibe you were into me." His arm around my waist falls away. "Sorry. My bad." His body floats slowly away from mine.

I bob in the rippling water, torn by indecision. Rox will be hurt if she finds out what just happened. But we made a deal. We would let *him* decide who he wanted. I think he just decided.

He's drifting away from me.

If he drifts any further, I might never be in his arms again.

"No, wait!" I blurt and lunge toward him.

Water splashes around us as he sweeps me into his powerful arms.

With the power of a fifty foot monster wave, the kind of wave that has the power to snap surfboards in half and bash careless surfers into oblivion, our lips crash together. Our tongues fight and our passion explodes like huge breakers against craggy shoreline rocks. White water and sea foam spray high in the air, glittering in the sun.

Oblivion.

oOoOoOo + O+O+O+O

You remember what happens next.

Me.

My stepbrother.

Our intense make-out session in the middle of the wave pool at Blazing Waters.

My horrid realization that I've made a huge mistake.

But we're not even related by blood, right?

And the stepbrother thing is a technicality, right?

And me and Rox pinky swore that we would let Dante, The Bod God, Mr. Miracle, decide for us. And no hating, no matter *who* he picked. We swore.

Trust me, none of that matters.

Things just get worse from here.

Chapter 3

AFTER THE KISS

"What happened to you guys?!" Rox yells as she swims toward where Dante and I stand on the artificial shore. "I lost you three waves ago. Where'd you guys go?"

The wave pool is huge and totally crowded. It's not that hard to lose someone.

"Uh, we've been riding them," I lie. More like riding him.

I *hate* lying to Rox. But I'm not ready to share news of my illicit kiss in the swoon lagoon or the drama bomb that dropped after. Or about how I let myself get sucked under water, hoping I would drown, even if only for a second, because falling for Dante is wrong in too many ways to count. Luckily, Dante was quick to save me, just like he did with that baby earlier. I guess helping people is second nature to him. It took only a second for him to grab me and swim us to the shallows, making him twenty times more awesome and desirable than he already was. Maybe it would've been better if he let the wave put me out of my misery.

"Are you ready to go again?" Rox beams, her excitement shooting off of her.

"Uh, I guess?" I say uncertainly. The only thing on my mind is when to tell Rox the news. She's gonna wanna know both that Dante picked me *and* he's my stepbrother. My gut tells me that Rox might argue the stepbrother thing is grounds for him picking her by default. It's not a bad argument. I'm already leaning in that direction myself. For Rox's sake.

Oh, goodness, what have I done?

Judging by the confused look on Dante's face, he's not entirely sure what he did either. But he can't stop sneaking glances at me.

Rox is bound to notice eventually.

I can't tell her now.

I just can't.

"Having fun?" Ashley Masters says from out of nowhere. She is walking out of the wave pool toward the shore, flanked by Monica and Brittany. When did they end up out here?

Rox rolls her eyes.

Ashley makes my need to barf a hundred times worse.

"Did you enjoy that last *wave*, Nightlight?" Ashley demands, glaring at me.

"Huh?"

"How was it? The *wave*?" she says pointedly. "The one that *carried you away*?"

Oh my god. Did she see me and Dante? This is not good.

Rox looks confused. She mutters to me, "What is she talking about?"

"I don't know," I lie. I glance at Monica and Brittany. Do they know too? If they do, word of my kiss with Dante will spread faster than a San Fernando forest fire in the height of summer, which is right now. The gossip grapevine of my high school is like a tinder box of dried out old grapevines waiting for a random spark to set it off.

I stare at Ashley. I can only imagine the look on my face is a cross between a deer in headlights and revulsion. If you don't know what that looks like, have your friend hit you in the face with a baseball bat, then run and look in the mirror immediately afterward.

But I digress.

If Ashley saw us kiss, that's bad. If Monica and Brittany saw, that's way worse. One witness can be written off as snarky jealousy, but three witnesses is proof. Maybe it's better that Rox knows now, instead of hearing it fifth hand from someone at school. Either way, I so don't want to do this right now.

At least Ashley doesn't know Dante is my stepbrother.

Or does she?

Was she or Monica or Brittany close enough in the wave pool to overhear me and Dante talking? Who knows? The pool is packed. She could've been one person over from the do-gooders telling me and Dante to get a room. I don't know, I don't know!

The not knowing is making me crazy.

In case of emergency, RUN!

I grab Rox by the wrist and pull her toward shore.

"Where are you going, Nightlight?" Ashley demands. "Did you inhale too much *water* during that last *wave*? Maybe you *swallowed* something and need *mouth to mouth*."

She is completely awful.

I can't look back. If I say anything, the truth is all going to come out like vomit.

What a mess.

oOoOoOo + O+O+O+O

"I don't know about you two," I groan, "but I think I'm getting sun fatigue or something. I'm totally nauseous right now. Do you guys want to go?"

Dante, Rox, and I stand on a crowded pathway near the kiddie area of Blazing Waters. A bunch of kids clamber all over the playground style equipment that is raining water everywhere. Those kids are having way more fun than I am.

Dante looks at me sympathetically. "You're probably dehydrated."

"How can I be dehydrated?" I say. "We're at a water park. Surrounded by water."

"Yeah, but you're sweating in all this heat. We've been running around for hours."

"He's right," Rox says. "We should get some drinks and take a break. Maybe get some shade. I don't know about you, but I've had all the sun I can take."

Although we're all tan, we've been in the sun for hours.

"Sounds like a great idea," I nod.

We get our stuff from the locker and buy huge sodas from one of the outdoor snack bars. Next to the snack bar are dozens of round cement tables with big sun umbrellas. We sit down at one.

I sip on a 7-Up with no ice, gulping it down. The water and the sugar totally hit the spot.

Rox has Mountain Dew, because it has more caffeine than Coke. Dante got a big bottle of water.

After sipping from her straw, Rox says, "Isn't it weird?"

"What?" I ask.

"How we're getting along so well for a bunch of strangers?" She laughs and grins at me, "Well, you and I know each other, Angelina, but Brad here is a complete stranger to both of us. But somehow I feel almost like family or something."

I choke on my 7-Up and nearly blow it out my nose. My nostrils tingle painfully all the way to the back of my throat. I start coughing.

"You okay?" Dante asks, concerned.

"Yeah," HACK! "I'm—" HACK! "...fine."

"Easy girl," Rox cautions. "You don't want to go drowning in your 7-Up."

"Thanks," I wince. That sounds like a good idea. It might take some work, but it *is* possible to drown in a cup of 7-Up if you try really hard.

"So I've been thinking," Rox says suggestively.

"About what?" I ask.

"That we should all come clean."

I almost gag. "Clean?" Does she know too? Did she see Dante kissing me and she's just trying to get me to spill it so she doesn't have to pry?

"Yeah," she smiles, giving me a pointed look. "Should we tell him?"

I try not to panic. "Tell him what?"

"You know," she hints.

"No, I don't know," I frown.

"Come on, Angel*iiiina*." She drawls.

"Huh?" I glance at Dante for support.

He shakes his head, totally lost.

She rolls her eyes impatiently, "Angelina? Jennifer? *Brad*?" she laughs.

"Oh!" I blurt. "The names." Relief.

She nods, "Now you're picking up what I'm putting down."

The wave pool in my stomach slowly calms. But only for a second. Because Rox knows my mysterious stepbrother is named Dante. If we go there, she's bound to figure it out. But if I resist and make an issue out of it, she'll grill me later for sure. I can't win for losing. "Sure, whatever."

Rox smiles and reaches a hand across the table toward Dante. "My name is Roxanne. You can call me Rox. This is my friend Skye."

Dante shakes her hand, "Nice to meet you, Rox." He winks at me. "And Skye."

"What's your name?" Rox asks.

"Dante."

She shakes his hand and smiles, "Hey, Dante."

Please don't figure it out, please don't figure it out, please…

"Hey, Skye," she smiles at me, "Isn't your stepbrother named Dante?"

I slump. Then I fake smile. "Yeah. That's right. My stepbrother, the one I've never met, is named Dante." I give her an odd look because odd best describes my state of being at the moment. I tilt my head to the side and hope that it somehow rolls off my neck all by itself, and tumbles into the nearby bushes, and everyone forgets I exist.

"I guess there's a lot of Dantes in the world," she grins.

"Yeah," I agree hastily. "Totally." That was *way* too close. At least I don't have to tell her now.

Roxanne chuckles, "Hey, you're not Skye's stepbrother, are you?"

Fuck me. I roll my eyes.

Dante snorts.

Rox crinkles her nose and shakes her head. "Sorry. I know, it's dumb. It's like when you meet someone from London or wherever, and you're like, 'Hey, I have a cousin who lives in Wales. Do you know her?'" She shakes her head. "I can be such an idiot sometimes."

"Noooo," I say with overly dramatic sincerity, "it's an honest mistake. For a second, the same thought crossed my mind." Why did I say that?

"Really?" Rox asks, chewing on her straw.

I hastily sip my 7-Up, needing a moment to collect myself. "Um, yeah. I guess. No, not really. Maybe?" I stop myself before I spill everything.

"So, Dante," Rox turns to him, "You never did tell us where you're from? Do you live around here? It kind of looked like you were just passing through on your motorcycle or whatever."

Dante shrugs, "You could say that."

What? I don't want him to "just pass through"!!! I want him to stay forever! I mean, uh... I don't know *what* I mean. This whole situation is tragic. Romeo and Juliet thought they had it bad. Imagine if they had been step siblings.

"So where are you going?" Rox presses.

"Actually..." he trails off.

Please don't say anything. We made it this far without Rox figuring it out. I almost choked to death on my 7-Up and drowned in the wave pool. Don't let all that go to waste.

Dante continues, "Actually, I'm just here to visit some, uh, *friends*..." He looks at me pointedly.

Phew.

"That's cool," Rox says. "How long are you staying?"

He shrugs. "Until I feel like leaving."

I hope he means years from now. Why am I so anxious about this? His being my stepbrother is a huge problem! Isn't it better for him to leave sooner rather than later? So I can get over my crush in private? Because chances are really good he's going to be staying at my house while he's visiting. And it's just a crush. I don't even know the guy.

"What do you mean 'leaving'?" Rox asks.

"I never stay in one place too long."

Rox turns to me, "Isn't your stepbrother like that?"

Damn it, she's figuring it out. I regret ever mentioning my mysterious stepbrother to her. How was I supposed to know that telling her about Dante was a bad idea? I didn't know things were going to play out like this. Geez, I don't know why I'm torturing myself. She's going to find out sooner or later. I just won't tell her about the kiss until absolutely necessary. "Rox, this *is* my stepbrother."

"Shut up," she says casually, sipping on her Mountain Dew.

I nod slowly and dramatically, smirking with distilled discomfort.

She winces explosively. "Seriously?!"

I arch my eyebrows, still nodding.

"No way. You're such a liar, Skye." A moment later she grins casually at Dante, "You're not her stepbrother." She pauses thoughtfully. "Are you?"

He arches an eyebrow and nods. "Yup."

Rox's face knots up. "What? Wait, no way. Skye? Is this for reals?"

"Totes," I say morosely.

She shakes her head, "Why didn't you tell me?!"

"I didn't know," I moan. If only I had...

"This is stupid," Rox laughs innocently. "You are *not* her stepbrother."

"I am her stepbrother," Dante says.

"For reals?"

"For reals," he smiles.

Rox blinks a bunch of times and stares at the sky, embarrassed. Her fingers flutter in front of her. "Oh my god, Skye! We have been flirting with your stepbrother all day! What is wrong with us?" She is laughing now. "I can't believe us!! We're terrible!"

"I didn't know," I sigh quietly.

Rox doesn't hear me. She frown-smiles at Dante. "You guys *really* didn't know?"

He shakes his head. "Nope."

"Well, when did you two figure it out?"

Red alert! Time for distraction by omitting certain key facts. "In the wave pool. He, um, asked if my name was really Angelina. We, uh, we figured it out then."

Rox cocks her head. "Really?"

I bite my lower lip and clasp my hands between my knees like I need to pee or something. I must look guilty as hell. "Yup. At the wave pool."

Rox stares at me, a half smile on her face. Her wheels are turning.

Oh no.

This is it.

The big blow up where my life falls apart the rest of the way and Rox disowns me.

She shakes her head dismissively and leans down to sip her Mountain Dew. "That is too funny. Well good thing we found out now, before something weirdly incestuous happened," she wrinkles her nose and shivers.

"Yeah," I wheeze.

Oh boy.

Can things get any worse?

Of course they can.

oOoOoOo + O+O+O+O

"Since Dante is off limits to you," Rox says in the Toyota on the way home, "Does that mean he's all mine?"

"Uhhh, gosh, Rox. Isn't he a little old for you? He's almost 22." I know he's still 21, but I say "almost 22" just to make it sound worse. Cause the extra few months totally make him a geezer. Not. But I'm desperate to talk Rox out of it.

She shrugs, both hands on the wheel. "Like that matters. It wasn't stopping us earlier when he offered us beer. Why should it matter now?"

"I don't know, because he's my stepbrother?"

"So? It's not like you two are related."

Thank goodness for that much.

"And he's never around anyway," she says. "How long do you think he'll stay in town?"

"Who knows. And all the more reason for you not to get involved. With my stepbrother." This is horrendous. I am trying to trick my best friend into not pursuing my stepbrother so I can.

"All the more reason to jump right on this. You saw his body. And we both saw his cock. He looked sizable, but you never know. He could be like a tree stump when he's hard," she giggles. "Or a redwood. You never can tell. Do you think he's a show-er or a grower?"

Grower. Definitely grower.

I blurt, "How the heck should I know?!"

Rox frowns, "You don't have to get defensive. I'm just asking. Anyway, I'll find out for both of us. I need to learn everything I can about his body. And how he uses it. Sort of as a courtesy to you."

"What?!" I gasp.

She giggles, "Come on. You know he's hot. He's just a guy who happens to now be your stepbrother. But he's a total stranger. And don't tell me the incest fantasy hasn't crossed your mind."

"Of course it hasn't! As soon as I found out he was my stepbrother, that door closed like a bank vault." I am such a liar.

She rolls her eyes and chews her lower lip thoughtfully, her eyes pinned on the freeway ahead.

Afternoon traffic is starting to pick up.

"Well," she says, "that's why you need me to find out for you. We can't very well have you hooking up with your stepbrother, can we? So, I'll handle it. Then I can fill you in on all the sexy details." She giggles with excitement.

Handle it? Which IT is she talking about? Duh. I search for an argument. "What about our pinky swear? What about him doing the choosing? Aren't we still bound by that? No action until he makes the first move?"

She glances over at me, her brows knit, "That was only if we were both going for him. You're out of the running by default, sister." She snickers. "No pun intended."

I stick out my tongue and make a barf face. "Right. I forgot. My stepbrother."

I look in the side mirror and see Dante on his motorcycle. He left his backpack and leather jacket in Rox's trunk. Right now, he's only wearing his T-shirt, jeans, boots, and helmet. The wind whips the cotton shirt like a fluttering flag, revealing his flat stomach. His tan arms, the ones with the flames tattooed on the forearms, grip the bars of the bike. It seems like every muscle in his arms are flexed sexily.

He is too damn hot.

And chances are, he will be sleeping in the guest bedroom right next to mine.

Will he be having sex in that guest bedroom? With Rox? With me? Because, yeah, I'm still thinking about that kiss. I can remember how his lips felt on mine, how his tongue felt inside me… I mean, inside my mouth. I shiver. Oh my gosh. This is so wrong. And the wrongness of it turns me on twice as much. In fact, my bikini is damp, and not because of spending the day in the water.

Well, maybe because of that.

But I'm damp.

For my stepbrother.

Oh, gawd.

I drop my head back against the headrest and close my eyes. Except the first place my mind takes me is to me with my legs wrapped around Dante's waist in the wave pool and feeling his raging hard on pushing between my legs.

There's a knock at my window.

My eyes flicker open.

Dante's motorcycle is inches away from Rox's Toyota. We're going like 75 mph because Rox always speeds. One wrong move and she'll knock Dante off his bike. I imagine 75 mph road rash in a thin cotton shirt is a bad idea. My heart cinches inside my chest and I gasp. Dante winks, slaps the roof of the Toyota twice, gives us a thumbs up, then revs the motor on his bike and pops a frickin' wheelie on the freeway.

At 75 mph.

"Wow," Rox muses lustily, "who knew your sexy stepbrother was such a bad boy?"

O. M. Groan.

I squeeze my hand over my eyes. Can this get any worse?

Yes it can.

Just watch.

oOoOoOo + O+O+O+O

"Let's go to your house," I say to Rox as we get off the freeway and drive toward home.

"I thought we told Dante to follow us to your house."

"I changed my mind."

"Why? Isn't he going to want to get settled in and see his mom?"

What I'm not going to say is how weird I'm still feeling about what happened today.

Let's recap:

1) Dante, who is 21, offered beers to two random teenage girls and suggested we all go someplace intimately private. I can only imagine what my dad would do if he heard the whole story. Picture a bunch of nuclear missiles with my dad's angry face painted on the front coming out of missile silos in the ground before rocketing toward Dante's head. Then picture my dad calling the cops and pressing charges against Dante for giving alcohol to his underaged daughter.

2) I hooked up with my stepbrother in the middle of a water park!! I don't think that would go over well with my dad *or* Dante's mom. I mean, even if they *don't* disown us, I don't want to endure a lecture from them about "not doing it again" or "how it will make them look". For my dad, it's *always* about how things make *him* look. Anyway, can you say AWKWARD with a capital INCEST? No, I'm not going through that.

In short, I'm not ready to face Dad or Catarina. I need to strategize with Dante and Rox to prevent any of the aforementioned disasters from happening.

Maybe there's a reason why you're not supposed to hook up with your stepbrother.

We park in Rox's driveway, which is only a few blocks from my house.

Dante pulls up and parks on the street. He peels his helmet off and sets it on the handlebars of his motorcycle. He looks so damn sexy doing it. I can't believe he's *my* stepbrother. Swoon. I mean, why does he have to be *my* stepbrother? Can't he be Rox's?

Roxanne and I hop out of the Toyota.

Dante winks at me. "Hey sis, is this our house?"

I'm torn by the thrill of him saying "our house" and the weirdness of him calling me "sis". O. M. Awkward. You and I are going to be besties, aren't we, Awkward? Awkward grins with smarmy satisfaction. Awkward should stick her head in a toilet and flush until she drowns.

"This is my house," Rox says.

"Nice place," Dante says.

"Thanks," she smiles. "My parents are both at work. Do you want to come in for a drink?" I'm sure she's imagining all kinds of things other than drinking.

"Sounds like a plan," Dante says.

We end up in Rox's kitchen. She opens the fridge. "Do you want anything, Dante?"

"Sure," he says. "What have you got?"

"Just about everything. Why don't you come take a look."

I watch all this curiously. Usually when I'm at Rox's, I just take what I want from her fridge. She does the same at my house. But I guess Dante is a guest, so to speak.

Rather than move, Rox holds on to the refrigerator door. Dante comes up behind her and leans his forearm against the top of the fridge door, which is above the freezer, so it's really high, but Dante is so tall, he does it easily. He also traps Rox between him and the fridge.

Is he doing that on purpose? If he is, it's *really* irritating. For whatever reason, I walk around the kitchen counter so I can better see what Rox and Dante are doing. Not because I'm jealous or want to make sure they don't do anything. It's because I want a drink too, obvi.

"Let's see…" Dante says. "Milk. Soda. Juice. Those Heine's I bought this morning are probably all hot and nasty by now. Hmmm. You don't have salted lassi, do you? I'm kind of in the mood for something savory."

"Salted what?" Rox wrinkles her nose.

"Lassi," Dante says. "It's a salted Indian yogurt drink with cumin in it."

"That sounds gross," I snort.

He shrugs. "You should try milk and cow's blood."

"Eww!" Rox gags. "Have you actually drunk milk and blood?"

"Yeah," he grins. "It's good. You should try it."

"Maybe if I was a vampire," Rox chuckles.

I can't help but laugh.

"Fine," Dante relents, "I'll have OJ."

"That's what I was going to have!" Rox grins at Dante.

I can totally tell she's flirting. "Funny," I say, "me too. Here, give me the carton and I'll pour for everyone." I'm just trying to break up her moment with Dante without being completely obvious.

"I've got it," she barks and pulls out the carton. She grabs glasses from the cupboard and pours. Dante leans against the counter behind her. I don't want to keep hovering, so I take a seat at the bar. This means the island is between me and the two of them. If I make a big deal out of it, I'm going to look weird. I don't want Rox knowing how much it's driving me nuts that she's closer to him.

Jealous?

Okay, maybe a smidge.

"Thanks," Dante says when Rox hands him a glass.

"My pleasure," Rox purrs.

She did purr. I'm not exaggerating. Maybe she didn't bat her eyelashes, but I heard purr.

Dante raises his glass like he's toasting. I didn't know you could toast with orange juice, but I guess you can. "To new friends," he says.

"To new friends," Rox says, clinking his glass.

Did they forget me? I have to lean way over the kitchen island to clink, "To friends," I say.

Dante grins, "And stepsisters." He clinks my glass.

Rox swallows some OJ and narrows her eyes at Dante. "So, Dante, I'm curious. Since you didn't know us this morning, what were you doing giving beers to a couple of teenage girls?"

He shrugs. "I wasn't going to toss the cans in the trash. You guys were there."

"Yeah," Rox says, "but I'm 17 and Skye just turned 18. We're not even close to 21. Don't you think that's kind of pervy?" She says it like she likes the idea.

Not that I can blame her. I like the idea of Dante having ideas about me just as much as she does.

"Pervy?" he chuckles and shakes his head. "I told you guys earlier, the legal drinking age is 18 in tons of countries. Less in some places.

I've been buying beer and wine legally for years. You guys looked old enough to me."

"Okay," Rox sighs, "you're forgiven." She giggles. "So, did you just get into town today when we saw you at the 7-Eleven?"

"Yeah," he says.

"Have you seen your mom yet?"

"No," he says with discomfort.

"I bet she's looking forward to seeing you."

"She doesn't know I'm here," Dante smirks.

Rox doesn't know that Dante and his mom aren't exactly on speaking terms. It's not something Catarina likes to talk about, so I always played that part down with Rox. "What?!" Rox blurts. "You didn't tell her you were coming?"

Dante shakes his head sheepishly and stares at his orange juice thoughtfully while swirling it slowly in the glass. "It was a last minute thing."

Rox says, "Well, I bet she'll be happy to see you."

He nods, "Probably." This is obviously making him uncomfortable. It makes sense. They are estranged, after all.

"How did you find your mom anyway?" I ask. "I mean without her knowing you were coming?"

"I searched online for Catarina Lord and found her real estate website. She still uses my Dad's last name for her business. I tried finding her home address, but I couldn't find anything current. So I figured I could hit her up at her office."

"Is that why you were at the 7-Eleven?" Rox asks. "It's like two blocks away from it."

He nods, "Yeah. I was on my way there when I saw the 7-Eleven and decided I needed some liquid courage and some time to reflect before I met up with her."

I nod. "How bizarre you ran into us, right?"

"No shit," he agrees.

Rox asks, "And you never saw any pictures of Skye online? You didn't Facebook stalk her?"

He shakes his head, "I didn't know my mom was married. Her Facebook page is all business. There was no one to stalk."

"Really?" Rox marvels.

"Yup."

My cell phone, which sits on the laminate countertop next to my house key, suddenly buzzes. Incoming text. I pick it up and read it. I say out loud, "It's Catarina. She says she's stopping at the grocery store when she leaves the office. She wants to know if I need anything." I look at Dante. "Should we go to the house and surprise her?"

"Why not," he says flatly.

Once again, weird.

"That sounds like fun," Rox beams, all excited. "Mind if I tag along?"

"Um…" I say nervously.

Rox is practically a fixture at my house. My dad treats her like she's his adopted daughter and she gets along great with Catarina. It would be totally normal for her to come along. But I don't want her to. Of course, I can't tell her that. If Dante was ugly and we hadn't kissed, I wouldn't even think of telling her not to come with. Unfortunately, that's not how things went. Yes, I'm shallow as shit. But I really don't want her coming along. "Uh…" I stammer.

Rox sighs, "I get it. Dante hasn't seen his mom in a long time and he's never met your dad. You guys go. We'll hook up later." She grins at Dante.

"Sounds awesome," he says, returning her smile.

It doesn't sound awesome to me.

Hands off my man!

Err, my stepbrother.

oOoOoOo + O+O+O+O

Outside on Rox's driveway, I say to Dante, "Oh, hey. Do me a favor?"

"Yeah?"

"Don't mention to our parents that we went to Blazing Waters today, okay?" I expect him to ask why.

He doesn't. He just says, "Sure."

I climb into Rox's car. Why? Because, when we were inside and Dante asked to use the bathroom, Rox offered to drive me. She pointed out that Dante doesn't have a spare helmet. I reminded her it's like three blocks. She reminded me that most accidents happen close to home. By accidents, I think she meant the kind that involve me snuggling up against Dante and straddling him with my legs on the back of his motorcycle, not her. Rather than argue, I relented.

Dante throws a leg over his motorcycle and starts his engine.

Rox adjusts her rearview mirror so she can watch him. "He's so hot."

"I guess. Look, can you promise not to mention what happened today to my dad and Catarina?"

"What? Going to Blazing Waters? Why?"

"Can you just not mention it? I don't want my dad weirding out."

She knits her brows, "Why, because of the beers?"

I nod hastily, "Yeah. The beers." It's not the whole truth, but it's a part. "I don't want my dad getting a bad impression of Dante."

Rox nods, "I get it. I know your dad. He wouldn't like the beer thing. But what's wrong with us all going to Blazing Waters? Dante is your stepbrother."

"But we didn't know he was my stepbrother at the time."

"Oh, duh. It does sound kind of pedo, doesn't it? Especially with the beers."

"Uhhh, yeah." I say. Why did she have to say "pedo"? Now I feel dirty. The step-incest kissing is bad enough.

She shrugs her shoulders. "Sure. Hey," she says seriously, "You don't mind if I go after Dante, do you?"

"He's not too pedo for you?"

She grins, "He's the good kind of pedo. But seriously. I just wanna make sure you're cool if I try to hook up with him."

I am not cool with it. No way. But I'm also touched that she cares. We are besties, after all. "It's fine," I sigh and lie. "I mean, he's my stepbrother, not yours." I hope I don't sound too possessive.

"Just making sure. You seemed weird in the kitchen."

I'm not surprised she noticed. "I guess." I don't know why I'm making this so hard on everyone. The best thing is for me to close any doors to Dante that may have opened inside me. "He's—" I choke for a moment, "he's all yours." It nauseates me to say it.

It takes everything I have not to gag as a satisfied smile grows on Rox's face. She starts the car and drives to my house. When we arrive, she pulls into the driveway. Dante rolls up on the left side of her car. I open my door and stick one foot out. "See you later?" In other words, don't ask to come inside.

"Yeah, sure. Hey, if you guys go out later, call me, okay?" she asks hopefully.

I smile, "Of course." I'm totally lying.

I can't help it. I need Dante to myself for the evening. I need to get to know my stepbrother, right? Just the two of us?

Right.

oOoOoOo + O+O+O+O

The front door of my house latches behind me. I'm leaning up against the inside of it.

Dante is grinning at me from three feet away.

"Catarina?" I call out.

The house is silent.

We're alone.

Dante's eyes darken with hunger. "You looked fuckin' hot in your bikini today. I couldn't stop staring at your ass."

"You couldn't?"

"All I wanted to do was throw you into the bushes and rip your bathing suit off so I could ram my dick into you."

"Oh…" My voice quavers.

"You're wet just thinking about it, aren't you?"

"No…" Yes.

My heart is pounding in my chest. My skin sizzles with anticipation.

Oh my god.

I want Dante to kiss me so bad it hurts. I don't care if he is my stepbrother.

He saunters foward, sliding his arms out of his battered leather jacket, which falls to the floor. One of the buckles clinks in feeble protest. He pulls his T-shirt over his head, revealing his amazing body. I swear he's better looking than he was at the water park.

He presses me against the front door with his sculpted stomach. And his rock hard manhood, which rages against my flat stomach through his jeans. His mouth twitches and his lips curl over his teeth like he's going to eat me right here in my parents' house.

"But you're my stepbrother," I whimper. "It's against the rules."

"Fuck the rules. We're not related by blood."

If he was a sexy motorcycle vampire, I would beg for him to suck my blood right now.

I don't have to beg because his mouth dives for my throat, which he bites gently.

"Oh…" I moan. No boy has ever bitten my neck.

His tongue slides up my neck and along my jaw.

My legs give out, but with him pressing me against the door, I'm not going anywhere. He laces his fingers into mine and lifts my arms above my head, pinning them against the wood. His chest presses into my breasts. I feel his muscles grinding against my stiff nipples. Oh, gawd. This feels so good. He thrusts his hips against me. The buckle digs painfully into my stomach.

"Ow, your belt," I wince.

He responds by releasing our interlaced fingers. Just when I think he's backing off, he grabs both my wrists in one big hand and keeps them pinned up against the front door over my head. With his free hand, he yanks his buckle open and frantically unbuttons his jeans. His hot cock jumps out of the denim and he presses it against my stomach. Then he grabs a fistful of my cotton T-shirt and lifts it up until we are skin to skin. His scorching manhood burns against my stomach. I can feel it pulsing against my flesh.

This is so wrong.

I am losing my mind.

He licks my neck again with savage greed before smashing his lips into mine. His tongue stabs into my mouth and forces its way past my teeth.

I can't stop him. I don't want to stop him.

His cock thrusts slowly against my tummy.

I am drenched. My folds must be dripping wet.

I don't know what's going to happen next.

But I know what I want to happen next...

BRRRRR!!!

The garage door opener!!

Dante breaks our kiss and turns to look.

"Your mom!" I blurt.

He growls in my ear, enraged. He doesn't want to stop.

"Dante! Your mom is here!"

"Fuck!" he shouts.

Fuck is right.

Chapter 4

Guilt.

Ten tons of it weighs down in my stomach like a jagged boulder.

GUILT.

That's what I'm feeling the second Catarina walks into the laundry room from the garage, her arms loaded with groceries. "Von's was a zoo. It took forever to get everything."

"Let me help you," I say, taking all the bags from her hands. I don't want her dropping them when she sees Dante, who is in the kitchen with his shirt back on.

"Thank you so much, sweetie."

Catarina is a stunning woman. Her dark wavy hair is artfully tousled. It's so different from Dante's surfer blond hair. But they have the same emerald eyes. She wears a colorful blouse that shows a hint of cleavage and a tight black fitted skirt and red wedges that tie in with the red streaks in her blouse. Her cherry red lips complete the look. It's no surprise her son is as gorgeous as she is. You might think she was a snooty bitch from looking at her, but she's not. She's a normal person with a normal job and totally down to earth. She's always helping me with my hair or giving me makeup tips. And we love going shopping together when we have time. I guess I became the daughter she never had when she married my dad. And she became the mom I never had, even though I did have one before she came along. My real mom was just lame. Whatever.

Anyway, Catarina's awesomeness makes my GUILT a hundred times worse.

Her son, my stepbrother, gave me an orgasm back at Blazing Waters. And he just threw me up against my own front door and made out with me. With his dick out.

"Is that everything?" I ask Catarina nervously, trying my best to act normal.

"Yes, thank you. Oh, and why is there a motorcycle parked in our driveway?"

"Um… there's someone here to meet you."

"Who? One of your friends?"

"Sort of. He's in the kitchen."

Catarina gives me an odd look. When she steps through the doorway to the kitchen, she stops short and I bump into her back.

"Dante?" she gasps.

"Hey." He sounds uncomfortable. Actually, he almost sounds guilty. It's going around.

"Oh my god, Dante," she says, her voice breaking.

I squeeze past her and set the grocery bags down on the island's granite counter top.

Catarina's eyes are watering. She's frozen in place, afraid to move.

Dante steps toward her and stops two feet away from her.

Neither one of them is making a move.

"Is it really you?" Catarina whispers, her voice tight, looking up at her son who is much taller than her.

He nods. "Yeah. It's me."

"You're so handsome." She reaches up and pushes his hair out of his eyes. "You're a man. My son…" Tears spill down her cheeks. "What happened to my little boy?"

Dante's eyes are watering. He sniffs, holding in his emotions.

They still haven't really touched each other. That two foot gap lies between them like they're both afraid to close the distance. I don't know why Dante and his mom became estranged seven years ago. It must've been serious for Dante to move out and for Catarina to let him go. I wonder if he somehow hurt her? Or his dad did something to keep her away? I can't imagine a mother giving up on her child without some kind of drama.

Suddenly, Dante lifts a hand and *almost* touches Catarina's arm, but stops at the last second and lets his hand fall to his side. Catarina immediately steps forward and throws her arms around her son, squeezing her cheek against his chest.

Dante awkwardly wraps his arms around her back and pats her gently.

The floodgates open and Catarina sobs against his chest.

I start to tear up myself. I want to join them for a group hug, but this is their moment. They deserve it. They can have all the time they need. I feel honored just to watch the silent intimacy flowing between mother and son. It's beautiful. It's delicate. I won't do anything to disturb it.

"WHO THE HELL PARKED THEIR MOTORCYCLE ON MY SIDE OF THE DRIVEWAY?!" my dad yells as he thunders through the front door.

Great.

Way to ruin the moment, Dad.

oOoOoOo + O+O+O+O

"Who's this?" Dad demands when he sees Dante hugging my mom. He sounds suspicious. So much for first impressions.

My dad is possessive when it comes to Catarina. I can't blame him. He loves her. I do too.

Dad is wearing his customary charcoal gray suit. He's tall and has short blond hair the same color as mine and the same gray-blue eyes. Despite working as a banker in one of the skyscrapers in downtown L.A., he's tan and in great shape from playing plenty of tennis and golf. Money has its privileges.

"This is Dante," Catarina says.

Dad frowns, "Your *son* Dante?"

She nods, still weepy.

"What is he doing here?"

Can you say *gawk*ward?

Dante smirks at my dad, but says nothing.

Dad can be an embarrassment. Sometimes he's too blunt for his own good. I guess that's what you get with a take charge kind of guy like him. He also doesn't like it when people get in his way or interfere with his plans. Like blocking his side of the driveway.

"Dante came for a visit," I offer, since no one else is saying anything.

Dad takes a step toward him, but he's looking at me. "A visit?"

I can imagine my dad's wheels turning. He's wondering how Dante is going to mess up his schedule or what allowances he's going to have to make. Dad's mind is a running balance sheet of social debits and credits. He's a "What can you do for me?" kind of guy. It's made him successful, but it also makes him annoying at times like this.

"Dude, chillax," Dante says.

Dad glares at him like he's stupid. "What?"

I roll my eyes. "He means relax, Dad."

"I know what he means," Dad barks. He turns on Dante. "Don't tell me to relax in my own house."

"Dad!"

"Gordon," Catarina says, stepping toward Dad, "Please calm down."

"If you don't want me here, I can bail, bro," Dante says to Dad.

"No, don't go," Catarina gasps. "You just got here. Gordon, calm down." She smooths her palm against Dad's chest soothingly.

Dad shakes his head, "Sorry. Dante." He holds out a stiff arm. "Gordon Albright. Good to meet you."

Dante looks at Dad's hand for a moment before shaking reluctantly. "Good to meet you... *Gordon*." There's a hint of tease when he says Dad's name.

Dad grimaces slightly but manages to maintain a strained smile while he pumps Dante's arm.

"Easy bro, don't break it."

"What," Dad challenges, "Did I hurt your arm?"

I don't think my dad is strong enough to hurt Dante, but don't try telling him that.

"I meant *your* arm, bro," Dante smirks.

"Now you two," Catarina says, forcing a chuckle. "Do I need to send you to your rooms?"

"Is he moving in?" Dad asks. "We didn't talk about him moving in."

Dante moving in? That would be amazeballs. The guest bedroom is next to mine. We would be sharing the upstairs hall bathroom. Imagine what we could do to each other in that bathroom?

O. M. GUILT!

"Calm down, Gordon. I haven't said anything about Dante moving in. But he's welcome to stay for as long as he wants, wouldn't you say?"

Dad opens his mouth to argue but clamps it shut. "Of course. We would be happy to have you as our... *guest*, Dante." Dad smirks at him.

"Then show me to my room," Dante grins.

Dad glowers.

I'm loving every minute of this because Dante is matching Dad point for point.

Catarina also seems amused. "All right, enough," she chuckles nervously while shooting covert daggers at Dad. "So, Dante, when did you arrive?"

"Just got here today."

"Where were you before?" Dad asks suspiciously.

"Long story. Maybe I'll tell you over beers sometime."

Dad scowls. He probably doesn't like Dante talking to him like an equal. Dad rarely considers anyone his equal.

"And you've met Skye?" Catarina asks.

My guilt kicks in like a mule as I remember everything Dante and I have done today since we met. "Met" is such an inadequate word for it.

"Not officially," Dante winks at me.

Please do not wink at me in front of our parents!!! I want to scream it, but don't. I think the look on my face is shouting loud enough.

"What does that mean?" Dad demands.

"Well, we, uh..." Dante stammers. This is the first time he's appeared anything but unflappable in the face of my dad, which is an accomplishment in itself.

Don't start going all flappable on me now, Dante! No flapping! We don't want you spilling any beans about what your cock did to my bean today!

"He means," I blurt, "that we never shook hands or anything." We shook other things, shudder, but hopefully my hasty explanation will satisfy Dad's intrusive curiosity. Dads aren't supposed to know about their daughters' sex lives.

"Then you should shake hands, right?" Dad says innocently.

Damn him and his formalities.

Without missing a beat, Dante extends his arm to shake my hand.

I lean over and grab it, intent on pretending this is all no big deal. Guess what? It IS a big deal. When Dante's hand wraps around mine, electricity shoots up my arm and my whole body melts. Where did my bones go? It takes everything I have not to puddle up on the floor at Dante's feet. I don't know how he manages to affect me like this. I'm shaking hands with Dante and I never want to stop.

Ach! Why is he so damn hot! Even the feel of his hand is pleasant ecstasy.

Dad is giving me an odd look.

guiltguiltguiltguiltguilt

I'm supposed to be Daddy's little girl.

GuiltGuiltGuiltGuilt

Still shaking hands with Dante like it's the best thing ever. Can you have a hand orgasm? Cause I'm having one right now. Oh my goodness. I can't breathe. Not that I deserve to after all I've done with Dante today! There is a special place in hell for me, right next to the other sex criminals!

Help!!

Dante seems not to notice my discomfort because he's not letting go of my hand. He's grinning with obvious satisfaction.

"All right, that's enough," Dad laughs.

GUILT!!!!!

I yank my hand out of Dante's.

What have I done?

I. Am. Hot. For. My. Stepbrother.

I mean, just look at him!!

But we already figured that part out when he made me come in the wave pool!

GUILT!!!!!!!!!

"I don't know about all of you," Dad says, "but I have quite the appetite today."

He isn't the only one with an appetite. Oh! He means food!

"Anyone ready for a bite to eat?" Dad finishes.

Dante smirks at me like he wants to eat a bite of me.

He can do all the biting he wants.

Just not in front of our parents!!

GUILT!! GUILT!! GUILT!!

oOoOoOo + O+O+O+O

We end up ordering Chinese takeout because Catarina is too flustered to cook. Dante offers to pick it up, which scores points with Dad. Dad reminds him to park his motorcycle in the street when HE comes back. Dad never quits.

The four of us sit down at the dining room table, me across from Dante, Dad and Catarina at opposite ends. Side note: Dante is literally the hottest man who has ever sat at our dinner table. I mean, I've had cute guys over, but not swoon worthy Bod Gods. It's almost like having your favorite movie star or rock star or fitness model come by for dinner. I mean, can you imagine the giddy fan-girling you would do if your dream date was at your dinner table?

"So, Dante, are you in college?" Dad asks as he ladles Kung Pao chicken onto his plate with a serving spoon.

"No," he says as he takes the carton of broccoli beef from Catarina, "I skipped college."

"How old are you again?" Dad asks.

"Twenty-one."

"What did you do after high school?"

"I traveled."

"For four years?"

"Six."

"Six? That doesn't add up. You're only 21. Did you graduate high school early?"

"Nope. Dropped out."

Catarina frowns. She doesn't know any of Dante's history after the age of 14.

"You dropped out of high school?" Dad asks, shocked.

"Yeah. I didn't see the point."

"The point is to get an education," Dad chuckles and shakes his head in disbelief. "So, how did you manage to travel all that time without an education?"

"Well," Dante grins, "I got on a plane and went from Point A to Point B. When I got bored with Point B, I took a train to Point C. After that—"

Dad waves a dismissive hand, "What I meant was, how did you pay for it?"

"Dad," I interject. Sometimes he doesn't know when to quit.

"You can travel for cheap if you're smart about it," Dante says.

"I suppose that's true. Does that mean you work?"

"When I have to."

Dad smirks, "So you're a free spirit?"

"The freest."

"That must be nice. Not having any responsibilities."

Wow, Dad is just firing with every barrel tonight.

"He's young, Gordon," Catarina offers. "This is the time in a young man's life when he should be exploring the world."

"I spent a summer backpacking around Europe," Dad says to her. "But I also got a degree."

"Not everyone has to have a degree," Catarina says.

"You have one," Dad says. "Skye will also have one in a few years. What's wrong with getting a degree?"

Catarina smiles impatiently, "I didn't say there was anything wrong with it."

"Okay then," Dad says like he won the argument.

I don't know what to say, so I busy myself with biting into a fried pork pot sticker.

"Gordon," Dante says.

Dad winces, "Yes, Dante?" He sounds petty.

"Did you know that people all over the world get by without a college degree?"

"And they live in third world countries," Dad chuckles.

"Do you think there's something wrong with people in third world countries?" Dante asks.

"Well, no, but..." Dad trails off. "Getting a degree is the wise thing to do for an American. We don't live in grass huts over here."

I repress a snicker and shake my head. O.M.Groan.

"You could," Dante says. "If you were willing to reduce your bloated standard of living, cut back your carbon footprint, and sacrifice most of the luxuries you're addicted to."

Go, Dante!

Dad frowns, bemused. "I thought you said you didn't graduate high school?"

"I didn't," he answers. "I read books."

"Books," Dad echoes like it's the stupidest thing ever. "Books can't teach you everything. The world economy is a complex animal. It's all tied together. You can't just throw away the infrastructure and have everyone live in grass huts. Commerce would grind to a halt."

"You could, but people won't."

"Do *you* live in a grass hut?" Dad sneers.

"I have. And I would again. But there's other options. Have you heard of a hexayurt?"

"What in hell is a hexayurt?" Dad scowls.

"It's a way to make geodesic housing out of readily available construction materials like plywood or even high density cardboard and duct tape. All you need is a bunch of 4 by 8 foot sheets of whatever material and you can slap one together in no time. If you do it right, they'll last for years."

Everyone is stunned into silence.

I do my best not to giggle.

"Did you read that in a book?" Dad asks sarcastically.

"No. I read about it on the internet."

"The internet," Dad scoffs.

"Then I helped build a bunch for a displaced tribe in Brazil when the cattle ranchers kicked them out of the rain forest where they'd lived for generations."

Everyone stares at Dante in disbelief.

"You did not," Dad laughs.

"I can show you the website. We paid for all the materials with donated money. There's video on YouTube showing us building dozens of hexayurts for the tribe on government land. I'm in it."

Holy shit. Who knew Dante was this awesome?

"You did all that?" Catarina marvels, captivated by her son's story.

"Yup," he smiles proudly.

"Can you believe that, Gordon?" she smiles.

He chuckles, "I'll have to see the video."

"Don't you believe him?" she presses.

Dad shrugs. "Show me the video."

Dante says. "I'll show you after dinner."

"Sure," Dad says, scraping at his Kung Pao chicken with his chopsticks.

A tense moment of silence passes between Dad and Catarina. That's not good. Dad and Catarina bicker now and then, but they usually get along great. I've never seen this kind of tension between them. I hope Dante doesn't create a problem for them. That would totally suck.

"So, Dante," Dad says, "will you be staying in a hexa-whatever while you're here? Or will you be staying in our first world luxury accommodations?"

"Gordon!" Catarina blurts. "Be nice. Dante just got here."

Dante grimaces. "I don't need to stay here." He pauses for effect. "Gordon."

"Then don't," Dad says casually.

"Gordon!!" Catarina barks.

"Geez, Dad!" I groan. "Take a chill pill already."

Dad laughs nervously and shakes his head while staring at his plate and flicking at his chicken. "Sorry. You can stay here, Dante. If you want to sleep in the backyard, you're welcome to."

I grimace and shake my head, "O.M. Groan, Dad…"

oOoOoOo + O+O+O+O

"I think I'm gonna head out," Dante says after he clears the last of the takeout boxes from the table and puts more dishes in the kitchen sink. Dante did practically all of the clean up and told Catarina to relax when she tried to help. Of course I helped so I could be close to Dante. I simply can't resist him, not after the way he put Dad in his place and not after everything else today. It's been a nonstop swoon typhoon ever since Hurricane Dante dropped into my life.

Dante grabs his leather jacket from where it hangs on one of the stools at the kitchen island and slides it on.

"You're leaving?" Catarina says, disappointed.

"Yeah."

"But you're coming back, right?" She sounds half panicked.

"I just need some air. It's a bit stuffy in here." He shoots a glance at my dad.

Dad offers a phony grin. Poor Dad.

Dante won tonight's intellectual tennis game six to nothing. Somehow, I don't think the match is over. I repress another giggle, then say, "I can join you, Dante. If you wanna go for a walk or something."

"Sounds like a plan," Dante smiles.

Dad says "Skye, don't you have prep work for your SATs? The last time I checked, your math scores were still lagging below the 90th percentile."

Wow, way to embarrass me, Dad. I sigh heavily. Do I sound pouty? Of course I do. I've been studying all damn summer.

"I can help you with math," Dante says. "If you need any tutoring."

"She already has a tutor," Dad says. "He's quite good."

"You're a numbers guy, Gordon. Why don't you tutor her? I bet your daughter would appreciate some quality math instruction from her old man."

I don't know about that. Dad would be a horrible tutor, even if he does know numbers better than I ever will. But I do know that Dad hates being called "old man". The irritated look on his face is proof.

Dad smirks at Dante, "I would, if I had the time."

"Don't sweat it, Gordon. I've got nothing but time. One of the advantages of not having a mortgage or a shiny new Beemer." He saw Dad's shiny new BMW 760Li parked outside when he went to get the Chinese food. Dad just bought it a few months ago.

Dad scoffs, "If it wasn't for my mortgage, you wouldn't have a place to do any math tutoring."

"I hear the public libraries are free. And they don't even charge you for electricity. Skye, what time does your local library close?" Wow, he is *so* rubbing it in Dad's face. Yay!

"Nine," I say. "We could totally go there."

"No, you could not—*urp!*" Dad chokes.

Catarina just elbowed him. She says, "I think Dante makes a good point. It's one thing to talk about being green and saving electricity and reducing your carbon footprint, it's another thing to do it. The library sounds like a terrific idea. Don't you agree, Gordon?" She gives Dad a superior smirk.

Dad gives her a fake smile. "Dante, have you heard the saying, 'We'll have to agree to disagree'?"

"Of course," Dante smiles.

"That applies here."

"I can hang with that."

Catarina smiles at Dad, pleased with herself.

You'll notice that Dad didn't disagree with Catarina. He disagreed with Dante. Dad isn't an idiot. He knows how to pick his battles.

Dad chuckles and pats Dante heartily on the shoulder. "Go help my daughter with her math."

"At the library?" Dante grins.

"No. Do it here. You can use the dining room table. No sense letting my electric bill go to waste."

Catarina frowns at Dad. He just cut everyone off at the pass or whatever the saying is.

"Actually," Dante says, "the lights are on at the library whether people are there using them or not. So we may as well use those. If we stay here, we'll have to use extra lights. No sense being wasteful."

Catarina gives Dad a satisfied look. "What did I tell you, Gordon?"

"Aren't you wasting gas by driving there?" Dad asks, proud.

"We'll walk," Dante says.

Finally, Dad relents, chuckling mildly. "Fine. I get it. Dante is smart and he didn't go to college. Did you read all your books at a library?"

"I did, in fact," Dante grins. "Or checked them out so I could read them outside in sunlight."

Dad waves his hands, "Go to the library, you two. The opportunity cost of arguing this any further is approaching intolerable."

Dante grins, victorious.

Wow, Dante is whip smart. Did I mention he was hot? Now he's hot-squared or cubed or fourthed or whatever advanced math is necessary to multiply his awesomeness accurately.

oOoOoOo + O+O+O+O

"I don't get it," I sigh impatiently, tapping my pencil eraser on my notebook. I'm trying to solve an SAT practice question about how many tubes of lipstick sell at a certain price. "How could I end up with a negative number?"

Dante and I sit shoulder to shoulder at one of the work tables in my neighborhood library. He glances at my steps, which are all written out in pencil on my blue-lined college-ruled paper. "I see what you did," he says. "Read the question again."

"I already read it," I sigh. "Math has always been an epic pain in my ass."

"Look at me," he says in that deep and calming voice of his.

"Huh?" My brain melts when I stare into his glimmering emerald eyes. Math? What's math? I can't think about math right now. All I can think about is Dante. And how much better the world is with him in it. With Dante around, who needs math?

"Take a deep breath," he commands.

"Why?"

"Just do it."

I inhale and huff out a sigh. "Okay, now what? Am I supposed to have the right answer now?"

He grins that cute dimpled grin of his. "First, take a real breath."

"I just did. I'm alive, aren't I? If that was a fake breath, I'd be suffocating, right?" We've been working on math problems for an hour straight. I'm ready to throw it in.

"You need to relax. You're wound up tight as a drum right now."

"Of course I am! I'm all mathed out. I need a study break or something."

"What do you do if you get frustrated in the middle of the SATs? You can't take a study break then. You need a strategy to use during the test. I never took the SAT, but I bet you're stuck in one of those cramped high school desks, right?"

"Yeah."

"It's kind of like being locked in a prison cell with a guard and a timer telling you to 'DO MATH NOW! LIKE YOUR LIFE DEPENDS ON IT!!' Right?"

"Yeah," I chuckle. "When you put it that way, it sounds horrible, doesn't it? I'm in math jail, getting math tortured!" I giggle. "Oops, sorry. I'm being loud." I glance around the library. There's plenty of people around, but no one seemed to notice my outburst.

"Math jail," he quips. "At least you're not in third world factory jail."

"What?"

He shakes his mind, "Never mind. I'm getting off track. We need to teach you how to relax in the middle of a test."

"Okay."

"First, sit up straight in your chair. You're all hunched over. Your stomach is probably in knots."

"How did you know?" I marvel.

"Because I've watched you curl up like a hedgehog since you first sat down."

"A hedgehog?" I laugh. "Do I have pointy spines on my back?" I glance over my shoulder.

"No, but your mouth is plenty sharp," he jokes.

"Hey!" I swat his leg.

"Sit up."

I do.

"Close your eyes."

"You're not gonna do something weird, are you?"

"I will if I feel like it."

"Hey!" I glare.

"Relax. You'll be fine. Close your eyes."

I do.

"Take a deep breath. From your stomach. And do it slow. Count five in, five out. Slow and steady."

I do as he says. After several cycles, I start to relax.

"Feel your neck and shoulders loosening up."

Magically, hearing him say that in his soothing voice makes it happen.

"Let your arms dangle at your sides and wiggle your fingers."

"What if the test guy tells me to stop?"

"You mean the proctor?"

I grimace, "I hate the sound of that word."

"I know," he chuckles. "It sounds like an ass doctor."

I cackle joyfully but clamp my mouth shut. I lean against Dante, trying to keep my laughs inside, but my clicking snickering tickles the roof of my mouth and I blurt out more laughter.

"Easy, girl. You're ruining the library atmosphere." He rubs his hand vigorously on my shoulder.

"That feels good. I'm more relaxed already. Can I take you with me to the next SAT?"

"I'd be glad to go with you, but I don't think that would fly with the ass doctors."

I snicker again and slump into him.

"Okay," he says. "Back to relaxing."

Sensing a flirtatious opportunity, I allow my torso to slide into his lap. Then I twist so I'm looking up at him.

"That's not what I meant," he grins down at me.

"I'm already relaxed." I casually rub his abs through his T-shirt with the backs of my knuckles. "You know, you're way better than my math tutor Marvin."

"Marvin?"

"Yeah. He's 14 and he's uber smart. Kind of like you. But not nearly as cute."

"Nobody's as cute as me," he smirks.

"You have a giant head, you know that?"

"That's what she said," he winks.

I feel my cheeks glowing red as I think about everything I know about *both* of his heads. And how big they are...

"Let's talk about math, shall we?" Dante says.

"Let's *not* talk about math," I giggle. "Seriously, who needs math?"

"You totally need a study break."

"*We* need a study break. I'm not taking one without you."

"Okay. *We* will take a study break in a minute."

"Do we have to wait?" I whine.

"Yes, we do."

SLAM! A book drops onto the floor somewhere nearby, jolting me out of my romantic mood.

I'm suddenly convinced someone is watching us. I sit up quickly and glance around at the stacks of books. We're in the reference section of the library. People are busy getting books or flipping through them at the surrounding tables. It could've been anybody. I ignore it. But it's a good reminder that this isn't exactly the place to get romantic with Dante.

Reluctantly, I sit up with a sigh. "Where were we?"

"We were talking about the ass doctor? You asked what to do if he tells you not to wiggle your fingers during the exam?"

"Oh yeah."

"If he says that, just try sitting up straight. Take a few deep breaths, counting to five on the inhale and five on the exhale."

"What if he tells me not to do that?" I'm being a brat.

Dante snorts, "Then ask him if it says anywhere in the testing guidelines that you're not allowed to breathe or close your eyes during the test."

"Wow," I marvel, "You seriously need to come to the SATs with me. I don't know if I'd be able to think of all your witty retorts when the pressure is on."

"If you stay relaxed, you'll think of everything yourself," he says with utter confidence. "You don't need me. You need you."

I stop myself and let that sink in. Wow. That was profound. I shake my head, my eyes narrowed, gazing into his eyes.

His emerald gems sparkle back at me through his thick lashes.

I'm on the verge of swooning again. "How did you get to be so smart, Dante?" Now is totally a kissing moment.

He dodges the option and says, "Back to your lipstick price problem. Read the question again."

"Yes, sir," I joke, smiling happily. My cheeks are still warm. I'm high on Dante right now. Somehow, he makes math almost as good as kissing. Not quite, but close. You know what I mean. I re-read the question. I see my mistake instantly. "Oh shit! I totally glossed over the part where it says that P is the number of *thousands* of units sold. I put down 50,000 when I should've put 50!"

"You got it," he grins.

I punch all the numbers into my calculator and check the result against the answer in the back of the SAT prep book. "That's right!"

He holds up his palm, "High five."

I smack his hand with mine. "Yes!"

"See? Once you were relaxed, you saw your mistake right away."

"I did," I grin.

"Do you still feel like math is an epic pain in the ass?"

"Not with an ass doctor like you!" I giggle.

"Okay, now you seriously need a study break."

Chapter 5

"This way," I giggle as I lead Dante down the stairs to the lower level of the library.

There are a bunch of meeting rooms down here. Some nights they're in use. Tonight, they're all empty. I try several doors before I find one that's unlocked. I pull it open. "It's dark," I whisper. "Come on." I pull Dante by the hand into the meeting room.

Dante flips on the lights, revealing a bunch of tables arranged in a big square in the middle of the room. Dozens of chairs are pushed under the tables.

I pull the door closed behind us. I look for a lock on the doorknob, but it's just one of those push bars. Oh well. It's not like anyone is gonna come in here at this hour. I flip the lights off, "We don't need lights." It is now pitch black. "I can't see anything. Where'd you go!" I feel around in the air for Dante. I can't even see my fingers.

"This is my kind of study break," Dante growls in my ear, startling me.

"Time for Sex Ed?" I whisper. I gasp when he grabs me abruptly and spins me up against the wall. In the darkness, the sudden motion makes me feel dizzy and off balance. Or that could just be Dante. He does have that affect on me. His hot body presses up against mine, trapping me inside his hard arms. I can't go anywhere unless he lets me. Heat pours off of him. His musky scent invades me, going straight to my core. Something about not being able to see heightens my sense of smell. I'm overwhelmed by his scent. I inhale deeply and I swear it makes my breasts tingle as my ribs expand. "Dante," I sigh.

His hot mouth melts into mine and my knees nearly buckle, but he holds me up by forcing himself between my legs. It's like we're picking up exactly where we left off when Catarina showed up at the house earlier.

"I've been thinking about this for hours," he hisses. His manhood strains against me. Too bad his jeans are in the way.

I jam my fingers between us, trying to undo his buckle.

"No," he grunts.

"What?" Did I do something wrong?

"Now it's my turn." Hard hands grab my ass and he lifts me up by the butt and spins us again. He walks us away from the wall.

I float in the darkness. I have no idea what's going on. I hear the clatter of metal meeting room chairs. What's he doing? Suddenly I'm tipping back like I'm falling and I gasp. A powerful hand presses against my spine, supporting me. I relax against his arm as he lowers me gently onto one of the tables. The surface is hard, but I don't mind. I'm now on my back and my legs hang over the edge. My legs are too short to touch the floor. Before I can adjust them, his hands hook under my knees and pushes them toward my chest, opening me up. Although I'm wearing panties and cotton shorts, I know that I'm completely wet and fully exposed to this man. I gasp again.

"Do you want this?" he growls harshly.

I'm suddenly nervous. I'm not even sure how I feel about this. "Umm…" A second later, I feel my legs lowered slowly to the floor. It's dark and I can't see him. Based on his tone of voice, I imagine him looking brooding and angry. I'm a little bit scared. "Dante?" I reach out for him with my hands, waving them through the air, trying to find him. "Where'd you go?" I whisper.

My fingers brush against something and I feel his large hands close gently over mine. They are warm and comforting, despite their strength. Lips brush my palms and I shiver with pleasure.

"Do you want this?" he whispers, this time with compassion and concern.

"Want what?" I'm afraid to say yes, but I'm not ready to say no.

"I want to touch you, Skye. I want to drive you wild. I want to teach you things about your body that you never knew. I want to make you come so hard that you lose your mind. But only if you say yes."

I've never had a guy ask me anything like this. They're usually just pushy. It's all about them. For the first time ever, I feel like it's all about me. I'm so touched, I can't even speak.

"Skye, just give me the word and I will turn on the lights, open the door for you like a gentleman, and we'll go back to studying math like this never happened. It's totally up to you. Whatever you decide, we'll still be friends, and I'll still be your new stepbrother. The choice is yours."

Oh, gawd. What the hell am I supposed to say? And did he have to remind me he's my stepbrother? I mean, we're not related by blood. But come on! This is insane. It's also what I want. I want this. For me. I want to take this risk. No matter how crazy it is. "Yes," I whisper.

"Yes what?" He sounds pleased.

"Yes, you can do whatever you want. Just, uh, nothing with my butt. No ass doctoring. Okay?"

He chuckles. "Okay. Fair enough. No ass doctoring. We'll save that subject for later."

"Thank you," I half giggle.

"Okay. One more time. Are you saying yes?"

I roll my eyes in the darkness, even though he can't see me. "Yes. Go nuts. Err, I mean—" I gasp again as he picks up my knees and forces them to my chest once again. I almost yelp, but hold it in. I trust him. I don't know why, but I do. I am wide open to him. Sure, my shorts and panties are in the way, but I've never been man handled like this. With Dante doing it, I'm enjoying every second of it.

When it comes to sex in public places, I never fantasized about the local library. I always thought about parks or beaches with picnic blankets or sleeping bags. Not stacks of books or empty meeting rooms. Turns out the library is a huge turn on. I guess all those sexy librarians know what they're talking about.

Something presses against my folds through the material of my shorts and panties. I am definitely wet. Both his hands hold my knees, so I'm not really sure where his third arm came from. Is he using his chin or his, um, *third* arm? I don't know, but I like it. Electric thrills sparkle up my stomach. His chin or whatever makes slow gentle circles, massaging my core expertly. Every circle releases a spiral of pleasure that corkscrews outward in every direction, tingling my toes all the way to my nipples and up to my scalp. I've never been this incredibly turned on. I didn't know it was possible to be this turned on. Wow.

Strong hands slide down my hamstrings. Thumbs massage my inner thighs, slipping into the legs of my shorts.

Oh, wow. Here come his hands…

Thumbs pry their way under my cotton panties and stroke my lips. In the darkness, I hear the minute pops and clicks of my wetness. Holy cow, I'm soaked. I want this to go on forever.

Shoulders or chest muscles press into the backs of my knees, opening me up wider. I'm pretty flexible, so my knees go up to my chest. I feel like my womanhood is front and center for Dante's—

Oh!

Something warm slides up my crease, teasing right across my exposed clit. Shiver. "Ohhh… Dante." What is it? His thumb? I'm not sure. I hope it's his thumb…

This feels way too good.

I've masturbated plenty of times, but this is a million times better.

His thumb or whatever arcs up and down across my clit.

Fuck.

He eases up on the backs of my knees with his shoulders and lowers himself until he's probably down on his knees. My legs rest on top of his shoulders. I feel heat blow across my center. A hand hooks my panties and shorts to the side and more heat wafts across my hot wet center. I feel like a hot tart or some other kind of steamy sweet dessert with a juicy center. I'm about to giggle when electric sex spears my clit.

Tongue.

That is most definitely tongue.

It works a circle that spins my head faster than a spinner ride at an amusement park. I start to quiver on the table top. Every muscle in my body spasms like I'm having some sort of a seizure. I've never had a guy go down on me before. To tell the truth, I've never really wanted any of the guys I've been with to do it. The idea made me nervous. I'm not nervous now. All I want is more of the head heroin that Dante is giving me. Chills and heat waves criss cross their way through my nervous system. I feel an orgasm begin to build.

He continues to lick with hot need, his entire tongue tickling every millimeter of my feminine flesh.

The orgasm starts to tighten with familiar force. Just when I think it's about to release, it doesn't.

Wait, what?

I thought I just came, but the pleasure is still building.

Muscles deep inside me clamp down again as his tongue assaults me.

Oh, gawd.

It keeps getting better.

He hasn't even put fingers inside me.

Just tongue.

His incredible tongue.

Another orgasmic wave whips through me.

Oh my god. With tongues like this, who needs dicks?

Circles, circles, circles...

Pleasure, pleasure, more pleasure...

His dizzying tongue is making magic between my legs.

"Oh, god, Dante, that feels... oh! Dante! Dante!!"

A delicious bubble inflates inside my chest and pushes pleasure sensations out of every pour in my body. I tingle from head to toe as every muscle in my belly suddenly locks tight, pulling all of that pleasure back into me, concentrating every bit of it between my legs.

Everything has become tongue and come.

My clit is arcing with a billion volts of electricity. A sizzling current of pleasure crackles through my veins.

And then he's inside me, filling me up. It's the most perfect sensation I've ever felt. It's the only sensation I ever want to feel again.

Him inside me.

Is he wearing a condom? I don't know, I don't care, because this is right. I can't explain it, but my body tells me this is the exact thing I've wanted since I started noticing boys.

This.

Only this.

And that sends me over the edge.

I am coming harder than I ever thought possible. My eyes clamp shut and my mouth gapes in a silent scream. We are in the library, after all. A tiny squeak peeps from my throat. Actually, I don't think I *can* scream. Every muscle in my body is locked up with orgasmic spasms.

Just when I think I'm going to have a stroke—

Release.

Liquid warmth washes over me as every muscle in my body suddenly relaxes.

Release.

I drown in the pleasure that floods out from between my legs.

oOoOoOo + O+O+O+O

I heave heavily, inhaling and exhaling as the orgasm fades into the darkness of the nearly empty library meeting room.

I just came at the library. Put that on your bucket list!

Holy WOW!!

"Dante," I sigh, "That was, that was… I don't know *what* that was. Wow."

"You like?" His finger skims up and down along my slit. It's just hard enough to tickle, but light enough that I'm not sucked back into another orgasmic tunnel of semi-consciousness.

"Oh, fuck. Yeah, I like. What were you doing down there?"

"I'll give you one guess," he chuckles confidently.

Now that I'm coming down from coming, I avoid the obvious. I'm not quite ready to think about the ramifications of any unprotected ramming that just happened. I joke, "Yeah, yeah. But are you sure you didn't have help from like six vibrators or something? That was incredible."

"I know."

"You are such a cocky bastard, aren't you?"

"Want to check for yourself?"

I glance down between my legs, "I can't see anything. It's too dark."

"Feel. Give me your hand."

"I don't want to poke your eye out with my finger."

"Just hold your hand out near your pussy."

I smirk when he says pussy. I don't know why. But I hold my hand out. Something bumps my palm and my fingers close around his— COCK!! It's hot and heavy and pulsing in my hand. "Dante!" I hiss. "Did you just fuck me?!" I knew he was inside me, but still. This is proof. And I'm shocked. Sure, I did say he could do whatever he wanted, but I'm suddenly freaked out. What did I just do? "Dante, did you come inside me?"

"No."

"Really?"

"Yup."

"Are you *sure* sure?" My anxiety level is on the launch pad like a space rocket and the guys in the control room are doing that countdown to blast off:

Ten, nine, eight, seven…

He snorts, "I'm pretty sure I know what my dick has been doing for the last ten minutes."

"Yeah, but did you come inside me?"

Six, five, four…

"I told you, no."

That's what guys always say. I'm freaking out.

Three, two, one…

"There was some finger toward the end, but that's it."

"Wait, for sure? There was no cock involved?"

"Yeah," he chuckles. "I mean, no. No cock."

"None? No cock whatsoever?"

"Nope," he snickers. "I mean, I have a cock, but it was never in play."

"Oh, phew."

Launch Aborted. And other things I don't want to think about.

"But it was waiting on the sidelines, ready to go in if the moment called for it," he says. "You can feel it. The shaft is dry."

Panic averted, I sit up and hold his exquisite shaft in both hands. He's really big. "Oh. Duh." I sigh. Then I sort of caress him with my fingers, exploring his throbbing length, feeling how hot and hard and silky smooth he is. The veins closer to the base are pumping blood in a hypnotic rhythm.

"Easy," he moans. "Don't start something you're not going to finish."

"Oh. Sorry." I release one hand but slide my other up the length. I can't help it. I want to feel him. I unintentionally circle my fingers around the spongy head. "Wait, why is the head wet?"

"That's pre-cum."

I shake my head in the dark, "What the hell did you do? I thought you said there was no cock?"

"About half way through, I took my dick out and stroked myself while I was eating you out."

"Huh?" This is all so overwhelming. "Why were you doing that?" I sort of feel slighted, like he *should* have been inside me, not giving himself a handy.

"Because if I didn't, I was going to fuck you right here."

"Why?" Yeah, it sounds stupid.

"Because you turn me on like nobody else, Skye."

"Oh." I can accept that. Wow. "But you know what I mean. I mean, why not?"

"Skye, I wasn't going to put it in you without checking in first. I didn't want to ruin *your* moment."

"Oh." Is he serious? This is too good to be true.

A moment later, his hands rest on my thighs. I scoot forward to the very edge of the table and wrap my knees around his waist. His hands slide up my back and caress my shoulders. I loop my arms around his neck. My eyes have adjusted to the darkness. There's a faint line of light coming through the bottom of the door to the meeting room. I can make out Dante's face, but just barely.

We are nose to nose.

Our lips press gently together and we kiss deeply.

I can't believe everything that has happened with Dante in just one day. It's incredible. It's beyond words. It's—

CLANK!

The door to the meeting room opens a few inches and white light pours inside, blinding me.

I squint my eyes, trying to see who it is. All I can see is a silhouette in the doorframe.

Flash! Cha-CLICK!!

That's the sound of a cell phone camera taking a picture.

"Hey!" I bark, suddenly blinded by the camera flash.

The door closes.

"What the fuck?" Dante grunts. His belt buckle goes *tink tink* as he no doubt fumbles with his pants.

"Someone just took our picture!" I hiss.

"No shit," he growls and strides to the door a few seconds later, hammering the push bar open.

I'm right behind him.

All we see are jeans and shoes jogging up the stairs.

Dante bolts out the door and I follow. He hurdles up the staircase in five long strides. When I reach the top of the stairs, he's holding Brittany Price by the arm.

"What the fuck was that?" he demands.

"What was what?" Brittany asks innocently.

Oh, no. Brittany and Ashley Masters are besties. Or what passes for besties amongst their back-stabbing ilk. This is beyond bad.

"Gimme your phone," I growl.

Brittany smiles at me like I'm speaking another language. "I'm sorry, what did you say?"

"Gimme your phone so I can erase that photo you just took."

"What photo?" She sounds bemused. "I have no idea what you're talking about." She is totally lying.

Who the hell else could it have been? No one is standing near the staircase except her.

My mind races as I consider what has just happened. When the door opened, Dante and I were kissing. Luckily, his pants were mostly on, and my shorts were never off. But I can't remember if he turned to look at the door. When the photo snapped, were we both looking at the camera? Will Brittany's pic have a clear image of me *and* Dante? With my arms and legs wrapped around him? Oh gawd, if this gets out, I'm screwed. "Gimme your phone, Brittany. Right now," I hiss.

She arches her eyebrows snootily. "Sorry. I can't do that."

"You didn't have our permission to take that picture."

"What are you talking about, Skye?"

Wow, what a bitch. "Brittany, you better give me your phone," I seethe. I feel powerless right now. This is awful.

"Or what, Skye?"

"Or, or—just give me the phone!"

"Is there a problem?" a librarian asks, having just turned a corner. She's a middle aged woman with a frumpy blouse and slacks.

"Nope," Brittany smiles victoriously. "I was just leaving." She disappears around the corner.

The librarian glares at me and Dante with obvious irritation. "This is a library, you two," she admonishes, "not a playground. I would expect better behavior from people your age. Please respect the library rules, or I will have to ask you both to leave."

Is she done yet? "Yeah, okay fine," I say hastily. "Let's go, Dante." I pull him by the arm.

When we turn the corner, Brittany is gone.

oOoOoOo + O+O+O+O

"If Brittany shares that photo, I'm screwed," I say to Dante as we walk home from the library.

The suburban streets are empty but well lit by numerous orange streetlights. Dante carries my backpack over his shoulder. He offered to carry it when we stepped out of the library into the warm summer evening air. Such a gentleman. Sadly, what should be a romantic walk through my quiet neighborhood is fraught with anxiety.

He puts an arm around my shoulder and pulls me snugly against him. "She wouldn't do that, would she?"

"You don't know the girls at my high school. They are catty jealous bitches. They will do anything to make someone else look bad. Just to make themselves look better."

"Why?"

"Because they're bitches! Don't you know anything about high school social politics?!" I'm practically shrieking.

"Not really," he sighs.

I take a deep breath, trying to calm down. "Sorry. I forgot you dropped out."

"It's cool."

It may be cool, but he just let his arm fall from my shoulder. "I'm sorry, Dante. Now I'm being the bitch. It's just that I'm really worried about this. If Brittany shows Ashley and Monica, I can picture the three of them conniving and strategizing about how to best ruin my life by posting that photo at the most inopportune time."

"Would they do that?"

"Yes they would."

"Did you do something to piss them off or something?"

"No. I try to avoid them. I mean, I see them at parties and stuff, but it's not like we're close. I try to stay out of their way."

"Then why would they dump on you like that?"

"That's the thing. Those three will do anything in their power to remain at the top of the North Valley High School social ladder. They live to be on top. Part of staying on top is keeping everyone else on the bottom. If they can make me look bad, they will. Maybe not right away, but when the time is right, I guarantee you, that photo of us is going to show up."

"So what if it does?"

"Duh!" I bark. "We're stepbrother and sister! The kids at school will have a field day with that!"

He smirks.

"It's not funny! This could be the end of my life as I know it!"

"Now I know why I dropped out of high school. I've met nicer drug dealers."

"Drug dealers? What do you know about drug dealers?"

"Long story."

We turn the corner onto my street. My house is only a few driveways down at the end of the cul-de-sac. Now is not the time for Dante to go into his own sordid past, whatever it may be. I don't want my dad accidentally overhearing and jumping to any more conclusions about Dante. The truth about him and me is already bad enough.

What was I thinking back in the library?

I was thinking that Dante is ridiculously hot. I wasn't thinking that Brittany Price would document my indiscretions. Why me? Couldn't she have picked someone else to torment? What was she doing snooping around at the library anyway? It doesn't matter now.

Dante stops us when we reach our driveway.

Our.

I keep forgetting how weird this is. He's going inside that house with me. He's not dropping me off like any other guy would. We are going inside. What's going to happen then? Will we continue what we started in that dark meeting room? With our parents sleeping just down the hall? Ew. I don't want to think about the possibility of them finding out. Especially not after what Brittany did. There's already too much evidence of our indiscretion floating around.

"We just have to make sure no one finds out you're my stepsister," Dante says.

"Easier said than done."

"Don't worry. I don't go to your high school. Nobody is going to see us together."

"Rox!" I blurt. "She already knows."

"Would she spread word around?"

"What, that you're my stepbrother?"

"Yeah."

"I don't know why she would. She's not a gossip."

"What about what we... you know, what we did?"

"I'm not a gossip either. I haven't told her."

Dante grins, "You haven't told your best friend about me and you kissing? Don't girls share that kind of information?"

"Not when she has a thing for you."

"Oh, right."

"What do you mean, 'Oh, right'," I mock.

"It was pretty obvious both of you were into me at Blazing Waters."

I smack his stomach with the back of my hand, hurting my knuckles more than anything.

"Hey!" he chuckles.

"You don't have to be so smug and cocky about it."

"What? You know it's true."

"So?" I growl.

"Relax," Dante says, holding both my arms gently. "I'm not into Rox or anybody else. I'm only into you, Skye."

The front door opens and Dad comes striding out.

I jump back and Dante drops his arms to his sides.

"What's up, Dad?" I ask nervously.

"Catarina forgot to bring in the mail." Our mailbox is one of those communal mailbox things with 15 other boxes. It's a few houses down from our driveway.

"Oh, okay," I say, relieved. For a second I was sure he'd seen us looking inappropriately intimate.

Dad hovers next to us. "How was the library?"

"Great!" I lie. Translation: Please leave us alone, Dad.

"Did you get a lot of studying done?" Dad asks, ignoring my subtext.

"Skye is a fast learner," Dante says.

I can't decide if that's an innuendo laden pun about what we did in the dark meeting room or not. Now would be a good time for Dad to leave.

"I know," Dad says. Somehow, that comment makes this conversation even weirder.

I bite my lip and try not to think about Dante and orgasms while my dad stands two feet away. I suddenly picture a camera crew driving up in a big news van. The reporter jumps out, flanked by the camera guy. A bright light blares in our faces and the reporter stabs the mic in my dad's face and says, "Sir, how does it feel knowing that your own daughter is sleeping with your sexy stepson?" Can you say awkward bomb?

Cringe.

Fortunately, the street is empty and the news vans are nowhere in sight.

Feeling guilty and skanky at the same time, which I think is referred to as "gunky", I say to Dad, "Do you want me to get the mail for you? I can bring it inside."

"Sure," Dad smiles.

Thank goodness for small favors.

oOoOoOo + O+O+O+O

"Can you do me a favor?" I ask Rox over the phone. I'm lying on my narrow twin bed in my bedroom, still dressed. Dante is down in the kitchen talking to his mom.

"Sure," Rox says in my ear.

"Can you not mention to anyone that Dante is my stepbrother?"

"Why not?"

"I ran into Brittany Price at the library tonight."

"Oh? What were you doing at the library?" Her tone of voice has shifted from normal Rox to suspicious Rox.

"Dante was helping me with my SAT math. Dad was being really annoying tonight. Actually, he was kind of a jerk to Dante."

"Oh?"

"You should've seen him. Dad was giving Dante tons of grief for not graduating college and traveling the world instead."

"What kind of grief?"

I do my best to recreate the showdown between Dad and Dante. I can't do it justice, but Rox is clearly amused by the whole thing. Especially the thing about the hexayurts and grass huts and stuff.

"Damn," she says. "It sounds like he shut your dad up."

"Yeah," I chuckle, "It was awesome. Anyway, Dante convinced my dad that it would save electricity if we studied at the library. Dante was ready to leave because Dad was being so rude, so it seemed like going to the library was best for everybody." I'm trying to make it sound all innocent.

"And you guys just studied?" Rox asks pointedly.

Does she know? How can she know? Maybe our lifelong friendship and her knowing my moods has something to do with it. "Of course we just studied," I say dismissively. "We were at the library. What else would we be doing?" Lies, lies, lies!!!

There's a pregnant pause.

Is my nose growing? Because I seriously feel like Pinocchiette right now.

"Just checking," Rox says.

I can't help but think that if this was any other random situation, Rox would totally call me on my evasive behavior. She would accuse me of getting defensive and pry with a pick axe until she got to the truth. But sadly, I think she doesn't want to actually entertain the idea that Dante and I did anything other than studying. She wants to keep believing that nothing happened.

If I told her what *did* happen, it would break her heart. I just know it.

I am a horrible person.

I am lying to my BFSF.

"Anyway—" I stop to rub my nose, which is suddenly itchy. I better not wake up tomorrow morning with a six foot long broomstick nose. "Anyway, please don't say anything to anyone about Dante being my stepbrother. It's bad enough Brittany and Ashley and Monica saw us at Blazing Waters with Dante. I mean, what would they say if they found out he was my stepbrother? Can you imagine the rumors?" Unfortunately, those three won't have to do any imagining. Ashley totally saw me kissing Dante in the wave pool. Now they have photographic proof.

"I get it," Rox says. "Those three rumor groomers would love to make you look bad any way they can. Them knowing you have a sexy stepbrother is begging for trouble. I won't say anything."

"Good," I sigh, relieved. I feel like I've been half holding my breath this entire conversation. I can't believe it went this smoothly.

"Besides," Rox says, "it certainly wouldn't look good for me if I start dating my best friend's stepbrother, would it?"

"No," I groan. "It wouldn't."

"I can totally see Ashely accusing us of having a threesome. We can't have that, can we?"

I wince, "No, definitely not."

"Good thing it'll never happen," she chuckles. Not for the reason she thinks. "Don't worry, Skye. Your secret is safe with me."

"Thanks," I say, relieved.

"Bee Tee Double U, can you do me a favor?"

"Sure. Anything."

"Can you steal one of Dante's shirts for me?"

"Whaaat?! Why?"

"So I can sleep with it."

"Why would you want to do that?" I know exactly why, because I already thought of it.

"As a warm up. So his scent will seep into my brain while I sleep.

Then I can dream about him all night tonight. Have my very own trashy sex dreams about Dante," she purrs. "Like the Gaga song. Speaking of, I think I'll go listen to it right now. Cue up the Sexxx Dreams!"

"I can't do that, Rox."

"Well, try."

"Nokay."

"Did you just so 'nokay'?"

"Yeppers."

"Bitch," she laughs. "Fine. You don't have to steal one of his shirts. But maybe you can borrow one for me? I'll return it when he marries me."

Oh, groan.

Chapter 6

I wonder if I can somehow manage to steal one of Dante's shirts to put under *my* pillow. And speaking of sex dreams, I'm having some sex day dreams right now while looking at Dante. I sit on the queen sized bed in the guest bedroom, which is next door to my bedroom. "So, Dante, am I gonna be safe with you in the next room?" I joke.

"Only if you want to be safe," Dante winks suggestively, a wicked glint in his eyes.

Catarina already made the bed while we were at the library. She showed Dante when we got back, almost like the made bed meant he had to spend the night, no matter how annoying Dad behaved. The door is wide open. My dad and Catarina are in the master bedroom getting ready for bed or chatting or who knows what. I know instinctively that if I was in this room with Dante with the door closed, Dad would somehow know. Whenever I've had boys over before, the rule has always been "doors open".

Dante is squatting on the floor beside his backpack, removing the contents thoughtfully, setting everything on the carpet with great care. Two rolled up T-shirts, folded socks, a toiletry bag. Too bad he only has two T-shirts. He'll totally notice if one goes missing. If Rox asks why I didn't steal her one, I'll blame his small wardrobe. He also pulls out a first aid kit. A tattered copy of On The Road by Jack Kerouac. A journal with a knotted piece of twine holding it shut and a ragged pencil that looks sharpened by hand.

"Is your like, whole life inside your backpack?" I ask.

"Pretty much. Everything I need, anyway. And I don't need much."

"Wow. That's so cool. I can't imagine having so few possessions."

"You get used to it. The next thing you know, you don't miss anything you used to have."

"Do you have a cell phone?"

"Not right now."

"I can't imagine not having one. I'd feel naked without the internet."

He shakes his head, grinning. "That's too bad."

"Why?" I genuinely want to know.

"Come camping with me some time. We'll leave your cell phone at home. Maybe drive up to Yosemite. That's close to here. Spend a week in the woods. I promise you, by the fourth day, you'll forget all about the internet."

The idea of spending a week with Dante in the woods sounds totally romantic. "I could be into that."

Dante pulls out a wrinkled map of Venezuela.

"Did you go to Venezuela recently?"

"Yeah. I was there in the spring."

"Really?"

"Yup. I spent weeks camping in Canaima National Park with some friends. Have you ever heard of Angel Falls or Mount Roraima?"

"No."

"Angel Falls is the world's tallest waterfall. It's over 3,000 feet high. There's nothing like it in the entire world. It's majestic. Breath taking." He has a far away look on his face. "The water from the falls is just clouds of mist by the time it reaches the bottom. On a sunny day, it's rainbow after rainbow."

"Wow, that sounds beautiful."

"You've never seen anything like it."

I've never seen anything like the look on Dante's face right now. So dreamy. Literally. I can only imagine the sites he's seen. "What's that mountain thing you mentioned? Mount Roar-What's-It?"

"Mount Roraima?"

"Yeah," I giggle.

"It's one of the oldest geological formations on the Earth. It's a table-top mountain with—"

"What's a table top mountain?"

He nods, looking up and away, remembering. "It's like a huge flat chunk of rock thrusting up out of the middle of the jungle. The plateau on the top is 20 square miles of land surrounded by 1,300 foot sheer rock faces on every side. It's like a time warp up there, like you're back in the time of the dinosaurs or something, like the jungle floor lifted up a billion years ago, preserving an entirely different ecosystem than the newer one down below. The vegetation is ancient. The rocks are worn down into crazy shapes by a billion years of wind and rain erosion. There are natural pools of collected rain water everywhere because it rains all the time. Some of the pools are big enough to sit in. You can soak and stare off into the clouds for hours. It's one of the most tranquil places on earth. So peaceful. The native Pemon people who live near the base of the mountain say that their gods live on top of the plateaus."

"Did you see any gods?" I joke.

"No," he grins, "but I can totally imagine them wanting to live there. It's paradise. Spending the night up there sleeping under the stars is like being in the Garden of Eden or something. A gentle breeze blowing across your face, the clouds opening and closing to reveal twinkling stars." He shakes his head and sighs. "When the weather is good, it's literally perfect."

"Wow, that sounds amazing. I think I'm jealous," I giggle.

"You should go. You'll never forget it."

"Will you take me?" I joke.

"Yup."

"Wait, are you serious?"

He nods.

Taking a trip with Dante to such a magical place sounds like a dream come true. I can't imagine it happening to me. The only vacations I've ever been on involve resort hotels and theme parks. My dad isn't into roughing it. But Dante makes it sound like roughing it and getting back to nature is the only way to travel. "When can we go?" I tease.

"Whenever you want."

"You're serious, aren't you?"

"Yup."

"I sort of have senior year to deal with. It starts in a few days. I'm gonna be busy with AP classes and studying for the SAT in October."

"If you went to Mount Roraima, you'd forget all about AP classes and SATs and everything else. That place has a way of making you forget everything that doesn't really matter. We should totally go. Just you and me. We should go when you graduate."

Is he making long term plans with me? This sounds like the most romantic thing I've ever heard. And I barely know the guy! We just met this morning! Sure, he's my stepbrother, but I don't know him. How did he manage to hypnotize me so quickly? It's inexplicable.

Still kneeling beside his backpack on the floor, Dante gazes into my eyes. He has the sappiest grin on his face.

I smile, "That sounds like a wonderful—"

"Aren't you in bed?" Dad blurts at me, suddenly standing in the doorframe.

I'm so startled, I practically jump off the bed using only the clenching of my butt muscles. "Geez, Dad! Can't you give some advanced warning? You should wear a bell around your neck like a cat.

I almost had a heart attack."

Dad grimaces, ignoring my comment. "I'm sure Dante is tired and wants to get some sleep."

I'm sure Dad is checking up on me to make sure Dante isn't doing anything illegal. Good thing I left the door open. Too bad it allowed him to ruin my moment with the greatest of ease.

"Do you have everything you need, Dante?" Catarina asks, leaning around Dad.

"Yeah, I'm good," Dante smiles.

"I'm so glad you're here," she says.

Dad looks irked when she says it. He has more of a stick up his butt than usual.

"Me too," Dante says.

"Time for bed," Dad orders, leveling a look at me.

"It's only ten, Dad," I groan.

"You need to get back on a school night sleep schedule," he says. "You'll thank me when school starts and you have to crawl out of bed with the rest of us."

I throw a glance at Dante.

He shrugs, staying out of it.

The look on Dad's face says, "I'm in charge around here and I give the orders. Now, march!"

"Fine," I sigh as I stand up. "Good night, Dante."

"Sleep tight," he grins.

oOoOoOo + O+O+O+O

I totally can't sleep.

The house is completely silent.

Everyone is in bed, presumably sleeping. But all I can think about is Dante. He's in the next room. What's he doing in there? Reading his book? Writing in his journal? Thinking about me? Dreaming about me? I don't know and it's killing me. I'd love to knock on his door and hang out with him all night, chatting about Venezuela and everyplace else he's been. Dante is easily the most fascinating person I've ever met. My dad, who is easily the most annoying and boring person I've ever met, would surely not approve of my having a slumber party in the guest room with Dante.

Oh well.

At least Dante is sleeping in my, or should I say our, house for the time being. I have that much.

I sigh heavily and shift on my bed. A pink glow warms the walls, my desk, my vision board with pictures of SDU hanging over it, my posters and everything else. Yes, I sleep with a pink nightlight. Not because I'm scared of the dark like Ashley Masters thinks, but because I once tripped on the leg of my desk chair when I got up to pee in the middle of the night and nearly broke my toes. I realized night lights weren't such a bad idea after that, and nothing to be ashamed of. Of course, I can't ever let Ashley find out I have one. There would be no end to the "Nightlight" name calling.

I close my eyes, trying to force sleep.

It doesn't work because the second I do, the second I see darkness, I'm right back in that meeting room at the library with Dante between my legs. I shiver just thinking about it. He made me come hard. I never knew an orgasm could feel so good. I'm getting wet just thinking about it.

I slide my palms down my stomach and wedge them between my thighs…

Okay, this isn't helping.

I slap my hands on top of my sheet and huff heavily.

It's warm in my room because I have the window open. Normally I leave it closed when it's hot because we have A/C. But after hearing Dante's story about sleeping on top of Mount Roraima, all I can think about is how stuffy my house is. The whole climate control thing is bugging me. Even with the window open, I can't feel the breeze on my face and I can't see any stars. I'm surrounded by the uniformity of sameness I've known most of my life.

For the first time ever, it's bugging the fuck out of me.

All I've thought about all summer long is the SATs, college applications, AP classes, GPAs, blah, blah, blah. Before today, it all seemed normal. And that's just it.

Normal.

Sure, I've dreamt about going to SDU for years. After spending the day with Dante, I'm like, "Why again?" Was college my idea, or just something I thought of because I saw kids wearing UCLA and USC sweatshirts when I was in middle school and I wanted my own college sweatshirt? That peer pressure bullshit can be really subtle. Or was college just something I took for granted because Dad has been preparing me for it for years? I'm suddenly wondering if any of it was my idea. I mean, sure, some of it was. But was I just going along with everyone else like a lemming wearing a college sweatshirt?

Dante made me wonder if maybe I was.

I notice the SAT prep books on the shelf of my little bookcase on my desk. I have three of them and I've been through all of them cover to cover. I shake my head. I've put way too much effort into this whole college thing. I'm not going to up and throw it all away just because of —

Faint voices drift up through the air vent on my floor.

Dad and Catarina.

They don't know it, but I can sometimes hear them talking when they're in the master bathroom. I think they go in there to talk because they think it's harder to hear them from the hallway, which it is, but I guess they don't know about the vent.

"I don't trust him," Dad says in a low echoey voice.

"You don't even know him, Gordon," Catarina hisses. "You just met him tonight."

"Which is why I don't trust him. You don't know him either, Cat. You haven't spoken to him in seven years. He's not a cute kid anymore."

"What?" she laughs in disbelief. "He's my son, Gordon. My flesh and blood. I know him."

"I'm sure Jeffrey Dahmer's parents thought they knew him."

Geez, Dad. That sounds ridiculous. I shake my head and grimace.

"My son is not a serial killer, Gordon."

"He may not be a killer, but something about him bothers me."

"I think he bothers your delicate sensibilities."

That's the truth. Dad makes muscle cramps look relaxed.

There's a long silence.

"I'm sorry," Catarina says. "I shouldn't have said that."

"No, you're right. When it comes to my daughter, I have very delicate sensibilities. I only want what's best for her." There's something snide about his tone.

"Are you saying that my son is somehow bad for Skye?" Catarina asks with obvious disbelief. "Gordon? What are you saying?"

"I'm not saying anything. But you just said plenty."

"Gordon! I would never put Skye in any kind of danger! I love her like my own daughter. And I resent the fact that you're insinuating that my son is a bad influence. Or somehow dangerous."

"You saw how he was looking at her."

"What?!"

"At dinner. He kept smiling at my daughter. I know that look."

"Have you gone insane, Gordon?" She chuckles. "Were we at the same dinner table?"

"I know that look, Cat. Your son is attracted to my daughter."

Oh. Shit.

"Gordon! That, that's... that's just *insane*."

"Is it?"

She doesn't respond.

My guts lurch and I suddenly feel like I'm about to shit triplets.

Catarina finally speaks, "So what if he is? Skye is a beautiful young woman. I'm sure there are plenty of nice young men attracted to your daughter." She says it like this is all no big deal. This is getting dangerously close to disaster. "It's normal for a young man like Dante to be attracted to her."

"Is it normal for a stepbrother to be attracted to his stepsister? One who is still in high school?"

I want to shout through the vent, "I'm 18! What does it matter!" But I don't.

"She's 18, Gordon. She's old enough to make her own choices."

Go, Catarina! I cheer and fist pump and make a "Yes!" face.

"That's not the point. I don't want him distracting Skye from her studies. I don't want her throwing away college for..."

"For what, Gordon? For my son?"

"That's not what this is about, Catarina. It's not about your son. It's about my daughter and her future."

"Are you saying my son doesn't have a future?"

"I don't know what he has. I just don't want him doing anything... *inappropriate* with my daughter."

"Inappropriate?" Catarina huffs, flustered. "Gordon, I'm sure that Dante would never do anything *inappropriate* with Skye."

Yes he would. And did. Some of it in this very house. The rest of it in the local library. Have I ruined things already?

"I hope you're right, Catarina. Because if I find out that your son has put any moves on my daughter, we are going to have a problem."

We already do. Oh my god, what did I do? This is horrible.

"What's that supposed to mean, Gordon?"

"Let's just say that Skye is the most important thing in my life, Catarina."

Silence.

Bad silence.

They never use each other's names like this. They're much more lovey-dovey. Not so formal. There's a divisive quality to it, like they're trying to separate themselves from each other. Separate... We all know what separation leads to.

Shit.

This is bad.

This is *way* bad.

oOoOoOo + O+O+O+O

The red numbers on my alarm clock read 1:13.

I haven't been able to sleep since hearing Dad and Catarina arguing.

My guts are in knots. My eyes are hot and dry. I think I wept out all my tears two hours ago.

All of this is my fault. I should've stopped things the second I found out Dante was my stepbrother back at Blazing Waters. I'm an idiot. I got carried away. I let my hormones make my decisions. People like to joke about how guys think with their dicks. Well, it's pretty obvious that girls think with their... put me out of my misery.

Now.

I had the start of a good thing going and I already went and ruined it. In one freakin' day.

And now there's tension between Dad and Catarina. Because of me. If I had drawn a line in the sand with Dante, I don't think he would've stepped over it. He seems like the respectful type, despite what Dad thinks. But that doesn't matter anymore, does it? Worse, I could just hear the threat of divorce dangling from Dad's lips. Would he divorce Catarina because of Dante? I don't even want to think about it. I love having Catarina around. She keeps Dad from being too over-protective. Without her, my life would be stifling. I would be an idiot to let my attraction to Dante destroy their marriage.

I'm a selfish child.

I've made a huge mistake.

But I don't know how to fix it.

When I think about Dante, my heart races. So what if we just met? He's gorgeous, smart, and sexy as hell. I am most definitely in lust with him. And in swoon. If I never saw him again after today, he would definitely be the ultimate "one who got away". Wait, this is crazy. I've only known him for one day! It's makes zero sense to be spun out for a guy after one day.

Zero sense.

A ticking sound at my door catches my attention.

The door knob turns with creepy slowness.

What the hell?

My Dad, for all his annoying faults, *always* knocks. It's our agreement because he wouldn't let me put a lock on my door. Safety issues. In case there's a fire. Or I'm hiding drugs or boys in my room. You know, the usual stuff. It can't be Catarina. If she needs something, she waits until my door is open. She's great about respecting my privacy.

It can't be Dante, can it?

No. He wouldn't. Would he?

I push myself up into bed until my back squishes my pillow against my headboard. My knees are pulled up to my chest. Why does it feel like a prowler or something, I don't know, illegal? I guess when someone sneaks into your room in the middle of the night, your mind goes all over the place. It isn't a vampire, is it? No, you have to give them permission to enter. I saw it on an episode of Buffy once.

Slowly the door opens.

A dark shadow stands in the frame.

The soft glow of my pink night light washes over Dante.

He's dressed in his T-shirt and jeans and leather jacket. His backpack is slung over one shoulder. His boots dangle from one hand.

No!

He's leaving!

"Can I come in?" he whispers.

I'm too shaken to answer. My stomach is now see-sawing liquidly.

He arches an eyebrow.

I can't respond.

His socks hush across the carpet. He sits on the foot of my twin bed, resting his boots on one knee. His warm hand slides around my ankle, which is naked after I slid up to the headboard. A shiver runs up my leg. It's a mixture of arousal and fear at the same time. I don't like how it feels at all.

"I have to go," he whispers.

"Why?" I plead in a squeaky voice.

"I heard your dad arguing with my mom. I have to."

I thought I was all out of tears, but I guess I have a few more. "You can't go, you just got here," I whisper.

He lowers his eyes and stares at the floor. "I knew it was a bad idea for me to come here. I should've written my mom a letter or something. It would've been better for everybody."

"No it wouldn't. The only problem here is my dad."

"That's a huge problem."

He's right. I don't know what to say. I can't think of a good argument. All those stupid SAT essays I wrote, and I can't think of a single logical idea when it counts. Stupid tests. I knew they were useless. What's the point of all this stupid college bullshit again? I feel my nerves amping up. I want to jump out of bed and start screaming. But that would wake Dad, and I'm sure Dante would bolt that much quicker. This may be the last moment I have with him. I can't blow it. I remember Dante's advice about breathing during the SATs if I got nervous.

I inhale slowly. 1, 2, 3, 4, 5. Then Exhale. 1, 2, 3, 4, 5.

A moment later, inspiration floats into my mind like a summer breeze over the plateau of Mount Roraima. "Dante, take me with you."

He lifts his head and gazes into my eyes. In the faint pink glow of my room, his eyes sparkle tiny pink diamonds. The light is so faint, his eyes so dark, they don't seem green. But they have a luminous quality that sucks me in. I feel our hearts connecting. Without words, our feelings pass between us.

He's considering it.

I'm certain of it. Not wanting to let the opportunity of a lifetime slip away, I plead, "I'm 18, Dante. I can do whatever I want. There's no law that says I have to graduate high school or go to college or anything." Wow, I wasn't sure if I had it in me, but that was easier than I would've thought.

He inhales slowly, about to speak. Then stops.

Our connection is broken.

"I can't," he sighs despondently. "I'm not going to break your family apart. If you ran away with me, your dad would blame my mom. I can't do it. You have a good thing going here, Skye. Your dad loves you. So does my mom. They're your family."

"They're your family too!" I cry.

He drops his head to his chest. "I don't have a family." He stands up and kisses my forehead.

My throat seizes and I swear my heart stops. A cold gust of icicles blows across my scalp and tinkles down my chest like an ice storm in the dead of winter.

He turns away but I grab his hand. I won't let go. I won't.

He twists his wrist in a lazy kung fu move and I can't hold on. He never looks back. He pads across my bedroom and out the door.

I jump out of bed and follow him downstairs. I don't want to say anything until we're outside. If Dad wakes up now, he's bound to not only ruin my moment, he'll likely push Dante right out the front door while he holds me back by the neck.

Dante twists the deadbolt on the front door.

"Wait!" I hiss.

"Skye," he sighs, "I have to go."

"If you open that door, the alarm will go off. It'll wake up Dad and Catarina."

He stares up the stairs thoughtfully. Then he looks at me. "Can you disarm it?"

"No," I say defiantly. "Wait until morning. Sleep on it. Think about what you're doing."

He sets his boots on the floor then slides his free arm into the dangling strap of his backpack.

"What are you doing?"

He bends down and pulls on one boot.

"Dante!" I whisper.

He pulls on the other boot then stands up tall.

I glare into his eyes. They're flat. Depthless.

Our connection is gone.

"Will you turn off the alarm?" he asks.

I fold my arms across my chest.

"Fine," he says and turns to the door. In one swift motion, he twists the deadbolt and the doorknob with both hands.

SCREE-REE-REE-REE-REE-REE-REE!!!!!

I clamp my hands over my ears. The alarm is piercing and deafening.

Dante strides out the front door.

Banging sounds upstairs.

"WHAT IN HELL?!" Dad shouts.

I run outside, chasing Dante.

When I reach the driveway, he's already throwing a leg over his motorcycle, which is parked at the sidewalk. "Get back, Skye," he growls.

I run across the front lawn and throw my arms around his shoulders, but he pushes me away forcefully with one strong arm. I grunt and stumble backward, landing hard on the grass, both arms behind me. Pain shoots up my wrists. "Dante!" I scramble to my feet, ignoring the pain.

The motorcycle engine revs.

"Skye!" Dad shouts, running down the front walkway and across the lawn, wearing only pajama boxers. "Skye! Are you okay?!"

Dante hooks a hand through the open face mask of his helmet rather than putting it on and guns the engine several times. His bike lurches forward, tilting sideways as he circles it out the end of our cul-de-sac. When he straightens, the engine growls and the front wheel comes up off the ground.

"Dante!" Catarina screams, running past me and Dad. She doesn't stop. She trots right into the street, her open bathrobe billowing behind her.

"What did he do to you, Skye?" Dad demands, hovering over me, looking for wounds or injuries. "Are you okay?"

I glare at him and smack his hands away. No, I'm not okay. And not because of Dante. Because of him. The only wounds I have are the ones you can't see. The ones to my heart.

Dad puts a comforting arm around my back.

I shrug abruptly. "Get off me!"

Right now, I hate my dad more than I've ever hated him before.

oOoOoOo + O+O+O+O

"I hate you, Gordon!" Catarina shouts as she slams the front door behind her.

Having already sprinted upstairs, I stop where I am on the landing and spin to watch the two of them through the bannister posts.

Dad is half way up the stairs, chasing me. He stops in his tracks and slowly turns to face Catarina.

I've never heard Catarina sound this unhinged. She's a very together professional woman. Hearing Catarina say she hates my dad makes me feel like we're kindred spirits. I want to say sarcastically, "You too, honey?" Just to make Dad feel stupid. But I don't. I'm frozen in place. The dark look on Dad's face before he turned toward Catarina was scaring the shit out of me. I've never seen him so angry. The irony here is that I'm the one who has the right to be mad. Not Dad.

"YOU PUSHED AWAY MY SON!!" Catarina yells. And I mean yells. Catarina has never been the kind of woman to raise her voice. Not this loud, anyway.

"I did no such thing, Catarina," Dad says in an icy calm voice.

Catarina scowls at him.

"I was polite to him at dinner. I let him take Skye to the library to study. What did I do wrong?"

"Polite?" Catarina laughs. "That was polite? You practically rounded up a lynch mob to chase him out of town!"

Dad sneers at her. "You're being irrational, Catarina. You sound like a child."

"He heard you guys arguing!" I shout. "I heard you guys!"

Dad turns slowly, his head swiveling around like a tank turret. Then he fires his giant parental tank gun at me. "Go to bed, Skye. This doesn't concern you."

"It doesn't?" I scream.

Dad's eyes narrow like laser sights, like a sniper aiming for the kill shot. In a cold and amused voice, he says calmly, "Why is this bothering you so much, Skye? It's not like Dante and you are old friends. You just met him this afternoon, didn't you?"

Oh my god, is he reading my mind? I blurt, "I—" But I stop myself before I say anything else. Dad will use everything I say against me in a court of law or a family meeting or whatever.

"What?" Dad asks with deadly patience.

"Nothing," I deflate.

"Go to bed, Skye. Catarina and I will work this out. Like..." he turns to face her, "...adults."

I exchange a look with Catarina.

Her face trembles with restrained emotion. "It's okay, Skye. Your father and I will figure this out." Her obvious agony makes me question her confidence. "Go to bed."

"Are you sure?" I ask. I feel like she needs backup on this. I'm ready to go in guns blazing.

"Bed, Skye," Dad orders. "Now." He's using the big guns tonight.

Against my will, I turn and walk down the hallway toward my bedroom. I close the door most of the way, but leave a four inch crack. I sit down next to it and listen.

All I can hear are harsh whispers.

A moment later, footsteps, then the door of Dad's downstairs office closing.

I can't hear anything now. I'm tempted to sneak downstairs, but you can see into Dad's office from the stairs. The door has a huge piece of glass in the frame and he'll totally see me sneaking. Too bad the air vent trick doesn't reach his office.

Still, I wait, sitting with my back against the wall next to my door.

I'm wired with adrenalin, so there's no way I'm falling asleep any time soon. My mind races as I wonder what they're saying to each other. How bad is this? How angry is Catarina? What is she going to do? What is Dad going to do? Will she leave? Will they get divorced? I don't know. The suspense is burning a hole in my stomach. I think I'm getting an ulcer.

Can you get an ulcer in one night?

It sure feels like it.

Some time later, when my last drop of adrenalin has drained out of my system, I'm about to doze off. My head sags against the side of my desk. I can sleep sitting on the floor, right? I mean, it won't make me feel any more miserable than I already do, will it?

The office door clicks softly open and I jolt awake. Footsteps pad up the stairs and the master bedroom door closes a moment later.

For several minutes, every muscle in my body remains tensed.

What is going to happen? Will Catarina storm out of the master bedroom in the next ten minutes with a suitcase in her hand? Will Dad yell "Good riddance!" or something equally cruel as he slams the door behind her?

That's what happened when my real mom left way back when. Except my mom was the one who did all the shouting, and she didn't just shout "Good riddance!" It was much worse.

"Fuck you, Gordon! You worthless piece of shit!"

Shattering glass. Dishes thrown. Blood dribbling down Dad's forehead...

I shiver at the thought and do my best to bury the painful memory. I smack my palms against my eyes, trying to hold everything in. My entire body starts to vibrate as every muscle contracts in agony. This always happens when I remember that night. I make fists and dig my short nails into my palms. It doesn't take long for the sharp pain to bring me back to the here and now.

Not that it's much better.

If Catarina leaves, I might go too. Throw some clothes on and climb out my window. But where would I go? Rox's house? That's probably the first place Dad would check. Then he'd have to drag me back home kicking and screaming. I can't do that to Rox and her parents.

I sigh heavily.

If I don't know where Dante went, what's the point of leaving?

I mean, gosh, if I run away or whatever, I won't get to focus on SATs and dream about the AP classes I'm going to take senior year. Whoop-dee-fucking-do.

After pushing my door closed, I crawl across my carpet and climb into bed. It takes all my strength to make it onto the mattress. When my head touches the pillow, I'm out like a light.

What a day.

Chapter 7

"Don't you think Emily would love this for her birthday?" Rox's face glows with glee as she holds up the cutest Hello Kitty plushie ever. Emily is Rox's seven year old cousin and she's obsessed with Hello Kitty. "It's adorbs!"

"Defs," I say, forcing a smile.

We're in the Sanrio store at the Glendale Galleria shopping mall. Rox cradles the doll in her arm like a baby while continuing to browse the explosion of Hello Kitty paraphernalia. I drag along behind her.

"Is something bothering you, Skye? You've been morbid all day."

"Is it that obvi?"

"Are you kidding? I haven't seen you this glum since your dad said you had to study the SATs all summer."

I grimace. Thinking about my dad only makes me hate him that much more.

"What's going on? Spill it."

I roll my eyes, "My dad is the biggest ass master ever."

"What did he do this time?" she chuckles while browsing through a rack of Hello Kitty T-shirts.

"He pretty much chased Dante off last night."

She looks at me seriously. "What do you mean?"

"Dante is gone. He left last night and took all his stuff."

"He's gone?" Rox asks, surprised. "Like, for good?"

"I don't know," I moan. "I guess so."

"Oh, no! I never had a chance to hook up with him!"

Neither did I. Well, I sort of did, but I was hoping for more than we had. "That's only half of it," I groan.

"What do you mean?! That's all of it! He was going to be my senior fling!"

I ignore her comment. "Our parents are fighting."

"Wait, whose parents?"

"Catarina and my dad. They were totally yelling at each other after Dante left. Catarina blamed Dad for pushing him away, and Dad blamed Catarina for—" I stop myself. I can't tell Rox that Dad thought Dante was coming on to me. This is way too complicated.

"For what?"

"For, for… for mouthing off to him." It's somewhat true. "Dad thought Dante was being rude and disrespectful. He said, uh… he said Dante was a… a punk. Or something like that." I need to start preparing my lies in advance. This is way harder than I thought.

Rox scowls. "What an ass."

"Yeah," I sigh.

"How bad did your dad and Catarina fight?" Rox asks carefully.

"Bad."

"Like, divorce bad?"

"I don't know," I grimace. "Maybe?"

Rox looks distraught. "Hold on a second. Let me pay for this plushie. We'll talk about it more in a second." She takes the doll up to the counter where the Asian woman rings her up.

I wait near the entrance to the Sanrio store, watching people stroll past in the mall.

"What a surprise," Ashley Masters says as she comes to a stop in front of me, holding a Bloomingdale's bag at her side. "Nightlight shops at Hello Kitty."

Brittany and Monica are with her. They both snicker at Ashley's dig, also holding Bloomie's bags.

I smirk at them. I didn't think it was possible to feel any worse than I already do, but Ashley is an expert at dishing out misery. "We were buying something for Rox's cousin, *Ass*-ley," I growl.

"Ho, ho, ho," she laughs sarcastically.

"What, are you supposed to be Santa Claus?" I smile to myself. Usually I'm not so quick with the clever comebacks. Brittany and Monica both look surprised. Score for me!

"Good one, Nightlight," Ashley faux-smiles. "No, I was calling you a ho. Or didn't you figure that part out?"

Bitch. I try to think of another comeback, but I've got nothing.

Sensing my defeat, Brittany and Monica cackle in unison, rubbing it in. If this was a gladiatorial arena, they would be giving the thumbs down from the cheap seats, cheering for Ashley to finish me off with a net and pitchfork.

Rox walks up beside me and wrinkles her nose with disgust. "Ew. Now I know what stinks."

"Very funny, Slutter," Ashley says.

"It's Slaughter," Rox snarls. "My last name is Slaughter."

"Whatevs," Ashley yawns. "Either way, you might want to wax

your upper lip. Or didn't you know that hair traps odor better than anything? That mustache of yours needs to go."

Brittany and Monica both giggle. Is that all they have to contribute? What a bunch of hobots. Does Ashley program them to laugh on cue, or are they set that way at the factory?

"What do you want, Ashley?" Rox rolls her eyes. She doesn't have a mustache or anything close to it.

Neither does Ashley. As usual, nothing is out of place on the body of Ashley Masters. From head to toe, from her expensive hair to her expensive shoes, she is the picture of effortless perfection. There's nothing about her that can be picked apart. A gloat eases onto her face. "Oh, I was just asking Nightlight here how her *math* studies were *coming* along." She drills me with a hateful look. "Have you figured out how to solve all those *hard* problems yet? Or are you still in the *dark* when it comes to advanced *techniques*?"

Oh, no! She knows! Brittany must've shown her the photo! I'm sure she knew minutes after it happened. That's how these girls operate. No juicy gossip goes untold. I need to get Rox out of here before Ashley blurts out the truth. "Don't you know how to be nice, Ashley? Like, for once in your life?" I say it with righteous judgment. Sticks and stones and all that jazz. I turn to Rox and grab her by the wrist, "Let's go."

"Urp!" Rox blurts as I yank her along behind me. She stumbles not to trip over herself. A minute later, when we're passing Bloomingdale's, she asks, "What was that about?"

"Oh, you know," I grimace. "Ashley is a supernatural bitch. That's all the excuse she needs."

Rox glances back at Ashley with a thoughtful look on her face. "Ashley wasn't at the library last night when you were there with Dante, was she?"

"Huh? No. I don't think so." That much is the truth. It was Brittany who took the photo. I don't think Ashley was there.

"So how does she know about your math studies?"

Damn it. Rox is putting the pieces together. I have to throw her off the scent. "Uhh... remember when we were at Blazing Waters and we saw Ashley by the bathrooms?"

"Yeah?"

"I mentioned to her that I had spent the whole summer studying for the SATs. Math in particular."

"I don't remember that."

"Oh, it was when you were still in the bathroom. And me and Dante waited for you?" That part is definitely a lie.

"Really?" She sounds like she wants to believe me. Which makes me feel worse. "Why would you tell her that?"

I shrug. "Uh, um, oh yeah! I said something like 'I'd rather be studying math right now than talking to you.'" I force a smile. "I totally put her in her place." Wow, I barely believe myself. But I need Rox to believe me. Even if I am spinning more lies.

Rox processes it for a moment. Then a grin slowly shines on her face. "Nice. That bitch needs to be put in her place at least once a day. We should do it more often. Now, about your Dad and Catarina."

I shake my head. "Don't remind me." I now feel three times more nauseous than I did when we walked into Sanrio.

Rox smiles sympathetically. "I think you and I need a sugar high. I want to wash the taste of Assley out of my mouth, don't you?"

"That's what I called her before you came out of Sanrio," I chuckle.

"Great minds think alike," she grins. "Let's go to Godiva for a chocolate pick me up. Then we can brainstorm some good put downs for the next time we have to deal with Her Royal Assness."

"That bitch is such a butt barnacle," I groan.

Rox giggles, "That's the spirit!"

oOoOoOo + O+O+O+O

"Can you smell the teen spirit? It's the first day of senior year!" Rox squeals at the wheel a few days later. "Our last year of high school!"

I groan where I sit hunched over in the passenger seat of her mom's Toyota as we drive all of one mile to school first thing in the morning.

I don't even think the sun's awake yet.

Who decided school should start so early?

Rox is totally happy because her parents bought a new Toyota a few days ago, so now the old one is hers, meaning she gets her own car for senior year. Yay for her. If my Dad sold his BMW 760Li and bought a regular Mercedes like a normal rich person, he could easily afford to get me a car. But he doesn't want me getting into any more trouble than I already do. I'm not talking about Dante. I'm talking in general. It's been a running theme at my house since I started high school. Keep Skye out of trouble. Keep her on the straight and narrow.

Not that I want anything from my Dad at this point. Ever since he chased Dante off, I'm beginning to question everything my dad has given me. From the roof over my head to his insistence on college.

After a few minutes of driving, Rox turns the Toyota into the parking lot at North Valley High. It's crammed with cars. Parents dropping off freaked out freshman. Saucy sophomores acting like they're the shit just because they're not freshman anymore. Jubilant juniors excited to be upperclassmen who are old enough to drive themselves to school. And seasoned seniors pretending to be above it all but thrilled to be on top of the social ladder by default. The energy is bustling, but I can't rise to the occasion.

I'm exhausted.

I've barely slept since the night Dante left. It's been a stress fest at the house ever since. All thanks to Dad. Catarina isn't talking to him. I'm seriously worried about the two of them. They've never gone this long without talking. In fact, I don't think they've ever gone without talking. They've always managed to work through things.

Worse, Dante never came back. Nobody knows where he went. There's a black hole in my heart that wasn't there before Dante came along, so I think we can safely attribute my dark mood to his absence.

After a few days of missing him, I went online and looked up that hexayurt video he mentioned over dinner that first night. The one where he helped build housing for those tribes from the Amazon. Watching him talking to the camera about all the good they were doing for those displaced people made me miss him that much more. I had to stop watching the video half way through because tears were streaming down my face and I kept wanting to go find Dad and yell in his face about what an ass he was.

Does it make sense that I miss Dante so bad? No. So what if I only knew him for one day? He's a great guy. And we were… *intimate* together. Maybe it wasn't love, but it was the start of something. I sigh to myself so Rox doesn't hear me and ask me what's wrong for the thousandth time in the last few days. I'm so glad she cares, but I hate having to lie and say I'm just worried about Dad and Catarina. Sure, that's true, but only half of the truth. I've never hidden so much from Rox ever. It feels wrong, but I'm trying to get used to it. Maybe I'll tell her the truth in a few months when everything gets back to normal.

Rox pulls into a parking space and turns off the ignition. "We're here! Day one of our last year of high school! High fives!" She holds up both palms expectantly.

I slap them half-heartedly.

"Are things still strained between your dad and Catarina?" she asks somberly.

So much for hiding my feelings from my BFSF. "Yeah." My eyes heat with impending tears. "Can we not talk about this right now? You're going to make me cry. Seniors aren't supposed to cry on the first day of school. I don't want to look like a wimpy freshman."

"As if, Skye. You're too sexy hot to look like a freshman. Nice legs, girl."

I'm wearing denim short shorts, strappy sandals, and a baggy lace panel tee. "Thanks," I don't feel sexy anything today. The outfit is purely functional. It's the tail end of summer and I don't want to roast during class because our school doesn't have A/C.

"Let's go," she smiles, hopping out of the car. "I can't wait to see which guys got hotter over the summer."

"Yeah," I sigh, dragging myself from my seat.

We walk across the parking lot toward the sprawl of one story buildings that make up North Valley High. Well, the gym is two stories, but everything else is one story. Since this is California, we don't have indoor hallways or multiple floors. Just plain boxes connected by covered walkways. It used to rain more often in California, but with the drought we've been having lately, the covered walkways seem unnecessary. All the same, the school is a familiar sight that brings up scattered memories of my last three years here. Despite my morose mood, it actually feels good to be back. I wonder what senior year has in store for me?

The warning bell rings five minutes before the start of school.

"Don't forget to ask for a different locker if yours isn't next to the senior lawn," Rox reminds me.

Seniors don't get to pick their exact lockers, but they can choose which section they're in. Everyone wants a locker next to the senior lawn. It's a circle of grass with benches around it. Supposedly, only seniors get to use the lawn. Exceptions are made for popular juniors or the boyfriends and girlfriends of seniors, but that's it. If you want to be close to the social action at North Valley High, you want your locker by the senior lawn. "Yeah, okay."

"See you after homeroom!" she waves while walking across the quad, heading toward her homeroom. Our homerooms are assigned by last name, so Rox is in the room for kids with S last names and I'm in the one for A and B last names.

When I get to homeroom, I sit in my alphabetically assigned seat. After taking attendance, the homeroom teacher hands out locker assignments. I can tell my number is one of the lockers by the senior lawn. I hope it's near Rox's locker. The teacher also passes out our class schedules. Mine includes:

Trigonometry (I don't know how I managed to pass Algebra 2 last year, but I did)

AP English Literature & Composition (which I'm looking forward to)

Chemistry (not so much)

Spanish 4 (muy bien!)

AP U.S. Government (snore)

AP Psychology (I can finally figure out why I'm crazy)

Photography (My Instagram needs all the help it can get)

Yes, it's a tough schedule. When I planned it out with Dad, I suggested Study Hall for both electives instead of Psych and Photography, but he wasn't having any of that. Yeah, yeah, colleges don't want you slacking off senior year. At the time, I didn't argue. Today, I feel like I could use six periods of Study Hall. Not gonna happen.

Does cutting classes look bad on your transcript? Bland sarcasm.

When they let us out of homeroom, I sigh and trudge toward the quad to check out my locker and make sure my combination works. "Shit," I grumble when I find it. It may be at the edge of the senior lawn, but it's a bottom locker. I examine the locker assignment paper to make sure I have the number right. Yup, this is it. I guess I'll have to squat down below whoever has the top locker. This is annoying. I sure hope it's somebody nice.

"Excuse me, Nightlight," Ashley Masters says, bumping me aside. "You're in my way." She deftly twirls the combination on the locker above mine and opens the door. She pulls a round mirror out of her purse and peels plastic strips off the adhesive backing and presses the mirror to the inside of her locker door. Then she checks her hair and lip gloss, both of which are perfect.

O.M.Great. She's already moving in and I can't even get to my locker because she's in the way.

Ashley smiles at herself, pleased with the results of her primping. Then her eyes flick toward me and her face sours. "Can I help you, Nightlight?"

"No," I growl, crumpling my locker assignment in my hand.

She glances at it and chuckles. "Don't tell me that your locker is below mine."

My face collapses despite my every effort to shore up my decaying mood.

"How fitting," Ashley smirks. "I'm your top. I always knew you were a bottom, Nightlight."

She's making some kind of BDSM reference. I'm not sure how it applies here. From what I understand, BDSM relationships are consensual, and I don't consent to acknowledging Ashley's existence, much less being her bottom.

Before I can respond, Ashley closes her locker and sashays off with a satisfied grin beaming from her face.

I spin and march straight to the main office. Inside it's bustling with tons of students complaining about one thing or another. I have to wait in line behind two kids who didn't even get lockers. Eventually, I get to the front.

"I'm sorry," Mrs. O'Neal, the school secretary says, her voice overly buoyant. She sits behind her desk wearing a prim Peter Pan collar blouse that is *très* irritating. She looks 50 but acts like a peppy 15 year old. "The senior class is rather large this year. I'm afraid we don't have any extra upper lockers. If you can find someone to switch with, you could do that. Would that work?"

I can guarantee that no one on campus will want to trade for a locker below Ashley Masters. "There are zero other lockers?" I ask desperately. I can't spend senior year at Ashley Masters' feet. I may as well bend down and kiss her toes every morning.

Mrs. O'Neal palms her mouse and clicks around on her computer screen. She glances around furtively then leans forward conspiratorially. "If you can't make do with a lower, we do have a few freshman uppers. I can get you one by the Biology wing." She smiles at me like she just shared a national secret.

I groan. There's no way I'm going to slum it with all the incoming children. I doubt even Rox would come visit me way out in the boonies by the Biology wing. But we're talking Ashley Masters. "Fine." I roll my eyes. "Give me a freshman upper."

Mrs. O'Neal lights up. "See how easy that was? You'll be very happy with a freshman upper. Think of those other freshman who don't even have lockers. They'll have to carry all their books around in backpacks like pack mules. Can you imagine? Poor things." She smiles and jots down a locker number and combination on a 3 x 5 card and hands it to me.

"Thanks." I take the card and skulk out of the office.

"There you are!" Rox blurts, strolling toward me. "Where's your locker? You got one by the senior lawn, right?"

"Ha. Ha. Ha," I fake laugh. "Would you believe my locker was below Ashley Masters?"

"No way!" she gasps.

oOoOoOo + O+O+O+O

"No way," a boy faced freshman gawks when I open my locker right next to his.

I grimace at him as politely as possible. He's shorter than me and

I'm not exactly tall myself.

"Is this your locker?" he asks hopefully.

"I guess so," I groan.

"You mean your locker is next to mine?"

"That's what I just said," I grumble.

"No way." His eyes are literally goggling behind his thick glasses. He's kind of cute in a band camp meets the geek squad sort of way. His World Of Warcraft T-shirt doesn't do anything to age him up. In other words, he looks like he still belongs in middle school.

I try to ignore him.

"What's your name?" he asks. He's not making this any easier.

I want to say that I don't fraternize with freshman, but I'm not a bitch like Ashley Masters. I sigh, "Skye."

"My name's Jason Carpenter. Nice to meet you, Skye." He offers his hand.

Still not being a bitch, I shake his hand, which is clammy. I end our shake as quickly as I can without being rude, then turn to my locker to open it. I spin the dial back and forth, matching the combo Mrs. O'Neal wrote on the card. I squeeze the thumb latch on the door and try to lift it. It's totally stuck. "Damn it," I groan.

"Let me try," Jason says.

"Sure."

Jason has tiny twig arms and matchstick fingers. If he can open it, I'm going to be embarrassed. He grasps the latch and tries it. No luck. He uses both hands and puts his shoulder into it. "Wow, that's really stuck."

"I've got it," a big hand reaches between me and Jason and pops the locker open.

Luke Nash smiles at me with a scintillating grin.

"Luke!" I blurt. Luke is my Ex. We dated for most of junior year.

He has chaotic black hair that spikes out in every direction in black blades. A small silver spike pierces the corner of his right eyebrow and two more silver spikes poke from his earlobes. Faded black skinny jeans hang from his narrow hips and a chain dangles from his belt. A Daft Punk logo is splashed across his black T-shirt. People might think he's a weepy emo, but he's always smiling and has a lot of friends. Luke wants to be a DJ like Skrillex or Deadmau5. He DJs for a lot of high school parties. It's the cool thing to have Luke be your DJ. He's actually really good. I think I was attracted to him because he does his own thing. But he's also really popular. The weird thing is, he manages to transcend all cliques without being ostracized by any of them. He can make friends with anybody.

"Hey, Jason," Luke says.

Jason's eyes light up with bromantic hope. "Hey, Luke!"

"You know him?" I ask Luke.

"Yeah. Jason's older brother is a junior. Nate Carpenter? Nate runs track every year?"

"Oh! Right!" I have no idea who Nate Carpenter is. But somehow Luke makes me feel like I should, just out of politeness. It's weird. Luke can do that.

"You all settled in, Jason?" Luke asks.

"Yeah. Thanks, man." Jason grins from ear to ear.

"Any seniors giving you shit?"

"No way," Jason says nervously, shoving his hands in his pockets. He's totally acting like he's one of the cool kids. It's kind of sweet.

"If you have any trouble, let me know." Luke winks at him. "We'll shitbag the locker of anyone who gets up in your grill."

Jason's eyes gleam with adoration. "Okay, yeah!"

Luke grins at him, taking it all in stride. I'm surprised he doesn't ruffle the kids hair or something.

Everyone loves Luke's laid back attitude and friendly personality. He grew out of the high school bullshit a long time ago. You would think I would still be with him because he's so awesome. But Luke's popularity was the reason I broke up with him. Yes, I ended it. Luke always had so much going on in his life, I could never escape the feeling that I was just one more thing on his To Do list. I don't mean like I was a notch on his belt or bed post. Just that he was always busy. Yes, he made time for me. Yes, we did fun stuff together. Yes, we had sex. But something was lacking. Looking back, I think we were buddies more than boyfriend-girlfriend. I wasn't clingy or anything. I never made an issue of it. But I got sick of him pushing off our dates because he had to DJ a party or hang out with some group or other. We split after junior prom, which we went to together. It wasn't a romantic evening like I'd hoped. Just another party for Luke to be the life of. I know he had a blast. I was... I don't know... bored? So the next weekend I told Luke I wanted to break up. He was really cool about it. Very understanding. I don't think that's what I was expecting. I guess expected him to object, to fight, to beg me to stay. Or something. Not just, "Okay. If that's how you feel."

Immediately afterward, I became suspicious that he had been cheating on me. It was the only explanation I could think of for why he was so easy-going about the breakup. But I never found any evidence that he was. Neither did Rox or any of our other friends. By all accounts, Luke is a stand up guy. He stayed single all the way through the end of junior year, which was the last time I saw him until today. The truth is, I don't think I missed him. I never thought about him all summer.

BRIIIIIIIINGGGG!!!

The five minute bell.

"See you guys later," Jason says hopefully. He's gearing up to walk away, but not actually leaving.

"Catch you on the down low," Luke says to him.

"Nice meeting you, Jason," I smile. I doubt I would've said anything more than "Bye" if Luke hadn't been here. But like I said, Luke does that to you.

"Yeah!" Jason smiles at me, his eyes all starry. "You too!" He's still standing there.

"Bye," I wave suggestively. Time to go, young man.

Finally, he turns and scurries off down the hallway, bouncing with every step.

I hope Jason isn't developing a crush on me. It wouldn't be an issue if his locker wasn't next to mine. But I don't want him getting all weird during the year.

"Jason's a cool kid," Luke says.

"Yeah," I say dismissively.

"Can I walk you to class?"

"Sure."

"Where are you going?"

"Trig."

"Mr. Mendez?"

"Yeah. How'd you know?"

"I had him last year. He's great. You'll like him." Luke is also one of the kids who can talk to adults like they're besties. I don't know how he does it. "Hey, how was your summer?"

"Don't ask," I groan.

"Why not?" he chuckles.

"My dad made me study for the SATs all summer."

"That's rough. Your dad is a total dictator."

I snicker. "Yeah."

"Did you do anything fun?"

"No."

"Nothing? Not one fun thing?"

An image of my day at Blazing Waters with Dante flashes across my mind. I push it away. If I think about Dante, I'm going to go start feeling miserable again. "No. Just studying."

"That blows. We need to arrange something fun for you. I'm DJing a party this weekend at Josh Parker's house. His parents are out of town. You wanna come by?"

"If my dad will let me," I groan.

"I'll talk to him. He'll let you go."

Believe it or not, Luke and my dad got along great. It took awhile for Dad to warm up to Luke's gothish exterior, but when he realized that Luke got good grades and took AP classes like I did, and that his charming personality wasn't just an act to impress the adults, Dad really started to like him. Dad was actually bummed when I told him I broke up with Luke. Oh well. It's not like grades and AP classes are my top priority when it comes to who I date.

We arrive outside Mr. Mendez's classroom. The door is open and students are milling around inside.

"This is me," I sigh.

"Yeah." Luke runs his hand through his hair, which causes his T-shirt sleeve to climb up his arm. The bottom of a tattoo peeks out beneath the sleeve.

"Did you get a tattoo?" I blurt.

"Nah," he snorts, "I drew it with a Sharpie last night." He pulls his sleeve up over his shoulder muscle, which is more muscular than I remember, and reveals a black tattoo of the planet Earth wearing DJ headphones. "You like it?"

"Yeah, it's awesome!" I examine it closely. "You really drew that?"

He nods. "I had to use a mirror, but yeah."

"It's really good."

"Thanks," he says with obvious humility. Luke really is awesome. It's not an act. "I'm trying it out. My dad says I should wear it for awhile to see if I still want it after a month. If I get bored with it, he said I should wait on it."

"Really?" Wow, I wish my dad was that cool. He would kill me if I asked about getting a tattoo. Or drew one on myself. He thinks they're low class. "Don't you have to be 18 to get a tattoo?"

"Yeah. You can't even get one with parental consent. I checked. It's a misdemeanor for anyone to tattoo a minor in California. I have to wait until I'm 18. Dad thought that was stupid, but whatever. Maybe he's right. Maybe I won't get one. Who knows." He shrugs and drops his arm to his side. "For now I've got this one."

The tardy bell is going to ring any second. "I should go," I mutter.

"Hey, Skye?"

"Yeah?"

"I missed you."

My heart pings suddenly. I wasn't expecting this.

"It was kind of lonely this summer without you," he says quietly.

"It was?" This is news to me. I imagined he had a full schedule of exciting activities and raging parties to DJ.

"Yeah." He nods and frowns in a weird way that is the cutest thing I've ever seen.

"Why didn't you call me?" I ask.

He shrugs. "I thought you were done with me. I didn't wanna harass you."

What?! He *should* have harassed me. I think that's what was lacking with us. Too much of anything, even a laid back personality, is too much. "Luke, why didn't you say any—"

BRIIIIIIIINGGGG!!!

The tardy bell. Luke is going to be late for the first class of senior year. The way he's looking at me, it's clear that's the last thing on his mind.

"Are you coming inside, Ms. Albright?" Mr. Mendez asks, holding the door knob, about to close the door.

"Uh, yeah," I say absently.

"You're going to be late for class, Mr. Nash," Mr. Mendez says to Luke with a smile.

"Yeah," Luke grins at him.

"I wouldn't want you to get behind on derivatives and integrals on your first day of Calculus." Mr. Mendez says it not with judgement, but as a joke between friends. "Mrs. Liao isn't a patient woman."

"For sure," Luke smiles.

Everybody likes Luke.

Luke turns to go, "Can I see you later?" he asks me hopefully.

"Find me at lunch," I smile as I walk into Trigonometry.

Mr. Mendez closes the door behind me.

Wow, I feel better already.

Why did I break up with Luke again?

oOoOoOo + O+O+O+O

"I don't know why you ever broke up with Luke," Rox says while we stand at the sink in the girls' bathroom during brunch. "He's a good guy. You should totally get back together with him."

"Yeah," I say absently, checking my hair in the mirror.

Rox touches up her lip gloss.

"Is that new lip gloss?" I ask.

"Yeah. It's Too Faced Glamour Gloss." Rox looks great without lip gloss, but she looks even better with it.

"It looks good on you," I smile.

"Thanks."

"What shade is that?" It's a pale pink that goes perfect with her skin.

"Barely Legal."

"That's a color?" I snicker.

"Yeah." She reaches into her purse and holds up two tubes. "I also have First Time and Strip Tease. Wanna try one?"

"Maybe later, when I drop out of high school to become a sex worker," I quip.

"When did you become such a prude?" she chuckles as she screws the brush applicator back into the bottle. "Anyway, I say you reconsider things with Luke. He's a great guy."

Luke being great is a bit of a broken record. Even Rox likes Luke. Not *like* likes, but they got along great. The thing is, when I sat in Trig class listening to peppy Mr. Mendez go on and on about sines and cosines and right triangles, the only thing I could think about was Dante. You see, with Luke no longer around to elevate my mood, my mind drifted right back to Dante's departure and how much I miss him after mere days.

I never missed Luke, and that was after months.

Sure, dating Luke again would make me feel better. For a while. But it wouldn't fix things. When I ended things with him, I wasn't distraught. I wasn't mopey or depressed. I wasn't much of anything. When Dante rode off on his motorcycle, it felt like the end of the world.

Looking back, I don't know if I ever really had any real feelings for Luke.

Don't they say that the definition of insanity is doing the same thing over and over while expecting different results? If Luke and I ended up dating again, I know what it would look like: meh. Our porridge wasn't too hot, and it wasn't too cold. It was just right. But who wants bland baby porridge when you can have hot and spicy man meat stew?

"What?" Rox giggles.

"Huh?"

"The dreamy look on your face says yes to the idea of you getting back together with Luke. See? I'm such a good match maker. Here, try the Strip Tease lip gloss. That'll pull Luke right back in."

I stare at the tube in her hand. I can't do it. I can't lead Luke on. "No, I'm good."

Even if Dante never comes back, I have to listen to my heart.

Chapter 8

My heart doesn't know what to think.

"This feels good, doesn't it?" Luke asks suggestively.

We're all alone.

"Yeah," I mutter nervously.

"Kind of like old times."

"Uh huh." I feel really weird right now, like this is way too much intimacy way too soon.

We're sitting on the sidewalk in front of the school with our feet in the street. The two sack lunches Luke bought for us from the cafeteria rest on the concrete between us. Luke suggested we eat lunch out here because the senior lawn was too raucous. Normally, he would've wanted to hang where all the action was so he could say hey to old friends and re-establish the connections that had dwindled over summer break. Not today. Today he's all about focusing on me.

"You look totally hot today," Luke says casually after taking a swallow from his bottle of juice. "Did you get sexier over the summer, Albright?"

"Studying for the SATs will do that to you," I joke.

"Want a chip?" He offers me his open bag of Sun Chips.

"Okay." I reach into the bag and feel totally guilty taking food from Luke. Sure it's just food, but it's like I'm betraying Dante, which is stupid because Dante is gone. The safe assumption is that Dante is never coming back. Nobody knows where he is. I *should* let him go. But I can't. What if he does come back? What if—

I jam the chip into my mouth, crunching it, hoping the noise in my head will drown out my crazy thoughts.

"I think I figured it out," Luke says thoughtfully, staring off at the row of houses across the street from of our school.

"Figured what out?"

"Why a hottie like you dumped me."

I ignore his use of the word "hottie". Luke was always complimentary when we were together. I like that he still is, but I'm not sure if I want him knowing that. I don't want to encourage him. "I didn't dump you," I smile. "It was a break up. Not a dumping."

"Either way, you ended it."

"Yeah. Sorry." I'm not sure why I'm apologizing, but I feel like I should.

"No worries. I know why you did it."

"Why?"

"Because I was too busy for you. I mean, you told me I was too busy. I never listened. Sure, I heard you. But I never took it in. It's like, I don't know, I think maybe I was afraid to have feelings for you."

"Really?"

"Yeah," he nods, gazing into my eyes. "I think I was afraid if I liked you too much, if you knew how into you I was, you'd dump me."

"See how well that turned out?" I snicker. I'm trying to cover up my feelings because everything Luke is saying is having an unexpected effect on me. I always thought he was too cool for school. I didn't realize he could be so sensitive. It's kind of a turn on.

"What can I say? Guys can be dumb. Eat a chip." He pulls one out of the bag and points it at my mouth.

I frown and wrinkle my nose.

"Eat it," he grins. "You know you love Sun Chips."

I do. I open my lips and he slips it in. I crunch and smile.

Luke smiles happily too. He really fills out his Daft Punk shirt quite nicely. I don't remember his shoulders being so broad. Did he spend the summer working out?

A black blade of hair shields one of his brown eyes, which look amber in the bright So Cal sunlight. I reach up and push the blade aside. Luke has really nice eyes.

So does Dante.

What am I doing?

I bury my hands in my lap. I can't let myself have feelings for Luke.

"I thought about you all summer," he says, his eyes locked on mine. "The more I thought about you, the more I felt like I'd blown it big time. My dad told me sometimes you gotta take a risk on love. If you don't go all in, you never win the jackpot. Know what I mean?"

Am I his jackpot? I never felt like his jackpot before, as weird as it sounds. A moment later, I realize that our knees are touching. When did that happen?

"I never went all in with you, Skye. I should've put all my money on you. But I didn't." He rests his hand on my knee. "What am I saying?" he chuckles to himself and swallows nervously. "This isn't about money. I'm just saying that because I'm afraid to say what I want to say. What I need to say…" he drifts off and stares at the pavement beneath his feet.

"What, Luke?" Am I having feelings for Luke? No, I can't be. That's why I ended it. Lack of feelings. There can't be feelings now, can there?

Somehow, his fingers find mine, crawling into my lap like a sneaky spider. Not the scary kind of spider. The love kind, if there is such a thing.

"I need to put my heart on the table, Skye."

My own heart flutters, frightened to life by the love spider in my lap. I squeeze his hand.

He squeezes back, "No more hiding my feelings. Skye, I never told you this before, but I really, really—"

BROOOOWWWWWLLLL!!!

A dusty motorcycle roars up right in front of us, skidding to a stop.

"Dante!" I blurt, jumping to my feet, flicking away the love spider that had been attacking my hand a second ago.

oOoOoOo + O+O+O+O

Dante vaults off his motorcycle like he's about to attack Luke.

"Dante, don't!" I blurt, jumping between them.

Luke is already on his feet, standing his ground. I don't think Luke has been in a fight since grade school, but he doesn't look scared. "Do you know this guy, Skye?"

"Yes. He's uh, he's… um," I don't want to say he's my stepbrother. "He's my math tutor."

Dante already has his helmet off. He smirks at me.

"Math tutor?" Luke snorts, not buying it.

"Yeah," Dante grunts. The sharp edge of confrontation sizzles in his tone, "Do I look like I don't know math?"

Luke laughs, "I don't look like I know shit about math either, but I'm taking AP Calculus this year. Luke Nash." He extends his hand. "Nice to meet you." That's Luke. Always making friends.

Dante's face softens slightly, but he still looks suspicious. "Dante Lord."

They shake like men. There's a moment where they test the strength of each other's grip.

"Why don't you guys arm wrestle," I say sarcastically.

Luke chuckles, "We're good." He glances at Dante. They're still shaking hands aggressively. "Are we good?"

"Yeah," Dante says, releasing Luke's hand.

"Math tutor, huh?" Luke smiles. "I used to help Skye with math. Back in the day."

"Which day was that?" Dante asks pointedly.

"Oh," he laughs. "Last school year. When we were dating." He emphasizes the word "dating" ever so NOT subtly. Luke is smart. I'm sure he senses Dante's interest. If that's what it is.

I hope that's what it is. I'd love for Dante to explain himself this instant, but I'm not about to have a heart to heart with Dante while Luke is listening.

"You guys used to date?" Dante marvels like it's an impossibility.

"Yeah," I smile. I don't want to give Luke any ideas by siding with Dante. I want it to look like Dante is merely my math tutor. And... I wouldn't mind making Dante a teeny bit jealous. Just a teeny bit.

Dante's face wiggles between irritated and friendly. It's kind of funny to watch. "That's great," he semi-scowls.

These two are politely fighting over me. Pardon me if I don't step in and put a stop to it. It's not like either of them is going to get hurt. So I'm going to enjoy it for a moment.

"You don't go to school around here, do you?" Luke asks Dante.

"Nope."

"Are you in college? You look a little old to be hanging around a high school," Luke quips. Jab, jab, jab.

"Part of the job." Dante grimaces.

"Do you tutor other kids here at North Valley?"

"Sure."

"How's the pay?"

"By check."

"That's not what I meant," Luke snickers. "I meant—"

"I know what you meant," Dante grunts.

"Okaaaay," Luke says dismissively.

"Skye," Dante says, "can I talk to you for a second? It's about our next tutoring session."

"Uh, yeah, sure," I smile. "Luke? Do you mind if I talk to Dante for a minute?"

"Yeah, go ahead," Luke grins.

"Alone?"

"Oh, okay." Luke picks up both lunch sacks from the sidewalk possessively. "Do you want any more chips?" He holds up the bag. "I'm not going to eat them all."

"No, I'm fine, thanks."

"I'll eat 'em." Dante leans past me and snatches the bag from Luke. Then he pops one in his mouth and crunches dramatically in Luke's face.

"Sure, man." Luke's smile flutters on his face as he tries to hide his irritation.

I think the chip bag is a metaphor for me, and Dante just took *it*, a.k.a *me*.

"You want my apple too?" Luke asks with irritation.

"Yeah." Dante holds out his hand expectantly.

Luke stares at it. "I changed my mind. I'm still hungry." *CRUNCH!!* He takes a big bite and chews in Dante's face.

Now I'm the chips *and* the apple. There's a Garden of Eden metaphor in there somewhere. Because of the apple. But my name's not Eve, and there was only one Adam. Although Dante did write The Inferno, so maybe that makes him the devil in this scenario.

Dante shoves four more chips in his mouth and bites them all at once.

I repress a grin.

Men.

I turn to Luke. "I'll talk to you later, okay?"

"Sounds like a plan," he mumbles over his mouthful of apple, standing in place. Tiny drops of apple juice jump from his lips.

"Bye?" I say suggestively.

"Bye." Luke backs up slowly, taking another big bite of his apple. I guess once Eve gave Adam that apple, he ate the whole thing. Then bad stuff happened and everyone got kicked out of the garden. But I'm getting ahead of myself.

When Luke is gone, Dante is swallowing the last of his chips. "Good chips," he says.

To say that I'm thrilled to see him doesn't do my feelings justice. I'm ready to jump into his arms, wrap my legs around him, and kiss every inch of his face. The only thing stopping me is the random students coming back to campus as lunch winds down. I'm sure if we started making out right here in front of the main entrance, word would spread around campus like wildfire before the start of fifth period. It can wait. "What are you doing here, Dante? I thought you'd left town or something."

"Thought about it," he grins. "But I couldn't do it."

"No? Why not?" I'm twirling from side to side like a giddy girl, my hands planted on my hips.

He chuckles and his dimples pop out as his luscious lips spread over his pristine teeth. A spray of stubble covers his jaw. His blond locks drift over his well-tanned brow. Emerald specks glint in his eyes, catching sunlight. He is so handsome it's ridic.

"Well?" I grin, smiling so hard my cheeks hurt.

"I couldn't leave you, Skye."

My heart melts all over the sun kissed sidewalk. I laugh. In a good way. "You couldn't?"

He shakes his head, at a loss for words. His bashful mood elevates his gorgeousness to godlike levels.

"How did you find me?"

"You told me you went here," Dante smiles.

"I did?"

"When you were talking about Brittany and Ashley and your other chums."

"Chums?" I laugh. It feels so good to laugh. I haven't had a good laugh since Dante disappeared. "Who says 'chums'?"

"Me."

"That's so dorky," I giggle. His dorkiness only makes him that much hotter. I'm dying here. I want to jump him. I need to jump him. I glance around. More students migrate back onto campus as the warning bell rings. "Can we go someplace?"

"Don't you have class?"

I shrug. "Yeah. I can be late. This'll just take a minute. I promise."

oOoOoOo + O+O+O+O

"I could do this forever," I sigh as Dante nibbles my neck.

We're leaning against a stuccoed wall behind the church down the street from North Valley High. Nobody is ever here during the week. Even though we're outside, you can't see us from the street because tall bushes hide us from view. The school burnouts often come back here to smoke pot, but none are here today.

Somehow, making out with my 21 year old stepbrother behind a church is more of a turn on than if it was a random building. Are the nuns and priests watching our deviltry? I hope they're enjoying the show. Maybe we're giving them ideas. Cause you never know what those nuns and priests do when no one is watching. They're never as innocent as they pretend.

Dante's hands squeeze my ass through my short shorts as his tongue thrusts into my mouth. I moan and lift one knee up and hook my heel around the back of his leg. Our naked lips grind together with hot wet passion. His hand slides inside the bottom of my shorts and he squeezes my butt cheek. "Are you wearing any panties?" he chuckles.

"Wanna find out?" I giggle.

"Damn, Skye, you are crazy. Shouldn't you be getting back to class?"

"This is more fun." I bite my lower lip and lock eyes with him. I am so turned on right now I feel nuclear. The pent up emotions inside me, and all the grief and sadness from the past week, now transform into lusty desire. This is insane, I know. But I can't help what I feel. I reach down between us and squeeze his hard cock through his jeans. It's a guided missile ready for launch. Wow. It's burning hot. I whisper into his ear. "Do you have a condom?"

He squeezes his eyes shut hard, smiling his dimples and grimacing at the same time. "No."

I shrug, "It's okay."

"What, are you on the pill?"

"No. Just pull out." I can't believe I just said that, but I did. I can't help it.

"Fuck, Skye…"

That's exactly what I had in mind.

"We can't," he sighs.

I start unbuckling his belt.

"What are you doing?" He chuckles, amused.

"You know what I'm doing," I purr. I was never this forward with Luke or any of the boys I've been with. But Dante does things to me. He literally drives me wild. I finish with the belt and it dangles open, the buckle tinkling softly. I unbutton his jeans and reach my hands inside, finding his heat.

He moans when I stroke his shaft and run my cupped fingers over the head, grazing the tip with my palm. "It's slick," I say, thrilled to feel his pre-cum already. I push his jeans down to give my hand better access, until he's all the way out.

He grimaces, biting his lower lip. "Skye…"

I stroke his shaft again and again, establishing a rhythm. His whole body melts like jelly. The only hard part of him remaining is the hot rod in my hand. He arches his body and his head tips back. With my free hand, I grab the waist of his jeans and pull him toward me. He falls against me, pressing his raging hardness against my body. His big chest crushes me against the wall. His arms trap me, planted against the stucco on either side of my head. He leans his head forward until we are cheek to cheek. He hisses in my ear with animalistic pleasure.

I whisper, "Fuck me, Dante."

He growls with restrained frustration. "I can't."

"Fuck me," I tease. "You know you want to…" I've never been the vixen, but Dante brings it out in me. In fact, I never knew I had it in me.

And it's something I'm discovering I really like. Something unbridled, something daring and courageous and a little bit dangerous. At this moment, I'm not the well behaved teenager who studies all the SAT prep books and takes endless practice tests while worrying about her GPA. I'm Skye, the Goddess of Flight. Or something like that.

He groans and pushes away from the wall, releasing me. He wastes no time pulling up his jeans and buttoning them.

I give him a pouty look.

"We can't. Not without protection." He buckles his belt and slides the leather tongue into the belt loop of his jeans.

A plain old leather belt has never looked so much like a chastity belt as it does now. I sigh, "You're right. We should get a condom. There's a Ralph's a few blocks from here."

"Ralph's?"

"It's a grocery store."

"Oh."

I hold out my hands, wanting him to take them. "Shall we?"

He reaches out and pulls me into him. I smack into his chest and we're kissing like we never stopped. He's still hot and hard.

And I'm all wet and soft. I need him to fuck me. "Let's get some condoms."

"Then where do we go?"

"Back to my house?" I've never had sex in my house. It was always elsewhere, like at Luke's house, where his parents were never a problem. Sex in my house is a dangerous proposition. And it feels wrong. "Or here? We could come back here." Even as I say it, I'm not so sure how I feel about it. This isn't the most romantic place. We're standing on hard packed dirt, surrounded by a random scatter of pine needles and a litter of cigarette butts.

"No, Skye."

It hurts to hear him say it, but he's right. "I'm missing fifth period anyway. I should probably go. I'll make some excuse about having cramps and being stuck in the bathroom."

He nods but says nothing.

I jam my fingers in the pockets of my short shorts. "Hey, um, are you coming back to the house? Your mom misses you big time." I miss him big time, and I miss the coming—you know what I mean—but I'm not saying either. I don't want to scare him off. You never know with guys.

"Yeah."

Yeah, he's coming back to the house? Or is he simply agreeing his mom misses him? Wow, how did I go from wild abandon to worried so quickly? Maybe because I can feel Dante walling himself off from me. Did I push things too far? Was I too slutty just now? Does he think I'm trashy for being so bold? Damn it! What did I do? Did I ruin things just when Dante decided to show up again?

"I should go," he mumbles.

Shit! Panic sweeps through me. Now I'm desperate. I can't think of a roundabout way to ask him to stay, so I just go straight to the point. "Am I going to see you again?"

He just looks at me, his face devoid of all feeling.

I'm suddenly freaked out he's going to leave town forever. Every crazy thought I've had over the last week that involved him jumping on a plane to who knows where, or disappearing into the wilderness on his dusty motorcycle, comes crashing back. From what I know, Dante really is capable of leaving and never coming back. Grasping at straws, I say, "Should I tell your mom I saw you today?"

He blinks and lowers his eyes, shaking his head. "No."

"What? You can't leave without saying goodbye to your mom." I'm panicking hard.

"I'll tell her myself."

Does he mean he *is* leaving, but he'll say goodbye to his mom first? This is driving me nuts. "Why don't you come over for dinner?" I blurt.

He smirks at me. "I don't want to deal with your dad again."

Damn my dad! He's the cause of all of this. Things were going great before Dad destroyed them like a bull in a china shop. The kind of china shop that only sells cute romantic curios of childhood sweethearts and kissing kittens and lovebirds perching together. My dad wrecked my romance once. He's not doing it again. "I'll make sure Dad is on his best behavior," I plead. "Catarina will make sure he's on his best behavior! We'll put a muzzle on him! We'll chain him to his chair! I promise, he won't do anything to ruin the evening!" I pause, nearly breathless. "But you *have* to come over." I've never sounded so desperate in my entire life. I don't care. I literally hold my breath, waiting for an answer. *Please say yes, please, please, pleasepleaseplease...*

After an endless moment, Dante grins at me, "The muzzle should be enough. I don't think you'll need the chains."

"Does that mean you're coming?" I gasp.

"Sure."

"Okay! I'll make sure everyone is ready to sit down to eat at seven. Don't be late!"

oOoOoOo + O+O+O+O

"I think Dante is late," I say to Catarina as we set the table.

"It's only 7:03," Dad says, glancing at his watch. "If he's not here by 7:15, we'll file a missing person's report," he says sarcastically.

I don't think Dad is too keen on Dante coming over for dinner. Screw him. He was the one who drove Dante away in the first place by being so uptight.

"I'm sure he'll be here," Catarina says hopefully. When I called to tell her Dante was coming over, she left work early and bought a bunch of food at Vons. She's quite the cook when she has time for it. I think she wants to impress Dante with a home cooked meal he'll never forget. Or maybe one that reminds him of when he was little. The kitchen is an explosion of ingredients and saucepans simmering on the stove.

I've been helping her get the food ready since she brought everything home. She prepped the veal for the Osso Bucco and stuck it in the oven two hours ago. I made tomato bruschetta with sun-dried tomatoes and plenty of olive oil. I also wrapped slices of prosciutto around steamed asparagus spears. The skillet with the half-cooked Lamb Fritata is ready to add eggs and go in the oven. The broccoli salad with chopped avocado and citrusy basil dressing is ready to serve. I tasted it. Yum. I'm not a huge broccoli fan, but Catarina knows how to make anything taste delish.

Earlier, when the bulk of the cooking was done, I went upstairs and changed around 6:30. I put on a loose fitting lace panel tee and floral print jeggings. Just a bit of makeup. Not so much that dad will notice and say something annoying, but enough so that my face isn't plain. I look nice. After my unfinished make out session with Dante behind the church, "nice" isn't what I want to project. "Bad" would better suit my mood. But with Dad here, I have to be on my best behavior. I don't want to give him any ideas to support his suspicions about Dante. Tonight will be a careful balancing act of flirtation with Dante and setting Dad at ease. I know I can do it.

"If it gets any later, the Osso Bucco is going to dry out," Catarina says absently, watching the clock. Her voice is strained. She cracks the door on the oven and turns off the heat.

"When do you put the Lamb Frittata in?" I ask.

"That should wait until Dante arrives. It only needs a few minutes in the oven."

I'm sure she's as worried as I am that Dante won't actually show up. It would suck if all our hard work went to waste.

"Does anybody want wine?" Dad asks, holding up a bottle of

Merlot.

"Please," Catarina says nervously.

Dad pulls the corkscrew out of the drawer and pops the cork. He's acting on his best behavior, but it sounds forced. I'm sure Catarina lectured him about not being a jerk tonight. It was probably the first time they've talked since Dante left, but at least they're talking again. Dad pulls two wine glasses out of the cupboard and sets them on the counter. He pours one for her and a much bigger one for himself. Dad doesn't usually get drunk. He drinks now and then, but I'm not sure what he's like if he gets loaded. I'm afraid to find out.

Catarina looks at his overly full wine glass. "You should let it breathe for a bit before you drink it." It sounds like a warning more than a suggestion.

Dad is swirling the glass under his nose like a wine snob. "Right." He sets his glass down on the counter and walks away from it, like he might be tempted to hammer it. He plants his hands on his hips and looks back and forth from the kitchen to the dining room. "How long do we wait for him?"

Catarina glares at Dad.

"He'll be here soon, Dad," I sigh.

Dad drums his fingers on his slacks. He took his tie off earlier, which is about as relaxed as he ever gets. He stares at his wine glass on the counter. "Does it need more air?"

Catarina says, "Drink your wine. It might help you relax."

Dad grabs it and takes a huge swallow.

DING dong DING DANG dang Dong!! —

We have one of those really long doorbells. Dad loves it. I hate it. "That must be him!" I run to the front door, all smiles.

—Ding DING TING-A-LING Dang dong Ding DONG!!

Catarina strides after me, her heels clicking on the hardwood floor.

"Finally," Dad moans, dragging his feet.

I grab the doorknob, trying to calm down and not act like a giddy teenager (which I am). Excitement sweeps over me. I open the door.

Dante.

And some floozy redhead holding his elbow.

WTF?

My smile collapses into a frown. Who's *she*?

"Hey," Dante says.

"Hi," the floozy smiles. She's stunning. Tall, long limbed, flowing red hair that looks completely natural. Her off the shoulder black bodycon dress hugs curves that would make a straight line in any man's pants. The long sleeves are studded at the wrists. She's wearing knee length buckled black leather biker boots. *Knee* length. She looks totally trashy. Bitch! She is hot as hell compared to me in my "nice" girl outfit. With Dante wearing his customary leather jacket and jeans, they look perfect together.

Damn her!

My stomach sours and I fold my arms across my chest.

"Who's this?" Dad asks.

My sentiments exactly.

"This is Phoebe," Dante says. "Phoebe Saxon."

Saxon? Like Sexon? As in, 'the SEX is ON'? Because that's the vibe she's projecting like a 90 foot tall IMAX movie in her slut couture. Where the hell did he find this vamp tramp? Hollywood Boulevard where all the hookers hang out? I wonder if she charges by the hour or the evening?

"Phoebe, this is my mom, Catarina."

"Hi," Phoebe extends her hand.

Catarina shakes it, "Pleased to meet you, Phoebe." She doesn't seem annoyed, just confused. "I'm so sorry, I wasn't expecting another person. I'll need to set another plate."

"I'm sorry," Phoebe says. "Dante..." she twinkles her nose, "... didn't you tell your mom I was coming?"

Does she *know* him? She's sure acting like it.

"Sorry. I forgot," he says like it's no big deal.

WTF? Did he also forget that I basically begged him to have sex after lunch? Oh my god, who's the trash gash now? I am such a slut! What the hell was I thinking? I was ready to have unprotected sex with Dante?! Who knows where his dick has been?! I am so stupid!!

"Is this your dad?" Phoebe asks Dante.

"Gordon Albright," Dad says, reaching past me to shake her hand.

"Nice to meet you, Gordon," she smiles.

Don't shake her hand, Dad! She's the enemy!! You'll probably catch hand STDs!!! I want to yell it at the top of my lungs, but I just swallow my anger.

"This is my daughter Skye." Dad rests his hands on my shoulders.

Is he holding me back? Because I'm about to lunge at Phoebe and slice her neck open with my nails.

Phoebe offers her hand, "Nice to meet you, Skye."

I will look like a total bitch if I don't shake her hand. I'm okay with that.

"Shake her hand," Dad encourages.

Dad never says the right thing when it counts.

I shake her hand, but look away, avoiding her evil eyes.

"I love your outfit," Phoebe says.

Sure she does.

"It's very cute."

Cute? Like Hello Kitty cute or Dora the Explorer Cute? Is she trying to make me sound like a child? Like I buy my clothes from the kids' department at Target? "Thanks," I groan. I drill Dante with rusty eye daggers. I hate him right now.

He's not even looking at me. Does he even remember I exist?

"Good to see you again, Gordon," Dante says. "Sorry if we got off on the wrong foot the other day." Dante holds out his hand.

Traitor!

Dad shakes it like a normal person and says, "Don't worry about it." He has a huge smile on his face.

Do NOT take Dante's side!

"I'll set a place for Phoebe," Catarina says.

"I hope you made enough food," Phoebe says thoughtfully. "I'm so sorry to surprise you like this."

"It's no bother," Catarina waves her hands. "I made plenty."

You too? Don't take her side!

"Come sit in the dining room," Dad beams. "We can't leave you two standing in the foyer all night."

Now everyone is against me!

This is awful!!!!

oOoOoOo + O+O+O+O

"This is wonderful, Catarina," Phoebe beams after daintily blotting her lips with her napkin. She is so damn polite it's sickening. "What is it again?"

"Pumpkin risotto. Dante always loved risotto as a boy," she smiles and winks at her son. "Isn't that right, Dante."

"Yeah," he grins, chewing on a mouthful of risotto, his cheeks puffed out like a chipmunk. Not the cute kind of chipmunk. The conniving kind. Bastard.

Phoebe leans against his shoulder for a moment, smiling that conniving smile of hers. Yeah, it's cute. But conniving and cute go hand in hand, as we just learned.

Quit leaning on him, you skanky bitch!

I would kick her shins under the table, but I don't think it would go over well with everybody else. For those of you wondering what you missed so far, let me make a list:

1. Everybody loves Phoebe except me. I hate her.

2. Phoebe is very nice and has a great sense of humor that I don't find funny at all.

3. Phoebe owns her own clothing boutique and made her dress herself.

4. Phoebe, Phoebe, Phoebe. Dinner has been all about Phoebe.

5. I tried slitting my wrists under the table with my butter knife, but it didn't work.

6. I can't wait until dinner is over.

"I love your earrings," Catarina says to Phoebe. "Did you make those too?"

"No," she grins. "I have a jewelry designer who makes everything I sell at my shop. She made them. But these are my own design."

"They're beautiful," Catarina marvels. "I love the diamond in the center of the star. A nice touch."

"Thank you," Phoebe smiles demurely.

They continue to blather on about how awesome Phoebe is.

I lean over and whisper to Dad, "May I be excused?"

"We haven't finished dinner," Dad mutters. "Don't you want to wait until after dessert? Those cannolis Catarina brought home look delicious."

"I have homework. And SAT stuff. I don't want to get behind on math." That should do the trick. Dad never hesitates when it comes to me studying more math.

"Can it wait until after dessert?"

What the what? Who body snatched Dad? I gape at him.

"We don't get to have a family dinner like this every day," he smiles. "Do it for Catarina."

I scowl and stare at my plate, pushing my Osso Bucco bone around absently. This. Sucks. I noticed that Dad stopped drinking wine a while ago. He was having too much fun talking to Phoebe. And even Dante. No arguing about the economy or hexayurts. Just yucking it up about Phoebe this and Phoebe that. I would've preferred a drunken fist fight over the way he's kissed ass all night.

"So, Skye," Phoebe says. "Dante tells me you're quite the honor student."

I'm the opposite of whatever she says about me. And what is Dante doing telling her about my personal life? What else did he tell her?

"Yes she is," Dad chimes in. "I'm so proud of her."

Why don't you lift up Phoebe's dress so you can kiss her ass right on her brown star while you're at it, Dad? I bet she has a diamond there too, just like her stupid earrings!! You know you want to because she's protecting me from Dante better than you ever could. Not that I'm bitter about it.

"She wants to go to San Diego University," Catarina says supportively.

Is she ganging up on me too?

"I hear SDU has a great business program," Phoebe smiles.

She's probably just saying that because she knows I'll be far away from Dante and she can have him all to herself.

"It does," Dad agrees. "Skye has been talking about going to SDU for years. With her grades, she's bound to get in. Isn't that right, Skye?"

Still nudging the bone around on my plate. Do I have to say anything? Can't I just sulk? This is ridiculous. I roll my eyes at myself. This is stupid. I'm acting like a baby.

From here on out, I'm going to act like the young woman I am. I know better. I should've cut off everything with Dante from day one. Not pine for him like I have. Him going out with Phoebe is good news. This way, Rox can't have him either, so I don't have to worry about her being jealous of me or me being jealous of her. What a disaster that would've been, right? Way too complicated. I've got more important things, like getting a good SAT score this fall to lock in my admission at SDU. It's not a guarantee until they send me the acceptance letter. "Yeah," I say. "I just have to make sure I don't blow the math portion when I retake the SAT in October. Which is why I should probably go hit the books. I've got a lot of studying to do." I stand up from my chair. "Dad, may I be excused?"

See how mature I'm being about all of this?

"Don't you want dessert?" Dad asks.

"I'm not really hungry." I push my chair up to the table.

"I'll save you a cannoli," Catarina smiles. "You can have it tomorrow." It's like she's trying to push me out of here too. Then it'll just be the Phoebe Saxon show.

The SEX is ON!!

I hope they fucking enjoy it.

Since they all love each other so much, they can have a four way right on the dining room table.

Traitors!!

oOoOoOo + O+O+O+O

I'm not enjoying studying in my room one bit.

Why?

Because Dante is in the guest bedroom with Phoebe.

Turns out he decided to spend the night. Yay. Not. I hope Phoebe doesn't plan on spending the night too. If Dad doesn't say anything about it, you can be damn sure I will. No sleepovers with members of the opposite sex allowed.

I throw my pencil at my notebook and flap the cover of the SAT math book shut on my desk. This is so lame.

With Dante here, we're like one big happy family. Too bad everyone's happy except me.

I heard Catarina talking to Dante in the upstairs hallway earlier. It sounds like he'll be staying for a while. Great! Kill me now.

The next thing you know, he'll be hooking up with Phoebe in the next room!

Speaking of which, I find it impossible not to wonder what's going on with them. I push back my chair and kneel down next to the air vent. All I can hear is muted muttering from the guest room. Well, that, and giggling from Phoebe. Did I mention she has a cute laugh? Not annoying cute, but perfect cute? Yeah, it's perfectly annoying.

I can't make out what they're saying, but I'm sure everything coming out of Dante's mouth is super charming. He's an ass.

After a while, the talking stops.

It's only 9:00pm.

Way too early for them to be sleeping.

I don't hear a movie playing.

What do two people usually do when they're in a bedroom not talking and not sleeping?

Hmmm.

I can't imagine.

Maybe I should go knock on the door and ask if they need anything to drink? Or a condom? Or did Dante already get condoms so he could use them with Phoebe instead of me? Bastard! He wouldn't have any if I hadn't suggested it!

"Oh... that's wonderful..." Phoebe moans ever so softly.

Damn it. What is he doing to her? And why isn't he doing it to me? Damn him!!!!

I stand up and stalk to my door and rip it open. It's not loud because it drags on the thick carpeting. But when I go into the bathroom, I slam the door. Unfortunately, it doesn't slam very loud. I sit down on the toilet seat with my elbows on my knees and my chin in my hands.

"Dante..." Phoebe purrs, "That's so good." The sound from the vent is muffled but echoey in the tiled bathroom.

Great. I forgot that the air vent to the hall bathroom connects to the guest bedroom too. I flush the toilet and pound the lever with my finger a bunch of times while gritting my teeth, even though I only need to press it once. Then I wash my hands for no reason for a really long time, making as much noise as I can. Now would be a good time for me to take a shower and sing Since U Been Gone by Kelly Clarkson at the top of my lungs. Or maybe You Oughta Know by Alanis Morissette. Sometimes you gotta go with the classics.

Or maybe I just need to stick my head in the toilet and flush it over and over until I drown.

Stupid Dante!!

You are the biggest prick ever invented!

"That's amazing…" Phoebe moaning again, obviously enjoying herself.

Geez, Dad, I wonder to myself, *aren't you hearing any of this? Put a stop to it already!!*

But I've already determined that Dad is a total traitor, so why would he? I consider jamming my mouth against the air vent and screaming, "*QUIT FUCKING EACH OTHER IN MY HOUSE!!*"

Do I march out of this bathroom and bang on the door to the master bedroom? I'm sure Dad wouldn't be happy if he knew what was going on under his own roof. But I can't count on Dad at a time like this, not after how ass kissey he was at dinner.

I need to take action myself.

I whip open the bathroom door and pound down the stairs. I rip open the fridge in the kitchen and grab the plate with the cannoli covered in cling wrap. It's not for me. I grab two forks and march upstairs. I rap my knuckles against the guest bedroom door like bullets. I'm sure they're totally naked and screwing with abandon right now. It'll take them a minute or two to put clothes on. It's not like I want to see Dante naked doing the in-n-out with Phoebe or see her eating his cream filled cannoli. But I want to put a stop to it. I knock again, just to be annoying.

The door pops open mid-knock. "What's up?" Dante asks, fully dressed.

Phoebe sits on the bed, also fully dressed, holding Dante's tattered notebook in her hands like she was reading it.

Where's the sex part? I thought they were totally busy getting busy.

"Um…" I stammer. "I brought you guys some more cannoli?"

He frowns at the plate. "We had some earlier. They're really good."

"Then you probably want another one?" I sound idiotic.

Dante turns to Phoebe, "You want more cannoli?"

She shakes her head. "I'm good. Hey, have you read Dante's poetry? It's amazing." She holds up his notebook.

I tilt my head and glare at Dante. "No, I didn't know Dante wrote poetry. He never told me."

"I didn't?" he asks innocently.

"No." I try not to growl.

He shrugs. "I guess I didn't. You can read it sometime. If you want."

And be your sloppy seconds? I don't think so. "Sure."

The three of us exchange a look that says "Go away, Skye." At least that's what I think it says. "I guess I'll eat this cannoli then." I walk down the hall and slam my door to my room. With the thick carpet slowing it down once again, it swooshes more than slams. I drop into my desk chair and stab the cannoli with a fork and shove a bite into my mouth.

This is going to be a long night.

oOoOoOo + O+O+O+O

Two hours later, the bitch is still here.

When is she going to leave? I'm too tired to study more. I already washed my face and got ready for bed. But she's. Still. Here.

Can I throw her out? I live here. I have jurisdiction.

I shake my head, staring at the ceiling. When will my torment end?

Normally, I would get Rox on the phone so I could whine about it to her. But I can't tell her what's going on with me and Dante. Or what went on, because he and I are done, as far as I'm concerned. But something tells me I shouldn't tell Rox. If I do, it will lead to her being hurt because I kept her in the dark about everything Dante and I did already. I've had enough drama for one day.

A minute later, I hear a knock in the hallway.

I hop out of bed and open my door a crack as quietly as possible so I can listen and watch.

Dad stands in front of the guest bedroom. Light pours out when the door opens. "Hey, Dante," Dad says in a low voice.

"Hey, Mr. Albright," Dante says. When did he get all respectful? Probably when he realized Dad could supply him with a free fuckpad for him and his floozy.

"Don't you think it's time to take Phoebe home? It's eleven o'clock and it's a school night. Time for lights out, am I right?"

For once in my life, I can finally say it: *Go, Dad!! Kick the bitch to the curb!!!!*

"Sure," Dante says. "I'll take her home right now."

Good riddance!

After some muffled sounds, Dante and Phoebe walk out of the guest bedroom and Dad watches them go down the stairs. Then he turns to face my door. Usually it's closed this late. Luckily my lights are off or else he'd totally see me. I scramble toward my bed and slide under the covers. Feeling hella guilty, I pretend to be sleeping. No fake snoring. That's a dead giveaway.

I hope Dad isn't going to do a bedtime knock and talk. I'm so not in the mood.

Luckily, he latches my door quietly and walks away.

For once, I'm glad for Dad. He did something right this evening.

I doze off to sleep at some point, I'm not sure when.

Then my eyes pop open. I was dreaming of Dante. Sex with Dante. Steamy wet and slippery sex with Dante. Luckily, Phoebe wasn't in the dream.

Phoebe.

Is Dante with her?

Disgust turns my stomach. Or maybe it was that cannoli I inhaled before bed.

I glance at the clock. It's 1:30am. That's more than long enough for Dante to have driven her home and come back here. Okay, I have to know. I slip out of bed, my eyes adjusted to the pink glow of my nightlight. I twist open my doorknob and creep down the hall. The house is completely silent.

And the guest bedroom is completely empty.

The door stands wide open.

Maybe Dante is downstairs because he couldn't sleep? I pad down the stairs in my PJs. I check the whole house. It's dark and gloomy and just as empty as the guest bedroom. Damn it. I trudge back upstairs and get into bed. There's no way I'm sleeping now. I'm too irritated. Not angry. My anger subsided when she left the house. Now I'm disgruntled.

Is Dante spending the night with her at her place, wherever that may be? Is Phoebe the Saxon Klaxon riding him right now like he's a bucking bronco, screaming like a firetruck siren? With that biker chick outfit of hers and flaming red hair, you know she's a screamer.

Am I jealous? Of course. I wanted Dante.

But you know what? He's a total liar. I should call him Dante Lord of the Lies from here on out. Earlier today, he said he couldn't leave town because of me. I was all ready to buy his bashful bullshit. I was fully under the impression that he came back for me. So what the hell is with Phoebe? Did he meet her today? Did he already know her? Somehow, that intel never came out during dinner. But they sure got along like gangbusters. Or should I say, gang-*bangers*?

I roll my eyes. I don't want to think about them in the sack.

But, when did they meet? Was it the day after I met Dante? After he took off? Is that why he never came back to the house? Maybe he's been sleeping at her place ever since. That makes perfect sense! I am an idiot! Of course that's what happened! Any woman in her right mind would take one look at a hot stud like Dante Lord and sink her claws into him and hold on for dear life. I certainly tried. But that doesn't mean he won't get away.

I turn in bed so I'm flat on my back, staring at the ceiling. I sigh sourly and knot the sheets in my fingers.

Maybe it's better I found out the truth about Dante now. Who knows what kind of heartbreak I'd have been in for if things went any further with him? The good news is that we did *not* have sex. That's Phoebe's job from here on out. She's welcome to it. Good luck holding on to him. I hope she has sharp claws because he'll probably bring some new hot trollop over to *her* place for dinner a week from now.

Maybe Dad was right about Dante all along.

I'm starting to wish he never came back.

Chapter 9

"Why didn't you tell me Dante came back?" Rox demands, hurt.

I take a rolled up square of shag carpet out of my bag and set it on the bottom of my open locker during brunch. "Because I just found out yesterday!"

"Well, why didn't you tell me then?" she huffs.

"It all happened really fast," I lie. "He just showed up at the house for dinner." More lies. I reach into my bag and pull out a package of removable wallpaper. I tear the cellophane open and pull out a sheet. It has pastel pink clouds floating against a pink sky.

"You could've invited me over. You know I'm interested in him."

"Maybe you shouldn't be."

"What's that supposed to mean?"

"He's my stepbrother, Rox! How weird would it be for you to be dating him?" *I'm the one who should be dating him!* If he ever dumps Phoebe, that is. "I don't like the idea of you making out with him in the next room, you know? It's weird. Can you help me with this?" I hold up the folded sheet of wallpaper.

"Sure." Rox helps me unfold it.

It's way too big for the locker, but I brought scissors. Rox holds the paper up while I cut it to fit the inside of my locker door.

"What if I promised never to hook up with Dante when you were around?" Rox asks, still holding up the wallpaper. "You wouldn't need to know."

"But I *would* know, Rox. That's the problem." I shake the scissors for emphasis. All I can think about is how much it's tearing me up inside to know that Dante is doing who knows what with Phoebe. If it was Rox, I would go nuts.

"Easy with those scissors, Lizzy Borden," Rox blurts, leaning away defensively.

I roll my eyes and resume cutting the paper.

"I don't want to be selfish, Skye, but don't you think you would get used to it after awhile?"

"Why are you so hung up on Dante? He's never around anyway." I sound really irritated, but I can't hide it.

"Are you kidding? You were there at Blazing Waters, right?"

"Yes, I was there," I growl.

"You saw how hot he was. Right?"

"Yes!" I say stridently.

"So you know why I can't stop thinking about him."

Welcome to the club.

"Someone has to go there," she grins. "So, why not me?"

I sigh harshly. "Well, what if you guys *do* hook up, but then you have a bad break up? Then I'd have to choose between you and him. Right? Imagine how complicated that would be."

She chews her lip thoughtfully. She's thinking it over.

I press the argument, "Besides, when did you ever have any problems getting hot guys?"

"Never," she grins. "But Dante is a man, not a guy."

"So let's go down to UCLA on the weekend and I'll help you troll for a college man. How does that sound? Maybe we'll even find you a sexy med student. Then you can date a hot doctor."

Her eyes flash. "That could be fun."

"Then we'll do that." I finish cutting the wallpaper and peel off the adhesive backing.

We carefully press the paper onto the locker door.

"Nice," Rox smiles, admiring our work.

"Thanks for the help."

"So, um, if Dante has dinner with you again tonight, will you call me?"

I grit my teeth. "What about UCLA?"

She shrugs, "That's not till this weekend."

"Can't you wait?"

"Promise you'll call me?"

Wow, she's not giving up on this. "Fine," I groan. "I'll call you if he comes for dinner." Maybe he'll bring Phoebe and Rox will let it go.

"Hey, Skye!" Jason Carpenter smiles, walking up with a binder under his arm that says Magic The Gathering on the front. I have no idea what that is. He takes one look at Rox and nearly drops his binder. Rox is stunning. These things happen. "Uh..." he stammers and swallows hard. "Is this your friend?"

Rox smiles indulgently but says nothing. She usually doesn't notice any male who is shorter than 5'11".

"Rox, this is my locker neighbor Jason Carpenter."

Jason stares at her, transfixed by her beauty. "Uhh... Do you play

Magic The Gathering?"

"Magic the What?" Rox laughs.

Jason lifts up his binder and opens it. Inside are a bunch of plastic pages filled with some sort of trading cards. Jason stares at the cards, fascinated. "It's a collectible card game. See, you collect the cards and build a deck—"

"Anyway," Rox says to me.

I elbow her and hiss, "Don't be rude. Jason is telling us about his card game."

Jason glances between us, totally confused.

BRIIIIIIIINGGGG!!!

The five minute bell.

"We should go," Rox says. "We don't want to be late for class, do we?"

Jason deflates.

I say, "You can tell her about Magic the Wizarding next time, Jason."

His eyes light. "Oh, okay! But it's Magic the Gathering."

"That's what I said," I frown.

"No, you said Wizarding! That's Harry Potter."

"Oh," I giggle uncertainly.

"We should go," Rox says.

"Do you guys wanna play some time? Magic, I mean?" The way he says "play" sounds so cute. Like grade school. "Some really cool guys play Magic in the library at lunch."

I can imagine how "cool" said guys are. Erm, no. "Maybe later?" I say politely.

"Yeah, okay! I gotta go! I don't want to be tardy. Bye!" He runs off.

"Bye, Jason!" I wave.

"He's cute," Rox muses. "But too young for you." She breaks into a laugh. "You should stick to Luke. I heard you talked to him yesterday."

"You did? From who?"

"From him."

Oh, no. I hope he didn't mention Dante. Rox might figure things out. "Uhh... what did he say?"

"He said you guys had lunch together."

"What else did he say?" I swallow hard.

"Just that you guys never should've broken up."

Phew.

"You should totally get back together with him, Skye. I think he put on some muscle over the summer and grew a few inches."

"If you think he's so hot, why don't you go out with him?" I frown.

"Because," she rolls her eyes, "I'm saving myself for Dante."

Funny. I am too.

"And I can't date your ex," she adds. "Way too much drama."

And you dating Dante would equal less drama?

This is getting way too complicated.

There's a simple fix. I hate to do it, but it has to be done. "Dante brought some random biker chick redhead over to the house for dinner last night. She owns her own clothing store and makes her own dresses."

"Whaaaaaat?" she sings.

I nod. "After dinner, they were camped out in the guest bedroom with the door closed until my dad kicked her out."

"Really?" She looks disappointed. Good.

"Yeah. I think they were making out." I don't have proof, but it's a reasonable assumption. The important thing is that Rox knows that Dante is interested in someone else other than me. Or her. She may chase guys like the crazy flirt that she is, but she's never been a home wrecker. Hopefully now she'll finally back off.

"Well," Rox grins coquettishly, "That just means I'll have to step up my game. Let me know if he brings the skank with him for dinner. I'll wear one of my scoop neck dresses and show off the girls." She glances at her chest. "Bee tee double U, how was the chest on the redhead?"

"I didn't look," I scowl.

"No worries. I doubt her ta-tas measure up to mine."

Oh, geez. What happened to the little Rox who used to love her Bratz dolls more than boys, just like I did?

Maybe I need to hang in the library with Jason and his card game cronies and forget about men entirely. I wonder if Jason's friends like Bratz dolls? They could be like Bronies, except Bratzies. Do they have those? If they do, we'll totally get along.

When Rox turns the corner to head toward her third period class, she says, "Don't forget, if Dante has dinner at your house tonight, call me!"

"Okay!" I groan.

"See you at lunch!" she grins and sashays off.

oOoOoOo + O+O+O+O

At the start of lunch, I meet up with Rox in the quad.

"We should ask Luke to go with us to Subway," she suggests.

She is totally trying to push me back into the arms of Luke. She's not usually like this. Then again, Dante does that to women. He makes them crazy. He makes me crazy too. I sigh, "No men today. Girls Lunch Out. Okay?"

"Okay. But can we talk about men?"

"No! We can only talk about girl things like makeup or periods."

She chuckles. "Periods?"

"Yes!" I laugh. "Let's go." I pull her toward the gym and we go around the back, using the gate past the school pool to get to the parking lot. I don't want to bump into Luke and have him try to join us by default.

"You know what?"

"What?"

"If Dante does come for dinner, maybe you should invite Luke? So you'll have someone to talk to while I focus on Dante."

"Would you quit already?" I whine.

"Hey, Skye!" a girl calls out behind us.

I turn around and see Nicole Parrish and Kayla Horn. Rox and I have known them since freshman year. We hang out with them at school and do stuff outside of school like go to the mall or the movies or do homework at each other's houses. But we've never been as close to Nicole and Kayla as we are to each other.

Nicole has straight brown hair and she's really tall. She tends to stoop her shoulders a lot, like she doesn't want to be so tall. She's on the basketball team. Kayla doesn't do any sports, except shop and starve herself. I swear Kayla wears new clothes five days a week. Her dad is a plastic surgeon, which is how she pays for all her clothes. Kayla is pretty, but she tries way too hard sometimes. I try not to hold it against her. From what she's told me, I think her mom is kind of a bitch. It definitely rubbed off on Kayla, but she's not so bad.

We saw them yesterday during Mrs. Huffman's fifth period AP English Literature, which we all have together, but we didn't have a chance to catch up.

"Hey, guys!" I smile.

"Are you guys going somewhere for lunch?" Nicole asks. "I'm starving!"

"Subway," Rox says. "Wanna come? I'm driving."

"Sure!" Kayla shrugs. "Let's do this!"

We all pile into Rox's Toyota and drive to Subway. We all order veggie sandwiches, except Nicole, who orders a foot-long hot meatball sandwich.

"Are you sure you got enough to eat?" Kayla snarks.

"Shut up, twigs," Nicole snorts. "Maybe if you put some muscle on these skinny legs of yours, you'd have an appetite."

"What do I need muscles for?" Kayla retorts. "I have guys lift things for me."

Nicole rolls her eyes, "You are lazier than my mom."

Nicole and Kayla always banter and bicker like this. They're pretty funny together. They're not as catty one-on-one, but we usually hang out together, so I'm used to it.

We carry our trays to a booth and sit down.

"What do you guys think of Mrs. Huffman?" Nicole asks, unwrapping her meatball sub.

"She's supposed to be super laid back," Kayla offers. "And an easy grader."

"Sounds perfect because I like to nap fifth period," Rox giggles before biting into her veggie sandwich.

"Totes," Nicole giggles then looks at me. "She was way cool when you came in late yesterday, Skye."

"Yeah," I agree nervously.

"What was that about?" Kayla prods.

"Oh, uh... " I stammer. Damn. I can't tell them about me and Dante behind the church. "Uh, cramps?"

Rox narrows her eyes. "I thought you and I cycled together. You shouldn't be cramping for at least a week."

I shrug guiltily.

Kayla scowls, "Can we not talk about cramps and periods while Nicole forces me to watch her slobber all over her meatball sandwich?"

"You're such a prude," Nicole groans before taking a huge bite of her sandwich and chomping on it loudly. "Mmmm! Bloody meatballs!"

Rox grimaces, "Gross, Nicole!"

The three of them laugh while I breathe a sigh of relief. That was too close. Lying all the time sure is a pain in the ass.

"What is with those shoes?" Kayla scowls, watching a pair of older women walk in the front door. Both women wear business skirts and blouses with running shoes. "I wouldn't be caught dead wearing those shoes with that outfit."

Thank goodness for the distraction.

"Exercise isn't a disease, Kayla," Nicole sneers. "You can't catch it like a cold. You actually have to get off your skinny ass and do it."

"As long as my ass is skinny, why do I need exercise?" She glances at the women again and shivers. "It's not just the shoes. Those outfits are terrible." She fake gags. Then she plucks a tomato slice out of her sandwich, which sits uneaten on the Subway wrapping paper. She pops the tomato slice into her mouth. I think that's all she's gonna eat today.

"Don't worry," Rox says, "No one is making you wear them."

"I hope not," Kayla groans. "So, did you guys miss me this summer?"

My honest answer would be no. Instead, I say, "Why, did you go somewhere?" Because that's what she wants someone to ask.

"To Europe, silly! Don't you remember?"

"Oh yeah!" I remember her talking about it for the entire last month of junior year. "How was it?"

"Brills. My favorite place was Majorca. The guys there were incredible. Milan was second for guys, but the shopping was off the hook. Well, the guys were pretty hot there too, but it's hard to compare when the guys in Majorca were practically naked."

"Did you have a summer fling?" Rox asks.

"Oh!" Kayla rolls her eyes with dramatic satisfaction and makes a moan face. "You mean, did I hook up with any hot guys?" She says it like a foregone conclusion.

"Well, did you?" Nicole grumbles. If Nicole has ever had a boyfriend, none of us know about it.

Kayla splays her fingers out almost like she's getting her nails done by the rest of us. A conspiratorial look lights up her face. "His name was Santiago and every inch of his body was hard, and I mean *every* inch, and—" she rolls her eyes back in her head again, "—and, oh... my... god... did he know how to use it!"

"In other words, you made him do all the work," Nicole says sarcastically.

Rox and I both giggle.

"You would've too," Kayla snorts. "If you saw him, you'd be paralyzed by his godlike beauty." She says it reverentially.

"Godlike? Sounds like a myth to me," Nicole says. "Do you have any pics on your phone?"

Kayla focuses on her untouched sandwich and mutters, "My phone doesn't work in Europe. So I left it at home."

"If there even was a Santiago," Nicole challenges.

"There was," Kayla presses. "I met him in Majorca."

"Yeah," she snorts, "But his name was probably Herberto and he was *muy peludo*." *very hairy* "I bet the only thing hard about him was the crusty hair on his back."

"Ew!" Rox grimaces, grabbing a napkin to cover her mouth so she doesn't spit out her bite of sandwich.

"Well, who did you hook up with this summer?" Kayla demands, glaring at Nicole.

"Your dad," Nicole snorts. "Obvi."

That causes the rest of us to laugh. Nicole chuckles and joins in, which defuses the tension between her and Kayla. Sometimes, it's a wonder those two are friends. I guess it's because they've known each other for a long time.

We finish up lunch and head back to campus.

When locker assignments were given out yesterday, Nicole and Kayla managed to get a pair near the cafeteria and the senior lawn. A prime location. They stop to open their lockers. It's almost time for class. Numerous other seniors are at their lockers getting out books and binders. I guess the warning bell already rang and we missed it.

"Where's your locker, Skye?" Kayla asks.

"Oh, it's at the end," I fib.

"Okay, see you guys in English."

"Laters," Rox waves goodbye as we walk toward her locker.

The two of us pass more seniors. Some are getting out their books while others are delaying the inevitable and chatting with friends.

"Hey, Skye," Luke calls out, leaning out from a crowd of other seniors.

"Hey," I mutter, slowing for a second. Then I remember what happened at lunch yesterday and speed up. I don't want Luke mentioning in front of Rox that Dante was here yesterday and I talked to him and that he practically ran Luke off.

"Hey, Luke!" Rox says, grabbing my shirt and stopping me.

Great timing, Rox. I reluctantly turn to face Luke. Who happens to be standing right next to Ashley Masters. Brills. Grot! As in, groan + not = grot. Grot!

"Oh look, the Twatsy Twins," Ashley grimaces.

Luke flicks his eyes at Ashley. Were they just talking? It sure looks like it. Are they friends? I don't remember Luke ever mentioning it. But you know Luke. Friends with everybody. Even the Monarch of Snark. Maybe he got to know her after he and I broke up. I heard Ashley threw a lot of parties over the summer, so maybe he DJed them for her.

Ashley sneers at me. "I didn't see you at the locker today, Nightlight. I was hoping you could shine my shoes for me." She glances down at her ankle strap wedges. They look brand new. She must've bought them at Bloomingdale's the other day. Show off.

"I switched lockers," I scowl.

"What, didn't you like our upstairs-downstairs arrangement? It's only fitting that the help lives below the aristocracy, don't you think?"

I give her my best withering eye roll before turning away and pulling Rox with me.

"I'll miss you, Nightlight!" Ashley croons. "If you ever want to clean my locker for me, bring a broom and a dust rag!" She laughs.

I ignore her. But I spin around and smile at Luke. "Hey, Luke!"

"Yeah?"

"Wanna come over for dinner tonight?"

"Sure," he grins. "What time?"

"I'll call you."

"Sweet," he says. "Laters!"

Ashley snarls, her lower lip bent into a twisted knot.

You can shove a broomstick up your ass, you bitch!

oOoOoOo + O+O+O+O

The bitch is back.

Phoebe.

She shows up with Dante around 5:00pm.

I was hoping it would just be Dante, but now I'm glad he brought her to the house again because Rox can meet her and stop pestering me about Dante. But I'm mad because, well, because I hate Phoebe. Obvi. Doesn't Phoebe have work? Oh, I forgot. She owns her own dress shop. The boss can do whatever she wants, I suppose.

Catarina comes home shortly thereafter with groceries and offers to cook Mexican for everyone. I guess she and Dante coordinated things earlier.

I text Rox around 5:30pm, as promised. **Guess who's coming to dinner?**

She replies, **Ashton Kutcher? ;-)**

No, dumbass. Dante.

I'll be right over!

Of course she will.

She shows up an hour later. What happened to right over?

The bell rings out its usual three hour symphony of dings and dongs. I open the door and Rox looks like a billion bucks. Her dark hair writhes hypnotically against her slender tanned shoulders, which showcase her clavicles and cleavage. Her smokey eye look makes her blue eyes blaze. Her lips glisten like plump red candy. Her red dress is glued to her body. And yes, her ta-tas are a sight to behold. She's so hot, I would do her.

"Are you kidding?" I chuckle.

"What?" she asks nervously. "Is it too much?"

"Not for the Oscars." I joke.

"It's too much," she says, deflated.

"No, I think it's perfect." What I'm really thinking is how Rox looks so damn hot, she'll probably scare Phoebe right off. Or trigger Phoebe into doing something ultra bitchy, causing the poor woman to dig her own grave with Dante. Rox will be the perfect weapon tonight. "I think Dante will approve."

Her eyes flame with desire. "Where is he?"

Do I warn her that Phoebe is here? Nah. If anyone needs a warning, it's Phoebe. Rox is going to make mincemeat out the poor girl. If there's a cat fight, I'll jump in to help Rox. Then I can take some free shots at Phoebe and no one will hold it against me.

oOoOoOo + O+O+O+O

Everyone is against me tonight.

Phoebe absolutely loves Rox. They've chatted it up like besties since Rox arrived. In fact, the two of them and Dante get along so well, the obvious next step for them is a three way love fest. I hear polyamory is all the rage these days. It serves me right for having Rox come over to stir up drama. But it's not like I forced her to come over or wear that dress or throw herself at Dante. It was all her idea.

Rox fills the entire living room with her flashy dress and her personality. It doesn't take long for me to feel like a fifth wheel, even though there's only four of us. Rox more than makes up the difference. Between her and Phoebe, Dante pays zero attention to me. I wish I could think of something to shake things up, otherwise this is going to be a long night.

That's when I remember that I totally spaced on calling Luke for dinner. When I offered earlier, I was really just doing it to piss off Ashley. I know he'd be bummed if I forgot. Luckily I have the perfect reason to invite him. When I excuse myself to call him, he says he'll be right over. Unlike Rox, he rings the doorbell seven minutes later. Little do I realize that his arrival literally makes me the fifth wheel because Rox pulls him right into her conversation with Dante and Phoebe. The four of them are laughing it up immediately, leaving me wondering what the F happened.

So much for my master plan.

"Sit down next to me and Luke," Rox says, patting the couch cushion between them. She's match-making. Her couch patting is also making her breasts bounce in her dazzling dress.

Luke steals a glance.

I can hardly blame him. I can't help looking at her bouncing boobs either. They're truly impressive. Maybe Luke will take an interest in Rox and they'll end up together. Then I'll end up alone. Wow, I really suck at this manipulation stuff.

Rox looks at me expectantly, "Join us."

"I think Catarina needs help in the kitchen," I lie.

"I can help," Luke says enthusiastically, standing instantly.

"Relax," I grimace. "I've got it handled."

"Okay," he sits back down slowly.

It turns out Catarina really does need help with the cooking.

"I made plenty of enchiladas," she says, "but I'm not going to have enough guacamole. Can you run to the store and buy more chips and avocados?"

"Sure," I sigh before driving her car to Vons.

Once we all sit down to dinner, Phoebe continues to wow everybody with her charming stories about work and the people who come into her dress shop, including numerous movie stars and models. Catarina and Rox love that part, and ask a million gossipy questions, which Phoebe is happy to answer.

Yeah, she's totally annoying.

I'm half tempted to sarcastically suggest to Phoebe that she date Luke, because he gets along with everybody too, and they would be perfect for each other. But I would sound like a jerk. And she's all eyes for Dante. Can you blame her?

It's pretty clear that Luke wouldn't be interested in Phoebe anyway. He keeps bumping my hand under the dinner table. I think he's trying to hold it. The hand-holding doesn't happen because I'm busy wringing my napkin in my lap, twisting it beyond recognition. Why? Because Dante is totally ignoring me.

He's not ignoring Phoebe or Rox or Catarina. He's not even ignoring Luke.

Just me.

What the hell is that about?

At one point, Catarina asks, "Does anyone want more enchiladas? There's a few more in the kitchen."

"I'd love some," Luke chimes in before anyone else. "I swear these are like the best enchiladas I've ever had." Oh, that Luke. Such a sweetheart.

"Thank you very much, Luke," she smiles endearingly before walking into the kitchen.

"I love your Deadmau5 shirt," Phoebe says to Luke.

"Oh, thanks," he grins as he forks up the last lump of refried beans and guacamole on his plate.

"Are you into the DJ scene?" she asks.

"Actually, I am a DJ."

"Really," she says with fake surprise.

"Yeah. I do a lot of parties around town. And I DJ at a couple different 18 and under clubs in the Valley."

"That's great," Phoebe smiles. "You're already making a name for yourself."

Blah, blah, blah. Isn't she sweet?

"I'm sure you know about Deadmau5 coming to town?"

"Yeah. I can't go because he's only doing 21 and over shows."

"I can get you a backstage pass when he spins at the Roxbury."

"No way!" Luke blurts, dropping his forkful of beans onto his plate. "You could do that?"

"Yeah. I make dresses for the manager's wife. You might even be able to meet Deadmau5 if you show up early."

"Meet Deadmau5? Are you serious?" Luke sounds like he's ready to offer oral favors to a homeless person in exchange for backstage passes.

This is so annoying.

Phoebe nods. "I'll set it up for you."

Oh my god. Why do I even bother? She's not even trying and she's stealing Luke away too. I mean, seriously, what do I have to offer but the opportunity to be tutored in SAT math? Fun stuff. I hear cool guys beat down doors to help girls like me study math all the time. Grot!

"Excuse me," I stand up and sigh. "I have to go to the bathroom."

Everyone keeps talking like I'm not even there. Chatter, chatter, chatter. Well, Catarina glances at me and smiles for half a second, but she was in the middle of saying something to Phoebe, so she continues.

I roll my eyes and huff before storming off. I really do have to pee. I consider the downstairs powder room but change my mind at the last second and go upstairs to use the hall bathroom. I need some space from the love fest in the dining room. After I finish on the toilet, I wash my hands morosely in the sink. I could stay in here for another hour, but it would be more comfortable in my bedroom. I'm sure no one would notice I was gone. They're too busy watching the Phoebe Show. I reach for the doorknob.

There's a soft knock at the door.

Excitement spins my heart into motion. Who would possibly use the upstairs bathroom instead of the empty powder room downstairs? Oh my god! Is it Dante? Did he abandon his adoring ladies and come up here to comfort me? I open the bathroom door and instantly deflate.

Luke.

"Hey," he smiles.

"What do you want?" I try not to sound too bitchy. "There's a bathroom downstairs, remember?"

"I don't need to use the bathroom."

"Then what do you want?" I fold my arms across my chest.

"Are you okay? You seem all weirded out."

"I thought you were busy talking to Phoebe about Deadmouse tickets."

"Oh. Did you want to go? Should I have asked her for one for you?" He pauses. "Oh, shit. I'm such a dunce. You want to go, don't you? I'm sure Phoebe can get two since she knows the manager. I can ask her right now. Then we can go together. Wouldn't that be awesome?"

"Yeah, I guess." At least he's not going on and on about Phoebe. I know he loves Deadmau5, which means this is something he actually wants to do.

He stuffs his hands in his pockets, "Hey, um, can I ask you something?"

"What?" I sigh.

"I thought you said Dante was your math tutor?"

"Yeah."

"What's he doing here?"

After Dante's behavior with Phoebe and Rox at the dinner table, it should be pretty obvious to Luke that Dante isn't into me. I doubt Luke is going to think something is going on between me and Dante now. I certainly don't think anything is. I may as well tell Luke. "Dante is my stepbrother."

"What?! Since when do you have a stepbrother?"

"Since a week ago."

Confused, he narrows his eyes, "How does that make sense?"

"He's Catarina's son. She hasn't seen him in years. He surprised her and just showed up."

"So how did he become your math tutor?"

That part he doesn't need to know. One more white lie will fix that. "My dad mentioned to Dante I was studying SAT math and he offered to help."

"Oh." He nods and it makes his black hair bounce in this really cute way.

To my surprise, his cuteness affects me more than it should. I tease, "Are you bummed I didn't call you for math help?"

He grins that cute grin of his I remember so well. "Yeah." His hair bounces again.

I reach up and brush one of the black blades out of his eyes, revealing the sexy silver spike piercing his eyebrow. "Did you want to be my Sir Maths-A-Lot?" I wink at him.

He snickers, "Yeah." He pauses and his face changes. "What was up with him coming by our high school at lunch yesterday?"

"Who knows," I lie. "He's weird."

"He's not into you, is he?"

"What?!" I blurt. "No! Haven't you been watching him with Phoebe? Those two are totally hot for each other."

"He sure seemed into you when he rode up on his motorcycle and got in my face."

Damn it. Luke is sharp when it comes to people. I shake my head, "Like I said, Dante is weird. Maybe he was being the over-protective older brother?"

"He's not dangerous, is he?" Luke says it with obvious concern.

"No," I scoff. "He's my stepbrother. Believe me, you have nothing to worry about." I do my best to hide the disappointment I'm feeling. "Why, are you jealous?"

"What? No!" Denial.

He's jealous. I have to admit, I like that he is. "You don't have anything to worry about. He's my stepbrother, so, ew. *And*, he's with Phoebe. And Rox is into him too, if you hadn't noticed."

"Really?" Luke says dramatically. "I thought Rox dressed that way every day," he says sarcastically.

We share a laugh.

"Rox is nuts," I chuckle. "It's why I love her."

"Yeah, she's great." He offers his elbow like a gentleman. "Shall we rejoin everyone at the dinner table?"

"Sure." I wrap my arm around his and lean against him as we walk downstairs together. I guess I forgot how sweet Luke could be.

Maybe I need to rethink this whole Dante thing. Maybe he needs a grown woman like Phoebe Saxon the Screaming Klaxon. Maybe I'm better off with someone my own age. Someone like Luke. That only leaves Rox. I'll have to find someone suitable for her. Who am I kidding? She could walk out the front door in that dress of hers and every Prince Charming in the world will flock to her like flies, or some other more noble insect not associated with poop, like maybe butterflies or shiny dragonflies.

When Luke and I get back to the dinner table, Catarina says, "There you are."

"Did you miss us?" I grin, not bothering to look at Dante.

Chapter 10

"I so missed this," Luke says two weeks later. He sits on my bedroom floor, leaning against the comforter that hangs over the side of my twin bed, resting his notebook on his knees, working on math problems with the help of his calculator. His Calculus textbook is open beside him on the floor.

"Yeah, me too," I smile at him. I'm on my bed, working on my Trigonometry homework in preparation for tomorrow's weekly Friday morning quiz.

"Are you having any trouble graphing your functions?"

"No. Not after you showed me how to do it," I smile.

Whenever I have a question about Trig, Luke has the answer. He knows everything there is to know about triangles and tangents.

It's been two weeks since he came over for dinner, the night Rox wore her red dress to impress Dante. I haven't seen much of Dante since then, but I've seen a lot of Luke. I didn't plan it that way. It sort of happened. Every day at school, I would talk to Luke. He would always ask how I was doing with Trig. Since I'm struggling through it, he always offered useful advice. It naturally morphed into him coming over to my house to help out. Since Dante is out doing his own thing much of the time, it made sense. Luke is now my math tutor, which is good because the next SAT is coming up in a few weeks. I need all the math help I can get.

It's not like Dante is never around.

I pretty much see him every day for at least a few minutes. I can't escape the feeling he's checking up on me. Maybe it's just me. I don't know.

But I do know he's still seeing Phoebe. Every day he's with her, it makes more sense that I'm hanging with Luke. Whatever happened between me and Dante is officially over. It's probably for the best. I mean, he *is* my stepbrother. It's best to let it be. He doesn't make it easy though. Every time he uses the shower in the hall bathroom upstairs, he always manages to walk from his room to the bathroom in only a towel. I think he is rubbing in what I'm missing. Do I look? Obvi. Hot guy, duh. But I'm over the lusting part.

Rox isn't. I don't know what her deal is. I've never seen her obsess over a guy like this before. She's over at the house all the time, which isn't weird because she's always over at the house anyway, but she's always asking me where Dante is or what he's doing. My answer is always the same: I have no idea. It's the truth. I don't ask Dante what he does with Phoebe. I really don't want to know. I have Luke to focus on now.

At the moment, he's bent over his notebook, punching numbers into his calculator, focused on his Calculus. The black blades of his hair bounce in this cute way when his head turns back and forth between his textbook and his notebook.

Feeling bad, I reach down with my pencil and brush it across the tangle of hair on the back of his head. Unaware, he reaches up to scratch his head and I yank my pencil away. He combs his fingers through his hair then smooths it down before going back to his calculus problem. I repeat this process several more times.

He looks up and over his shoulder, "Is there a fly in here or something? Something keeps landing on my head."

"I hadn't noticed," I say innocently.

Downstairs, the sound of the front door opening and closing. Since it's only four o'clock on a weekday, it's not my Dad. It could be Catarina or it could be Dante, who now has a key to the house. He comes and goes whenever he wants and nobody seems to care. Even though I'm 18 and technically can come and go whenever I want, Dad makes it clear that as long as I'm living under his roof, it's his rules. I guess Dante is a guest, so he doesn't have to follow the same rules. Whatevs. Technically Luke isn't supposed to be in my room with the door closed, but since Dad isn't around, there's no way he's going to find out. Yes, I open the door when Dad comes home, but not when he's gone.

I'm about to tease Luke's hair with my pencil again when I hear heavy footsteps coming up the stairs. That's not Catarina. A minute later, the guest bedroom door closes.

"Is that Dante?" Luke asks in a low voice, sounding weird.

"Probably."

"What does that guy do, anyway?" His judgment is obvi.

"You mean like for a job?"

"Yeah."

"I have no idea."

"How much longer is he staying here?"

"I don't know. As long as he wants, I guess. Catarina really likes having him around, even though he's barely here. Why, does he still bug you?" I tease my pencil eraser across Luke's unruly hair once again.

He reaches up and spins around, grabbing for my pencil. "I thought there was a bug in here," he grins.

I yank my pencil back. Pretending to be innocent, I purse my lips and look around the room randomly. "Oh, there it is!" I point with my pencil. "That pesky fly that keeps bothering you just landed on my dresser."

He smirks, "The only bug in here is the big one on the bed."

I try not to giggle. Luke really is cute. I'm starting to wonder why I ever broke up with him. Looking back, it seems silly now. What was I thinking? He's a great guy.

Luke's phone buzzes on the carpet. He picks it up and reads the screen. A second later, he fires off a quick text and sets his phone down.

"Who was that?" I ask.

"Ashley."

"Ashley Masters?" My voice drips with disgust.

"Yeah. Is that a problem?"

"I guess not," I groan.

"She's not that bad. Besides, we have Calculus together. She was asking if I had the homework for today. She missed class because she was at the dentist."

I'm sure Ashley had to get her teeth whitened or capped or whatever the hell she does to make them perfect. Jealousy flares up inside me. Not only does she share a class with Luke, but she's a year ahead of me in math, which makes me feel stupider than her. "Do you tutor her too?" I ask petulantly.

"No, just you," he smiles.

Oh, that was *so* the wrong answer. My face drips as sour sauce pours across it. Not only is Ashley a year ahead, but she doesn't need constant tutoring like I do.

"What?" he grins innocently.

"Nothing." I spin away, facing my window and resting my head on my pillow.

Luke climbs up on the bed and sits next to me, laying his hand on my hip. "Hey," he says softly. "What's bugging you?"

I don't want to answer because I know I'm going to say something bitchy.

"You're not worried about Ashley, are you?"

"No," I blurt. That's not entirely true. I'm not sure where Luke and I stand, but I'm totally sure that Ashley is a total bitch and I don't want anything to do with her. "Are you guys friends or whatever?"

"You could say that."

"When did that happen?" I grumble.

"Over the summer. She was at a bunch of the parties I DJed."

"Sounds like she was stalking you."

"I hadn't thought about it. You know Ashley. She's always at all the sick ragers."

I don't know why I'm being so bitchy. It's not like Luke and I were dating over the summer. We broke up two months before summer started. I can't blame him for talking to other girls. I guess it wouldn't be so bad if it was someone other than Ashley Masters. "You guys didn't hook up, did you?"

He snickers, "No."

"Good." I sound so petty right now. I'm such a baby.

His hand slides around the front of my hip and for a second, I think he's going to slide it between my legs, but he doesn't. It comes to rest on my stomach. "Would it bother you if we had?"

"I..." don't know what to say. Luke and I haven't kissed or anything since we started hanging out again. I wasn't thinking we were dating or anything close to it. I just like having him around. I don't know, maybe I'm using him as a distraction from Dante. Maybe I secretly want him around because I want to make Dante jealous. Who knows? The only thing I know for sure is that Luke and I get along, and he really is a great math tutor.

Luke lies down behind me, spooning me, his warm hand still on my stomach. His nose nuzzles the back of my neck and I feel his warm breath blow across my skin. "I missed you, Skye." The emotion in his voice is obvious.

I don't want to leave him hanging. "I missed you too."

"You did?" It sounds like he doesn't believe me.

Did I? I suppose I did, in a way. At the moment, it sure feels nice having him cuddle with me. I haven't cuddled with anyone since we broke up. Luke was always a good cuddler. This definitely feels nice.

He pulls me into him, enveloping me with his warmth. "You don't have to worry about Ashley. She's just a friend."

I roll my eyes to myself. That's Luke, everybody's friend. I sigh. I can't hold it against him. Being nice is not a crime, even when someone is nice to a bitch. Especially then. It makes Luke a better person. He really is a good guy. I snuggle into him, basking in our touch. Maybe I could get used to this again.

KNOCK! KNOCK! KNOCK!

I jump and Luke tenses for a second before unwrapping his arm from around me.

I slide off the bed and trot over to my door and open it.

Dante stands in the hallway wearing a T-shirt and jeans, filling my doorway. His tattooed and muscled arms hang at his sides. He's not hot. Not hot at all. He looks at me for awhile, his eyes flicking across my body.

"What's up?" I ask, smoothing my own T-shirt.

"Do you need anything from the store? I'm going to Vons."

"Um, no? Not really, Luke, do you need anything?"

Luke sits up on the bed, smirking. "I'm good."

I shrug at Dante. "We're good."

Dante nods but doesn't go anywhere.

I arch my eyebrows expectantly.

He narrows his eyes.

Why is he acting weird? I smile sheepishly and gently close the door in his face. When it's almost shut, he hasn't moved, so I say, "Bye?"

He grinds his jaw.

What's up his butt? I don't know. I close the door and the latch clicks.

Boots thud down the hallway and downstairs.

I turn to face Luke. "Sorry."

"You were right. Dante is weird."

"He doesn't scare you, does he?"

"No," Luke chuckles.

I don't believe him. Dante is tall and broad-shouldered and bigger than Luke. How could he not be intimidated?

The front door latches downstairs. I pad across the carpet and sit down on the bed beside Luke.

He rests his hand on my knee and squeezes it.

"Wanna do some more math homework?" I ask.

Luke cocks his head to the side, smiling. He doesn't say anything. His hand slides up my leg, then back down.

I know where this is going. I'm not sure how I feel about kissing him or anything. So I pull my legs onto the bed and crawl up to the headboard. I grab my notebook and pretend to focus on my Trig homework.

Luke rubs my shin through my jeans.

I don't think anybody ever told him that shins are not an erogenous zone. I offer a nervous smile before focusing on domains, ranges, and functions.

"Skye?"

"Yeah, Luke?"

"Is there anything going on here? I mean, between us?"

That's so sweet of him to ask.

"Um, I don't know?" It's the truth. I really don't.

"If there is, you would tell me, right?"

"Yeah."

I can't get over how sweet Luke is. Such a contrast from cocky Dante. Dante is a take charge kind of guy. He knows how to get me worked up without even trying. I mean *really* worked up. Before Dante, sex was something I did just to do it. So I could say I had. But with Dante, it was different. Dante made me feel like sex is something I *need*. Only with him, of course. But the *need* is intensely overwhelming. Yes, in the past few weeks, I've thought about the sex I had with Dante plenty of times. The orgasm I had in the wave pool at Blazing Waters. Him pushing me up against the front door of my own house and pulling his cock out. Coming harder than I ever thought possible in the dark library meeting room. Begging him to fuck me behind the church across from North Valley. Yes, begging. I would happily beg again. Well, as long as he followed through. It's when you beg and the guy bolts that it's a problem. I don't want to think about that right now. It's getting me worked up for all the wrong reasons.

Luke crawls up the bed and sits down beside me.

I don't want to think about *this* right now, not with Luke.

He reaches over and takes my hand away from my notebook, squeezing my fingers in his. "I missed being with you, Skye," he says in a soft voice.

I wish I could say, "Me too," but I can't. I honestly haven't thought about sex with Luke since forever.

Luke's other hand slides between my upraised knees and strokes the inside of my thigh. He's being totally obvi. But we haven't even kissed yet. He's getting way ahead of himself.

"Luke," I sigh, and squeeze my legs closed.

He retracts his hand instantly. "Sorry. Maybe we should just study," he says gently. "I don't know what I was thinking. Between your AP classes and the SAT, you have a lot on your plate. I don't want to get in your way." Luke lowers his leg onto the floor, about to stand up. He sounds really hurt.

I'm an ass. I grab his wrist. "Wait, Luke."

He gazes at me longingly.

"Come here," I pull him back onto the bed. "I missed you too, Luke." He's such a sweet guy. Who wouldn't miss a sweetheart like

Luke?

His eyes dance, locked on mine.

The next thing I know, we're kissing. Luke rolls on top of me and his hips sink between my legs. We're both wearing jeans, so I feel safe. I don't know if I want to start having sex with Luke right away, but making out? I can totally do that.

Our lips press together as our tongues fight. I drape my hands behind his neck and he thrusts himself against me. My eyes are closed and I surrender to the tickling in my core. This isn't so bad. It almost feels like Dante—

Okay. This is wrong. I can't be thinking of Dante while Luke makes out with me. This isn't fair.

Does he notice? The way his tongue throbs in my mouth with obvious need, I think not. Luke is really into this.

I can't do this to Luke. I try to push his tongue out of my mouth with mine. It reminds me of when you're at the dentist and you push that sucker thing out and the hygienist removes it. *So* not a turn on. "Luke," I grumble.

He snaps his head back. "Are you okay?" His eyes search mine. "You're not into this, are you?"

"Sort of?"

He smiles, "It's okay. We can wait. I don't mind." He rolls off of me and—

He slides right off of the edge of the narrow bed. I grab for him, rolling to the side, and we both thump onto the floor in a tangle of limbs.

"Ow!" I shout. I land smack on my back and hit my elbow. It really hurts. I cradle my arm to my chest. What did I do to it? "Owwww!" I moan.

"Are you okay?" He touches my elbow and the pain is instantaneous.

"Stop! That hurts!" I whimper. Did I bust my funny bone?

He lets go, but he's still on top of me, on hands and knees.

WHAM!!

My bedroom door blasts open and Dante barrels into the room, shouting, "GET THE FUCK OFF HER!!" He knocks Luke onto his back. Luke skids across the carpet and whacks against the side of the bed. The bed jumps and knocks against the wall. Dante dives at Luke and grabs a fistful of Luke's black T-shirt collar, holding a threatening fist high in the air, ready to hammer down on Luke's face.

"What the hell, man!" Luke shouts, glaring up at Dante.

"Let go of him!!" I shriek, grabbing Dante's arm, which shakes with barely restrained rage.

Dante's face whips around, his brows dark with hot fury.

"Stop, Dante!"

"Get off me, man!" Luke grumbles.

Dante's arm relaxes and he releases his grip on Luke's shirt. "Sorry, man," he mutters. He offers his hand to Luke to help him up.

Luke bats his hand away.

Chastised, Dante backs up a step. "Sorry, man. I'm really sorry. I just thought..." he trails off.

"What did you think?" Luke growls.

I'm totally confused myself. "Didn't you leave to go to the store, Dante?"

"I..." he stammers.

"Yeah," Luke insists, "I heard the front door close."

Dante swallows hard. "Sorry, I, uh..." he glances between me and Luke. "I'm really sorry. I don't know what came over me." He's looking right at Luke. "Are you okay?"

Luke lifts his arm, which is abraded along the bone up to the elbow, examining it. It weeps red, the skin burned off from when Dante pushed him into the rug. "Fuck, man," he winces. "Look what you did." It looks bad, but he'll live. He won't need stitches. Just some antiseptic and a few Band Aids. Luke looks up at me, judgment in his eyes. "I told you this guy was crazy."

"I'm really sorry," Dante says sincerely. "I heard Skye shout 'stop' and I thought she was in trouble."

"In trouble?" Luke spits. "From me?"

I have to agree with Luke on this one. I've never been afraid of Luke. He's too nice.

Dante sighs, "I'm really sorry, man. I just reacted."

Luke frowns, "Reacted? All the way from Vons? How did you get here so quick?"

"Yeah," I say thoughtfully. "It was like two seconds from the time I fell off the bed to when you busted through the door."

Dante's features spasm when I mention falling off the bed.

"Were you standing outside the door?" I ask.

Dante turns away. Busted.

Luke sneers, "He totally was. He never went to the store."

"Is that true, Dante?"

Dante stands tall, his hands resting casually on the hips of his jeans. He shakes his head, his lanky blond hair dangling over his brow. A shaky smile spreads across his mouth. I think he's embarrassed.

"I knew it!" Luke barks. "He was spying on us, Skye."

"Dante," I demand in a friendly voice. "Were you spying?"

Dante looks at me and smirks. His cheek dimples and he rolls his eyes. "Sorry."

"That's fucked, man," Luke growls. "Do you think I'd do something to hurt Skye?" Luke is really pissed now.

"I don't know," Dante mutters.

"Dante," I snicker. "Luke is a sweetheart."

"Sorry," Dante says meekly.

"This guy is a dick," Luke seethes.

"He said he was sorry," I defend.

Luke snorts, "Are you taking his side? He tore my arm open."

"It's not torn open," I dismiss.

"Look at it!" Luke holds it up.

The only thing that got torn open was Luke's pride. "I'm sorry," I say. "Dante is sorry. He didn't mean to hurt you, did you, Dante?"

Dante represses his smirk, "No."

"Look at him," Luke accuses, "this is a big joke for him."

Dante rolls his eyes. "I didn't mean it, man."

I suddenly feel like I'm parenting a couple of fighting grade-schoolers. Now is the part where they're supposed to kiss and make up, or whatever boys do. Shake hands, I guess.

"Then why did you slam the door open and knock me down?" Luke demands.

"I told you, I thought I heard—"

"Me raping Skye," Luke cuts in. "I know what you were thinking. This is ridic, Skye. I'm outta here." Luke grabs his books off the floor and stuffs them into his backpack.

"Luke, relax," I sigh. "It's no big deal. Dante apologized. Can we go back to doing our math homework and forget about it?"

Luke sneers, "Yeah. Sure. Whatever." He zips up the main pouch of his backpack.

"Luke?"

He barges past Dante and stops in my doorframe. "If you want help with your math, I'll be at my house." Then he storms down the hall.

I consider going after him, but for whatever reason, I don't.

A minute later, the front door closes.

A moment after that, another door opens. Not the physical kind. The metaphorical kind. Dante is standing on one side of the threshold and I'm standing on the other.

oOoOoOo + O+O+O+O

"Sorry about that," Dante says, embarrassed.

"It's okay. Nobody got hurt too badly." I sigh.

"Maybe you should go after him? That was a dick move on my part. I don't know what came over me."

I search Dante's eyes. Why does it feel like he doesn't want me going after Luke? Is it the way his eyes glimmer when he looks at me? Is it that cocky smile stretching across his straight teeth, the one that melts me every time I see it? "He'll be okay." I don't know what else I'd say to Luke right now anyway. I think he needs some time to cool off. There's no sense talking to him while he's fuming. I'll call him later. Looking at Dante, I realize that this is the first time I've been alone with him since Phoebe showed up in his life. Phoebe. The Saxon Klaxon. Any warm thoughts I had toward Dante suddenly freeze. "How's Phoebe?" I ask sourly.

"She's good."

Does that mean that *they* are good too? Despite how much she irritates me, I'm dying to know what's going on with them. Just for general gossip reasons. That's all. "You two seem pretty serious. How are things?"

He shrugs. "They aren't."

"What?" I gasp. "Did you break up with her?"

"No."

"Oh." Disappointment.

"We were never together."

"What?!" I laugh. Hope.

He shakes his head.

"I call bullshit," I chuckle. "I've seen her hanging all over you plenty of times."

"And what did you see me do? Was I hanging all over her?"

I smirk and open my mouth to spew, then stop myself. "No," I say truthfully.

"It was a pretty good show, wasn't it?"

"Show? I'm totally confused."

"For your dad."

"What?" My nose wrinkles. "What are you talking about?"

A satisfied grin spreads across Dante's face. "I bet your Dad thinks I've been sleeping with Phoebe, right?"

That was my assumption. "Uh, yeah, I guess. Probably."

"I bet he thinks I'm totally into her, right?"

That was also my assumption. "Yeah."

Dante chuckles, "I should totally be an actor."

"I'm not getting it..."

"Do you know what a beard is?"

"A what?!"

"You know, a beard."

"Like a lumberjack beard?" I'm not following this at all.

"No," he snorts. "Like a gay beard."

"A gay beard? Oh! You mean, like when a gay guy pretends to have a girlfriend for work or whatever? Because he's not out?"

Dante taps the tip of his nose.

"You're not gay," I laugh, then stop short. "Wait, are you?"

"No," he chuckles.

"Oh yeah, duh. You're totally bi. Right?"

"No."

"Wait, then how is Phoebe your gay beard?"

"She's my straight beard. For your dad."

I squinch my eyes shut and shake my head. "What?!"

"Skye, do you think I hooked up with you at the library and every place else just because I wanted an easy lay?"

"Yeah, pretty much."

He grins, "You don't know me very well, do you."

"Not really."

"I don't hook up with people."

"You did with me." I roll my eyes.

His face does this thing that I can only describe as falling apart, but it happens so fast, it's put back together again a split second later.

"Wait, are you serious?" I marvel. Hot guys like Dante hook up with hundreds of girls. Usually, they don't remember the women's names the next day, if they ever knew their names at all. That's what hot guys do. It's in the U.S Constitution. We learned it in Government class the other day. I swear.

He nods slowly. "I'm totally serious."

It takes a moment to sink in. Part of my brain is unwilling to believe what I'm hearing. My heart, on the other hand, is going crazy, fluttering in my chest, trying to fly skyward and soar with the clouds, where hopes and dreams hang out. "Are you, you know... are you still into me?"

He nods. "All the way. Into you," he winks suggestively.

That wink sends a bolt of lightning shooting up between my legs, but I ignore it. "Dante, why didn't you tell me!"

"Did you not notice your dad? He knew what was going on with us from the moment he met me. Maybe not what we did exactly, but he's your dad. He knows your moods. He knew something was up, Skye.

And it freaked him out."

"This is insane." I'm smiling from ear to ear. "So, you're not dating Phoebe?"

"Nope."

"Or having sex with her?"

"Nope."

"Are you into her?"

"Nope."

"Come on," I laugh. "She's super hot. And smart. And nice. And funny."

"And?"

"Look, I may not be in Calculus or whatever, but I can do the math. Phoebe is a catch. And you're telling me you're not into her and didn't screw her once?"

"Nope."

"I totally don't believe you. She would know. She would be like, 'Dante, why aren't we having sex? It's been like twenty dates. Why aren't you making a move on me?'"

He nods. "We had that conversation."

"What did you tell her?"

"I go slow."

"What?" I laugh. "That's ridic."

He shrugs.

"Don't you feel like you're leading her on?"

He chuckles, "What's with the double standard? Women go out with guys all the time without giving it up. Sometimes, after a bunch of dates, they break it off without ever having sex with the guy. Nobody thinks that's strange. Why can't a guy do the same thing?"

"Because guys always want sex."

"Some guys save themselves until marriage. Or so the legend goes." He winks.

I snort, "You're not saving yourself. You're not a virgin. Wait, are you?"

He looks at me thoughtfully for a long time.

I gasp. "No way! You are NOT a virgin!"

He arches an eyebrow.

I laugh. "I *so* don't believe you are a virgin!"

"Why is that so hard to believe?"

"Look at you!" I wave my hands at him "You... you're *hot* Dante. Women throw themselves at you. Don't tell me they don't. And the way you act when we fooled around? Come on! You have tons of experience."

"Maybe I watch a lot of internet porn."

"You? Why would you need to watch it? You *are* porn!"

He smirks.

"You're not a virgin," I dismiss.

"No," he laughs.

"Ass," I slap his arm. "I knew you couldn't possibly be one."

"But it made me seem pretty amazing for a minute, didn't it?"

I roll my eyes. "Amazingly idiotic. So, did you make out with Phoebe?"

"A couple times."

"Then you're totally leading her on."

"Why? Because I made out with her?"

"Yeah!"

"A guy can change his mind. Or is that something only women get to do?"

"Well, no, but—"

"I changed my mind. I decided I didn't want to pursue her any more."

"When did you decide that?"

"Just now."

"Oh. So wait, you *were* interested in—" I stop myself.

Dante grins at me.

I narrow my eyes, "What did you just say?"

"I said, I decided I didn't want to pursue Phoebe just now."

I blink several times, unable to speak. "Dante? What are you saying."

His grin widens into twinkling territory.

"Dante..." I blush.

I stare at him in utter disbelief.

He arches an eyebrow.

I press my palms against my face and shake my head. "Is this happening?"

"Is what happening?"

"Us?" I peer through my fingers.

"I want it to."

"What about my dad?"

"We'll worry about that if it becomes a problem."

I drop my hands. "Are you serious?"

"About you? Very."

My heart spins out of control. "Dante?" It's all I can say.

"Yeah?"

I close my eyes and shake my head. "Someone pinch me, I think I'm dreaming."

He snickers. "You're awake. Open your eyes."

I do.

The hottest man on the planet stands in my bedroom.

The house is empty.

That only means one thing.

Chapter 11

"Oh my god," I gasp. "Oh my god, Dante…" I moan low as he ravages me with his skillful tongue.

I lay on my bed, naked. Well, my shirt is still on and my unhooked bra swims around my arms somewhere under the shirt. Dante unhooked it expertly at some point without my noticing. Not that I'm thinking about any of that now. Because Dante's entire face is attacking my drenched folds and it is mesmerizing.

"Ohhhh…" I moan again.

I've never been this naked in my room with Luke or anybody else. It feels entirely naughty. Does it heighten things knowing Dante is my stepbrother? Of course it does. So what if our siblinghood is just on paper? It's still deliciously dangerous. I don't have a lock on my bedroom door. Our parents could walk in at any moment, but neither of us are thinking about the consequences.

My fingers are knotted in his thick blond hair. My heels rest on his naked shoulders and I start bucking against his face as a powerful orgasm wracks my body. Every muscle clenches sweetly as heat burns through me. I am soaking wet as his fingers probe deep inside me, tickling what must be my G-spot, which I never knew I had until now. Yeah, there is no way Dante is a virgin. He's a veteran sexpert.

As I come down from the intense orgasm, he nips my clit with a final kiss and lifts his glistening face, grinning from ear to ear. "Was that good for you?" he asks.

"Oh my god," my head falls against the edge of the bed, hanging backward because I'm lying crosswise. I think this is the reason my dad never let me get a queen sized bed. He wanted to prevent exactly this kind of thing. I guess his plan didn't work. "That was beyond good," I huff, breathing hard, my rib cage heaving as I try to recover.

The heel of his hand presses against my wetness and he circles it slowly, sending electric puffs into my body. Every time he bumps my clit, it sings. I think I'm going to come again. I close my eyes and lift my head up. With it hanging over the side of the bed, so much blood is rushing to it, I'll pass out if I don't. He's licking my clit again, sending shivers up my tummy. It feels so painfully good, my entire torso clenches like I'm doing a sit up. I put my elbows behind me and prop myself up, almost like I'm trying to get away because the intensity of his tongue has suddenly become too much. But he doesn't stop for a second. His arms wrap forcefully around my thighs and he pulls me back to his face. His mouth won't stop. This feels too good. Way too good. Suddenly the only thing I want is to find out how good it can feel. Because once again, Dante has led me to a whole new world of sex way beyond anything I thought existed. This is too good to be true.

And I want more.

I hiss and seethe with restrained screams, biting my lower lip. "Mmmm!" I moan. I can't let it out because we're in my house. I have to keep it a secret. Somehow, holding it all in heightens the intensity. Every inch of my skin sizzles with pleasure. Another orgasm is coming. It starts with my toes, which curl. My knees start to shake. My thighs vibrate. The spray of sensation tickles up to my core, where it spirals out wider and wider, swimming through my abdomen, spinning across my breasts, singing in my nipples, then climbing right up my throat.

I'm going to do it.

I'm going to scream.

I bite my lip. I can't scream. I *shouldn't* scream. But if I don't let it out, this orgasm is going to tear me apart when it finally explodes.

I *have* to scream.

Some corner of my mind reminds me to check the time. The alarm clock beside my bed says 4:30pm. My dad is never home this early. Catarina probably won't be home for awhile either. They'll never hear me if I scream. But I can't. Not in the house. Their bedroom is just down the hall. So what if they aren't here? It's the idea of them that I can't escape. But I have to scream. I have to!

Dante's mouth eats me alive. His fingers thrust inside me forcefully. He's fucking me like crazy.

My orgasm is coming.

I'm going to die.

I have to scream.

But I can't.

The pleasure is so strong, it is literally going to kill me.

"Dan—" I heave. "Dan..." Hold it in. Don't scream. I can't. I can't! "Dan!"

He won't stop.

There's nothing I can do.

"DANTE!!"

He growls and grunts against my feminine flesh, devouring me, tearing my body apart, shredding it with wicked pleasure.

"DANTE!!" I cry out.

One of his hands is squeezing my ass as I come all over his face. His fingers dig into my flesh like he's tearing me apart.

"DAAAAANTE!!"

A restrained roar cracks from his throat, like he's enraged that he's not inside me. He *should* be inside me. His manhood should be spasming and fountaining his seed into me right now. It hurts my heart that he is *not* inside me. I almost feel guilty that he's not enjoying any of this. But the heat haze of my orgasm wipes that thought away as I float through pink clouds of ecstasy. All my strength is gone and I slump against the bed, my arms dangling over the side, my head hanging upside down.

A red haze of blood rushes to my brain once again. I'm going to pass out, but I don't seem to care enough to stop it. I'm floating somewhere else. If Dante wasn't holding onto me, I would slide off the bed and smack my head on the carpet. Luckily, he pulls me back onto the mattress. He lies down next to me. His shirt is off but his jeans are still on.

My body continues to heave, trying to recalibrate, trying to gulp oxygen like I haven't breathed in days. "Dante…" *Huff.* "That…" *Huff.* "Was…" *Huff, huff, huff.*

He chuckles. "I know."

"Cocky…" *Huff.* "Bastard…" *Sigh.* I smile, spent and satisfied.

He kisses my cheek and I turn to him, our mouths meeting, our tongues kissing and twirling like rose petals floating on the wind: dancing, spinning, swirling. The spiral of my orgasm echoes up my spine and through my mouth. I try to breathe my pleasure into him. I reach down with a lazy arm and squeeze his hardness through his jeans.

"Mmmm," he purrs.

I slide my fingers across it, but it's difficult to do much with the denim in the way.

"Here, let me," I whisper languidly.

"You sound like you need a nap," he chuckles.

"No," I moan. "I need to touch you."

"Aren't our parents going to be home soon?"

"Do you have to remind me?" I groan. Not wanting to think about it, I continue to stroke him through his jeans.

"Sorry. Forget I said anything," he chuckles, shifting his hips so I have better access.

I stroke softly for awhile, struggling to stay awake. He wasn't kidding. I could sleep for a week. But I try hard to stay awake, because he's raging hard, pulsing under my fingers, ready to burn a hole in his pants with his hot rod of iron. He deserves to have an orgasm too. "I want to make you come," I whisper so softly I can barely hear myself.

"What?"

At the moment, I'm paralyzed with anxiety and can't speak any further.

See, when I was with Luke, the male orgasm was always his department. What can I say? I tried giving him a blowjob one time, but it was a disaster. I didn't know what I was doing. Luke actually asked me to stop after a few minutes. He was very apologetic, but he said I was hurting him. I wasn't even using my teeth! That didn't matter. Anyway, I felt totally stupid and he never asked me for another blowy after that. I sure wasn't going to press the issue. It was embarrassing. After that botched blowjob, I became super insecure about my bedroom skills. The only solution I could think of was to graduate to actual sex. I knew I couldn't possibly screw that up (no pun intended). We found a routine that worked. Mostly for him. The sex was okay but never great. Luke *loved* doing it. Me? Not so much. The important thing was that I became one of the girls at school who had a sex life. Not that I gossiped about it or went into detail. I didn't want the truth of my sexual ineptitude coming out. So, when people like Kayla or Nicole brought up sex, and inevitably asked if Luke and I did it, all I ever said was yes and left it at that.

With Dante, I feel like it's time for a change. I clear my throat. "I want to make you come."

"Sounds like a plan," Dante chuckles quietly. Other than that, he doesn't do anything.

I guess I'm supposed to take the reins? I reach over and undo his belt. That part is easy. I fumble with buttons and the zipper next. I'm even brave enough to reach down and grab him. Wow. His cock is huge. Is it supposed to fit inside of me at some point? I'll worry about that later. Right now, I have bigger fish to fry. So to speak. I grab his velvety shaft and pump it slowly.

"Mmmm," he moans.

That's a start. I keep at it. The flap of his fly keeps getting in the way. "Can we, um, push your pants down or something?"

"Sure." He arches his back on the bed and pushes them down to his knees, causing his cock to flip up before slapping back down against his thigh.

I almost shout, "Timber!" but don't because now his rod is all out in the open and I'm overcome by giddiness. Dante Lord is all out and about in my bedroom! My very own male supermodel, naked! In *my* bed! Well, mostly naked. His jeans are around his knees. But close enough. I suppress a girlish giggle.

"What?" he chuckles.

"Nothing," I grin. I nuzzle him and kiss his cheek, working the shaft up and down. Despite my failure as a blowjob operator, I did give Luke a few successful hand jobs in the beginning. I remember the first time he came after literally like five pumps. I barely had to do anything. After that first time, before we started having sex, I could make him come in thirty seconds or less with my hand. Probably because we'd make out for like an hour before and he'd be totally worked up. With Dante, that's not the case. Obvi. He seems like he's going to last all day despite all the fooling around we've done since Luke left the house.

I continue to stroke Dante's cock, but it's not working. Why is he taking so long? Is he getting bored? He's still hard, but he's not moaning or anything. Overcome by insecurity, I stop. "Am I doing this wrong?" I sigh, frustrated.

"No. I was enjoying that."

"Yeah, but you're not like, I don't know, getting super into it."

"There's no rules about how things are supposed to work in the bedroom, Skye. I'm not keeping score."

I guess I am. I'm too embarrassed to say it. "I want to make you feel like you make me feel. Maybe we should just have sex?" Guys *always* want sex.

"We could do that. Or you could give me a hand job. You were doing fine, Skye."

"I don't want to be fine," I pout. "I want to be hooker fabulous, I want to be a hand job expert. I want you to go crazy like I did."

"Relax, *Cielo*."

I recognize the Spanish word for sky instantly. "Did you just call me *Cielo*?"

"Yeah." The sound of his voice is a warm blanket of affection that settles over me.

Wow, I really like the idea of him calling me *Cielo*.

"Should I not call you that?" he asks.

"No! I luh—I mean it's great." Whoops, don't want to go using the L-word, even in regular conversation. Way too soon. "Maybe I should call you *Fuego* or maybe *Tierra*."

"Either works."

"I forgot, you know Spanish, don't you?"

"Yup."

"That's awesome. You know I take Spanish, right?"

"Yeah. Catarina told me."

"Awesome." Suddenly, I realize I'm completely relaxed chatting with Dante like this. Sure, I'm still holding his hard-on, but I'm not worried about it anymore. I resume stroking him. "So which is it, *Fuego* or *Tierra*? Flame or Earth?"

"You could use both and call me *Tierra del Fuego* if you want," he chuckles.

"That's a bit much," I giggle. "But I can't decide. You're definitely hot, which is why I went with *Fuego*, but you're also so grounded, which is why I thought of *Tierra*."

"Use either. I love both."

Whoa. He said love. He said it! I didn't!

"Easy does it," he blurts.

I just squeezed his dick really hard when I was thinking about him using the L-word. Whoops! Now I'm blushing. "Sorry," I mutter.

"If you want," he says gently, "I can give you some ideas about how to work the machine."

"Wait, what?"

"My stick shift? It seems like you're stuck in first gear."

My cheeks suddenly burn. I burry my face against his chest. "Sorry. I know, I suck at this," I grumble.

"It's okay," he soothes. "I'll give you a few tips, like what to do with the tip, and let you take it from there. How does that sound?"

Still hiding, I say, "What if you don't like it?"

"Don't worry, *Cielo*, I will like it."

"But I don't know what I'm doing!" I'm getting more anxious by the second. "It was so easy with Luke! He came in like two seconds!" Whoops. You're not supposed to mention other guys in the bedroom. Total sex *faux pas*. "Sorry." Can I crawl under the bed now? Wait until Dante leaves so I can cower in peace?

"It's okay, *Cielo*. You're nervous for no reason. Let me show you. Trust me. It'll be fine."

"What if I can't make you come?"

He snorts laughter. "I'm not worried about that. Are you?"

"Yeah."

"*En serio?*" *Seriously?*

"*En serio.*"

He hugs me with his powerful arm, "You're getting worried over nothing, *Cielo*. I've had a raging hard on for you since I laid eyes on you at 7-Eleven that first day. I haven't been able to stop thinking about you for more than a minute or two at a time."

Remembering the moment, I look at him and grimace, "Me and Rox were total klutzes that day! I dropped my water bottle like a total dunce! I can't believe you bothered to offer us those beers."

"Are you insane? You don't know this, but when you and Rox were stumbling all over yourselves in line, I was totally checking out your ass. I had to hold that six-pack of Heineken in front of my wood."

"B.S.! You did not."

"I totally did," he grins, lifting himself up on one elbow.

I push up on one elbow too. "So you weren't just giving away those leftover beers?"

He snorts, "Fuck no. It was an excuse to talk to you."

"Perv," I laugh. "Did you know I was 18?"

"I was *praying* you were 18."

"Lucky you."

"You said it."

"Huh?"

"I'm the lucky one, *Cielo*."

I try to let that sink in, but it's hard to believe.

"Hey," he asks, "did you want to take your shirt off?"

"Not really," I mutter.

"Why not?"

"I have small breasts, duh." I search his eyes, looking for any hint of an impending insult, but I see nothing but kindness. I sigh heavily and roll onto my stomach, hiding my breasts. "I'm not all big like Phoebe or Rox." When Rox asked me the other day if Phoebe had big breasts, I lied and said I hadn't noticed. Of course I had. And they were bigger than mine. Other women's breasts are *always* bigger than mine. And I'm sure Dante is used to women with large breasts, be they natural or artificial. In either case, I don't measure up. Isn't it funny how in school, the best grade is an A, but in the breast department, you never want an A? You want the breasts that get bad grades? The Breast School dropouts? The ones that get Ds and Fs? Hilarious. Grot. Anyway, I'm totally an honor student when it comes to breasts. Even my bikini tops have padding.

"You're beautiful, *Cielo*. I saw you in your bikini. You have a killer body."

I'm not about to mention the padded top.

"Let me tell you something about your beauty and how it affected me the day we met."

"How?"

"When I was staring at your ass at 7-Eleven, I couldn't get over how incredible it was."

"Thanks," I blush.

"But when I got a good look at your face? I was struck down."

"What do you mean?"

"*Cielo*, I've been all over the world. I've seen a lot of pretty women in every country on the planet, I mean tons."

I can't help but feel jealous, but I keep my mouth shut.

"Inside the 7-Eleven, I knew you were cute. But I didn't see your face. Not straight on. Just a bit from the side. But when I opened the doors and you spun around and I got a good look at you? My heart stopped."

"It did?"

"No, that's not quite right."

"Oh." Disappointment.

"Saying 'your heart stopped' is just a metaphor. Let me tell you what really happened. It was more like time stopped or something. Normally, I'm cocky as fuck, right?"

I snicker.

"I know it," he chuckles. "I'm not afraid to talk to women. I always know what to say. It just comes easy for me. But when I walked outside and saw your face, my mind went blank. It was like my brain just shut down. Boom. I've never experienced anything like it. I almost didn't know what to do. That's why I pretended to ignore you while I walked to my motorcycle and started packing my beers in my backpack."

"So all that business with the beers was because you were too nervous to talk to me?"

"Yeah."

"No way! You're such a liar!"

He shakes his head seriously, "If you saw what I saw, what I'm seeing right now—" he skims his thumb across my cheek, "—you would've done it too." His green eyes glimmer darkly in the dim light of my bedroom. The blinds are down, so the daylight seeping inside is muted. But his eyes sparkle nonetheless.

Those frickin' eyes…

They make me feel like the most beautiful woman in the world.

He continues, "When you stripped down to your bikini in the parking lot at Blazing Waters, I literally flipped."

"Weren't you staring at Rox's chest? I know I was."

He frowns, "Are you kidding? When I got a good look at you in your bikini, I don't know, every cell in my body literally screamed, 'THIS ONE!! THIS IS THE BODY YOU'VE DREAMT ABOUT SINCE PUBERTY!'" He chuckles to himself. "*En serio.*"

"No way."

He nods, "I can't explain it, *Cielo*. But that's exactly what happened. Maybe it's some genetic thing. I have no idea. But there was no denying it."

After a compliment like that, I think I can manage to at least take my shirt off. I grab the hem. "You sure you want to see them? You won't be disappointed?"

"Nope. I already know they're perfect."

I lift my shirt over my head and toss it across the room. Despite my moment of confidence and his reassurances, I instinctively fold my hands over my chest, hiding my disheveled bra and half-exposed breasts. My bra hangs at an angle, one strap down by my elbow, the other clenched against my arm pit. Suddenly, I'm not in any hurry to go completely topless. Without the extra padding of my bra, I have almost nothing to show. So I'm loathe to take it off and reveal the truth.

"Do you want to leave your bra on?" he asks gently, sensing my distress.

"I don't know, maybe?"

"It's up to you *Cielo*. You can leave it on if you'll be more comfortable." He means it.

His willingness to accept me for who I am and take my needs into consideration has a powerful effect on me. Feeling suddenly adventurous, I relax my arms and peel my bra off. Then I stretch it like a slingshot and fire it across the room, like I'm shooting an arrow of insecurity way out into space, never to be seen again. Bye, bye, insecurity! I grin at Dante. I also clasp my hands in my lap and squeeze my arms together, which sort of makes my breasts look bigger, but it's not like they go up an entire cup size. I smile down at them, "What do you think?"

When I don't hear an answer, I look up to see what's wrong.

Dante is staring at my chest. I mean *staring*. Gawking, his jaw slack.

"Fuck," he gasps. "Why are they so perfect?!" He looks up and locks eyes with me. "They're perfect, *Cielo*. Fucking perfect! I don't get it. They're just perfect! These are them, these are the breasts I dream about!" He's 100% serious. It's written all over his face.

A smile spreads across mine.

No guy has lost his marbles looking at my breasts. Not once. The few guys who have seen them never said anything about them. Sure, they felt me up, but it wasn't like they spent a lot of time on my breasts. This is the opposite of that feeling.

I launch myself at Dante, aiming my mouth at his and pushing him down on the bed. Our tongues twist and our lips writhe. His hands grab my breasts, squeezing what little there is, massaging them and pinching the nipples. Luke never did anything to my breasts, not after the very beginning. It's like he forgot about them. And I forgot how sensitive they were. My nipples explode with pleasure. Dante slides me upward, breaking our kiss so that his mouth can claim my breasts. His tongue spins around one nipple, then the other, sending waves spiraling through my ribcage.

I feel so alive it's ridiculous.

I start breathing hard as one of his hands squeezes my ass and the other works between my legs, slipping right inside me. I'm still so wet it goes in easy. I pump my hips against his finger, my breasts flickering with intense pleasure.

I come hard, riding his hand while his tongue tickles one of my nipples.

oOoOoOo + O+O+O+O

"When is it going to be your turn?" I chuckle breathlessly, now lying beside him on the bed.

"Whenever you want. Or we can wait."

I had to roll off of him a moment ago, as soon as my orgasm passed, because I realized his hard cock was throbbing like four inches away from my core. It was just too much, too soon. I'm not quite ready to go all the way. Plus, I want to focus on him for once. He has been so generous. I grin, "No, waiting wouldn't be fair. What if the world ends and I never get to make you come?"

He snorts, "I'm not worried about that."

"You're never worried about anything, are you?"

"Not really," he smiles.

"Well, *juuuust* in case the world ends in an hour," I say it in a comical high pitched voice, "Maybe I oughta do this..." I reach down and start pumping him gently.

"Mmmm, that'll work."

We start to kiss again and he moans into my mouth. That's good. But the truth is, he really is big, and my hands aren't exactly large. I need to use two hands, which is really awkward lying down. I push myself until I'm sitting on my heels. "Can we sit up? So I can get a better angle?"

"If you want. But we don't have to, *Cielo*. I'm happy just kissing you and chilling like this."

"Yeah, but are you enjoying my handy?" Although I'm still

pumping, it doesn't seem to be doing much. "I feel like I could be doing it better." My insecurities about my hand job tactics come rushing back.

"You're doing good, *Cielo*."

Good is not what I was aiming for. Everything he did to me already belongs in the Guinness Book of World Sex Records or whatever. I slump my shoulders and sigh, hanging my head. My loose hair falls in my face and I swipe a lock behind my ear. "You don't get it. I suck in the bedroom, okay?" It's ultra embarrassing to admit.

He pushes more of my bangs out of my face. "*Cielo*, it doesn't matter. You can learn. I'll show you. Nobody starts out an awesome lover. You have to learn things. I'm not going to bolt because you're not a walking Kama Sutra."

I giggle, picturing a book with arms and legs walking across a room. "Are you sure?"

"Yup." He says it with such confidence, I can't help but believe him.

"So, what do I do?"

He scoots himself up to my headboard and kicks off his jeans until he's completely naked. His arm muscles tense and bulge. The flame tattoos on his tanned forearms flicker like they're actually on fire. His body is mesmerizing, that's all there is to it. The other thing that's mesmerizing is his huge cock that lays across his lap at an angle.

"First," he says, "Get comfortable. Wrap your legs around me."

I climb over his knee and plant my butt between his legs. My nude wet crotch is inches from his. We're both completely naked. It would be so easy to lift myself up and slide down onto his hot rod. *So* easy. But I'm not quite ready for that yet. I hook my heels around his waist and grab his dick. "Okay, now what?"

"I like to start with the balls."

"Huh?"

"You want to wake those guys up. Let them know they'll be needed later."

"Whaaaat?" I sing.

"Please. Sex is all about the balls at the end of the day, right?"

I wrinkle my nose, "I thought it was about the penis or whatever."

"Naw, the penis is just the balls' butler. He does all the work, but the balls pay the bills. They don't call them the family jewels for nothing."

"Okay," I laugh, "That is so stupid."

He grins. "And yet so true."

"Yeah, but isn't the penis the one who has all the fun and does all the work?"

"What can I say? Balls are lazy fuckers," he winks. "But they still want some love."

"What do I do?"

"Just play with them. But be gentle. A little goes a long way."

"I know," I grouse. I reach between his legs and cup them gently with one hand. They're so smooth. He must manscape because they're pretty much hairless. I swirl my fingers around them, enjoying their weight. "What would you do if I squeezed them really hard?" I can't help it, I feel all-powerful with them in my hand. I wink wickedly.

"They'd probably pop like grapes."

"Ew! Let's not do that."

"No, let's not."

"So, why am I doing this again?"

"Because balls aren't just lazy. They're also insecure and want attention too. They need to feel just as important as the cock."

I shake my head and laugh, "Okay, whatever. Can I use my hand now? I mean, on your penis or whatever?"

"Go for it."

"What do I do with the head?" At the moment, it's dry. "What happened to the pre-cum?"

"Did you notice the wet circle on my jeans? I've been pre-cuming the whole time I was going down on you. The jeans soaked it all up. For the moment, anyway." He arches an eyebrow. "I've got plenty more."

"How do I make it come out? The pre-cum, I mean? Do I have to talk to the balls?" I jiggle them in my hand. "Wake up, lazy balls! The butler bone needs your help!" I giggle and grin at him. "Sorry, I'm being stupid."

Dante smiles, "It's totally fine. Sex is ridiculous when you think about it. All that grunting. You'd think you were pushing a boulder up a mountain from all the effort that goes into it. But it's just an ounce of fluid traveling a few inches."

"Ha!" I laugh, "Yeah." Dante is doing an incredible job of setting me at ease. Luke and I never talked in the bedroom. We were pretty much silent. It always felt so separated somehow. This is much better.

"If you want some lubricant now, you can spit on the head."

"Ew!"

He smirks, "It's not like I'm asking you to hock a loogie on me. Just work up some saliva and let it drizzle on the head."

"Are you sure?"

"What do you think happens when a woman gives head? Spit goes everywhere. It's the same thing."

"Oh, duh. Okay." I work up some saliva and purse my lips. It dribbles on his lap. "Whoops! Sorry." I wipe it away with my fingers.

"It's okay. Try again."

I do, and this time my saliva finds the bull's eye. Or should I say, ball's eye. I laugh to myself.

"What?"

"I just hit your *ball's* eye."

He chuckles, "Yeah. Isn't there some saying like, 'here's spit in your eye'?"

"I think it's 'here's mud in your eye', but same difference." This is awesome. I'm having fun. No nervousness. Sex should always be this easy. Why isn't it? Who knows. "What do I do now?"

"Smear that spit around. And maybe work the shaft with your other hand."

"Won't the balls get lonely?"

"They have each other. They're never lonely."

I shake my head and grin, "You are such a dork."

"Is that a problem?"

"No. Just don't make anymore ball jokes. I need to concentrate." I slowly work my spit around on the head with my fingers.

"Mmmm," he moans instantly. "That's good…" he murmurs.

I pump the shaft a few times while massaging the head. Why didn't I think of this? I add more spit and work it down the shaft until both hands are slipping and sliding all over it. Oh, I get it. No wonder women get so wet during sex. Duh. I keep at it and the next thing I know, his eyes are rolled up into his head and he's sinking into the bed like his entire body is melting. "How's that?"

"Keep doing that," he moans. "Fuck, keep doing that."

And like that, I go from being a frightened newbie to feeling like maybe I'm not so bad in the bedroom. With new confidence, I work my hand along his length, thrilling in the feel of it, sliding and squeezing and releasing. My other hand teases the bulging head, which seems to be getting harder. In fact, he's thicker too. There's no doubt he's turned on now.

"Fuck," he hisses. "Yeah…" His head lolls against his shoulders, his face tightens and he releases a strained, "Ahhhh…"

Wow. I like this. Every time I knead the head, closing my fingers around him and pulling upward, his whole body shivers and his pelvis spasms on the bed. I remember him making my body do this earlier. It's fun being in the driver's seat. I'm learning all kinds of things today. My hands are nearly dry, so I add more spit. This process continues for a long time. I make him moan and shake, adding more spit which makes him moan again. I absently wonder if I'm going to need a drink of water before he finishes, otherwise I might run out of spit.

I also realize I'm getting turned on again. Watching him lose himself to my touch is seriously hot. His muscled body shakes. Because of me. His gorgeous face strains with ecstasy, all because of me. I could do this forever.

But I don't think I'll have to. Each time I slide my circled fingers down his head and shaft, he groans louder. His knuckles are white, fisting into my sheets.

"*Cielo…*" he moans.

Slide.

"*Cielo!*"

Sliiiiiiide.

His whole body tenses.

"*Cielo!*" he grunts.

Sliiiiiiiiiiiiiiide.

His cock trembles in my hands, hard, hot, dark red, bulging, swollen. His mouth opens in a silent scream.

Sliiiiiiiiiiiiiiiiiiiiiide.

"*CIELO!!!*" Dante's back arches and his butt lifts up off the bed, his arms tensing, supporting his weight. His cock is inches from my face.

I marvel at it, watch the head swell like it's going to burst…

WHIR!

The garage door opener! Someone is home!

Shit!

Dante is about to come!

I can't stop now! It might kill him! Or something really bad!

SLLLIIIIIIIIIIIIIIIIIDDDDDEEEEE.

POP!

A stream of semen shoots up into the air, arcing back and literally flying over Dante's shoulder, hitting the wall above my bed.

Splat!

Before I can even think about it, he's fountaining cum out of his cock. Luckily, only the first spurt missiled into the air. But the rest of them are flooding out of him. There's a ton of cum covering my hand and dripping down the back and puddling in his lap.

Thud.

The door between the garage and the house closing! Someone's in the house! Time to hurry this up!

Someone tell the balls enough is enough!

The butler is done!

Time to clean this place up!

Chapter 12

Dante sits up, suddenly alert, "Who's here?" he hisses.

"I don't know! Your mom or my dad!"

His eyes bulge. "We gotta clean up. Quick." He scrambles past me on the bed and grabs for his jeans.

"You're dripping!" There's a glistening hand-sized smear of cum on my pillow. Ew. That doesn't look good.

"Sorry," he says, frantically jamming his legs into his jeans.

What do I do with my pillow? Turn it over. Duh. Then I remember the splotch of cum on my wall. I grab the pillow and use the corner to wipe the splotch. A droplet of cum from the pillow falls behind my headboard. Shit! I peer down and see a big white drop on the carpet. Well, no one's gonna notice it back there. At least the wall stain is mostly gone, or no more than a damp smear. If anybody asks, it's glue. No, nail polish. That makes sense. Somehow. I turn my pillow back over, wet side down, and drop it onto the bed. I'll be washing my sheets this evening. Good thing Catarina doesn't have time for laundry and I do it for her. Er, that might be too obvious. It'll have to wait till the weekend so no one asks questions. Hopefully, dried cum comes out easily in the wash.

Footsteps coming up the stairs. That doesn't sound like Catarina.

"It's my dad!" I hiss. "Get out of here! He'll kill you if he finds you in here!" My door is currently closed. But not locked. Remember? No locks allowed. If dad were to open the door and see inside, he would go ballistic. There's no way this looks good.

Dante jumps off the bed and grabs his shirt and boots off the floor.

Footsteps in the upstairs hallway, coming toward my room.

"Too late!" I whisper. "In the closet!"

Dante's eyes flash and he pads naked across the carpet and squeezes between the clothes on the hangers, then faces me. "Wait! You —"

There's no more time. I slide the mirrored doors shut in his face. That was close.

Knock, knock, knock.

"Skye?" It's Dad.

I whip my head around the room one last time, making sure I didn't miss anything, obvi. Dante's clothes are out of sight. Check. Cum stained pillow face down, check. Cum stain on the wall behind my bed, mostly invisible. Check. I think that's it.

And that's when I notice myself in the mirrored closet door.

Totally. Naked.

Dad knows I'm not a nudist, so this will *not* look good!

"Just a second!" I spin around frantically, looking for my clothes. I grab my shorts, which somehow ended up on top of my desk, and shake my legs into them. Where's my shirt?! Shit! I don't even worry about my bra.

"Skye?"

"Hold on! I'm changing!"

"Okay."

Guilt!

Where the F is my shirt! I don't have time to search for it. I yank my dresser open and the shirt drawer is empty! F BOMB! My hamper is inside my closet. I don't have a choice. I open the door quietly and Dante's arm juts out holding a blouse. One of the nice ones I wear when I have to get dressed up. A blouse? With shorts? I don't have time to worry about it. I jam my arms into it and button it up. When I get to the bottom, there's an extra button! Crap! I missed the top button hole!

"Skye?"

No time to fix it. I lunge toward my door and notice my bra dangling from my bookcase on my desk. I hurl it behind the bed and whip the door open just enough to stick my head through, breathless. "Hey, Dad!"

"Are you okay?" he asks, eyes narrowed. Looking over my shoulder, he searches the room behind me. "Is someone here?"

"Nope! Just me! What are you doing home so early?" Do I sound nervous? Understatement.

Still looking around my room, Dad says absently, "I thought I'd surprise Catarina. I've been coming home late a lot lately. So I thought I'd take her out for dinner and drinks." He's obviously paying more attention to my room than what he's saying. He's totally on to me.

Geez! Now he decides to leave work early?! Couldn't he have picked tomorrow?! "That's great, Dad," I lie frantically.

Dad's brows knit. "Skye, are you high?"

"Uh, no! I was just, uh, dancing? That's why I'm out of breath, see?" I do a really bad pirouette and nearly fall over.

"Careful," Dad warns, reaching out to catch me.

I recover my balance, but I'm hopping from foot to foot anxiously. "And, um, I was trying to remember this complicated dance step when you knocked."

"I thought you said you were changing?"

"Oh! I was! I had to change outfits for the dance!" This sounds way too stupid to be believed.

"How come I didn't hear any music when I came in? The house was completely silent."

At least he didn't hear us banging around in here. "Because I was changing! Duh!" I smile at him hopefully.

"All right," Dad nods. "You should open a window. It smells... *sweaty*... in here."

I cringe. Or cummy. Oh, gawd. "Yeah! Good idea!"

Dad looks around the room one last time. "What's that spot on your wall? Above your bed?"

"Nail polish! I spilled it!"

"On the wall?"

"Yes!"

He narrows his eyes, staring at me.

LEAVE!! He doesn't listen. I didn't shout it, but you get the idea.

Dad's phone rings in his suit jacket, which dangles from his hand.

"Isn't that Catarina's ringtone?" I suggest maniacally, sounding completely insane.

"Yes." He glances down at his jacket.

Phew. Saved by the ringtone.

He fishes his phone out of the jacket pocket and strolls down the hall toward the master bedroom, "Caaaat," he drawls. "I have a surprise for you, honey..."

My daughter is having sex with your son!

He doesn't say that, but damn, that was close.

I push my bedroom door shut. Too bad I can't lock it. Thanks, Dad. At least he didn't surprise me by opening the door without knocking. But there's always a first time. Now that he's wondering if I'm high, who knows what he'll do next time.

I step toward the closet to strategize with Dante about what to do now. We have to get him out of my room pronto.

Knock, knock, knock!

My eyes saucer and I spin around because innocent people never hesitate when answering the door. "Yeah?"

"I saw Dante's motorcycle outside. Is he here?"

I bite my lip. *Why, he's in the closet getting cum all over my dresses! Do you want to say hello?* "Uhh… he went for a walk!"

"Okay. When he gets back, tell him to call his mother."

"Yeah! Will do!"

I close the door and wait until I hear the shower running faintly in the master bedroom. I open the closet. "You need to climb out the window and—"

"I heard," he grunts, looking really mad as he leans out from between my clothes, still naked.

"Sorry, it's just, my dad, and… well, I don't want to—"

He puts his hands on my shoulders. His face softens and he whispers, "I get it, *Cielo*. It's okay. We have to be careful. Now you know why I brought Phoebe over for dinner."

"Yeah." I hate hearing her name. But at least I'm the one who just made Dante come everywhere, not her. Speaking of which, I'm staring at his naked mansicle. I shouldn't be looking at it right now. Bad timing. But I really want to touch it and… I squeeze my eyes shut and shake my head. *Not now!*

"You didn't get cum on my dresses, did you?" I quip, trying to be humorous and not horny.

He smirks, "I think I got it all on your bed. But I have more, if you know where to find it." He winks. He's already getting hard again. His cock is twitching and growing, going from a slumped curve to a proud column in like four seconds.

I watch it, transfixed. Oh, damn. Do we have time to have sex or something while my dad is still in the shower?

Hardly.

Hard… *Rock* hard. Throbbing… Pulsing… Oh, my…

I mean, no! Not enough time!!

I roll my eyes and smirk at him. "Get dressed and climb out the window before my dad decides to go water the grass in the backyard or whatever. Then you'll be stuck up here."

"I'm okay with that," he says suggestively.

"Get dressed," I grin and turn away. Not because I want to, but because if I don't, gazing at the hypnotizing hotness of naked and rock hard Dante Lord in my very own bedroom will lead to nothing but more cum-soaked trouble.

Not that I'd mind…

Goodness!

oOoOoOo + O+O+O+O

"Goodness," Catarina says as she walks across the kitchen on her heels, adjusting an earring. "We're going to be late for our reservations at ReaXion." ReaXion is the trendy restaurant Dad is taking her for dinner. It's on Melrose, on the other side of the Hollywood Hills. It's supposed to be the coolest place in town, but I've never been.

"We're fine on time," Dad says. He's dressed in a blazer and black silk shirt.

"Where's your tie, Dad?" I say sarcastically.

He smirks at me, "I don't *always* wear a tie, Princess."

"Your father looks dashing," Catarina insists. She walks up to him and kisses him on the lips before stroking her hand through his hair. "Now let's go before we lose our table."

I take a moment to be grateful that the discord between Dad and Catarina evaporated the moment Dad had a change of heart about Dante. They had me worried for a while. Now they're back to their usual affectionate selves. I just hope Dad doesn't find out about me and Dante now. Something tells me that would ruin everything.

"Let me get the door for you guys," Dante says to Dad and Catarina, wearing his leather jacket. "I've got a date too."

"With Phoebe?" Dad asks.

"Yeah," Dante grins.

Wait, what the F? I'm shocked. My heart clamps and my throat locks.

"Phoebe is great," Dad says.

"I really like her," Catarina says.

Assholes! Every last one of you!

"Yeah," Dante agrees.

"Are you two serious?" Dad asks.

"I think so," Dante smiles bashfully.

Oh my god! I'm an idiot! No wonder I need so much math tutoring! No wonder I'm taking the SAT a second time! I'm too stupid! I can't believe it! I drill Dante with a hateful gaze.

Catarina kisses Dante on the cheek, "Say hi to Phoebe for us," she smiles.

Say hi to Phoebe for us, I snivel in my mind. How about murder Phoebe for us? Drive a truck over her stupid red head? Crash a jet airliner into her dress shop while she's in it?

"Goodnight, Skye!" Dad calls as he walks down the front porch. "Don't stay up too late! The SAT is right around the corner!"

"Bye, sweetie!" Catarina calls.

Thunk.

The front door closes behind Dante. He didn't even look back to say goodnight.

Thunk.

My jaw drops to the floor.

I stand in my empty house, staring at the door, abandoned by my entire family.

How the hell?

This isn't happening.

But it just did.

I'm incredulous, which is another SAT word. I grimace at myself, disgusted by who and what I am.

Since I'm alone, this is a good time to cry. The tears flow like fountains. I trudge upstairs and slam my bedroom door. I won't need a lock for it now. Dante is never going to set foot in here again, and that's a promise.

Everyone in this world is a liar and an asshole.

My phone buzzes on my desk. My heart jumps. Dante! It has to be him calling to say he was just pretending about going out with Phoebe. I swipe my phone off my desk.

A text from Luke, **Hey.**

Disappointment weighs down on me. Well, at least Luke isn't a liar or an asshole. I text back, **Sorry about earlier.**

It's okay. Can we talk?

Do you want to come over?

Is Dante there?

No. He went on a date with Phuckbe.

Phuckbe? :-)

I grin to myself. **That's how I spell it.**

Riiiiight. I'll be over in 5.

I'm waiting at the door when Luke shows up. I open it before he knocks.

"Hey," I sigh.

He runs his hand through his black blades of hair. "Hey," he smiles. His other hand is thrust in his pocket nervously. "Can I come in?"

"Oh, sorry," I smile and lead him into the kitchen. "Do you want something to drink or anything?"

"Sure. Er, have you had dinner yet? I'm kind of hungry."

My stomach is still knotted up. "I guess."

"Do you want to get some Mexican? I'm in the mood for a burrito."

"Okay." Anything to get out of the house. "Let me grab a sweater." I run upstairs and get it. When I come downstairs, Luke is waiting by the front door. A shadow outside moves behind the cloudy glass. Oh no. Don't tell me that's Dante! Did he not go to Phoebe's? Oh shit! I'm so stupid! Of course he didn't!

Luke reaches for the door to open it.

Don't open that door!

I need to do something quick, before they see each other! I imagine Shakespearean hijinks that involve dragging Luke into the living room while marshaling Dante upstairs. But they would hear each other and it would be useless. I sag as Luke opens the door.

Dante.

Damnation.

Luke's smile snaps in half.

Dante's smile torques into a frown.

I hope they don't fight. Luke will lose and it'll all be my fault.

"I thought you said he was gone," Luke growls, glaring at me.

I feel so small and petty right now. "He was," I mutter.

"We can fix that," Luke laughs. "Now I'm gone." He shoulders past Dante.

Dante turns and watches him for a moment before Luke drives off.

When the sound of Luke's car fades, Dante says, "Care to explain?"

I wince. "You probably hate me right now."

"I don't hate you, *Cielo*."

"You don't?"

He smiles and shakes his head, "I could never hate you."

Relief. "I'm so sorry, Dante. I thought you were actually going on a date with Phoebe."

"My bad. I didn't think of it until our parents were heading out. When I started imagining what we might do to each other once they were gone, I freaked. I was convinced your dad was reading my mind when we were standing in the foyer. So I went with the obvious. After I left, I hopped on my bike and rode a couple of miles away so I wouldn't run into them on the way back here. Then I, uhhh, ran an errand before coming back." He suddenly narrows his eyes. "But you didn't waste any time calling Luke, did you?"

"I am *so* sorry. He texted me right after you left. I was hurt, I thought you were serious. You didn't give me a high sign or a wink or anything when you left."

He grins and shakes his head, "I'm telling you, I knew your Dad would know. He's fucking smart."

"Yeah, unfortunately," I smirk. "But I'm *really* sorry about Luke. I don't know what I was thinking."

He shrugs. "It's okay. He's gone, right?" It sounds like he's trying to convince himself.

I grab Dante's arm with both hands and pull him into the house, closing the door behind us. "I'm an emotional girl, Dante. I was hurt. I can't tell you how hurt I was. When I believed you were going from my bed to Phoebe's, I was kicking myself for being so stupid. For, I don't know—" I have to stop myself, because I can't think of a good word that describes how I feel for Dante right now. The obvious word is way too scary to say. And way too soon for me to be feeling. I've only known Dante for a few weeks. I can't feel *that* way for him already, can I? Whatever I'm feeling, one word that captures it is the word 'powerful'. "Am I making any sense right now?"

He smiles that perfect smile and bends down to kiss my forehead with those perfect lips. "Yeah. I get it. And I'm sorry. I would've said something if I'd thought of it sooner."

"Are we okay?" Whoa, why did I say that? That's what people in a relationship usually say.

"Yeah, we're okay. Better than okay." His dimples flicker under his cheeks. "So, what do we do now that our parents are out for the next couple hours?"

My eyes widen. I laugh, "Uhhh..."

"Remember I said I ran an errand while I was out?"

My stomach flips.

He reaches into his leather jacket and pulls out a small box of condoms.

"Oh, fuck..." I mutter.

"That's what I was thinking..."

Okay, I'm wet all over again.

Good thing I drank a bunch of water earlier.

oOoOoOo + O+O+O+O

Dante stalks toward me, shrugging off his leather jacket. He drops it on the floor.

We stand in the foyer.

I'm frozen in place.

He stops a foot away, smirking at me, gazing down from way up high. Dante must be at least a foot taller than me. God damn it, he is so hot and manly. I smell his scent, which is that same dusty biker smell. I think part of it is the leather jacket, but the rest of it is seasoned world traveler. Adventurer. Nomad. A man who knows no boundaries. It is intoxicating. I inhale deeply.

His eyes flicker with hunger.

"What?"

I'm still wearing my blouse from earlier. Re-buttoned properly, of course. I thought it would look less guilty if I left it on. Dante wraps his fists in the material near my throat, almost like he's going to choke me to death. The feral snarl on his face frightens me. My heart starts to hammer.

RIP!!

He tears the shirt open and buttons clatter across the hardwood.

I'm not wearing a bra. I didn't bother putting it back on earlier. Cool air blasts across my breasts. My nipples harden instantly.

"Wet yet?" he chuckles in his deep rolling baritone.

"Uhhh…" I stammer. Obvi.

He releases my blouse and the two panels hang open. I almost feel violated, but not in a bad way. All I can think about is how he flipped earlier when he saw my breasts for the first time. The way he treasured them, the way he made me feel proud of them for the first time ever. I arch my back, thrusting them toward him. I slide my hands onto my hips seductively, doing it in such a way that I also casually pull the panels of my blouse open just enough to expose my nipples. Both are tight buds of feminine sexuality. I feel suddenly powerful.

His face curls into an approving snarl as he gazes at my chest. He nods approval, then commands darkly, "Take your shorts off. Now."

His voice is so powerful, so forceful, so dangerous, it jolts me out of the fantasy and back to reality. Anxiety floods in. I'm standing in my parents foyer, my shirt torn open by a caveman, my breasts on display, and he wants me to get completely naked? What if they come home? What if they forgot something? There's no convenient closet to hide in now. I swallow hard.

"Your shorts," he growls.

"What if our parents come home!" I hiss.

"What if I fuck you right here on the floor and make you come so hard and scream my name so loud the neighbors call the cops? What if I tell you I don't give a fuck what anyone thinks, because you are mine and I'm going to make you forget everything in this world that isn't me?"

"Um…"

"When I'm done with you, the only word you'll know how to speak is my name…"

He sounds serious. Like, this is not a game. I'm overwhelmed. I'm scared. I don't know what to do. But I know I want what he's offering. I want it more than anything ever. "Can I at least remember your nickname? *Fuego* or *Tierra*?" I giggle.

"Okay, that's it. But only my name." A grin flickers across his face.

"Your personal dictionary is now down to three words."

With that corny comment, I know I'm safe. For a moment, I'm actually bummed, because I don't want to be safe. I want to be scared of this nasty gorgeous man.

"Now take your fucking shorts off before I tear them off," he growls.

Okay, scared again. Oh so yummiliciously scrumptiously scared. "Okay," I warn, "But can I turn around first?"

He responds with a grunt.

I'm thinking about how much he said he'd admired my ass at the 7-Eleven. As I push my shorts down to my ankles, I arch my back and cock my hips, presenting my ass, teasing him.

He grumbles approval. "Take your shirt off. I want to see every inch of you."

I drop my blouse to the floor, revealing my naked back. I plant my hands on my hips defiantly and turn my head to the side. I watch him from the corner of my eye. "What are you gonna do now?" I feel so confident right now, it's incredible. No man has ever made me feel like this. Somehow, this all seems like a game, a fantasy, but I know I'm being the woman I've always wanted to be. Not some frightened high school girl. I am sexuality incarnate. I cock my hip to the side, teasing him with my ass.

"Now your panties. Get rid of them."

"No," I taunt.

He strides up behind me and grabs a handful of the stretchy cotton material. It pulls against my wet folds pleasantly. He pulls harder and harder, the panties getting tighter and tighter until the sensation is almost painful, then he releases it just a fraction and pleasure floods through me. Somehow, he knows my body better than I do. He wraps a big hand around me and presses his hot palm against my flat stomach, yanking me into his body. I nuzzle my head against his muscled chest and moan. His hand rubs down my tummy and pushes under the waistband of my panties. His finger slides across my wet clit and dives inside me.

"Ohhhh…" I sigh. "Dante…" I drop my arms to my sides.

Dante slides his free hand over my breasts, squeezing them lustily and twisting the nipples softly. His other hand thrusts his finger in and out, rubbing it across my magic bud, casting a hypnotic spell over me. I sag into him, but he supports me. I am so turned on, quivering with anticipation, that I can't think. I forget everything except the hot man burning behind me. I push my ass against his jeans, feeling his hot cock rigid against me. His finger strokes me and I start to shake.

"*Tierra*," I moan. "*Dame tu fuego.*" *Give me your fire.*

His finger goes deeper and I start to come. My core tightens around him and I shiver as an orgasm erupts around his hand. I rain down on him, dripping wet, the only sound in the foyer the clicking echoes of my wetness as his hand massages my folds.

"*Tierra*," I whimper and bite my lip. "Oh… it's so good…"

"Yeah it is," he grunts in my ear.

"Fuck me, Dante," I whisper, snaking my arms over my head and around the back of his neck.

He bends down and hooks an arm under my knees and lifts me up, cradling me in his chest like I'm weightless. He carries me into the living room.

The living room has a big U-shaped sectional couch. I have watched The Real Housewives of Beverly Hills and Pretty Little Liars on this couch. My dad watches CNN and Bloomburg News on this couch with Catarina curled up beside him. This is the family couch. Meant for family things.

Dante tosses me onto the middle of it. He rips my panties off my legs. There's nothing "family" about the way he does it. Dressed in his boots and jeans, he hovers over me like a brutal intruder, his eyes on *fuego* as he peels his lips back over clenched teeth. "I'm going to fuck you senseless, *Cielo*."

I run my palms down my stomach and slide them across my cleft, feeling my hot wetness. "Do it, *Tierra*. Take me. Make me yours. I'm ready."

The gleam in his eye sparks into fiery desire. He kicks off his boots and socks. Then he pulls his T-shirt over his head. His abs ripple and his chest and arms bulge. So hot. He tosses his shirt onto the couch. With exaggerated slowness he unbuckles his belt and pries open his fly. His cock springs out proudly, hot and throbbing. It's huge. I don't know how I'm going to fit it in me. But I want it. "Are you ready?" he asks.

Frightened, I nod, still sliding my hands across my wet entrance.

He tears the condom box open and bites the top packet with his teeth. He yanks on the strip of condoms and the packet tears open. He peels the condom out of the wrapper and drops the rest onto the glass coffee table. Then he rolls the condom on his cock.

He turns me and lays me down on the couch. I let my knees relax and fall away, opening myself to him. He kneels between my legs and crawls toward me. With a fist around his dick, he rubs the slick tip of the condom against my wet heat. "I'll go slow," he warns. Because yes, it's a warning, like he's going to torture me with his manhood in a way that only he ever could.

I'm so wet, the tip slips in with ease. But oh my, is he big. I try to relax. I've never felt anything this large inside myself. Sorry, Luke. Dante is in only an inch, but I swear I'm having a baby or something. He leans down and kisses me on the forehead, the tip of my nose, my lips. "Does it hurt?"

"I'm not sure." I'm scared more than anything.

"Relax, *Cielo*. I'll never hurt you."

The hushed tone of his voice is so kind, so calming, I let go of my worry. It relaxes me down there, and he inches farther in. To my heart. No! I mean, into my body. Into my body!

Zing!

His hips touch my clit and pleasure springs up my spine. He's all the way in. I really thought I wouldn't be able to fit him in, but I do. And I am full. Oh. My. Cock. This is what it feels like to have a man inside you.

The *second* greatest sensation I've ever felt is the slow drag as he withdraws. It tickles my lips in this amazing way. But the greatest sensation is definitely the feeling of him pushing back into me, filling me back up, and the way he makes a silent growl, his eyes half-shut like he can't take any more of this but at the same time can't stop himself, like it's too good to endure even another second, but he's *forced* to fill me up. Yeah, it's incredibly awesome. We could stop right now and I would never need to have sex again. This is the pinnacle. Right here. Smokin' hot 21 year old surf stud man deep inside me. It doesn't get any better than this.

Oh, wait. I was wrong.

He withdraws and pauses then eases himself back home.

It gets better every time.

pull…

Every.

push…

Fucking.

pull…

Time.

push…

If I didn't come just then, I don't know what's going to happen when I *do* come, because right now, this is unreal.

push…

pull…

He does the slow thrust again and again and I lose my mind. I lose track of time. I lose track of where I am. All I know is that Dante is deep inside me, thrusting in and out with tremendous need, a need that matches my own.

"*Cielo…*" he moans desperately. "*Cielo…*"

I can't even speak to respond. All I can do is whimper and squeal pathetically. "Nnnn…" I'm a tiny mouse being ravaged by a fiery lion. I float on a firestorm of pleasure. Dante lowers his weight onto my chest and I wrap my arms around him, pulling my palms against his rippling back muscles.

push…

"*Tierra…*" I cry. Literally. Tears leak from my eyes. This is heaven.

pull…

"*Cielo…*"

push…

Somehow, he gets bigger inside me. My impending orgasm expands around him.

pull…

"*Dejate venir, Cielo…*" *Come for me, Skye…*

"*Sí, mi amor…*" *Yes, my love…* "*Sí!*" I squeal. I don't even realize I've said it. "*Sí!!*"

The orgasm tears through me. My core clamps around him and he howls.

"*Cielo! Me voy a venir, mi Cielo!*" *I'm coming, my Heaven!* "*Estoy viniendo!*" He arches his back and his eyes point toward heaven. "*Cielo!! Mí amor!*"

I scream as he explodes inside me.

The sound of my scream echoes throughout the empty house.

As every cell in my body tickles with sweet release, I finally realize what we've both just said…

Mí amor…

Somehow, it's not the same because we were speaking Spanish.

It's not the same.

It's the same.

My love…

oOoOoOo + O+O+O+O

After.

I am freaking out.

Not because our parents came home in the middle of it, because they didn't.

The reverse.

sees it and Ted tells her it's conditioner and she puts it in her hair. When the scene cuts to the bar, and Mary's hair is standing up, Dante releases my hand and guffaws, literally slapping the couch and folding over himself with belly busting laughs. Even though I've seen the movie a dozen times, I laugh almost as hard as Dante.

"What is so funny?" Catarina asks, leaning into the living room.

I guess we never heard the garage door opening when they got home.

A moment later, Dad is standing behind her. They both look happy. Their night out went well, I can tell.

"Mom!" Dante cries, "You have to see this! Skye, rewind it to the beginning of the bathroom scene." He reaches for the remote, but I do it for him since I know where the buttons are.

This is the first time Dante has ever called Catarina "Mom" in front of me. It might be the first time he's called her "Mom" in seven years.

Her face lights up and her eyes twinkle, but she pretends like it's nothing. "What is it?" Catarina asks, sitting down beside Dante.

Dad remains in the archway to the living room. He slides his hands in his pockets, still smiling, but still separate.

"Trust me, Mom," Dante gasps, "You have to watch this."

I don't think Catarina has seen the movie. I know Dad has. We watched it together. A father-daughter bonding moment I forced on him last year. He actually liked it.

"I remember this scene," Dad says casually.

I rewind to the beginning of the scene, where Chris Elliot, who plays Dom, a.k.a. Woogie, is talking to Ben Stiller about having "baby batter on the brain" and "flogging the dolphin" so he's not nervous around Mary.

I start the scene. As it unfolds, Dante is snickering the whole time, but he's holding it in so Catarina can hear the audio.

"What is this?" she chuckles. Catarina isn't exactly a raunchy comedy kind of women. She's too classy for that.

But as the scene unfolds, it does something magical.

Dad starts to chuckle and he sits down next to me. "Baby batter," he chuckles, shaking his head.

When the cut happens to Cameron Diaz's hair sticking up at the bar, Catarina cackles and squeals like a teenager. She looks at Dante, her eyes shining, "Her hair! It looks like wild grass!"

I've never heard her laugh so hard before.

And never in my life have I felt such a powerful sense of family as I do right now.

Me, my dad, and my mom. Because Catarina really is my mom.

She's always been there for me in a way my real mother never was…

"You stupid little cunt!"

SLAP!!

Shocked, I hold my cheek and feel the needle sting of hate coming from someone I love.

"You ruined my life, you little shit! I never should've had you!"

Thoughts of my own mom make me want to cry, but I don't let them. I push them away so they don't ruin this moment.

I'm too happy right now. I want to enjoy it.

Sadly, this is the last time we'll feel like a regular family ever again.

But I don't know it at the time.

All I know is that I'm in love with my stepbrother.

And he's in love with me.

Chapter 13

The kid sitting in front of me passes back the stack of blank Trig quizzes on Friday morning. I take one and pass the rest to the girl behind me. I smooth the test paper out on my desk and look at it. Shouldn't it be illegal to make people take math tests this early in the morning? I vote yes. It's cruel and unusual punishment.

I try to read through the first problem, but it swims in my vision.

Am I tired?

Yes.

Did I not sleep well after making love to Dante? Because let's be honest, that's exactly what it was. The answer is no, I did not sleep well. It felt plain wrong that Dante and I slept in separate bedrooms while Catarina and my dad got to share their bed. Why do they get to cuddle up at night while Dante and I have to pretend we barely know each other? It's criminal. At the same time, I felt an amazing sense of contentment that he was just one room over. My frustration gave way to bliss and eventually I went to sleep. But I kept waking up all night long, thinking about Dante, imagining what would happen if I snuck into his bedroom or he snuck into mine. Sadly, it was not to be. Would I have slept better in his arms? Who knows.

But I do know: I. Am. Tired.

And I never finished studying for this quiz.

Can you blame me? When Dante chased off Luke, I was only a quarter way through studying for it. After that, do you think I went back and hit the books? Ha! Hardly.

Math ceased to exist after Dante Lord made love to me.

No time to think about that now. No more Dante. I'm all about math at this moment.

Math, math, math.

Dante.

Tierra...

Swoon.

This isn't getting me anywhere. We only get 25 minutes for the quiz.

I've wasted five already thinking about Dante.

Focus!

Mi Cielo… My Heaven…

Side ratios and right triangles!

Creo que Te amo… I think I love you…

Sines and Cosines and functions!

Yo nunca te dejaré ir… I'll never let you go…

I shake my head, trying to block out thoughts of Dante. I check the clock. Fifteen minutes left.

This is ridiculous. I haven't even done the first problem! Now I'm starting to panic. I read over the question again and do my best to hammer out an answer. I hope it's right. I set to work on the second problem. When did this all become so unfamiliar? I did the homework during the week. Why can't I answer the quiz questions? After scribbling down an answer for question two, I check the clock. Five minutes left. Crap. I rush through the remaining problems, jotting down my best guesses. The last two may as well be random answers. Good enough.

I turn in my quiz with two seconds to spare.

At least it's Friday and the weekend's right around the corner.

I'm sure by Monday, I'll forget all about this quiz.

oOoOoOo + O+O+O+O

"So I heard you fucked your stepbrother, Slutbright," Ashley Masters says in school on the following Monday. Her words cut like iron spikes that slam straight through my breast bone and tear my heart apart.

My eyes bulge. I stumble to a stop, stunned, dropping my notebook onto the cement walkway. It flaps open like a dead bird.

How the hell did she know?!

"Thought so," Ashley sneers. "It was that guy Brittany saw you with at the library, wasn't it? The one in the picture?"

Oh my god. She knows! How does she know?!

"He's the same guy I saw you kissing at Blazing Waters, isn't he?"

I try to hide my reaction, but my eyelids peel back farther.

"It is," she says victoriously. "And it all makes sense. There's *no* way a guy that hot is related to you," she says venomously. "Not by blood, anyway. But that doesn't change the fact you're having incestuous sex with your brother! Ha ha ha!" She laughs. "How awesome is this! I can't wait to share the news. Skye Slutbright, Brother

Fucker." She chuckles gleefully and walks toward her locker by the senior lawn while typing something into her smart phone.

This isn't happening!

But it is.

It just did.

Only one thought crosses my mind over and over and over again:

Who told her?

Because there's no way anyone in the world knows that Dante and I had sex in our house on Thursday night. Nobody could possibly know. Not one single soul except me and Dante!

Unless…

Luke.

Oh, no…

Did he spy on us?

What did he do?

Why did he do it?

Oh, no, oh no, oh no, oh no!!!

He's jealous of Dante! It was *so* obvi!

I'm screwed.

In the worst way ever invented.

oOoOoOo + O+O+O+O

"How could you tell her?!" I seethe dangerously, digging my nails into Luke's forearm.

He spins around from his locker, caught totally off guard. "What the hell, Skye!"

"You told Ashley, didn't you?" I am rage incarnate. I've never been so angry in my entire life. I've never hated anyone like I hate Luke right now. I want to claw his eyes out. I want to stab a number two pencil through his heart. I want to jam his scrotum in my three ring binder and puncture his testicles in the clawed steel rings. I want him to die. But only after I hurt him worse than he hurt me.

He yanks his arm out of my grasp, tearing the skin, drawing blood. "What are you talking about, Skye?"

"You told Ashley that I had sex with Dante, didn't you? You lied to her and made up a story because you're jealous of Dante!"

"No I didn't!" he denies vehemently.

"Oh really?" I hiss. "Then *who* told her? The Gingerbread Man?"

He rolls his eyes dismissively.

"I knew it," I growl. "You told her! And what's worse, you lied to make me look bad!"

"I didn't tell her you guys had sex," he snaps.

I glance around, noticing all the other seniors milling around us. "Lower your voice," I whisper.

"I didn't tell Ashley you had sex with Dante." He looks at my shrewdly. "Wait, did you?"

"That doesn't matter," I grunt guiltily. "What did you tell her?"

He rolls his eyes again and sighs like I'm no more than an annoying rash he has to begrudgingly tolerate until it goes away.

Well, he's in for a rude awakening if he thinks he can ignore me. I'm not going anywhere. "What did you tell her, Luke?" I demand.

"I told her that I was into you and you weren't into me." He says nothing more.

"That's it? You can't expect me to believe that's all you said."

"I may have mentioned that you had a thing for Dante. And that he was your stepbrother."

I stamp my foot. "How could you, Luke?!"

"I don't know!" he says defensively. "That part just sort of came out. Maybe I was mad at you."

Him mad? He has no idea what mad is. I grind away at him some more. "How could you possibly think that Ashley Masters, of all people, wouldn't take that to the gossip bank and cash it in for a million dollars worth of rumors?!"

"I never told her you guys hooked up! I just said you liked him. And maybe I told her what happened at the house. That you and I were making out and Dante barged in like an animal."

"You told her that?! What were you thinking, Luke?!"

His brow furrows, "I was thinking that Dante is a total dick, and he basically thought I was a rapist or some shit. How was I supposed to feel? Look at my arm." He holds up his forearm, the one Dante abraded when he knocked Luke down. There's a thick pebbly scab running the length from elbow to wrist.

"Oh," I grimace.

"Yeah," he spits. "Oh," he mimics.

"Sorry. I didn't realize it was so bad."

"It's no big deal. I'll live. But that's not what hurts." His face softens and he looks totally dejected.

My stomach sours. He doesn't have to explain himself. I chose Dante over him. Then I stood beside Dante after Dante made Luke look bad by attacking him and being jealously suspicious of his intentions. "I'm sorry, Luke," I mutter.

"It's no big deal," he sighs.

That's Luke. Always being nice.

But I can tell it is a big deal for him. Luke and I got along really well. Maybe not in the bedroom, but looking back, we had fun together plenty of times. Maybe not often enough for what I expected out of a relationship at that point in my life, but we had fun tons of times before I ended it, for good or bad.

"Luke. I'm sorry about your arm." I wave my hand toward his wrist. "And the nails."

He holds up his other arm, the one I grabbed, and smears away the blood seeping from my claw wounds. He shrugs, "It'll heal."

Damn it, Luke. Stop being so understanding. You're impossible to hate.

oOoOoOo + O+O+O+O

"I hate you!" Rox jams her smart phone in my face. It shows the photo of me and Dante wrapped around each other in the dark meeting room at the library, looking guilty as sin. It's the photo from that very first day we met.

We're both dressed, except Dante's pants are obviously unbuckled and hang an inch too low around his waist, revealing the top of his tan and dimpled ass. Because of how I'm positioned behind him in the pic, I almost look naked. All you can see is my naked knees wrapped around his unbuckled jeans and my arms around his broad shoulders. But I remember having all my clothes on. Well, skimpy cotton shorts and a T-shirt. But from this photo, I may as well be totally naked. Worse, over my shoulder on the back wall, there's a library poster of a dinosaur wearing glasses and reading a book. The caption reads, "Don't let your love of reading go extinct." The library logo is on the corner of the poster. Jesus, this looks *really* bad.

I can't respond. I'm shell-shocked for the second time today.

"This was that day that Dante tutored you at the library, isn't it? The day we met him at 7-Eleven and went to Blazing Waters." She's tearing up. "You *lied* to me, Skye! You lied!"

Like black lightening, her words damn my soul to you know where.

I am horrid.

I am despicable.

"But..." I whimper weakly.

"You said all you did was study math! This isn't studying math! How could you?" she pleads. "You've been lying to me since this all started, haven't you?!"

"I—"

"You've been hooking up with him this whole time, haven't you?!"

"No, I..." I feel like I've stolen her heart and soul and thrown both into the sewer for the rats to feed on. I hold out my hands in a half hearted gesture. "Rox—"

She spins away and runs off before I can stop her.

I can feel my own heart start to crumble piece by piece.

How did she get that photo?

I can think of one likely source.

On wobbly legs, I make my way toward my locker in the freshmen section. I pull my smart phone out of my bag and open my ChatBrat app and wait for it to connect.

ChatBrat took North Valley by storm two years ago. It's a social networking app that lets you post text or pics or video anonymously, and it sends your message out to every user within a ten mile radius. In other words, anyone at North Valley can post anonymously to ChatBrat and everyone at North Valley will know about it one second later.

Yes, everyone at North Valley uses ChatBrat. It's a one-stop shop for the latest North Valley insider info and ghoulish gossip. Who's dating who, who cheated on who, who is hot and who is not, who's fake, who's real, blah, blah, blah. I was obsessed with it sophomore and part of junior year, but I got over it after a while. I decided the constant stream of stupid mean hater gossip was best avoided, so I quit using it.

But now, I have to check it one last time to find out if the worst has occurred.

Like a person gawking in slow motion past a freeway accident, I watch the disaster unfold before my eyes when the app connects. The top post on my ChatBrat page is that photo of me with Dante in the Library. Below the photo is the following text:

Town Pump Skye Slutbright getting used and abused at the local library! Someone slap a scarlet A on that girl's chest!

Gosh, who could've come up with such a clever caption? Could it be Ashley Masters? Sarcasm. Who else could it be? Only she is that cuttingly clever. She is the ultimate snark shark. Whenever she smells blood, she starts an offending frenzy.

The other thing about ChatBrat is that it uses up-voting and down-voting, similar to "likes" on Facebook. On ChatBrat, you either "kiss" or "diss" a post. The photo of me and Dante already has 586 kisses. How ironic, because usually you kiss people you like. This feels more like the kiss of death. My heart is cracking into pieces. And 586 kisses? That's almost half the North Valley student body, and I'm guessing Ashley only posted the photo a few minutes ago. I'm sure by brunch or lunch, it'll be all over the school. Social networks are evil. Grimacing, I jab the "diss" button for the post with my finger, which brings the total number of disses to 3. I wonder who has my back? I want to personally thank them. It's safe to assume that Luke is one of the dissers because we all know how nice of a guy he is. Who was the other? I hope it was Rox. I *doubt* it was Rox because of how hurt she is. But I'm still going to hope that she has my back after all these years as BFSFs.

I quit out of the ChatBrat app and shove my phone in my purse. Unfortunately, quitting the app doesn't kill that post. I'm pretty sure it's about to take on a life of its own.

Nausea sloshes through my stomach in a cold rippling wave.

Can this day get any worse?

oOoOoOo + O+O+O+O

The sound of rustling papers surrounds me during first period. Mr. Mendez is passing out last Friday's graded trig quizzes. The students sit in their chair desks flipping through the graded pages. Some kids stuff their quizzes into their binders or under their Trigonometry textbooks without looking at them.

All I can think is the only reason they aren't all on their phones goggling at Ashley's latest ChatBrat post is because it's against school policy to use your cell phone during class. But at some point today, everyone will have seen the photo of me and Dante. Can you say, 'The calm before the perfect storm?'

Normally, calm is a good thing. Right now, it's the worst thing I've ever experienced. I am in hate with calm. I will never speak to calm again. Because calm is a bastard waiting to bite. Can I stop time and not have to deal with what is inevitably about to happen to me? Can I leave the country and not come back? Fly to the Moon or Mars and live there? This is jacked beyond all proportions.

And the fun hasn't even started.

"Miss Albright," Mr. Mendez smiles, offering me my graded quiz.

I take it from him politely, "Thanks."

He gives me a disappointed look before stepping past me.

On my paper, scrawled in careful red pencil at the top of the page, is yet another death sentence:

47%

For those of you who don't know, that's an F.

As in, fail.

As in, fuck.

Below the score, written in elegant cursive almost like a personal note from a caring Mr. Mendez are the words: *"What happened, Skye? Your first three quizzes were B's. Don't drop the ball now!"*

I'll tell you what happened. Dante happened. I may have dropped the trigonometry ball, but I didn't drop Dante's balls. I had those well in hand on Thursday when I should've been studying for this damn quiz. Stupid math quizzes! Who invented them anyway? The last thing on my mind has been math. Because seriously, who needs math when you're in *amor* with a hottie like Dante?

The good news is that Dante can actually help me with my future math homework. We just need to make sure we devote as much time to math as we do to sex education. I can do that. The idea puts a smile on my face.

What puts a frown on my face is seeing Anna Schmidt sneak her phone out of her purse and check ChatBrat during class. She sits one seat forward and to the right of me. I can see the photo of me and Dante on her screen. Anna turns and leers at me like I smell, which I don't. She gloats with rancid superiority and silently mouths the word, "Slut," her lips peeling across her teeth and her tongue tapping her teeth on the T.

I am not a slut.

Sluts sleep around.

I am in *amor* with Dante and I will only be sleeping with *him*. So what if he's my stepbrother? That totally doesn't make me a slut.

I glare defiantly at Anna.

Anna's response is to snort derisively and tap the "kiss" button on her phone with great satisfaction before putting it back in her purse and turning her back to me.

I want to shout, "You can 'kiss' my ass, you squirrel faced fuck! You could chew through a truck tire with those buck teeth of yours!" But I don't because I'm not a bitch and we're in the middle of math class. But I do sneer and shoot a million daggers into the bull's eye on her back, which makes me feel infinitely better.

Remember how I was totally focused all summer on preparing for the upcoming SAT retake in a few weeks? Because I need to do better on the math portion so I can secure a spot at SDU next year? That hope is about to be sunk by the rippling ramifications of one bad decision: sleeping with my stepbrother. Oh, and the fact that Ashley Masters had to tell the whole world. Love her timing. Grot.

Like most impending disasters, the first signs are seemingly insignificant. Mr. Mendez's disappointed smile. Anna's silent snooting. Both are easily ignored. But, in a very short period of time, the adult disappointment and the peer disdain are going to balloon out of control. And, like the captain of the Titanic, I'm too drunk (on *amor*) to care about the tip of the iceberg. It's just the tip, as they say.

How bad of a problem can that be?

I have Dante in my life. That's all that *really* matters, right?

Despite my optimistic denial, my slide down the slippery slope to academic and social irrelevancy starts here.

oOoOoOo + O+O+O+O

The brunch bombshell explodes, as per the warning signs.

It goes off like a chain reaction the second I set foot in the quad, which is packed with people. But I don't care about them. I need to find Rox so I can explain things and apologize to her. That's my top priority. We usually hang out in the quad on the senior lawn during brunch. But I don't see her anywhere.

What I do see is the rest of the student body entranced with their smart phones. Then, one by one, people look up from their phones and notice me. Word of my presence passes through the crowd like a virus until it seems like everyone is staring at me.

My first thought is to run. No. I won't. I'm not going to let a little gossip make me hide my head in the sand. I'm going to stay strong. Screw everyone and their petty rumors. Besides, I'm a senior now. I have more important things to focus on, like my future. I take a step forward, heading toward the senior lawn, which is on the far side of the quad. My skin tingles with hot irritation while I walk, like I'm wearing an itchy wool jumpsuit that has never been washed. Who knew that so many dirty looks could make you feel so unclean?

As I pass through the thronging gauntlet of people sitting on the numerous benches around the quad, everyone is literally whispering my name like I'm a social disease, which from this point forward, I may very well be.

What I hear the girls say:

"I didn't know Skye Albright was such a slut."

I'm no slut. I'm in amor.

"Girl, don't you see the way she walkin'? That a slut strut right there."

I'm not slut strutting. I don't even know what that is. All the same, I try to walk as plainly as possible.

"Didn't she sleep with the football team last year?"

"I heard it was the swim team."

"Bitch probably did both."

I haven't slept with any member of either.

"O.M.G, who did she piss off?"

We all know the answer to that one: Ashley Masters. Don't get on that bitch's bad side.

"I always knew Skye was a skeevy slunt."

"Look how she walks like she's a princess or something."

I'm not walking like a princess! I'm walking like normal! Just plain walking!

"That ChatBrat pic proves she's nothing more than a whore."

Oh, the pic. It is going to ruin my life, isn't it?

What I hear the guys say:

"I'd fuck that."

"I already fucked that."

No he didn't. I know who I've had sex with, and it wasn't you!

"Mmm, mmm! I'd like to tear that ass up!!"

"That" ass belongs to a human being! Me, you jerk!!

"Get her drunk and we'll both hit that shit."

No you won't, and don't call me shit, you shit!

"No need. She's DTF, bro. Everyone knows Skye Albright is a slag hag. She'll fuck anybody."

I'm not Down To Fuck, and everyone knows that I've barely slept with anybody. Well, that was the word on the street about me an hour ago. Isn't it amazing what a single photo with a clever caption can do to sink your reputation in seconds?

"Who's the dude with her in the photo?"

"Her cousin."

"No, bro, it's her brother."

"Her *actual* brother?"

"Yeah. He went into the Army when he was 18. Now he's out."

The Army? Where the hell does all this misinformation come from? I almost want to laugh. But it would be tragic laughter, not happy laughter.

"I could kick that guy's ass. Fuck the Army."

"The only thing I wanna fuck is Skye Fuck Me All Night Albright."

"Heh, heh! Yeah!" another voice laughs and hollers behind me. "Hey! All Night Albright! Whyn't you suck my dick, bitch?"

I spin around to glare at whoever said it, but all I see is a bunch of guys and girls smirking and chuckling and looking away like they weren't just literally talking about me behind my back.

Everybody heard that comment. And everyone thinks it's A-okay.

"All Night Albright," some girl cackles.

"All Night Albright!" another girl sings.

I spin around trying to see who said it, but I can't tell for sure. There's way too many people around.

Welcome to North Valley HATE School.

Great. I'm sure the cheer squad will work up a cheer in my honor by lunch time.

Let the waking nightmare begin.

I speed through the gauntlet of haters and beeline toward the senior lawn. Since I don't see Rox anywhere, I stride right past it, heading toward the gym and all the grass fields behind it. Since we're not allowed to leave campus during brunch, the fields are the only place I can be alone right now. I pass right by the girl's restroom. There's no way I'd risk going in there. My loving peers would probably corner me and start casting stones at the village slut. I'd end up murdered for sure.

oOoOoOo + O+O+O+O

Sitting through third and fourth period is murder.

I can't concentrate on what my teachers are saying. All I'm aware of is the eyes of everyone clawing away at my back. I try to focus on my notebook and taking notes, but I can't figure out how to move my pen. That's not true. I know how to use it. But I'm afraid if I start writing, I'll just jot down all the horrid gossip I've been hearing for the last two hours.

When the bell rings at the start of lunch, I feel a mix of relief and wretched dread. Relief because I need a break from the hate I've been getting, and dread because I know there's going to be more judgment waiting for me outside.

I go to my locker and dump my books in it. I notice the pink cloud wallpaper that Rox helped me put up a few weeks ago. Rox. I need my BFSF right now. Badly. I need to find her and apologize profusely. I have to remind her that we pinky swore the day we met Dante that we would let him decide between us. I know she'll understand. And I know she'll stand beside me in the face of all the hate I'm going to be forced to endure for the next few weeks. Hopefully it won't take long until the gossip about me is replaced by some other gossip and I become yesterday's news.

"Hey, Skye," Jason Carpenter says as he puts his school books in his locker and pulls out his Magic The Gathering binder.

"Hey, Jason," I smile uncertainly. Has he seen the ChatBrat post?

Does he care about that sort of thing? The genuine grin on his face says no.

"What are you doing for lunch?" He asks hopefully. "Me and the guys are playing Magic in the library today. If you want to join us."

"Oh, thanks, Jason. That's sweet. But I have to find my friend Rox."

His shoulders sag, disappointed. "Oh, okay."

"But thanks for offering. It means a lot." It really does. Not everyone has been so kind today.

"Maybe next time?" he suggests.

"Yeah." I don't know if I'll ever spend a lunch in the library with the geeks playing games, but it sure is nice of him to offer. "See you later," I smile and wave as I walk away.

"Yeah!" he beams hopefully.

I text Rox as I walk toward the main parking lot: **I'm sorry, Rox. Can we talk? I need to explain.**

She hasn't responded by the time I make it to the parking lot. I look around for her car. It's not where she parked it when we came to school this morning. There it is! I see it driving down one of the parking lanes. I trot toward it.

Rox is at the wheel and Nicole sits shotgun.

That's *my* seat.

Kayla sits in the back seat.

"Rox!" I shout. "Wait up!"

She doesn't hear me. Or if she does, she's ignoring me.

Nicole grimaces when she see me and Kayla rolls her eyes with obvious disgust.

The car drives away and turns into the street.

I slow to a stop and watch them disappear.

This is too many kinds of wrong to count. I can't believe Rox ditched me! She's never ditched me! My world is officially falling apart. My best friend has abandoned me. I glance around the parking lot. The kids who leave for lunch are already gone. It's just me and the parked cars in an empty suburban high school wasteland.

I feel totally alone.

This blows.

I really don't want to be alone right now.

It's killing me that Rox blew me off like that. I don't know what hurts worse: all the slut hate, or Rox abandoning me like this. I'm about to fall apart. But I can't do it out here. It feels too vulnerable, like some kids might see me and point and jeer while I cry.

I pull myself together.

What are my options? I'm not going to the senior lawn. The quad is a minefield of gossip bombs. I could go to the bleachers and hang with the burnouts. But I don't really know them. Maybe I'll walk to Ralph's by myself. No, that won't do. I need to call Dante. I pull out my phone and call him. He bought a pre-paid phone over the weekend so we could stay in contact. But he doesn't answer. I text him: **Call me. It's important.**

"Don't you have any friends, Slutbright?" Ashley Masters shrills behind me.

I don't want to turn around. I tilt my head up and stare at the sky. Nobody up there seems to be listening.

"Were you just calling your brother for a lunch time hookup, Slutbright?" Monica Webb asks.

Now she's calling me that too?

Brittany Price chimes in. "Maybe you can fuck him in the school library and I can take your picture again."

"Yeah," Ashley laughs, "we'll post it on ChatBrat. I wonder which will get more kisses. I see here the current photo has 1,277. But I bet a good X-rated photo will triple that. Get all the local pervs and pedos sharing it around town. Maybe you can make a career out of it like Kim Kar*TRASH*ian."

Bitches.

If only I'd managed to take Brittany's phone away from her the day she invaded my privacy in the meeting room at the library, none of this would be happening right now. If it wasn't for that stupid librarian, I would have. Too late to worry about it now.

"Do your parents know you're fucking your brother, Slutbright?" Ashley asks. "I'm sure they'd love to know."

I whip around, my fists clenched at my side. I'm ready to cut a bitch with my claws. "He's my stepbrother," I hiss.

"Same diff..." Ashley smiles pleasantly, holding an E-cig in her fingers She sucks on it with great joy and the tip lights up blue. "... *buuuuut* you're still fucking him."

It's true. I can't deny it. All I can do is glare. The good thing is it's not like Ashley knows my parents. And my parents don't frequent ChatBrat. I don't think they know it exists. What are the chances they'll find out? I mean, only every kid in school knows. Is it possible one of them will mention the photo to their parents? This is bad. Then again, the reason ChatBrat is hip is because parents *don't* know about it. Maybe that's my one saving grace. I can hope. Either way, there's nothing I can do about it now.

Since Dante hasn't called or texted, I need to go elsewhere. I don't want to spend my lunch being taunted by these three heathens. Rather than turn my back on them, I march straight at Ashley like I'm going to kill her.

Her eyes goggle, which looks so very much out of place on her effortlessly pretty face.

Seeing her shock thrills me to no end. I stop with my nose an inch from hers. Well, a few inches, because she's taller and I have to look up at her. But I'm seeing red, not measuring distances. "Do whatever you want, *Assley Masturbates*."

"Whoa!" Brittany chuckles. "I think she's butthurt!" She too has an E-cig and takes a fake puff.

I ignore her dig, still focused on Ashley. "Just remember who you're messing with," I finish with as much danger as I can muster. I'm not exactly known around campus as a badass, but now seems like a good time to change that reputation.

For a moment, Ashley looks unsure of herself. It's a look she rarely wears. A second later, it's gone, replaced by her usual superior contempt. "We'll see who gets messier in the coming weeks, Slutbright."

I have nothing to say to that. I grimace and shove past her, heading back toward campus.

If my Dad somehow finds out about me and Dante, things are going to get much worse.

What am I going to do with the rest of my lunch?

I need to regroup and figure out how to do damage control.

Chapter 14

"How much damage does that guy do again?" Jason Carpenter asks the kid sitting across from him in the library at one of the dozens of tables in the room.

The other kid, who has a hair helmet that practically hides his entire face, and tiny glasses that make his eyes look really big, says in a sniveling voice, "My Bogardan Hellkite does five damage. He also has five toughness. Your Elemental Shaman doesn't stand a chance, Jason." He giggles in this sputtering way that is really strange.

Maybe the library was the wrong place to spend lunch.

Jason and his friend haven't seen me yet. I turn to leave before they do.

"Hey, Skye!" Jason hollers. "What are you doing here?"

I wince, freeze in place, then slowly turn around, "Hey, Jason," I say in a shaky voice. I *so* don't belong here.

Jason's friend stares at me. I swear, his eyes get even bigger than they already were. He blinks at me like maybe I'm a ghost or a mirage.

"Hey," I smile.

Jason says. "This is my friend Trevor. Trevor, this is Skye. She's a senior."

Trevor gulps audibly but doesn't say anything. He just stares with his giant eyes through his tiny glasses. I think he's never seen a girl up close before.

"Hey, Trevor," I say nervously. He's kind of weirding me out.

Trevor looks really nervous. He leans over the table toward Jason and whispers, "She's a girl!"

That was so cute, I can't help but chuckle. "Yeah. And I can hear you."

Trevor just stares at me.

"Do you want to learn how to play magic?" Jason asks.

"I guess?" I say tentatively but also hopefully.

Jason stands up like a little gentleman and pulls out the plastic chair next to him.

"Thanks," I smile and sit down.

After the dirty looks I've been getting all day, I'd rather do something goofy like play games in the library with two nice guys like Jason and Trevor than endure any more hate from the all the other rabid animals at North Valley.

For the remainder of lunch, Jason and Trevor attempt to explain the game to me. It's totally confusing, and obviously requires math skills, which I find ironic, but I do my best to follow their instructions. The alternative of stewing in thoughts about my social downfall is way too painful.

Magic it is, then.

Jason is more than happy to help me learn the game. Trevor is nearly speechless at first. Slowly, I'm drawn in by all the fantastic art on the cards and the story that goes along with the game mechanics. It's all fantasy creatures like in the movies, and it seems like fun, like Harry Potter on steroids or whatever. The more questions I ask, the more comfortable Trevor gets. Whenever he explains what a card does, or how to use it in play, he gets impassioned, like he's telling me something super secret or life altering. It's kind of cute. More than anything, I'm struck by the fact that Trevor and Jason are both so completely nice. Something tells me that even if they've seen my illicit photo on ChatBrat, they don't care, which makes them five times awesomer in my book.

The next thing I know, the warning bell rings, signaling the end of lunch.

"Wow, that was cool," I say. "Thanks for showing me how to play, guys!"

"You want to play again tomorrow?" Jason asks with bright hope.

"Maybe," I smile. "I'll have to check my social calendar first," I wink. We already know I'm clear through eternity after this morning.

"We're here every day if you want to play more," Trevor smiles.

These guys are too nice.

Lucky me they were here today. It's nice to know not everyone in the world is a terrible asshole.

oOoOoOo + O+O+O+O

"It was terrible, Dante. Everybody knows." I jump into his arms the second I walk in the door after school that day. And I do mean walk, because Rox was nowhere to be found after sixth period when it was time to go home, so I walked. I didn't mind the exercise, but every footstep felt like failure, like embarrassment, because I no longer had my BFSF driving me. It didn't help that she, Nicole, and Kayla all ignored me during fifth period English. Is it ironic that we're reading The Scarlet Letter by Nathaniel Hawthorne for AP English Lit, and my closest friends are now all shunning me? I'll let you be the judge. Whatever. Sooner or later my friends will get over it and re-friend me, right? Maybe? Hopefully?

I fight back tears and gaze up at Dante's loving, I mean *amoring* eyes.

"What happened?" he asks, surprised, holding me gently by the arms.

His pure beauty melts my heart. For a moment, I forget that I'm just a high school girl living at home with her parents. For this moment, it's like I've walked home to my own beautiful house and my own beautiful man. Too bad it's tinged by the events of the day. "Remember that photo that girl took of us at the library?"

"Oh yeah," he grins. "What about it?"

"It's out."

"Out?"

"Someone posted it on ChatBrat. Now the whole school has seen it."

"What?"

I open ChatBrat on my phone and show him the post. It now has 1,764 kisses. Geez, it's spreading.

Standing beside me, he puts his arm around my shoulders and reads the caption. "What the *fuck*?" he hisses. "Who posted this?"

"ChatBrat is anonymous. Nobody knows. But it's probably Ashley Masters."

"Was she the chick at the library?"

"No, that was Brittany. Ashley was at Blazing Waters the day we met. She was the gorgeous blonde. The one we talked to outside the bathroom?" I forget that none of these people are a part of Dante's life like they are mine.

Dante frowns. "She did this?"

"Probably."

He shakes his head. "If your dad sees this…"

"I know."

"Can you email ChatBrat and have them remove the pic?"

"I can try. But the company is somewhere in like Latveria or wherever. They're not known for responding to emails from random teenage girls in California. Besides, I'm sure plenty of people have already saved it, so it's bound to show up elsewhere if it gets removed."

Dante's eyes grow distant as he stares off into space. "Fuck..." he mutters.

"Yeah," I snort. "My dad and your mom are going to find out. It's just a question of when."

Dante winces and runs his hand through his shaggy blond hair, "That pic doesn't look good, does it?"

"Not really. The caption doesn't help either."

He looks at the phone and reads the caption. "Used and abused? That doesn't make me sound too good, does it?"

"It's just stupid gossip," I dismiss. Then I quit the ChatBrat app so we don't have the picture staring back at us. "We know what happened. You didn't abuse me."

He arches his eyebrow, "I know, but..."

I sigh. "Yes, this is a disaster. But at least we can go through it together." I look at him hopefully. For a second, I'm deathly afraid that he will disagree, that he'll bow out and skip town, never to be seen or heard from again. If that happens, I'll have to pick up the pieces alone. My Dad would probably love it if Dante disappeared, but I sure wouldn't. The last thing I want is to do this without Dante.

I need him.

I hope he needs me.

He places his big hands on my shoulders and turns me to face him. Damn it, he's so handsome. His emerald eyes shine from beneath that ruffle of hair that always falls over his brow in the sexiest way possible. "Don't worry, *Cielo*. We'll get through this. Together." I wrap my arms around his waist and he pulls me into his chest, folding his arms around my shoulders while he kisses the top of my hair. "Everything is going to be all right, *Cielo*. I promise."

Remember when I said way back in the beginning that I knew Dante was going to fight for me, no matter what? Yeah, that. Wrapped in his muscular arms, I know I was right to feel that way.

Dante *is* going to fight for me.

He's going to fight for us.

We're in this together.

No matter what evil people throw at us.

oOoOoOo + O+O+O+O

I want to throw my phone across my bedroom.

I've texted Rox a million times since I got home from school, but she totally ignores me. It hurts ten times worse than it did at lunch or during fifth period. She really is blocking me out and abandoning me. But she's my BFSF. She's not supposed to do that.

I sigh heavily.

I've *always* been able to talk to Rox. Especially when things went bad. We have always been there for each other. What's worse, I don't know what her deal is. I've never seen her get this attached to a guy who wasn't into her. Then again, I can't get over how attached I am to Dante myself. It totally scares me. But at least I know he's in this with me.

And that's another thing. I should be sharing all of my giddy glee about Dante with Rox. We're always the first person either of us talks to about boys. The good stuff and the bad stuff. I don't get to share either with Rox. Total bummer.

For now, Dante and I agree to play it cool at the house, especially under the circumstances.

For the next several days, we act like what we're *supposed* to be. Plain old stepbrother and stepsister. Dad and Catarina totally buy it. The whole family has dinner together every night. Dante and I sit across from each other. Never once do we flirt or play footsies or anything. But the secret knowledge of our connection makes it something special. A wink here, an arched eyebrow there, nothing too obvi, but enough to let each other know that we're connected deeply.

Ever since the night the four of us watched There's Something About Mary together (we ended up watching the remainder of the movie that night), Dad has made a huge effort to be home in time to eat with us every night, and spend more time afterward just hanging out with all of us. There's been a continuing closeness we've never had as a family. I hope this closeness lasts forever. Somehow, I know it won't. But I can wish for something, even if I don't have a magical lamp and a genie to grant me three wishes.

Sadly, the first sign that things are starting to crack comes one night at dinner.

Dad passes me the platter of meatloaf, which Dante suggested when Catarina asked what to cook earlier in the afternoon. I fork a slice onto my plate.

Dad asks me, "What happened to Luke? I haven't seen him around in a while. Wasn't he helping you study math for the SATs?"

"I guess he's been busy or whatever."

"That's too bad," Dad frowns. "I really like Luke. He's a good kid."

I hide my scowl. Luke isn't exactly number one on my list after what he told Ashley.

"Why did you two break up again?" Dad asks, spooning sliced green beans onto his plate.

I smirk, "Because he was too busy all the time." It's the truth. I glance briefly at Dante. He doesn't appear bothered by Dad's line of questions.

Dad nods, "I suppose that makes sense. Well, the important thing is that you're preparing for the SAT. How is that going?"

"Great," I lie.

The truth is, I'm a little worried about the upcoming Stress.A.T. I've been trying to study, but I swear, all the drama surrounding that photo is a constant distraction. You tell yourself that you're going to rise above the negativity and focus on higher things or whatever. But it's turning out to be much harder than I thought.

Every night I try to study, it seems like I spend more time worrying what people are saying about me online than I do working my practice math problems. I stopped checking ChatBrat right after the fact. But that doesn't stop hate messages from showing up on my Facebook feed. I check Facebook because I'm stalking Rox to see if she's forgiven me or forgotten me. I can't really tell. She seems to be avoiding Facebook right now. There's also the constant stream of notifications I get from Ask.fm. I forgot I even had the account. But half the people at North Valley have blown it up with incessant hate questions. Every single one comes from an anonymous person.

How long have you been a skeevy slut?

Why are you such a skank?

Do you sleep with anybody who asks? Or only family members?

I saw u hook up with Dominick R. at Ashley's partay. Duz ur brother no?

This person means Dominick Rodriguez. He's a senior who plays varsity football at North Valley. I would never go to any party Ashley threw, and I've never hooked up with Dominick. I don't think I've talked to him for more than a minute since I started at North Valley.

Are you pregnant? You look it.

Do you think you and your brother's baby will be retarded?

That's stupid, because Dante and I aren't related *or* pregnant.

Your sick for liking your brother

Satan is smiling right now. When are you going to join him in hell?

Wanna hook up?

Why don't you die already?

Pap of yor titz

I think not. Pap means "Post a pic".

How many guys have u slept with?
Show us you're sex tape
Ur no princess. Ur a slut.
Is it true u r a homewrecker? Or does it not count cuz it was your own home ur wreckin?

The questions go on and on like this. There's over 400.

When I started high school at North Valley, I had felt confident that I could play it smart and avoid cyber bullying all the way through graduation. And I made it all the way to senior year without having to endure more than a minimal amount. I guess I jinxed myself by being cocky. In just two weeks, I've received three years worth of hate from my peers. No wonder they killed that kid Piggy in Lord Of The Flies.

Teenagers are evil.

For a moment, righteous rage flares up inside me. Armed with all my SAT vocab words and critical writing skills, I would love to lay into these jerks and give them a piece of my mind. I could answer every one of their stupid questions with a smart and clever response. If I was still 14, I would probably do exactly that right now. But I'm not 14. I'm 18 and I know better.

So I delete my Ask account with a huge smile on my face.

Screw you, cyber bullies.

"You look happy," Dad says, standing in my doorframe. "Did you conquer your latest SAT practice test?"

I grin, "Something like that."

"Well, don't stay up too late. You want to be well rested going into the real thing. When is it?"

"A week from Saturday." In other words, well over a week from now.

"Then it's good to get on your sleep schedule now," he offers with infinitely parental wisdom.

"Yeah, okay." I smile at him.

He leans over and kisses me goodnight on the cheek. "Goodnight, princess. You're going to do great on that test."

"Thanks, Dad."

Yawning, I close my laptop and stretch my arms over my head. Then I head to the hall bathroom to brush my teeth and wash up before bed. Right before I pass the guest bedroom door, it opens.

Dante.

Every night, he says goodnight to me too.

It's our ritual. It's dangerous to do it in the hallway where the master bedroom door is in clear view, but it feels important to us. He doesn't even step out of his room. He just stands in the doorframe. It's like we're in some Victorian era romance novel where it's considered adultery to show your ankle to a man before marriage. We just stare at each other and heave our breasts with repressed longing. Somehow, it's the most romantic thing ever. Dante's eyes twinkle. I bite my lower lip. He leans forward, as if to take a step, which is tantamount to ravaging me. But he restrains himself. I resist the urge to faint. Since I'm not wearing a corset and a hoop dress, and there's no fainting couch nearby, I never actually do it. That would certainly bring Dad running with the dueling pistols in a polished wood box. He would slap Dante across the face with a leather glove before the two of them charged down to the front lawn where they would take ten paces apiece, turn and fire. That never works out well for anybody. Luckily, none of that happens. Not yet, anyway. You never know with my dad.

When I finally emerge from the bathroom, face scrubbed and teeth clean, Dante is still standing in his doorframe, stalwart as ever. Well, he's leaning casually against the doorframe looking more like a lazy surfer than an aristocrat, which is fine by me.

"Buenas noches, mi Cielo," he mutters. *Good night, my Heaven.*

"Buenas noches, mi Tierra," I sigh. *Good night, my Earth.*

Then I do go to my room and swoon.

I hug myself to sleep, knowing Dante is in the next room, likely also hugging himself to sleep.

Since he's a guy, he's probably, you know, *hugging* himself the way guys usually do in private.

Two can play at that game.

Lying on my bed, enveloped by the warm pink glow of my nightlight, I slide my fingers against my waiting wet heat and imagine Dante's magic mouth lulling me to sleep.

It works like a charm.

oOoOoOo + O+O+O+O

On Saturday afternoon, I wash Catarina's car for her. It's warm out and I need a study break. So I suds up a bucket of water with dish soap and unroll the garden hose in the driveway. Dad won't let me wash his BMW because he doesn't want me messing up the paint. He pays a fortune to have it professionally detailed. Catarina isn't so anal about these things and was grateful I offered.

While I'm sponging the roof of her Lexus, an older Honda Civic pulls up in the driveway next door. Out steps Kamiko Nishimura. Her family lives next to us. She was two years ahead of me at North Valley.

When she graduated high school, she went to SDU for pre-med. Her family wants her to become a doctor. The passenger door of her car opens and Romeo Fabiano floats out. Romeo is Kamiko's GBF. Gay Best Friend. They were inseparable in high school and graduated together. Romeo goes to SDU too. He's an art and theater double major. I've seen Romeo at Kamiko's house plenty of times, and got to know both of them pretty well.

"Hey, Romeo! What's up?" I ask tentatively. If there's one person I know who won't judge me for falling in love with my stepbrother, it's Romeo Fabiano. Not that I'm going to come out and tell him. But considering everyone else is shunning me, I could really use a friend or two right now.

"Skye! So good to see you, darling!" He walks onto the driveway. "If you're thinking about hosting a wet T-shirt contest, I'm not your audience."

"Oh, no," I laugh, looking down at my shirt, which is damp on the chest. I'm wearing my bikini top underneath, so it's no big whoop. And Romeo's gay.

Romeo has a fancy embroidered black steampunk coat that reaches nearly to his knees. The coat has a high collar that circles above his jawline. It looks very aristocratic. He also wears black skinny jeans and pointy black leather shoes. An old-school monocle dangles from one button on his coat. The outfit is similar to what I saw him wearing in high school, but this is fancier. Everyone at North Valley knew who Romeo was because you couldn't miss him walking around campus looking like a gothic vampire five days a week. He also wore the monocle back then, and the same short black faux-hawk hairstyle. But this coat looks brand new. "I love your new coat," I say. "Did you make it?"

He fans his fingers against his chest, "Me? *Make* something?" He shakes his head vigorously. "Oh no, Skye, you must have me confused with someone else. I would never do anything as *gauche* as lift a finger when I can have a servant do it for me."

"Don't lie, Romeo," I chuckle. "I saw A Midsummer Night's Dream when North Valley did it your senior year. The costumes you made for all the kids looked incredible. If it wasn't for your sewing skills, people would've worn two dollar plastic costumes from the Spirit Halloween store on stage. Your outfits brought that show to life."

Romeo smiles bashfully, "Thank you for noticing."

Kamiko also looks nice. She wears a loose fitting scoop neck sweater over a knee length dress with cute combat boots and print socks.

"Are those Adventure Time socks?" I ask.

"Yeah," she smiles. Kamiko is an Adventure Time über super fan. I've watched the cartoon at her house a few times when I was younger because it's *all* she ever watches.

"I told her to throw them out and buy socks made for adults," Romeo sneers, "but she simply refuses to grow up. I think she has Peter Pan syndrome."

Kamiko smacks Romeo on the arm. "I'll show you Peter Pan syndrome. I'm going to keep hitting you until I stunt your growth."

Both of them are short, although Romeo is a bit taller than me, but he's short for a guy.

"That's fine with me," Romeo grins. "I like to look up at my men. It makes me feel more feminine." He runs his fingers through imaginary long hair.

"You are such a bitch, Romeo," Kamiko growls.

"I know, right?" he laughs.

We're all distracted by the sound of a motorcycle. We turn to watch Dante ride up on his dusty bike and stop beside the sidewalk. He pulls off his helmet and tosses his lanky blond surfer hair.

"Who is this vision of perfection?" Romeo gasps while frantically jamming his monocle into his eye socket.

Dante's brows furrow in amusement as he climbs off his motorcycle.

"Romeo Fabiano, at your service," Romeo says, twirling one hand in the air while backing up a step and bending into a courtly bow. Then he pops up his head and winks at Dante, "And your dream come true." The wink causes the monocle to pop off Romeo's cheek. His hand flutters for it, trying to catch it as it swings. He finally manages to slap it against his chest.

Kamiko groans audibly.

Romeo titters nervously, "Don't mind the monocle. It has a mind of it's own. Unlike Kamiko." He glares at her.

She rolls her eyes and smacks his arm.

Dante is shocked into confusion and glances between me and Romeo, "Uhhh..."

"He's cool," I reassure.

Romeo straightens and leans toward Dante, gesturing with his hand to shake. He waits patiently. "Don't worry, I won't hurt you. Unless you want me too..."

Kamiko huffs, "Romeo couldn't hurt a fly even if he tried."

"You wound me, Kamiko," Romeo says, distraught. "I'm very manly."

"Wearing a monocle doesn't make you manly," she snickers.

"I'm a man of high society, dear. Muscles don't make the man. Did you fail to notice my sartorial splendor?"

"Your what?"

He tugs on one cuff of his coat, then the other, with deft precision. "My elegant finery?"

"Huh?"

"My clothes?" he sniffs petulantly.

Kamiko shakes her head. "Oh. Why didn't you just say clothes? Then *maaaybe* we could all understand you?"

I suppress a giggle.

Dante smirks.

"Heathens," Romeo dismisses. He closes his eyes, lifts his eyebrows, and says in a snooty voice, "Why say diamond when you can say pebble? Why say ruby when you can say rock? Why say dandelion when you can say garden weed?" He glances at Kamiko. "Need I continue?"

"Shut up," she barks.

"So modest," Romeo chortles.

"I think I have to agree with Romeo on this one," I say. "Dandelion is much prettier than weed."

He smiles indulgently, "Thank you, my dear Cerulean Skye."

"Cerulean?" I wrinkle my nose.

"Yes. It's an expensive shade of blue paint, one that is befitting of your priceless beauty."

Dante puts a protective arm around me. "Are you hitting on my girlfriend, *amigo*?"

Romeo tosses a dismissive hand in the air. "I'm hitting on you, *Mi Hombre Hermoso*." *My handsome man.*

Dante bursts into laughter. "Where did you learn Spanish?"

"I took it at North Valley, just like *esta bella flor*," *this beautiful flower.* Romeo nods at me.

"Romeo," I scoff, rolling my eyes. "Anyway, how is SDU treating you?"

He bites his lower lip indulgently, like he's tasting something yummy. "Fabulous, dear. Simply fabulous. You really should go. Is SDU still your first choice?"

I sigh, my shoulders slumping, "If I can get in."

"If? What do you mean if? If I recall, you were the inspiration of bookworms everywhere."

"Yeah, right," I laugh.

He grins, "Well, not by your choice. But I remember your dad being quite the taskmaster, right?"

"For sure," I groan.

Romeo looks off, musing. "You know, Gordon really is quite handsome. I've often wondered what it would be like to have him tie me up and force me to recite Shakespeare's sonnets with a whip at the ready in case I badger the pronunciation. Just the two of us, locked up in a gloomy room, with nothing but our shirtless bodies glistening—"

"Romeo!" I bark. "Eww!! So gross!"

"What?" he asks, offended. "Your dad is a handsome man. And so terribly controlling." Romeo shivers with obvious delight. "There's nothing gross about him!"

I grimace, "You are *so* wrong, Romeo!"

He pretends to toss his imaginary hair. "He's not *my* father. To me, Gordon Albright is the picture of Armani suited manhood. He can do anything he wants to me in *my* fantasies!" He practically giggles with glee.

"Oh, gross!"

"It's weird," Kamiko says. "I'm both repulsed by everything Romeo says, but at the same time, I have to agree. Your dad is hot, in a Fifty Shades of Graying At The Temples sort of way."

"You guys are seriously grossing me out." I stick out my tongue and gag.

"Are you all talking about the same Gordon Albright I know?" Dante asks.

"Are you hot for him too?" Romeo gasps intently.

Dante chuckles, "No. Just his daughter."

"She *is* a looker," Romeo smiles. "But I prefer the masculine version," he winks. "And what is your name anyway, you jewel of a man?" Romeo's eyes crawl up and down Dante's entire frame with naked desire.

"Dante. Dante Lord."

Romeo purrs, "You can be the *Lord* of my manor any time, you heartthrob."

"Hands off!" I bark but also giggle.

"Wasn't that your stepmom's married name?" Kamiko asks.

Dante and I exchange a guilty look.

"I saw that," Romeo says conspiratorially. "What are you two hiding?"

I cringe.

Dante shrugs.

Romeo's eyes widen and he gasps. "Stop the gossip presses! Are you two stepbrother and sister?"

I wasn't planning on bringing it up. But if there's one person in the world who might not judge, it's definitely Romeo. And I might just be getting a bit sick of hiding it like it's shameful, because it's not. I wrinkle my brows and nod uncertainly, not quite sure how Romeo will react.

"You harlot!" Romeo pouts. "Some girls have *all* the luck! Why couldn't *I* be the one with the sexy stepbrother?" His eyes suddenly gleam. "I can imagine all the *dirty* things he and I would do behind closed doors." He bites his lower lip. "Mmmm. *So* taboo. And here I thought there was nothing more delicious than being gay. But I never once imagined what it would be like to have a hot and sexy gay stepbrother!" He shivers and stares at Dante with open desire. "I think I'm going to swoon right here."

"If you do," Kamiko says, "make sure you change your underwear."

Dante chuckles.

"Ew," I giggle.

"Well, this is good news," Romeo smiles at me.

"Um, not really," I sigh.

"Oh?" Romeo says thoughtfully.

"It's not exactly helping my social standing at North Valley. If you can imagine."

He nods, "North Valley isn't exactly the pinnacle of progressive thinking, is it? Do people know? Are the rumors flying to and fro?"

"Yeah," I grumble.

Romeo suddenly appears shocked. "Skye, do your parents know?"

Dante and I exchange a guilty look.

"Not yet," I say fearfully.

"Ooh! Intrigue!" Romeo gasps.

I snort, "Romeo, how do you manage to make my worst nightmare sound like gossipy good fun?"

"Talent," Romeo says with finality. "Skye, listen to me." He sounds suddenly serious. "Do you two love each other?"

I exchange a look with Dante. He gazes into my eyes. His twin emerald jewels, which are definitely not rocks or pebbles, glow with warmth and affection. He takes a deep breath and sighs, "Yes."

"I do. I—I mean, me too!" I sputter. What did I almost just say? Geez! It's not like he proposed to me just now. But why does it feel like he did? I don't know. I'm not a genius. It's just a guess.

"I can tell," Romeo says sweetly. His tone then changes to completely serious. "Skye, if there's one thing I've learned from being gay, it's that true love will overcome all adversity. Gay people are heroes. When society literally hates them for loving one another, they stand proud. They get married even when it's banned in some states. They remind every last one of us that it's okay to be different, especially when it comes to who and how you love. If you two truly love each other, then follow your hearts. Don't let society tell you it's wrong." He snorts. "Especially if said society are the gossip ghouls at North Valley High."

Everyone is silent.

After a moment, Kamiko says, "Wow, Romeo. That was profound."

He smirks, "Of course it was, dearest. I'm not just a cheap gimmick."

"That's funny," Kamiko quips, "because I heard you'll give it up to any hot guy for free, as long as he's hot enough."

He waves his hand, "When it comes to hot beefcake, I'm as cheap as they come. *Come*, Kamiko. I said *come*." He moans the word.

"You definitely need to change your underwear," Kamiko winces and waves her hand at him, shooing him away.

Romeo tosses his imaginary hair once again.

I grin from ear to ear, "Wow, Romeo. I can't thank you enough for your encouragement. It means a lot. Seriously."

"'Tis nothing, Skye. Don't let others tell you who to love. You'll regret it if you do. What seems like the easy way out now will eat away at you later on. Follow your hearts. Both of you." He glances at Dante. "And, if for some reason you decide she's not worth it," he winks at me, "look me up. You can have your way with me any time you want."

Dante chuckles, "I'll keep that in mind. But you might be waiting a long time." He wraps his arm around my shoulder. "I think your advice about Skye is spot on."

I feel warmth and *amor* radiating off of Dante. I melt into his side, where I fit perfectly, like we were made for each other in some cosmic artist's studio where souls are crafted by the gods, two lovers made as one, then split apart and cast into the world of man to enjoy the adventure of reconnecting for eternity. Or something like that.

Then I remember that Dad could walk outside at any second and I reluctantly pull away.

Back to hiding my feelings from the world.

It could be worse.

oOoOoOo + O+O+O+O

"You sure are all the rage on ChatBrat today," Ashley Masters says as I pass her in the hall on the following Friday morning.

I ignore her. Too bad I didn't turn around and go the other way the moment I saw her. But she saw me see her, and there was no way I was letting her think I was backing down. That's why I hold my head high and wait until I'm at my locker to check ChatBrat.

Once again, I'm infamous.

This time it's a new photo at the top of the ChatBrat feed.

In it, me, Dad, and Catarina stand together with our heads sticking through one of those boards that has cartoons of perfect hard bodies in bathing suits and bikinis painted on the front. We had the photo taken at the Venice Beach boardwalk last summer. Usually tourists pay two dollars to stick their heads through the holes and have the guy take their picture. It was my idea to do it, and amazingly, Dad was happy to look foolish for the fun of it. We had a blast that entire day, so I posted the pic on my Facebook. One of the few family photos I put up. Yeah, it was dorky, but so what?

The only problem with this version on ChatBrat? Someone has Photoshopped Dante's head from the library meeting room photo onto the fourth cartoon body. Worse, the cartoon people painted on the board are obviously a dad, a mom, a son, and a daughter.

Guess where Dante's head is?

You got it.

The caption below the photo reads:

NEWS FLASH!! It turns out Slutbright's hookup is her BROTHER! Slap a scarlet I on her chest! Can you say incest?

I am furious.

Whoever made the photo stole it from my Facebook. I doubt it was Ashley. She's never been a Facebook friend and I limit access to my page. But considering I've got several hundred friends, many of whom are acquaintances who go to North Valley, one of them could've passed the photo on to Ashley. Or posted it themselves. Because it seems like lately the cool thing to do is trash Skye Albright on ChatBrat. Too bad there's no way to know who is posting all this crap.

I can't blame Luke, because I distinctly remember he said he told Ashley that Dante was my stepbrother. Not my actual brother. Either Ashley posted this to hurt me more, or someone else ran with whatever misinformation they had and now I have to deal with it.

This is going to make things worse.

Why can't people be more open-minded like Romeo? He was right. Gay people are heroes. Having people hate on you because of who you love is the worst thing that's ever happened to me, or probably anybody it happens to.

Not wanting to deal with people's gossipy whispering, and since

Rox, Nicole, and Kayla are still avoiding me, I spend another lunch in the library with Jason and Trevor playing Magic The Gathering. Or should I say, pretending to play, because it really isn't my thing. But I do seem to meet more friends of theirs by the day. Today it's Brian and Stuart. They play Magic head to head, but spend more time talking about geeky tech stuff that I can barely follow. One thing I catch clearly is both of them plan on working for either Google or Apple when they graduate college. Based on the way they talk, it sounds totally feasible.

Does hanging in the library with the freshman geeks make me irrelevant in the North Valley social hierarchy? I hope so, because if the ChatBrat hate flaming continues, I'd rather disappear.

Do I care? No, because I have Dante at home, and screw everybody else. They're assholes anyway.

My badass attitude doesn't stop the dirty looks I get when lunch ends and I have to traverse campus from the library to my locker. I also hear more whispery trash talking behind my back when I walk to AP English. I try to ignore it. My skin gets thicker every day. But I can't decide if the insults are rolling off my back or if I'm shoving them down and repressing them. Well, if I die my hair black and consider piercing my eyeballs or whatever, I'll seek help then.

Who knows.

For now, I'm staying strong. If worse comes to worse, I'm outta here in June and I'll never see this shit hole school or these shit hole people ever again. Even if my entire senior year turns out to be a horrid nightmare, I'm sure things will be much better at SDU.

Assuming I get in.

All I have to do is ace my SATs tomorrow, and I'll be golden.

That shouldn't be a problem.

Chapter 15

"We've got a problem," Dante says when I get home from school that afternoon.

My fantasy of coming home and falling into his loving arms is instantly incinerated. I close the front door behind me, suddenly scared. "What?"

Dante heaves a heavy sigh. His face is at war.

What the hell happened? Do I even want to know?

I'm hot from walking home from school. There's always a heatwave in the Valley every October. Since Rox still isn't driving me to or from school, I have to hoof it. It's no big deal, but I'm parched. "Hold on. I'm dying of thirst. I need a drink." I'm just delaying disaster, I can feel it. Who wants to face bedlam when you're dehydrated?

"Sure. Let me get you a drink." Dante strides ahead of me into the kitchen and pulls a clean glass out of the cupboard next to the refrigerator.

So thoughtful.

His little touch of generosity, even when things get stressful, eases my fear. With Dante by my side, how bad can *anything* really be? I bet we could get through a post-apocalyptic nightmare together. If The Walking Dead was real, Dante would be my Daryl and I would be his Carol or whoever Daryl finally ends up with. I can totally picture Dante with a big old crossbow resting on his shoulder and his shaggy blonde hair hanging in his face. The image brings a grin to mine.

Dante hands me the cold glass of water.

The sides of it are cool. I take a few swallows of the cold water and feel instantly better. I'm almost afraid to ask, but I do anyway. "What's going on, Dante?"

His jaw grinds. His eyes dance desperately. He heaves a sigh. "Your dad knows."

I gasp and cover my mouth with both hands, dropping my glass of ice water. It shatters on the kitchen floor. "Oh my god... how?"

Normally, if someone dropped a *glass* glass and it shattered on the floor, everyone would be bending down with a broom to pick up pieces and sweep things up. For an elongated moment, Dante and I simply stare at the shards of glass and spilled water. Is it symbolic? Has our pipe dream finally blown apart? Is this it? Is *this* the moment when my perfect daydream comes to an end? Because we all know this whole setup was *way* too good to last. I mean, come on: super hot surfer hottie moves into my parents house and we fall hard for each other? Oh, and it turns out we're step-siblings? Can you say: not gonna last?

"What happened?" I ask, my voice shaking.

"Your school principal called your dad. I guess there's some social network site that has the library picture online with some harsh comments? Do you know anything about that?"

"No! I just left school! Everything was normal! I have no idea what's going on!"

"Not anymore," he sighs. "My mom called to warn me. Your dad is on his way home now."

Paralyzing panic smacks me as I remember what happened the last time my dad was mad at Dante. "What do we do? If Dad finds out…" I can't even finish the sentence. If he finds out what me and Dante have been doing under his nose, this is all coming to an end. Dad really will chase Dante out of town with a lynch mob this time. They'll be shooting rifles and waving torches in the air and Dad will be the one with the hangman's noose dangling from his saddle as the gang runs Dante down. He and his motorcycle boots will be swinging from a tree by sunup. "Dad is going to freak out." Understatement.

"That's what I was thinking," Dante says with zero humor.

My mind races. The first thing I think of is packing some clothes in a backpack and jumping on the back of Dante's motorcycle so we can both ride off into the sunset together. But that's just a fantasy. I need a real solution. But every solution leads back to a confrontation with Dad. That will end badly. Period. "Let's go."

"Go where?"

"Anywhere," I say it with desperate haste. "Pack your stuff. I'll grab some clothes. But let's get out of here. Now."

A faint smile drifts across his face. "*En serio?*" Seriously?

"*En serio.*" I step toward the stairs but stop myself. I grab a dustpan and whisk broom from under the sink. I sweep up the broken glass. I'm picking up the pieces. Yes, it's symbolic. Dante grabs paper towels and blots up the water.

"How long will it take you to pack?" I ask.

"Me? Five minutes."

I smirk, "You're such a wanderer."

"And?" He grins dimples.

I shake my head and snort, "Me too." I never was before, but you gotta start sometime. I rush upstairs and jump into jeans and throw my arms into a hoodie. I dump my books out of my knapsack onto my bedroom floor. Won't be needing those. I throw some clean panties, shirts, socks, and a tooth brush into my school knapsack. I unplug my cell phone charger by my desk and dump it into the bag. Then I dash into the guest bedroom, holding my knapsack. Dante is already cinching his backpack shut. "Are you packed?" I marvel.

"Yeah."

"Um, do I need a warm jacket for the motorcycle?"

He looks me over. "Yeah. Stuff your hoodie in the knapsack and wear your coat on the bike. Do you have a leather jacket?"

"No," I say, disappointed.

He grins, "We'll have to get you one."

Those words thrill my heart. We are *doing* this. O.M.Jesus. I run back to my room and grab a ski jacket and stuff the hoodie in the knapsack. I stuff my purse into the knapsack. I can't think of what else to bring.

"You ready?" Dante asks, leaning casually against my doorframe. Damn, he looks hot in his leather jacket and jeans and boots and beard stubble.

"Tampons!" I'm gonna need them sooner or later. Who knows how long we'll be gone? I run into the bathroom and grab a bunch from under the sink. I also grab a hair brush from the drawer and some hair ties. I look at my makeup: eyeliner pencils, mascara, lipstick tubes, foundation, blush, blah, blah, blah. I turn my back on it and bump into Dante on my way out the bathroom.

He chuckles.

I look into his eyes. They glint a precious shade of green. A jovial flicker dances across them as they swallow my heart.

"We're doing this?" I ask.

"Yeah."

"Road trip!" I giggle.

"Let's go," he smiles, offering his hand.

I take it, feeling its warmth and strength. I sigh pleasantly, on the verge of swooning. But we need to go! Before dad gets here.

"Shit," he huffs.

"What?!" More panic.

"You need a helmet. We're not gonna get far without one. Some cop will pull us over."

I run back to my bedroom and pop open my laptop. I do a quick search for motorcycle dealerships. "There's a Honda dealership near the freeway. They'll have helmets, right?"

He nods proudly, "Yup."

I slap my laptop closed. "Let's go!"

We trot down the stairs and he says, "There's no room for you on the seat if I strap my pack on it. Can you wear my pack and I'll wear yours?" He hands it to me at the bottom of the stairs.

I shrug mine off, he takes it, and helps me into his. "It's kind of heavy. But I'll manage."

He slips his arms through the straps of mine.

We both look like idiots. He because he's wearing a girl's backpack that's way too small for him. Me because his pack makes my ski jacket puff out around the straps. "Remember that crazy puffy snowsuit that Randy wore in that movie A Christmas Story?"

"Who?"

"You know, Ralphie's little brother Randy? He had that burgundy snowsuit and he couldn't put his arms down once he got it on?"

"Sorry," he smiles. "I missed that one."

"Well, I can barely put my arms down. I feel like Randy."

"Oh. Was Randy cute in his puffy snowsuit?"

"Yeah, I guess."

He kisses my forehead, "You are too. We should go."

We walk out the front door and I'm way too hot in this jacket. Dante sweeps me off my feet and sets me on the back of the motorcycle. Then he does this martial arts looking move with his leg to put it over the front seat without kicking me in the arm. He lowers his helmet onto his head and adjusts the straps. Then he starts the engine and it vibrates between my legs. It's not as big of a turn on as I would've imagined. Then again, we're on the run. And while it seems sexy, the reality of it is nerve-wracking.

"Put your arms around me," he commands.

"Gladly." I circle his waist with my arms and squeeze up against him. "I could get used to this."

"Hold on tight. You don't have a helmet, so I don't want you flying off. Head injuries aren't pretty."

"Yeah," I snort. You'd think we would've worked this out already, but do you think my dad would've liked the idea of me getting a helmet so Dante could ride me around town on the back of his motorcycle? Exactly. Not!

I glance toward the end of our cul-de-sac. My dad's fancy 760Li Beemer is turning the corner.

"Oh shit!"

"I see him," Dante growls. "Hold on."

The engine revs and I'm thrown backward by the force of the acceleration. But my arms are wrapped tightly around Dante, and I manage to hold on, just barely. My chest seizes instantly with fear and adrenalin. I have a moment to wonder if Dad has seen us and what he might be thinking. Is he going to suddenly swerve and lay down black stripes of rubber, creating a road blockade like a cop? And then Dante reacts a second too late and the back wheel of the motorcycle slides out from beneath us and I tumble across the cement at thirty miles an hour, with no helmet and nothing but a flimsy ski jacket to protect me, only to slam into the side of Dad's car? Can you say, 'Coma'?

Luckily, none of that happens.

But the front wheel of the bike lifts off the ground as we jet past Dad.

Dad slams on the brakes of the BMW and slides to a stop in a straight line.

We rocket down the street and Dante leans the bike over as we turn the corner. I'm not sure if I'm supposed to lean or not, so I just squeeze Dante as hard as I can and clamp my eyes shut. I'm scared out of my mind.

For the next several minutes, we weave our way through the sunny suburban streets near my family home, cutting corners, running stop signs, breaking the speed limit and just about every other driving law there is.

As we approach our first stop light, Dante aims the motorcycle at the red taillights at the back end of two lines of idling cars waiting for the light to turn.

"What are you doing!" I scream. "There's totally not enough room for us between those cars!"

"I've got this," Dante grunts.

"Holy shit!" I yell, squeezing my eyes shut. I can't watch.

The motorcycle missiles between the two columns of cars. I know, because I hear them whipping by.

Fup! Fup! Fup! Fup!

I peek from one eye and see nothing but fenders and bumpers blurring by, only inches away from my knees.

He brakes hard and we suddenly slow to a stop at the front of the line of cars.

I'm breathing hard like I just ran a sprint. "Oh my god, Dante! That was way too close! I don't want to die today!" I half laugh, but mostly mean it.

He flips his visor up and turns his head to the side. "Relax, *Cielo*. I've got you. I'll keep you safe."

"You better! If you get me killed, I'm gonna kill you!" I jerk my wrists, which are locked together around his waist, into his hard stomach once. "No dying today! For either of us!"

He chuckles, "Don't worry, *mi amor*. It's not gonna happen. Which way to the bike shop?"

"Turn left here. Oh, um, you're not in the left turn lane." There's a lane between us and the left turn lane.

"I'll take care of it."

Tires screech behind us.

I twist in my seat and see Dad's BMW grind to a stop at the back of the row of cars. "Shit! It's my dad!"

"I see him. He's not gonna catch us from way back there."

The door of the BMW opens and Dad jumps out. He sprints straight up between the cars behind us.

"Dante! He's running after us!"

Dante glances at his side mirror on the handlebars. "Hold on tight. This just got real." He revs the engine loudly and it growls angrily between our legs.

The intersection we're at is a big one. Three lanes of cross traffic in front of us in both directions. The road we're on is two lanes each way plus a left turn lane in the middle. Cars whip by left and right at 40 mph, kicking up wind. There's no place for us to go. Is Dante going to shoot through traffic? Like in that old video game Frogger? I so don't want to go splat and get turned into a frog pancake!

"Dante, don't!!" I squeal.

"Hold on! The lights going to change in two seconds!" he shouts.

The engine barks over and over as he gooses the throttle.

I twist back and Dad is four steps away. He's about to grab me!!

"Now!!" Dante shouts.

REEEEEENNNNNG!! the motorcycle screams.

We surge forward.

The light has not yet turned green.

"Dante!!" I screech.

Coming like a freight train, an SUV barrels through the intersection on the far side of the intersection, blasting from right to left. It's going to Frogger the shit out of us!!!

"Dante!" I scream again, holding on for dear life.

The bike tips and swings left. We're going to spill and slide right under the wheels of the SUV!

Hard acceleration as we veer left, leaning so far over my left knee is inches from the asphalt.

"Shiiiiiiiiiiitttt!!!" I wail.

The motorcycle tires are clamped to the pavement. The bike starts to come up slowly. The SUV is two feet to the right. I could reach out and touch it, but my arms are locked in a stony death grip around Dante's waist. A second later, the SUV disappears behind us as Dante cycles through gears, the engine growling and shrilling in quick succession. We must be going at least 90 miles an hour. We blast past cars like they're standing still. The cars parked on the street to my right are a blur. The wind whips against them:

—*fip fip fip fip fip fip fip fip*—

Up ahead, two cars drive neck and neck, blocking the road. We barrel toward them. Dante doesn't slow down. He cuts right up the middle of them. *Wiiiiiiing!* The sound of the engine slaps off the two cars as we thread the needle between them.

I can't believe I'm not wearing a helmet. Just my ski jacket.

Insanity.

oOoOoOo + O+O+O+O

Several blocks later, we slow to a mere 40 mph. "Which way?!" Dante shouts.

"The Honda dealership should be up ahead on the right, just past the hot tub dealership!"

Dante slows when he sees it. You can't miss it. There's like ten hot tubs in front of the store, all tilted up facing the street. We turn into the Honda parking lot two stores past it. Tons of ATVs and dirt bikes with colorful fenders are parked out front in rows.

"Let's make this quick," Dante says, pulling me inside the store, still wearing his helmet.

The showroom is filled with higher end street bikes parked in rows. Dante pulls me toward a wall of helmets. A salesman walks up. He's tall and lanky and has short blond hair. "You guys look like you need a helmet."

"Yeah," I smile.

"I saw you ride in just now. My name's Tim," He holds out his hand to shake it.

"We're kind of in a hurry," I smile.

Dante is scanning the wall. "This one's good." He pulls down one with slick pink and black graphics.

"Do you know what size you are?" Tim asks me.

"I have no idea."

"This one's an extra small," he says. "I think you need a medium.

He reaches up and pulls down a similarly styled helmet. "Try it on."

I slide it over my head and it's snug, but not too tight. "It fits?" My hair hangs out the back.

Dante checks it, looking me over. He bends down and adjusts the chin straps. "Yeah, it's good. How much?"

"Ninety," Tim says.

"Jacket," Dante says, pulling me toward a rack of leather jackets with the helmet still on.

"I'm a small," I say, following Dante around the circular rack toward the smalls. I guess head and body sizes don't always match. "Can I take the helmet off?"

"Leave it on," Dante grunts as he flips through jackets. "Do you want classic or modern?"

"How about cheap? I don't have much cash in my account."

"I'll cover it." He holds up a black jacket with pink cursive script across the chest that says Vixen below a row of pink studs across the shoulders. "Goes with the helmet. I like the modern look on you." He winks. "You're a twenty-first century woman. None of that dated rebel biker stuff for you."

"But I wanna be a biker rebel," I pout.

"Next you're gonna ask for one of the chrome German helmets with a spike on top, right?"

I wrinkle my nose, "Maybe not that. But how about the kind Marlon Brando wore in The Wild One?"

"Haven't seen it. Hold this." He jams the Vixen jacket at me and I take it while he flips through the rest of the smalls. "I don't see any rebel jackets."

"Fine," I grin. "How much is this one?" I hold up the jacket on the hanger, looking for a tag.

"I think this one's three hundred," Tim says.

I wince. "That's too much."

Dante kisses my cheek. "You're worth a million times that much. I'll pay for it. Put it on."

I switch my ski jacket with the pink on black Vixen jacket and stuff the ski jacket in my knapsack, which is on Dante's back. The pack now bulges like a balloon.

"Let's go," Dante says. He grabs pink and black gloves on the way to the counter with the register and Tim rings everything up. I have to lean over the counter so he can point the laser scanner at the tag hanging from the neck of the helmet.

Tim totals everything and smiles, "$479.59."

I wince. That's not a price to smile about.

"Are you guys in a hurry?" Tim asks.

"Yes," Dante spits, pulling out his wallet. He hands Tim a Visa card.

"Dante," I sigh and smile. "This is way too expensive."

"I'm buying it," he says with finality. "Put the gloves on." He jams the receipt from Tim into his front pocket. He nods at me admiringly, "Sexy hot biker chick."

"Damn right!"

"Let's go." He pulls me toward the door.

"Oh shit!" I gasp and stop.

"What?"

All I can do is point. Outside the double glass doors, Dad is striding toward us. He doesn't seem to have seen us.

"Go!" Dante grunts.

We push out the right side door as Dad pushes through the left. With our jackets and helmets on, I don't think he recognizes us. Seven strides later, we're at Dante's bike.

"Hey!" Dad shouts behind us.

Dante vaults onto the motorcycle like a puma.

"Stop!" Dad roars. "That's my daughter!"

I try to climb on behind him, but I'm too short, as usual. I only manage to get my knee over. "My leg! I can't get it over the seat!"

Dante reaches down and hooks my thigh with his right arm, hoisting me powerfully over the seat.

"Crap!" I flail my arms as I spill over the far side of the seat. I grab his waist at the last second and stop myself from tumbling onto the pavement.

The motorcycle revs.

Luckily for us, there's a driving lane that circles all the parked ATVs and dirt bikes. We don't have to turn around.

Dad runs up behind us in slacks and his button down shirt, his loafers slapping the ground. "Give my daughter back, goddamnit!"

"STOP!!!" he shouts.

"Go!" I scream.

I swear I feel a breeze when Dad grabs for me. But he's too late. The motorcycle lurches forward.

Seconds later, we pull into traffic and race to the freeway, which is only blocks away. The on-ramp is packed with two more lines of cars waiting at the metering lights. The paved shoulder to the right is wide open, so Dante takes that.

With rush hour traffic already clogging every lane on the 101, Dante slows as we approach the slow moving cars. I glance back and Dad is driving right down the shoulder at the metering lights like a madman.

"He's coming!" I shout.

Dante accelerates and speeds along the shoulder until it shrinks to nothing. Then he brakes and cuts to the left, sliding through a gap between a minivan and a big delivery truck. Without slowing, he slices between lanes, putting more and more distance between us and Dad.

I glance back constantly while holding on tight. It's hard to keep a good grip on Dante with my ballooned knapsack on his back pressing into my face, but I manage. A moment later, Dad screeches to a stop where the shoulder ends, blocked by the guardrail where the freeway passes over a surface street below. Horns honk as Dad tries to jam his way into the flow of traffic, but no one lets him in.

It doesn't take long to lose Dad.

That's the last we see of him as we disappear into the setting sun.

Like I'd always thought, Dante really does ride off into the sunset. But it's with me on the back of his steel horse.

Cue up Bon Jovi's timeless hit.

Richie Sambora sings the refrain in his gravelly voice, *"Waaaanted!" Dead or Alive…*

oOoOoOo + O+O+O+O

"Mmmm, that's good Al Pastor," Dante says before taking another bite of the foil wrapped pork burrito.

We stand on the end of the Santa Monica pier watching the sun drift toward the horizon. "Yeah," I mumble, munching on mine. I drizzle salsa from the little plastic cup onto the end of my bitten burrito and take another bite, enjoying the heat of the jalapeños and the tang of the Al Pastor pork.

Our motorcycle helmets sit on top of our backpacks, which lean against the weathered wood railing of the pier. Waves lap the posts twenty feet below. Dozens of men and boys dangle fishing rods over the railing, many of them trying to catch a free dinner. Some have buckets beside them already half full of fish.

"Have you ever fished for your dinner?" I ask Dante.

"Plenty of times. You can't live in Baja and not eat fresh caught fish. If I had a rod I'd catch something and grill it up for you."

"We need to get you a fishing rod," I grin.

"Maybe we can rent one from one of these dudes."

"Tomorrow," I smile. "This burrito is plenty for tonight."

"You got it," he grins, peeling back aluminum foil from his burrito. He chomps off more meat and tortilla. "So good."

"What do we do now?"

"Anything you want, *mi Cielo*."

"Anything?"

"The world is our oyster."

This is the most romantic thing that has ever happened to me. Me and Dante against the world. Heaven on Earth.

Cielo en la Tierra.

Not once has Dante mentioned our parents or school or anything. Yes, there are probably 100 voicemails on my phone from Dad, but I turned it off after 75. I don't need him yelling at me like I'm a child or accusing Dante of being a bad influence or a criminal or whatever the hell else he might say. Since I'm 18, I could technically ditch my entire life. Leave behind everything and go wherever the wind blows us. I mean, why stay? Dad hates me. Rox hates me. Everyone at school hates me. Who needs all that stupid hateful gossipy bullshit back at North Valley? Who needs college? Who needs tests and homework and studying for the— "Oh shit!"

"What?"

"I'm supposed to take the SAT tomorrow!"

He snorts, "Fuck the SAT." He means it.

My eyes search his. They flicker with hope and promise and dreams fulfilled. I grab his free hand and ask, "Are we doing this?"

"Doing what?"

"I don't know, running away?"

"I meant what I said. Whatever you want, *mi Amor*. I will take you anywhere you want to go on the entire planet."

"Santa Barbara!"

He chuckles. "It's not exactly what I'd call exotic, but I hear they have great beaches."

oOoOoOo + O+O+O+O

We worm our way through traffic on the 101 north as the sun sinks into the Pacific Ocean. Traffic is horrendous during rush hour. But we're not in a hurry, so that's okay. The funny thing about having no set plans is that you're never in a hurry. Why do people live stop-and-go lives again? It doesn't make any sense to me.

Traffic starts to thin by the time we pass Camarillo and head toward Oxnard. Our motorcycle cruises along at a sedate 45 mph.

Suddenly the bike slows for no reason and we're pulling over onto the shoulder. When we stop, I lean around Dante, who has his boots on the ground, and holler over the rushing wind of passing traffic, "Is something wrong with the motorcycle?!" I hope we didn't run out of gas. Not that I care. A walk to the nearest gas station might be fun.

He glances back and shouts, "Cop!" He hooks a thumb behind us.

A California Highway Patrol car stops twenty feet behind us, its reds and blues flashing. I didn't realize he was back there. He never used his siren.

"Should I stay on the motorcycle?" I ask.

"You can climb off. Just don't run away or you might get tazed."

I smack his back. "I'm not going anywhere without you, *mi Tierrai*"

He peels his helmet off and sets it on the seat, grinning at me.

Geez, even getting pulled over by the CHP is romantic when it's with Dante. As always, he looks totally hot.

I unstrap my helmet and set it on the seat beside his. They make a cute couple. The helmets, I mean. Grin.

The CHP officer turns out to be a tall woman with broad shoulders. Mirrored sunglasses cover her eyes and her hair is up in a businessy bun. A super fat gun belt circles her waist. Never a good look. For whatever reason, I stare at the gigantic gun in her holster.

"What's the problem, officer?" Dante asks.

"Good afternoon. Can I see both your licenses and registration?" she asks.

"Sure," I say. "Um, mine is in my backpack. I mean his backpack," I smile anxiously. "Is it okay for me to get it?" I don't want to scare her by doing something weird.

She glances between us for a moment, assessing us. Now she's probably wondering if I'm high on crystal meth. I never should've said anything.

Dante hands her his passport, a Mexican driver's license, and a folded slip of paper, which I'm guessing is the registration. "Here's mine," he says casually.

The officer takes both. "Thank you, sir. Please remove your backpack so your friend can get her license."

"Sure," Dante shrugs, taking off the backpack.

The officer watches me closely as I unzip it. My ski jacket balloons out and I giggle as I drape it over the seat of the motorcycle. "It's in my purse." I pull out my wallet and hand her my license. "Here you go," I smile. "Were we speeding or something? I swear we were only going 45." Cops always make me feel like I have to prove I'm not a guilty criminal. They probably do that to everybody, but Dante seems super relaxed.

"I need to run these," the officer says blandly. "Hang tight." She walks back to her car and sits down behind the wheel. She types away on the laptop mounted off to the side.

"Why did she stop us?" I ask Dante.

"Who knows."

"Why are you always so calm?"

"Because I deal with stuff as it comes. No need to worry about what isn't happening."

"Wow, that's really smart."

He winks at me.

Yeah, I made the right choice this afternoon. This is way better than enduring a tirade from Dad.

It takes the CHP officer almost twenty minutes to finish up in her car. She talks to someone on the radio a bunch of times. About what, I have no idea. But it's making me increasingly nervous.

"This is taking forever," I sigh as a thousand more cars pass us by. Every time a big SUV or 18-wheeler passes by, a huge buffet of wind slaps into us.

The officer steps out of her car and strolls toward us. "Are you Skye Albright?" She's all business behind her mirrored shades.

"Yeah?"

"Can I speak to you over here for a moment?" She motions toward her car. "Alone?"

"Um, you're not arresting me, are you?"

"No."

I glance at Dante.

His eyes narrow. He's obviously irritated. "I'm the guy driving the bike. What do you want?"

"I just need to ask her a few questions, sir," the officer warns. "Please remain with your vehicle while I speak with her."

"And you're not arresting her?" Dante demands.

The officer's lips thin. "No, but I will arrest you if you don't let me do my job."

Now I'm scared. "Calm down, Dante. It's okay." I *hope* it's okay. I follow the woman to her car. We stop next to the front bumper.

"Ma'am, are you aware that your father filed a missing persons report on you about an hour ago?"

Fury pops in my chest like a thousand firecrackers. "What?! No. I had no idea." I stamp my foot. "I mean, I'm not surprised, but no, I didn't know."

"Is this man holding you against your will? Did he force you to go with him?"

"Whaaaaat?! No! Is that what my dad said?"

"I don't know exactly what he said, ma'am. I wasn't there when he filed the report. I only know that you are currently classified as missing, and an APB was put out for your friend's motorcycle."

"Oh." I glance at Dante.

He stands with fingers splayed on cocked hips, looking highly irritated.

"Dante! It's okay!" I holler. "Hold on a second, all right?"

He smirks and nods before smearing his hand across his mouth. "Take your time," he yells over traffic.

I say to the officer, "I thought if someone went missing, the police waited 24 hours before starting a search. To, you know, make sure they're actually missing. I just left like two hours ago."

"That's a myth, ma'am. If you have a legitimate reason to believe that a family member or loved one has gone missing, you should contact law enforcement immediately. The sooner we're aware that someone has gone missing, the better the chance that we'll find them."

"Oh. So… what happens now?"

"I ask a few more questions."

"Okay."

"Did your friend take you under duress?"

"No."

"Are you here of your own free will?"

"Yes."

She nods. "Since you're over 18, and as long as your actions are voluntary—"

"Yeah, totally," I cut in.

"Then you're free to go. If that's what you want. Or I can take you to the station in the cruiser. Your father can pick you up there. The choice is yours."

I picture myself sitting at some Highway Patrol office, waiting for my dad to show up and take me home. Can you imagine the car ride home? Not gonna happen!! "What are you going to tell my dad?"

"Only what you want me to tell him."

"Seriously?"

"Yes, ma'am. Should I let him know you're safe?"

"Yeah," I sigh, feeling kind of jerky about everything.

"Anything else? Your whereabouts? Your destination? Your expected return?"

When she lays it out like that, I'm suddenly thinking about this completely differently. It was romantic when it was me and Dante and the wind in our hair, I mean motorcycle helmets. But there's other people involved. What about Catarina? I'm sure she's freaking out.

Who knows what kind of argument she and Dad are having. Based on what happened last time, it can't be good. My stomach sours thinking about it. I'm causing all of this. Correction: I went and made things worse. It was Dad's attitude toward Dante that lit the fuse of this drama bomb in the first place. Which takes me right back to why we bolted in the first place.

"Well?" the officer prompts.

"Um…" For sure I'm not going home tonight, I feel like I need to send Dad a message. I wonder what he'll do when the cops tell him I don't want to be found? Will he be mad? Probably. He'll probably shout at the cops and demand to know where I am. An image of his rageful face flashes in my mind. Screw him. My brows knit with determination. "Just tell him I'm fine and I'll be home when I'm home." I fold my arms across my chest for emphasis.

The officer doesn't seem to react. I doubt she'll add my folded arms to her official report. Oh well.

"Anything else?" she asks.

"No," I sigh. "Thanks."

"Then you two are free to go. Here's your IDs and the registration."

"Thanks." I notice Dante's license is from Baja. It says *Gobierno del Estado de Baja California* and *Licencia de Conducir* at the top. Dante's picture is on it, and it does indeed say Dante Lord. Not that I was wondering who he was or anything.

"Drive safe," she smiles faintly before getting back in her car. She doesn't leave right away.

I think she's watching us. I walk up to Dante and explain everything.

"Makes sense," he says casually. "He loves you."

"Yeah," I frown.

"Do you wanna go home?"

"What? And deal with Dad's inevitable blowout?" I shake my head. "There's no way I'm subjecting myself to that tonight. Maybe next year. Let's go to Santa Barbara, okay?"

He swings his arms toward the motorcycle and bows, "Your steed awaits, fair lady."

oOoOoOo + O+O+O+O

It's almost 11:00pm.

We're strolling along State Street in downtown Santa Barbara, people watching and window shopping. Orange streetlights cut the

of our stuff while the rangers watch.

We trudge through the cold sand to the sidewalk that runs along the beach.

"Where to now?" I sigh.

"Let's get a hotel room," he offers.

"They're way too expensive, Dante. Can we even get a room this late anyway?"

"If they're any left."

I sigh again and look around. We're in a random suburban Santa Barbara neighborhood. The houses this close to the beach are really nice. Way better than mine. But the windows are dark and the doors are closed and there's no way we're crashing in any of these mansions. Defeated, I mutter, "Let's go home."

He arches his eyebrows compassionately. "Are you sure, *Cielo*? We can find a hotel somewhere."

"I have the SAT tomorrow. I have a warm bed waiting at home for free. *You* have a warm bed too."

"Those beds come at a price, *Cielo*."

"You mean my dad?"

He nods.

"Maybe he'll be glad I came home."

"What happens after he knows you're safe? What does he do tomorrow or the next day? What about the photo? What about us? What's your dad gonna do about us?" He shakes his head and sighs. "I can protect you out here, *Cielo*. I can't protect you in your dad's house. He made that his job a long time ago and takes it very seriously. I'll just be in the way."

I take in his words and mull them over. "What if we don't go home?" I ask with a shiver of trepidation.

"I have to warn you. Life out here isn't always easy. It's not like living at home with your parents. Believe me. I've done it enough to know." There is hidden weight to what he says. Dante hasn't told me anything about what happened after he stopped living with Catarina way back when. I've asked, but he doesn't want to talk about it. It's obviously a painful topic for him.

"Stop scaring me," I chuckle nervously.

"I'm not scaring you. But this is the real world. If you want a warm soft bed and hot running water, you have to pay for it. If you don't have money, you have to rough it." He arches an eyebrow.

I don't have an answer for him.

"If we rough it," he offers, "we'll be fine. But it won't be *Casa de Albright*."

I'm so tired and wired and cold that my body literally jitters. "I can't take any more of this tonight, Dante. Let's go home."

Chapter 16

On the way home, I have the ski jacket on over the leather jacket. It's freezing. Unlike in a car, where you can sleep if you're not driving, the back of a motorcycle is a wide-awake deal. I don't want to fall off and go bouncing down the road at 75 mph. I do feel relief when we exit the 101 and drive down the familiar suburban streets of the Valley toward home. When we turn onto my cul-de-sac, I finally relax. I climb off the motorcycle on weary legs. It feels like we just rode for a thousand miles instead of a hundred.

The outside of the house is dark. I hope coming home wasn't a mistake. Hopefully Dad is asleep and won't bother us. My plan is to sneak into my bed and crash like a log under the warm blankets. All I can think about is sleep.

Sleep, sleep, sleep.

Me and Mr. Sandman are gonna be besties tonight.

Dante and I creep quietly up to the front door. I imagine Dad armed the alarm. I'll have to disarm it as soon as I open the door. At least I know the code by heart and can punch it in in the dark. I pull out my house keys and aim them at the deadbolt.

The porch lights pop on.

The front door whips open.

Dad stares at me. He's still dressed in his button down shirt and slacks. He never got ready for bed. "Skye," he chokes out and steps over the threshold, throwing his arms around me in a big hug. "Are you okay?"

"Yeah," I groan. My arms are at my sides, so I can't really push him away, but I do hunch my shoulders forward to let him know I'm not in a hugging mood. This was not what I was hoping for. I guess sneaking into bed is no longer an option.

Catarina trots up behind Dad, belting a bathrobe around her waist. "Oh, thank god. We were so worried about you two." She slides past me and Dad and hugs Dante.

"We're fine," Dante reassures.

"Where were you?" Dad asks.

"Can we talk about this later?" I sigh petulantly.

Catarina hugs me next. "You're so cold! Let me make you some hot tea. Come inside."

We end up in the kitchen, sitting around the granite island. Dante leans against a wall with his hands behind his back. I relay the day's events to Dad and Catarina. I start with what happened after we left the Honda dealership, namely burritos on the Santa Monica Pier and the sedate drive north. I make it sound like it was just a regular evening out. I skip the part about the Highway Patrol pulling us over and the Park Rangers kicking us off the beach. Catarina chuckles with amusement a bunch of times, but Dad does not.

Dad doesn't look at Dante once.

Dad doesn't say anything to Dante.

Dad pretends Dante doesn't exist.

Also, Dad never mentions the missing persons report. I don't want to know how he reacted when the cops told him I didn't want to be found. I'd like to sweep that bit under the rug.

When I finish the story, my cup of hot tea is empty. I feel warm and sleepy. "I'm super tired, you guys," I yawn. "I really need to get to bed." Mainly I want to get away from Dad. I know he's a ticking time bomb. His Mr. Mellow act isn't fooling me.

Dad's eyes pop, "Damn it, that's right! You have the SAT tomorrow! I can't believe I almost forgot."

Too bad he didn't.

He glances at his expensive wristwatch. "It's almost three in the morning. What time is the test?"

"I have to be there by 7:45."

"Oh, Jesus," Dad blurts. "You're not going to get much sleep."

Dad's theatrics turn my stomach. I grimace, "All the more reason for me to go to bed now."

Dad nods, "You're right. Let's get you to bed."

I roll my eyes, "I think I can manage that on my own." I slide off the barstool. Despite the fact that Dad is hovering right in front of me, my first instinct is to take Dante by the hand and lead him upstairs. I turn to Dante and smile sweetly, "Are you going to bed, Dante?" It's like I'm asking him to come to bed right in front of our parents.

He still stands in the shadows, separate from the family. "Sure," he mutters.

"Dante," Dad says, "I'd like to talk to you for a minute."

The room goes silent.

Catarina's face tenses.

I watch Dad carefully. I can see him hiding his anger. "No, Dad," I growl. "You can talk to him tomorrow. Afternoon."

Dad's brow darkens, "You don't tell me what to do, young lady."

And like that, the facade of our friendly late night tea splits apart. Bye-bye, Mr. Mellow. Here comes Mr. Hell No. I won't stand for it. I jam my hands on my hips. "Oh yeah? How about I skip the SAT tomorrow?"

"Then you can take the next one in November," he fires back.

"The registration deadline is already past," I say victoriously.

"Then you'll take the one in December." Dad always has another ace up his sleeve.

So do I. "I'll skip that one too," I challenge.

"Don't play games with me, young lady. I won't have you throw away your future because of..." he glares at Dante, "...him." Dad says the word like it's poison.

"*Him*?" Catarina barks. "*Him* is my son, Gordon."

Everyone stares at Dad.

The room bristles with restrained rage.

Someone is going to explode.

Dante's eyes are locked on my dad. He no longer waits in the shadows leaning against the wall. He's on the balls of his feet, ready to react in a split second.

Dad pivots toward Dante. "I saw the photo, Dante," he growls. "Are you sleeping with my daughter?"

Dante stares at Dad from under his own feral brow. He doesn't answer.

"I'm 18, Dad," I scoff. "I can sleep with whoever I want to."

"Not in my house you can't," he jabs.

"Fine!" I shout. "Then I won't sleep here and screw the stupid SAT!"

Dad turns on Dante and shouts at the top of his lungs, "I WANT YOU OUT OF MY HOUSE RIGHT NOW!!" He shoots a stiff finger toward the front door.

"No, Gordon!!" Catarina yells. "You can't kick my son out of this house!"

Dad yells in Dante's face. "YES I CAN!! GET OUT, DANTE! OR I WILL CALL THE POLICE! DON'T THINK I WON'T!"

Dante sighs heavily, shifting from foot to foot, shaking his arms loosely at his sides like he's ready to throw a punch or block one if necessary.

Catarina grabs Dad's arm and hisses, "Gordon, stop this! You're acting crazy!" She takes a deep breath. "Calm down. We can talk about this tomorrow. After Skye takes her SAT."

Dad rips his arm from her hand and grumbles, "We're dealing with this now. I've had enough of your rebel son. He's turning my daughter into a loser, just like huh—" he stops himself short.

"Just like who, Gordon?" Catarina drills with icy calm. "Like *him*? Like my son? Is that what you were going to say, Gordon? Is it?"

"No, I wasn't—" Dad stops himself and his eyes dart around at the three of us. He reeks of guilt.

Just like her…

I flash back:

"Fuck you, Gordon! Fuck you!" my mom shouts at Dad, throwing another glass, aiming for his head. It shatters against the wall, spraying shards in every direction.

He ducks this one, but the last one cut blood. He shouts back, "You're a loser, Crystal! A low-class loser! Get out of my house and don't come back! Don't ever come back!"

I shivered then and I shiver now. I wrap my arms around myself, but it doesn't stop the shivering. The chill in my heart has never thawed.

Catarina glares at Dad and seethes in a low and dangerous voice, "God damn you, Gordon. I won't have you—"

"Fine!" He throws his arms up in the air. "You win! What do I know? I'm just her father!" He grabs his car keys from the console table next to the laundry room door.

"Where are you going?" Catarina demands.

"Out."

"Gordon…" she calls apprehensively. "We can talk this out…"

Dad stops in the laundry room with his fist around the garage doorknob. He glares at her, "No, Catarina, we can't. I can tell when I'm not wanted in my own god damn house." He whips open the door leading into the garage then slams it behind him. The walls vibrate as the garage door opens. A moment later, the BMW engine rumbles to life. It fades as the car backs out of the garage and drives off.

Catarina looks at me with sad eyes. "I'm so sorry, Skye, I…"

oOoOoOo + O+O+O+O

The pink cocoon of my room is not enough to put me to sleep.

Dad never came home.

To my surprise, it's making me anxious. Catarina tried calling him, but he never answered.

It's now 4:45am and I still haven't slept.

I whip the covers back and pad toward my door.

The hallway is somehow more quiet than usual. It feels lonely. I walk up to the guest bedroom door and hold up my knuckles. Instead of knocking, I try the doorknob, twisting it silently. It's open.

Dante lies on his side, his back facing the door, asleep.

I tiptoe across the carpet and climb into bed. I spoon up against his back and circle my arm around his chest.

He turns to face me and whispers, "*Mi Cielo.*" He kisses me sleepily and envelopes me in his warmth and scent.

I fall asleep instantly.

oOoOoOo + O+O+O+O

"Skye! It's 7:20! Wake up!" Catarina whispers frantically. "You're going to be late for the SAT!"

My eyes crack open creakily and I sit up in bed, disoriented. I'm in the guest bedroom. With Dante. I blink away sleep.

"Get moving," Catarina insists, her face harried.

My adrenalin kicks in. "I need to shower!"

"There's no time. Get dressed and grab a yogurt. I'll drive you."

For a moment, all I can think about is the fact that Catarina hasn't said a single thing about the fact I'm sleeping in bed with Dante. In case you still haven't noticed, Catarina rocks the awesome sauce by the gallon.

"What are you waiting for?" she demands. "Move it, Skye!"

"Yeah, okay." I jump out of bed. My head is foggy and I'm super groggy.

Dante stands up, "I'll come with you."

I glance at Catarina, "Is Dad home?"

She lowers her eyes and shakes her head.

Oh. That's not good.

"I'll worry about your father," Catarina encourages. "You worry about the SAT."

Ten minutes later, the three of us are in Catarina's Lexus. I shovel raspberry yogurt into my mouth while Catarina drives us to the test center. It's at Herbert Hoover High School in Glendale, not North Valley. She drops me off in the parking lot out front.

I jump out of the car.

"Take these," Catarina calls, leaning over the center console, holding out two energy bars.

"Thanks."

Dante hops out and gives me a big hug. He kisses me on the lips briefly. "Remember, stay relaxed. Breath in and out on a five count if you get nervous. If that doesn't do it, sit up straight and wiggle your arms. You've got this, *mi Cielo*."

Him believing in me makes it twice as easy for me to believe in me. I feel warm all over. "I've got this, *mi Tierra*," I grin.

I dash up the front steps with my calculator, number 2 pencils, admission ticket, and snacks in hand. A bunch of printer paper signs taped to various columns and walls lead the way. The signs read <u>SAT</u> and have pointing arrows. I end up in an empty classroom. A woman sitting at a desk looks up my name on a sheet and points me toward Building 10, second floor.

Inside a random classroom, which is entirely unfamiliar, the test administrator checks my Driver's License. Then he points me to my assigned seat and I sit down. I watch other kids dribble into the room over the next ten minutes. I don't recognize any of them. Just like last time. The administrator closes the door at 8:00am. After he reads the instructions like a robot, we start the test. The first section is writing. I'm going to ace this.

The reading section is first. I breeze through sentence completion with ease. All the vocab studying I've done pays off. The questions go something like this:

27. Whoever wrote these questions didn't know that Skye Albright is _____, and she's totally going to _____ the SAT.

A) a leopard .. eat
B) a doorknob .. fail
C) a genius .. kill
D) a dimwit .. bomb
E) a battleship .. sink

The obvious answer is C, although I am half tempted to chose E, because it sounds more dramatic.

I do all the sentence completion questions first, skipping over the passage based reading, which always take longer. Then I go back to the beginning of the test booklet and start with the reading. The first passage is some random thing from some old book about a French guy named Poussant and his grandmother, who is apparently a bitch. I skip over sentences and have to go back and re-read the passage again and again until I get the gist of it. I think my adrenalin is starting to wear off and my exhaustion is starting to take over, seeping out of my bones like a sleeping potion. I sit up straight and take a deep breath like Dante suggested. I'm not about to conk out, but I would really like to lay my head on my desk for an hour or two before continuing. But I only have 25 minutes to finish all the questions in this section.

I take another deep breath and go back to the passage. When I try to answer the questions about what I just read, I'm totally guessing. Oh well. Next!

The administrator calls time before I finish the last question in the booklet. I scribble in a random answer on my answer sheet. I pick A, because A is the best grade you can get. Who knows. I shrug because it's better to guess wrong than not answer at all. There's always a chance the guess is right. I can hope.

By the end of the third segment of Critical Reading, I'm exhausted.

Only nine more sections to go!

When we get our first break, I'm frazzled. I can tell I'm missing more questions than I'd hoped. Running away yesterday was obviously not a smart way to spend my day before the SAT. Too late to do anything about it now. After Dad's bad behavior last night, I sort of don't care. All this college admissions stress can suck it.

I get up and go outside to use the unfamiliar girls' restroom. After, I gobble down one of the energy bars Catarina gave me. Peanut Butter crisp with chocolate chips. Whatever works. I'm starving. The five minute break is over before it started.

I dive back into the questions. When I hit the math section, it kicks my ass. I should know this stuff, but I'm so tired, I can't think. I sit up and shake my arms and breath in and out. I half expect the administrator to say something, but he doesn't. Too bad relaxing isn't helping me feel less tired.

I put my shoulder into it and muscle through the rest of the test. Easy answers evade me, well except for the vocab ones. Those I do well on. But the rest? Forget it.

By the end of the entire exam, I'm done. Zombie tired.

I slog out of the classroom and head toward the parking lot. Can you die from lack of sleep? It sure feels like it. I try to smile when I see Catarina and Dante waiting at the car, but I'm sure it looks more like I'm frowning. Both of them appear fresh and showered, unlike me. I probably look like I went ten rounds in an MMA fight. Brutalized.

"How'd you do?" Catarina smiles hopefully.

I sigh.

Dante places a comforting hand on my shoulder. "Don't sweat it. I'm sure you did great. If you didn't, there's another test in December, right?"

"I am *so* not doing that again," I moan.

oOoOoOo + O+O+O+O

"What time is it?" I moan when I wake up in my own bed.

"Four," Dante says, sitting on the mattress. "You slept for three hours."

I wipe my face with my palms. "It feels like I could sleep three more." Can I pause for a moment to say that being woken by a hottie like Dante is the only way to wake? If you've never been woken by a rugged surfer super model, I suggest you try it. Enough said.

I reach up to rub his stubble with one hand. "Do you need a new razor?"

"Huh?"

"You always have stubble. Is that a thing?"

"My razor is fine," he snickers pressing his hand to mine on his cheek. "But I think you're delirious. Go back to sleep."

I say nothing, but I take a moment to stretch like a cat and smile at Dante. I could lay here all day staring at him. Too bad reality starts to bleed in around the edges of my rose colored fantasy. "Did my Dad come back?"

"No."

My chest seizes. This is very bad. Dad never does this.

"But he called my mom and told her he would be home this evening. She said he said something about calling a family meeting?"

"Oh, grot!" A nausea balloon inflates in my stomach faster than one of those helium balloons when you fill it from one of those big tanks. Only my stomach doesn't fill with happy helium laughing gas. It fills with sewer fumes.

"Grot?"

I roll my eyes, "Groan plus not."

He grins and chuckles. "You're weird, you know that?"

His beautiful face doesn't pop my sewer balloon, but it does diminish it. I feel four percent better than a second ago. All the same, I huff and pull my covers over my head. "Don't wake me until after the family meeting is over," I grumble. "I'm going to sleep through the entire thing."

oOoOoOo + O+O+O+O

"Are you two sleeping together?" Dad asks bluntly, or should I say point blank, which best describes the way his question hits me at the beginning of our family meeting.

It's like getting shot in the face from a foot away.

I gulp. I think the sewer balloon in my stomach is back, only now it's the size of a hot air balloon. It has a basket and passengers and everything, only it's not going to lift me skyward, it's going to sink me straight to Hell.

Dante shifts uneasily on the edge of the couch, a foot to my right.

I can't escape the feeling that we're two kids who've been called on the carpet for something serious like stealing Dad's Beemer and driving it off a cliff, or burning the house down. Not two consenting adults having sex. So what if we're stepbrother and sister?

"Are you going to answer me?" Dad demands, standing in front of the couch, fists on hips.

Catarina sits to my left. She sighs and wrings her hands in her lap.

"Uhhh…" I stammer.

"Yes," Dante says.

Dad winces like someone just ran over a puppy dog with a steam roller right in front of him.

"Relax, Dad," I grouse. "People have sex."

"You're my daughter, Skye," Dad groans. "You're not some random person I've never met. There's a difference."

"It's not like he de-flowered me," I say sarcastically. Since this conversation is already fraught with discomfort, I'm trying to make light of it.

"Skye!" Dad barks. "Do you have to put it that way?"

"What?!" I protest. "Flowers are beautiful. It's not like I said he popped my cherry."

"Stop!" Dad grunts.

I repress a giggle. "Sorry. Anyway, that's not what happened."

"I got it. And I don't need details."

"Then why are we having this discussion?" I twinkle.

Dad turns and smirks at Dante like they're drinking buddies, which is super weird. "My daughter. Can you believe her? Smart as a whip. I hope you know what you're getting yourself into," he chuckles.

For a second, it's like Dad is extolling my virtues, telling Dante how rad I am. I hope it's not a smokescreen. Dad can be clever like that. He might be trying to set Dante at ease so he can blindside him ten minutes from now.

"Her intelligence is one of her most attractive qualities," Dante smiles. "I think that's what attracted me to her from the beginning." He places a possessive hand on my knee and squeezes it affectionately.

"What…" I quip, "I thought you said it was my beauty."

"That too," Dante grins his dimples and flashes his perfect teeth, which glow from his tanned face.

"Oh, you two," Catarina chuckles easily.

And for a moment, it feels completely normal. Like this isn't a doom-and-gloom "family meeting" dripping with drama. It's almost like Dante and I are both older, with jobs and lives of our own, and I'm just introducing Dante to Dad. Like an hour from now, Dad and Dante are going to go out back with shot glasses full of whiskey so Dante can ask Dad for my hand in marriage. Dad will give him a hard time, but eventually he'll say yes and start calling Dante "son". Roll happy ending.

I remind myself that that rosy fantasy isn't what this meeting is, and my Dad's not the movie version of Dad. This is the cranky, stubborn, short-tempered real Gordon Albright, warts and all. My dad doesn't have any warts, but you know what I mean.

"Let's try to keep this family meeting on track," Dad admonishes.

Of course.

Dad continues, "Can either of you explain the photo that Principal Brown brought to my attention?"

"You mean the one of us—" I almost say "at the library" but decide it best to leave that part out, "—on ChatBrat," I finish.

"Is that what's it's called?" Dad asks. "Chat brat?"

"Yeah. I have no idea who put the photo there."

"Well, who did?"

"I don't know!"

"Do you at least know who took the picture?"

"A girl at school. She did it without my permission."

Dad frowns, "At school? Is that where this picture was taken?"

"No!"

"Then where did it happen? And how?"

"I don't know, Dad!" Is omitting the truth a lie? I don't really care at this point.

He rolls his eyes, frustrated. "Do you at least know the name of the girl who took the photo?"

"Brittany Price."

"So you know her?"

"Yeah," I whine. "Didn't I just say that?"

Dad's eyes scrunch closed and he pinches the bridge of his nose in agony. "Then why didn't you tell me, Skye? Perhaps we could've talked to this Brittany girl's parents and put a stop to this before the photo went online."

"Uhhh…" I laugh, "because I knew you would freak out if you saw me and Dante together?"

Dad squeezes his entire face with his hand and shakes his head, "Maybe you're right." He smears his hand down his chin then plants both hands on his hips and stares at the ceiling, shaking his head several more times. He looks like he just got fired or something equally traumatic. He doesn't know what to do. My dad *always* knows what to do. This is so weird. He asks, "Have you contacted the website and demanded they remove the photo?"

"The company is in Latveria or someplace," I mumble. "They don't care."

"Have you at least tried?"

"No, Dad!" I moan. "It's not worth it. Everybody already knows anyway. I mean, *everyone* at North Valley knows. What difference will it make now? The photo is out. It'll probably be on the internet forever."

Dad hisses, "Why did you let this Brittany girl take that photo, Skye?" He's almost pleading.

"I didn't, Dad." I'm raising my voice now. "We tried to stop her. It's not like I could just steal her phone and smash it to pieces."

Dad nods forcefully, then turns on Dante, "Where were you when all this was happening? Huh? Why didn't you put a stop to it? You're the adult."

"What did you want me to do?" Dante protests. "Mug a 17 year old high school girl and take her phone?"

Dad's face flickers. "A better question is what were you doing with my daughter in a compromising situation like that? And where the hell were you two, anyway?"

Neither Dante nor I answer.

"Well?" Dad prods.

"At the library," I sigh, slumping over, elbows between my knees.

"The *library*?" Dad chortles. "Why did you have to pick the library?"

I snip sarcastically, "Because I'm pretty sure the living room wouldn't have worked for you."

Dad leans over at me and goggles, "You're right. It wouldn't. Nowhere in this house would've worked. Because you shouldn't be fooling around with your own stepbrother."

"Is that what this is about?" Catarina asks warily.

Dad shoots her a look. Dad opens his mouth to speak, then stops himself. He starts again, then stops. He runs his hand through his hair and swivels his head in frustration. "Yes, Catarina. Yes it is. My daughter is sleeping with your son. We're married. Do I need to go on?"

Catarina shakes her head, "I don't understand what the problem is,

Gordon."

Dad laughs, "You don't understand what the *problem* is? Do I need to spell it out?"

"Yes, I believe you do."

Dad closes his eyes dramatically. When they open, he gestures at Catarina with both hands, "Your son..." he swivels toward me, "my daughter. Get the picture?" Dad is usually more articulate than this.

Catarina nods, "I understand how strange this is, Gordon. But the kids aren't related by blood. Maybe we should hear them out."

"Maybe we should move to Utah," Dad chuckles.

"That's polygamy, Dad," I offer.

"What?" he gawks.

"In Utah, men have multiple wives. It has nothing to do with stepbrothers and stepsisters."

Dad blurts, "Does it fucking matter? It's wrong all the way around. I won't have you sleeping with Dante under my roof," Dad says, "no matter what state we live in."

I scoff and roll my eyes.

Dante says, "With all due respect, Gordon, I mean, Mr. Albright, that's not your decision to make. It's Skye's."

"If she's living in my house, it sure as hell is my decision to make," Dad warns, folding his arms across his chest. "Remember, Dante," Dad says acidly, "this is my house. If I want you gone, out you go," he grins with full on crazy eyes.

"Gordon!" Catarina barks. "This is not what we discussed!"

"I don't care what we discussed, Catarina! We've had nothing but problems since Dante arrived." Dad spins on me. "How did your SAT test go, Skye? Did you do well? Were you well rested going in? How do you think you scored? 2,000 combined? I hope?"

"I don't know," I whine. I do know, but I'm not about to tell him that I think I did worse than the first time I took the SAT last year, which means I scored *waaaay* below a 2,000.

"Well, we'll find out when you get the results in a few weeks. We can evaluate this situation then."

"Evaluate?" Catarina asks.

Dad narrows his eyes and an evil smile spreads across his face, "If it turns out that Skye did poorly on the SAT she took today, then we're going to have to reconsider whether or not Dante will be staying here any longer."

"We will not," Catarina gasps.

"We will too, Catarina. I will not have your son ruining my daughter's future. And if that means Dante goes, then so be it."

"If Dante goes, then I go!" I shout.

"You'd throw away your future for *him*?" Dad seethes.

"Yes!" I jump off the couch and get in his face. "I'm 18, Dad! I don't need to go to college! I don't need the stupid SATs! I can live fine without them!"

Dad glares at Dante, "Did you put this idea in her head?"

"Yeah. So what?"

"So what?" Dad takes a step toward Dante, who still sits calmly on the couch. "So what? She's my daughter, you imbecile! Her future is of the utmost importance to me! Don't you get it?" Dad shakes clawed hands in Dante's face.

"Easy, Gordon," Dante warns in his low baritone.

"What, are you going to punch me?"

"I will if you don't back the fuck up."

I try not to laugh at Dad because that is probably the funniest thing I've ever heard in my entire life. I also resist the urge to cheer, "Go, Dante!"

"Get out of here!" Dad growls, grabbing the shoulder of Dante's T-shirt.

"Let go of my shirt. Gordon," he warns.

"Then get the hell out of here!"

"Stop it, you two!" Catarina shrieks, shooting to her feet.

What happens next is a tragic accident of epic proportions.

Dad spins in reaction to Catarina's sudden movement, but his foot catches on Dante's big boot, causing Dad to trip. Trying to regain his balance, Dad releases Dante's shirt while reaching out to stop his fall with his free arm, which lands hard on Dante's knee. This agitates Dante, who hops up a mere two inches. Unfortunately, Dante's sudden movement is enough to cause Dad's other arm to arc wildly toward Catarina. The edge of Dad's hand catches her cheek in a feeble slap.

Catarina stumbles back a step, holding her hand to the side of her face. Her eyes are wide with shock. Not from the pain, because she wasn't hit very hard, but because the moment is charged and everyone is at DefCon 1.

"You hit my mom!" Dante hisses and thrusts all the way to his feet instantly.

"I didn't—" Dad starts, but doesn't finish.

Dante slams Dad in the chest with both palms, knocking him backward.

"Dante!" Catarina shouts.

Dad's feet juggle beneath him and he trips over the coffee table.

"Dad!" I shout as he flails his arms, trying to keep his balance while spilling backward.

CRACK!

He hits the back of his head on the corner of the big ceramic vase against the wall. The dried branches poking out the top shudder and buzz when the vase thumps the wall.

"Dad!" I scream, running over and falling to the floor beside him.

He's unconscious.

"Call 911!" I cry.

"Oh my god!" Catarina gasps, kneeling beside Dad and placing a hand on his forehead.

I twist and glare at Dante, "Why did you do that?!" I shout.

His face is ashen, his expression shocked. Dante says nothing, but his eyes dance around crazily. His fingers quiver at his sides.

I look back at Dad.

His face is slack.

I don't know what to do.

Don't "they", whoever "they" are, say that some of the most deadly accidents often happen in the safety of our own homes?

Chapter 17

"Where am I"? Dad mutters from the hospital bed.

Catarina stands from the hospital chair she has pushed up next to bed. She leans over him. "Gordon!" she whispers with relief, cupping his cheek. "You're in the Emergency Room."

I push up out of my chair, which is next to hers and smile at Dad.

He doesn't have a bandage around his head or anything, but he is wearing a hospital gown and has an IV tube going into his wrist and the heart rate monitor pincher on his finger. "Dad," I sputter, my eyes hot.

Dante is standing in the corner, removed from the rest of us, but he steps toward the foot of the bed and rests his hands on the footboard.

"How'd I get here?" Dad asks in a meek whisper.

"You hit your head on the vase," Catarina says.

"I did?" he asks. "Which vase?"

"The one by the TV."

Dad's face squeezes as he tries to sit up in the bed.

"Don't," Catarina cautions softly, "try to relax."

Dad complies and looks at me, "How did I hit the vase?"

Do I tell him? I really don't want to tell him. "You fell," I half-lie.

Finally, Dad sees Dante.

Catarina and I suggested that Dante wait outside until after Dad came around, but he insisted. He felt terrible about what happened.

Dad narrows his eyes, "I remember we were having a family meeting. About the photo." Dad's tone changes from wispy and uncertain to clarity. Here it comes. "I was angry. We were arguing about Skye's future. I was standing over… you," Dad glares at Dante. "You pushed me." Dad's face starts to boil. "You pushed me into that vase, didn't you? You pushed me." His anger rises. "God damn it, get him out of here," Dad grunts, trying to push himself up on his elbow, but lacking the strength. He sags back against the mattress.

Dante's face flickers between confrontational and defeated. He backs up a step.

"Get out!" Dad hollers, although not in his loudest voice. He's not back to full strength. "Leave!"

Something starts beeping on the vitals monitoring screen beside the bed.

A nurse walks in a minute later. Her scrub top is black with a rainbow of hundreds of party balloons. She trots over to the bed, "His blood pressure is up," she says with minimal concern. "Nothing to worry about. What just happened?" She glances at me and Catarina.

"I just happened," Dante mumbles before spinning on his heel and walking out of the room.

It only takes a moment for the beeping on the box to slow.

"What happened to my head?" Dad asks the nurse.

"You had a concussion. But your CT scans and X-rays were normal. You're going to be fine," she smiles.

Dad nods sourly. "Good."

I head toward the door, intent on finding Dante.

"Skye!" Dad barks.

I halt and spin around, "What?" My irritation is bright and sharp.

Dad closes his eyes, "We'll talk about this later."

We all know what "this" is.

Dante.

"Relax, Gordon," Catarina soothes.

My sentiments exactly.

oOoOoOo + O+O+O+O

"Wait up," I call down the long hospital hallway.

Dante is at the far end, like three blocks away. He turns the corner.

I guess he didn't hear me. I jog to catch up, hoping I'm not disturbing the other patients. I nearly run into a nurse walking around a corner. "Sorry."

"Please walk, miss," she says curtly.

I power walk down the corridor and turn at the end and go out the double doors that lead to the Emergency Room's waiting area.

Dante is already heading toward the automatic front doors that lead outside.

I resume jogging and catch up with him in the circular driveway in front of the building.

Some woman with lustrous black hair is helping an old man climb out of a PT Cruiser and into a wheelchair. The old man is too big for the little woman to move. She's trying hard to lift him, but she's not strong enough.

Dante immediately stops to help. He hooks an arm under the old man's shoulder.

"Come on, Dad," the woman says. "Let's stand up."

I can't help but wonder if I'd be helping my dad like this woman is when I'm her age. Right now, the answer would probably be no.

"We'll lift him together," Dante says to her. "On three."

The woman nods, "Okay."

"One, two, three! Lift!"

With Dante's help they stand the old man easily and lower him into the hospital wheelchair.

"Thank you so much," the woman says. "I can handle it from here."

"You sure?" Dante grins.

She smiles at him, her eyes twinkling. She's not thinking about her father any more. She's drooling over Dante. "Thank you for the help. Really."

I don't say anything.

Dante says to her, "Any time."

The woman is still mesmerized. "We should probably get inside." She doesn't sound like she's in a hurry to go anywhere.

Jealousy starts to flare up inside me. Why is Dante still talking to her? She's not that beautiful. Well, maybe she is. But she's way too old for him. She's at least 30 or 40.

I fold my arms across my chest. I consider turning and going back inside. But something tells me that if I go, Dante will be gone.

"You should probably get inside," Dante says to her. "There's a long wait."

"Oh, right," the woman smiles. "Thank you again, so much," she gushes.

Okay, enough! I almost shout it, but don't.

Finally the woman pushes the old man through the automatic doors.

Dante is looking at me. He says nothing.

"Hey," I sigh. "Where are you going?"

"Away."

"Where away?"

"Anywhere but here."

"Here as in the hospital? Or…"

He shrugs.

I'm afraid to ask. "Dad's just mad. He'll get over it."

"I'm not so sure about that."

I'm not either, but I won't admit defeat yet. "Stay, Dante."

"I'd like to, *Cielo*."

Hearing him use my nickname gives me hope. But we're not out of the woods yet. "*Buuuuut...*" I offer.

"But your Dad doesn't want me around. We've both known that since the beginning. Me being at the house is making things worse."

"Not for everybody," I frown-smile. "You made things a whole lot better for me."

"Did I?"

"Of course you did!"

"How did you do on that SAT yesterday?"

"I won't find out for a few weeks."

"Yeah, but how do you think you did?"

I sag. "Not very well."

"Exactly."

"So?"

"So? Don't you want to go to college? I thought you wanted to go to SDU since you were a kid."

"I thought I did. Now I don't know. Maybe I don't want to go to college."

"Did you feel that way before we met?"

"Well, no, but—"

"My point exactly."

I frown, "But isn't that what relationships do to people? I was never into DJ music before I met Luke. He turned me on to all kinds of music I never listened to before."

Dante smirks, "Musical tastes are one thing. Doing a one-eighty with your life is a bit more drastic."

We're standing five feet apart and it feels like a million miles. I close the gap and throw my arms around his waist, staring up into his shining green eyes. "Don't go, Dante. We'll figure this out."

He smoothes the back of my head and kisses the top of it.

My heart melts and the rest of my body follows as I sink into his skin. Relief.

"Okay. Maybe I'll stay."

oOoOoOo + O+O+O+O

"He's not staying," Dad grumbles as Catarina and I help him into the house that evening.

Dante is in the garage parking the Lexus.

"Gordon," Catarina sighs. "Can we talk about this later?"

"We can talk about it in five minutes or five hours or five weeks. My response will be the same. Dante cannot stay here. Period. Am I making myself clear?"

Catarina purses her lips, her eyes wet. "We'll talk about this later," she mutters.

"No, we won't. He leaves now."

"Dad!" I protest.

"Zip it, Skye. Dante is going. Tonight."

"Fine!" I shout. "You can walk yourself upstairs!" I march toward the kitchen.

"Skye!" Dad hollers.

I ignore him and turn into the laundry room and open the door to the garage.

Dante is already on the step, reaching for the doorknob. "Oh, hey."

"You don't want to go in there," I warn.

"Why?"

I press the garage door button and the door starts to open. I grab Dante's wrist and lead him out to the driveway, where we stop. "We're going."

"What?" he says, confused.

"You, me. We're going. Now."

"*Cielo*, what's going on?"

"Dad doesn't want you in the house. He just said it when we were inside. Let's go. I don't care where. Let's just go. I'm serious this time. No wimping out like Friday. I'm done. I mean it."

Dante's emerald eyes search mine for a long, long time. Then he blinks and his face suddenly goes dead.

What is he thinking? Now I'm worried.

Then he starts to smirk.

Better.

Then he grins full on, flashing his even teeth.

Good.

Then his eyes twinkle and he starts chuckling.

Even better.

Now he's full on laughing.

"What's so funny?" I ask, half-giggling myself.

"This is insane."

"I know, right? Dad has lost his marbles. I think he knocked them all out when his head hit that—"

"No," Dante laughs. "This!"

"What?" I'm confused.

He motions between me and him. "This. Us," he snorts.

I'm not liking where this is going.

"Did you really think I'd be into a high school kid like you, Skye?"

Wait a second...

"I mean, it was fun for a while, but did you really think we would run away together?" He's grinning from ear to ear like we're at a comedy show.

But nothing about this is funny. "What about Friday?" I press. "What about Santa Barbara?"

"Fuck Santa Barbara. I do shit like that all the time."

"Like what?" Now my chest is starting to tighten.

"Take chicks places on my bike just for fun. I usually fuck them for the weekend, and that's that."

"You're hurting me, Dante."

"What can I say?" He shrugs. "Did you not figure out that I don't like to stay in one place too long? It was pretty obvious from the beginning. The only reason I went to Blazing Waters with you and Rox in the first place was because I wanted to fuck both of you," he snorts.

I can't believe he's saying this. My mouth quivers. I'm trying not to sob. I shake my head, "You don't mean that."

Dante narrows his eyes. "I would've fucked you both, but I changed my mind when I found out Rox was only 17. Not worth the hassle. But you were an easy target."

"Target?" I'm about to fall to pieces. This is turning ugly way too quick. "What about *'mi Amor'* and *'mi Cielo'*?"

"What about it?"

"I thought it meant something."

He smirks, "Don't you know guys will say anything to get laid? And the shit they say when they're *getting* laid never means anything. Don't you know that?" he chuckles abrasively.

I gape at him, shocked into silence.

"You were just one more fuck."

"Dante," I mewl. My heart is getting squeezed so hard right now, I can barely breathe. Tears dribble down my cheeks. "Don't you love me, *Tierra*?" Calling him that is one last desperate attempt to hold on to something that I suddenly fear was never there.

"I never said I did."

Technically, he didn't. He said he "thought he loved me" and it was in Spanish. *Creo que Te amo.* I guess that doesn't amount to anything when it comes from Dante.

His mouth curls into a hateful twist, like he's enjoying the pain he's causing me. "You'll get over it. I gotta go." He pats my shoulder twice like a consolation prize before strolling past me and walking into the garage and the house.

I collapse on the driveway and I can't stop the sobs.

Five minutes later, Dante walks out of the garage with his pack and helmet.

I sniffle and wipe my tears off my cheeks with my fingertips.

"You can sell the helmet and jacket and gloves. Keep the money."

"I don't want the money," I mumble. I want to be strong and stand up, but I can't. I want to pretend this isn't breaking me, but it is. I want to pretend I don't care, but I do.

"Go to college, Skye. Forget about me. You'll be glad you did. Find someone like Luke. He's a good kid."

He climbs on his motorcycle and rides off into the night.

oOoOoOo + O+O+O+O

"Did Dante leave?" Catarina asks as she trots out of the garage. "I was helping your father get situated in the living room." She sounds frightened.

I can't answer her. I just stare at her as more tears spill down my cheeks.

She squats and wraps her arms around me. Her whole body quivers. "What happened?"

"Dante's gone," I sob.

"Gone?"

"He left."

"No! Why?"

"I told him Dad wanted him gone."

"And he just left?"

I can only nod my head.

"Damn that Gordon!" she hisses and hugs me hard. "Did Dante say when he was coming back."

"No."

"No he didn't say, or no he's not coming back?"

I start sobbing again. It's all I can do.

Catarina comforts me, but she's shaking. I'm sure she's mad and sad and everything else. After several minutes, she says, "Let's go inside. We can't sit on the driveway all night." She helps me to my feet.

My legs are wobbly and I'm ready to sit down after two steps, but we make it into the house and she helps me up to my room and guides me onto the bed.

I sit on the edge, hunched over, my arms in my lap, nearly catatonic.

She pulls my shoes off and I manage to swing my legs onto the mattress and lie down.

She plants an arm on the bed and leans over me, smoothing my hair, "We'll find Dante."

My face knots and I start to cry again when I hear his name.

"Don't worry, sweetie, we'll find him. I promise. He's my son." She looks at me thoughtfully. "You love him, don't you?"

I stare at her, afraid of what she might say next. Is she going to lecture me about how I'm standing in the way of her marriage and her son?

She smiles, "You do. I can tell. I suspected something was going on between you two, but I didn't say anything. When you're young, it's normal to develop feelings for someone very quickly. Believe me, I know. I was 18 once too. There were times when I liked a different boy every day of the week," she smiles, reminiscing for a moment. Then her face slowly returns to thoughtful and comforting. "But those feelings are often fleeting, Skye. Teenage crushes usually are..."

Dread tightens my throat. Is she saying that my feelings for Dante didn't mean anything? Is she going to try to convince me not to love Dante, just so she can have him back?

She sighs, "But I could tell there was something special between you and him after a few weeks. You were always watching him whenever you were in the same room, always asking if I knew where he was or what he was doing when he was gone. And when he brought that Phoebe girl over?" She rolls her eyes. "Hmph, I can't believe you didn't attack her at the dinner table." She smoothes back a lock of my hair. "But you've never been the confrontational type. Your father handles that for the rest of us."

I nod minutely, but I completely agree. "Is—" I stop myself.

"What, sweetheart?" she asks softly.

"Is it weird that I fell in love with your son?" Yes, I said it. I love him. Maybe I'm stupid to feel that way, especially after how he treated me on the driveway just now. But the pain in my heart is born out of lost love, not lost like or even lost 'live'. Live, as in, halfway between Like and Love. This is the real deal, and it hurts worse than dying.

"No, of course not, sweetheart. It's completely natural to fall in love with someone."

Why is Catarina so cool and my dad such an ass?

"But it's what you do with your feelings that counts," she finishes.

I'm about to say something when the pain slams into me again. How could Dante be so callous? So hateful? I didn't think he was like that. And the things he said about Rox? I shudder at the thought.

Maybe there was a dark side to Dante I never wanted to see. Maybe Dad saw it from the beginning and I ignored it like a foolish girl.

I'm so confused right now. I'm not ready to share any of this with Catarina yet. I'm not even sure how I feel about the whole situation myself.

"Don't worry, Skye, we'll find Dante and bring him home."

I'm not sure if I want that to happen.

"No matter what your father says…"

oOoOoOo + O+O+O+O

"No!" Dad shouts from downstairs. "Absolutely not!"

I'm still in my bedroom and Dad is in the living room, but he's loud enough to be heard anywhere in the house.

"Damn you, Gordon!" Catarina barks. A few minutes later, the garage door hums and a car drives off. It sounds like Catarina's.

Where is she going? When is she coming back? *Is* she coming back? Or is it going to just be me and my mad dad from here on out?

I half consider getting up to go down and yell at Dad, but I don't think I could move right now even if I wanted to.

Surrounded by the womblike cocoon of my softly glowing pink room, I stare at the ceiling and sink deeper into my bed. My next thought is to call Rox and pour my heart out to her, but she probably wouldn't answer even if I did.

This is awful.

I need to talk to someone, but there isn't anyone.

How am I going to face school on Monday?

I close my eyes and try to die.

oOoOoOo + O+O+O+O

Sunday morning, Catarina knocks on my bedroom door. "I made breakfast. You should come have some."

Thank goodness she came back.

It takes me forever to drag my butt downstairs, but I make it to the kitchen and sit on a bar stool.

Catarina is pouring pancakes on the cast iron skillet. Bacon sizzles in another pan.

"Where's Dad?"

"In the living room. Resting."

"Skye?" Dad calls.

I sag and sigh.

"Go see what he wants," Catarina says.

I roll my eyes and slide off the stool and trudge into the living room. "What?"

Dad's in an Abercrombie & Fitch T-shirt and fancy sweats. They almost look like slacks. Leather loafer style slippers cover his feet. He never dresses down. "Something is bothering me."

"You too?" I quip.

"I'm serious, Skye."

"What?" I don't look him in the eyes.

"I've been looking over this ChatBrat site and it has me worried." His phone is in his lap.

I grimace. "And?"

"And I can't figure out where all these comments are coming from."

"From kids at school. Duh."

"Yes, but why?"

"Because high school kids are evil?"

Catarina walks in with a tray covered with a plateful of pancakes and bacon. A butter pat is centered on the pancake stack and syrup drizzles over the side. A tall glass of orange juice sits next to the plate. She sets the tray down on the coffee table near Dad.

"Yes," Dad says, "but all those comments have a specific... *tone.*"

"You mean hateful?"

"It's more than that."

"I don't know what you're talking about, Dad," I groan.

He scrolls through his phone. "The town pump?" He's talking about Ashley Master's first post. "Why would anyone call you that?"

"I don't know," I groan.

"And all these other comments calling you a slut? Care to explain all that?"

"Me?"

"Yes, you, Skye."

"I didn't make the comments!"

"But there's dozens of them calling you a slut. How did that happen? Is there something you're not telling me, Skye?"

My mouth gapes open. "I'm not a slut, Dad!"

"Then why is everyone calling you one?"

A jagged memory cuts through me.

Dad yelling at Mom: "Is there anyone in town you HAVEN'T slept with, Crystal? Because I'd really like to know."

"Maybe if you knew how to use that useless dick of yours, I wouldn't have to, Gordon!"

"You're a slut, Crystal! Nothing but a lowlife slut!"

Rage burns up my throat and I scream, "Because I'm just like Mom?!" I'm referring to my real mom, not Catarina. "Is that what you want me to say?"

Dad's mouth clenches. His lips shake as they peel over clenched teeth. "Watch your mouth," he snarls.

"Do you want me to say I have sex with every guy who comes along?!" I scream.

"Shut up, Skye!"

Catarina halts in the doorway, holding another tray of pancakes and bacon. Her eyes bulge in surprise.

I'm assuming she doesn't know anything about my real mom Crystal, because Dad never mentioned her name again after the divorce. Mom is Dad's dark little secret, the biggest skeleton he has in his closet, an embarrassment. A mistake, well, except for me, but he *hates* Mom. She cuckolded him for almost their entire marriage. When I was little, like 3 or 4, I started noticing Mom had a lot of male friends. It was normal to me. Guys came over to the house when Dad was at work. I didn't think anything of it. We lived in a different house then. It was smaller and out west in Reseda. Mom would spend a lot of time in the guest bedroom with her male friends. She always turned the living room TV on really loud and told me I could watch whatever I wanted. I didn't exactly know what was going on at the time, but I knew something wasn't right. After the man would leave, Mom always said to me, "Don't tell your father about this. Okay? He wouldn't understand." So I never did. When I got older, the men stopped coming over. But she didn't stop having affairs. She just hooked up with them outside of the house.

I grunt, "I'm not Mom, Dad."

"Don't say another word," he warns, glancing over at Catarina.

All of my anger toward Dad for pushing Dante away comes rushing up like a geyser. Dad ruined everything. This is all his fault, and he needs to pay for being such a jerk. "Why not?" I tease. "Aren't you supposed to talk about your feelings?" I cut. "Maybe Catarina would like to know all about what mom did when you weren't around."

"Shut your mouth, young lady."

I smile at Catarina, who still holds the tray of food at her waist, looking completely stunned. I grin, "Mom used to have guys over all the time when Dad was at work. Right under his nose. He didn't find out for years. That's why they got divorced." I smile at Dad.

"Stop it, Skye," he grunts.

"Why? You ruined my life, so why shouldn't I ruin yours? Maybe

Catarina should know about the time you caught mom with that mechanic? The one with the tattoos? The one who gave you a black eye when you caught them at Motel 6?" That happened right before the divorce. I was old enough to know exactly what was going on then. I wasn't there, but Mom told me all about it afterward. She made it sound like it was all Dad's fault. My mom wasn't exactly a model housewife.

"You stupid idiot! You ruined my new dress! How many times do I have to tell you to stay out of my closet, you little shit! You really are dumber than a doorknob."

But Mom's parenting is not the issue here.

Dad stands up suddenly from the couch and takes a step toward me, but instantly stumbles and holds his hand to his head, wincing. He drops back on the couch, looking woozy.

"Easy, Gordon," Catarina says, rushing over. She sets the second tray next to the first and sits beside Dad. "The doctor said you need to take it easy for a few days. In case the concussion was worse than they thought." Her concern is obvious. She turns to me, her brows knit. "Please, Skye. This isn't the time."

"He started it!" I yell, feeling righteously justified.

"Then be a bigger person and you be the one to stop it. You're an adult. Act like one."

I wince. I thought Catarina was on my side. I feel like an idiot. But that doesn't mean I'm not mad. "I'm not a slut, Dad," I hiss as I walk out of the room.

It hits me when I walk up the stairs to my bedroom.

Dad thinks Dante is just like the men Mom ran around with. He probably wants to protect me from them since he couldn't keep Mom away from them. They certainly didn't help make her life any better. But that's a whole other story.

I close my bedroom door behind me and stare at myself in the mirrored closet door.

You know what, Skye Albright?

Dad was right about Dante.

I shake my head and grimace at myself.

I really am an idiot.

Chapter 18

Catarina drops me off in the bus circle at North Valley on Monday morning,

I practically crawl out of the car. I don't want to be alive right now. I'm more exhausted than I was when I took the SAT Saturday morning, and I must've slept fourteen hours Sunday night.

I walk through the front entrance and stroll past the main office. Someone opens the office door so I skirt around it.

"Morning, Slutbright!" Ashley Masters beams behind me.

I guess she just came out of the office.

I halt in my tracks, fists clenched.

"Any new incestuous hookups to report from over the weekend? I can post them on ChatBrat for you, if you want." She sounds so sweet and helpful. So fake.

Rage. Black, blind rage clamps down on me like a falling piano. I spin and take one step toward Ashley and slap her right in the face.

CRACK!

"Oh!" she yelps.

I smile. "Shut the fuck up, bitch, or there's more where that came from." I stare her down.

Her eyes widen. My white hand print glows on her pink cheek. A look of shock is frozen on her face.

Priceless.

I whip my phone out of my purse and snap a photo. I turn around and walk away, already opening the ChatBrat app. I post the photo of Ashley with the following caption:

Ashley Masters just got pwned by Skye Albright

Entirely satisfied with myself, I walk to my locker. I say good morning to Jason Carpenter, who is sliding his Magic The Gathering binder into his locker, then make my way to Mr. Mendez's trig class with a bouncy step. Any time someone whispers my name or gives me the stink eye, I flip them off. People are surprised by my reaction. Good.

I'm not taking any more shit from anybody.

They've already fucked with my life enough.

During class, Mr. Mendez does some example problems on the board. "...then divide both sides by three X minus one and—"

The door to the classroom opens and some kid leans inside.

"Yes?" Mr. Mendez asks.

The kid holds up a slip.

Mr. Mendez walks over and takes the slip, reading it. "Skye? You're wanted in the office." He holds the slip out for me.

The class rustles and there's a few mumbles.

I ignore them while I pack my notebook and calculator in my handbag. Gee, I wonder why I'm going to the office?

Grot.

oOoOoOo + O+O+O+O

"Would you care to explain your actions, Miss Albright?" Principal Brown asks. He's a very tall African-American man with a bushy mustache and an easy smile. He wears a tweed sport coat and red button down shirt. Even now, despite his size, he's not intimidating. He's very friendly. His fingers are laced together on top of his desk. There's a window behind him with venetian blinds, but they're open and early morning sun pours through. Plaques and school photos cover the wall on both sides of the window.

Ashley Masters sits next to me in the cramped office, her nose wrinkled with piggish pride.

I sigh casually, "Ashley said something nasty. So I slapped her."

"Now, Miss Albright," Principal Brown says in his deep voice, "I'm sure you're aware that school policy is no fighting, no hitting, no punching, and that includes no slapping."

"What about no insulting?" I glare at Ashley. "And no posting photos that are an invasion of privacy on ChatBrat."

"You're referring to the photo I called your father about?"

I arch my eyebrows at him with proud acknowledgment.

He glances at Ashley, "Do you have anything to add on that topic, Miss Masters?"

She smiles, "I have no idea what you're talking about."

I roll my eyes, "Everyone knows you posted that photo, Ashley. Who else calls me Slutbright?"

"I'm sorry, what?" she asks innocently.

I make a sour face. "Don't pretend you don't know what I'm talking about, Ashley. You posted that photo, you wrote the caption. End of story."

"I have *noooo* idea what you're talking about."

I sigh, "She's lying. She did it."

Ashley's arms are folded over her gray cardigan. Her legs are crossed and she bounces one foot repeatedly. She probably sucks at poker because she's obviously nervous.

Principal Brown nods thoughtfully. "I'm sure the two of you know that ChatBrat is anonymous and we have no way of knowing or proving who posted what."

Ashley smirks.

His eyes dart toward her. "Be that as it may, I have to wonder about the name calling Miss Albright is referring to."

"You mean her calling me Slutbright every time she sees me?" I blurt.

Ashley's leg stops bouncing. More precisely, it freezes in mid air. Thought so.

Principal Brown represses a smile, "Yes, that."

"I've *never* called her that," Ashley growls.

Oh, geez.

"And anyway," she continues, "she slapped me! Then she took my picture and posted it on ChatBrat with *her name* on it!" She glares at me. "Isn't that right, Suh—" she stops herself and purses her lips, "...*Skye*." She says my name almost like it's admitting defeat.

"Gosh, Ashley, let's find out." I reach into my bag and pull out my phone. I'm still on the ChatBrat app. "Well goodness, almost three hundred likes already! And we're still in first period. What do you think will happen at brunch when everyone gets on their phones?"

Ashley narrows her eyes and catapults a huge basketful of eye daggers at me.

I smile pleasantly as the daggers bounce off. I'm bulletproof this morning. Because I stopped caring the second I walked on campus.

"Now, Miss Albright," the principal intones, "let's not gloat."

No, let's gloat. Let's gloat very much. Let's throw a gloat party. The first round is on me. "Are we done here?" I demand.

"No," the principal smiles. "I'd like to know what Ashley said to you to provoke you."

"She asked if I had incest sex over the weekend," I grumble.

His face twitches imperceptibly while he maintains composure. He would be much better at poker than Ashley. He turns to her, "Is that true, Miss Masters?"

"That's not what I said," she whines.

"Close enough," I chuckle.

"What *did* you say, Miss Masters," Principal Brown asks.

She curls her upper lip, "Can I plead the fifth?"

"You could," he chuckles, "but you would end up in detention."

"If I tell you, will I not end up in detention?" she whines.

"That will depend on what you say," he offers.

She rolls her eyes. "Just give me detention. What about her? She gets detention too, right?"

"I'm afraid so," Mr. Brown says, giving me a compassionate look.

"Can we have detention together?" I ask snidely. "I totally want to spend it with Ashley." I turn to her. "You do too, don't you, Ashley? We can be like the kids in The Breakfast Club and become BFFs before the end of the movie."

"I don't think so," she groans with superiority.

"Detention is in the cafeteria, as you know Miss Masters," Mr. Brown says pointedly, "but I will give Mr. Rhodes instructions to seat you on opposite sides of the room. Please report to the cafeteria after your last class."

oOoOoOo + O+O+O+O

SLUT

That's what's lipsticked red on my locker door when I go to it at the beginning of brunch.

I stop short and marvel at it. I wonder what shade of red it is? Scarlet Harlot or Crimson Tart?

Several freshman notice the red writing as they walk by my locker. The guys giggle or laugh. The girls whisper and glance at me. Everyone at North Valley knows who I am. I don't even need the Scarlet A or I or whatever the hell other letter Ashley Masters would have me wear on my shirt.

Fucking Ashley.

It had to have been her.

First, SLUT is written in a bouncy girlish hand. Second, SLUT wasn't written on my locker when I came in this morning. The word is underlined twice because everyone knows underlining is meaner and two underlines is twice as mean. Shiver. Sarcasm. I can totally picture Ashley sneaking over here after leaving Principal Brown's office so she could vandalize my locker. She probably thought she was Zorro when she slashed the underlines onto the door. In her case, she should be called Slutto, because she's the one who tirelessly defends the reputation of the entire community from sluts like me.

What a joke.

Ashley.

This school.

And everyone in it.

It's all a big joke.

I stuff my bags in my locker. Then I get an idea. I close my locker door. Then I take a picture of it and the word SLUT. Then, since I'm wearing a white V-neck T-shirt, I step up to my locker, slide my palms up under the cotton material, and press the chest of my shirt against the lipstick.

"What are you doing?" Jason Carpenter asks, walking up behind me.

"Making a new shirt. Here, take my picture." I stand beside my locker facing the camera. I hand Jason my phone. "Make sure you get me and the locker."

"Why?"

"Just do it, Jason. Please?"

He's frowning with uncertainty.

"Please?" I beg.

"Okay. I won't get in trouble, will I?"

"No. Don't worry." I glance down at my shirt and you can read SLUT but it's backward and kind of mushy and blurry. I smirk a cocky disinterested smile and flip off the camera.

Jason snaps the photo and hands me my phone.

In the picture, you can read SLUT on my shirt just fine, even though it's backward. "Thanks, Jason."

"I guess," he says. "Are you okay, Skye?"

It's so sweet that he cares. No one else does. "I'm fine."

"Are you gonna play Magic with us in the library today?"

"Maybe. I don't know. I might skip school."

"Don't do that." He sounds so serious.

"Want to come with me?" I offer.

He shakes his head, "No, I don't want to get detention."

I shrug. "I already have detention today. What's another hour or two?"

"Um, okay. I should go."

I'm freaking him out. "Bye!" I wave. I sigh when he's gone.

Then I upload my SLUT lipstick photo onto ChatBrat with the caption:

Someone defaced my locker between first period and brunch. If you saw who did it, let me know. Skye Albright.

Then I walk to the nearest girls' restroom and sit in a stall until brunch is over. I hear girls come and go, chatting and giggling and gossiping beyond the steel isolation of my stall. All I see are some shoes. Their banter is nothing more than white noise to me. I coil a lock of my hair around my index finger over and over. I pick a few split ends. When the warning bell rings, I flush the toilet for no reason and walk to third period.

I have Chemistry third period. When I walk in the classroom, Mr. Goldberg takes one look at my SLUT shirt and sends me to the office. I walk right past it and stroll out the main entrance.

Fuck school.

oOoOoOo + O+O+O+O

I begged him to fuck me right here, across from the school.

I'm standing behind the church where I wanted to have sex with Dante back in the beginning, before things blew up.

What was I thinking?

My stomach knots so I turn around and go back to the sidewalk.

The last thing I want to think about is Dante.

I don't know where to go. I don't want to go home. That sounds too dreary. Too many memories of Dante and Dad and everything.

I look up and down the street in front of school. Just parked cars and buildings but no people. So lonely.

I've cut school a few times since I started high school, but it was always with Rox. I sigh when I think about it. I miss her so much, she doesn't even know. I wonder if she knows how much she hurt me when she abandoned me when all this slut shit started.

SLUT

It's on my shirt.

I guess that makes me the slut. Just like mom.

"You're a slut, Crystal! Nothing but a lowlife slut!"

Sigh.

I walk aimlessly down the sidewalk, heading in the general direction of nowhere. I end up at the mall that's close to school. Why didn't I think of this before? Retail therapy is every girl's best friend. Macy's is calling my name. I think I need to try on shoes today. You can never have too many.

The saleswoman in the shoe department is sharply dressed. Her brassy blonde hair is pulled back in a snooty hair pin barrette. Her chiffon blouse and wool skirt scream "uppity". She sneers when she sees me wander in with my lipstick SLUT shirt. I don't think it's to her liking. When I ask her if I can try on a pair of leopard print pumps, she scowls, "Shouldn't you be in school?"

"I graduated," I lie. "I go to UCLA. I'm in the fashion design program. I need shoes for one of my design classes." I love the fantasy version of me. She doesn't get slut shamed. She's too busy getting her collection ready for Mercedes Fashion Week.

Ms. Uppity purses her lips before snipping off to fetch the shoes.

I leave before she returns.

Bitch.

I wasn't going to buy the shoes anyway. I wander upstairs and try on a few outfits. It's no fun by yourself. I wander through the mall for over an hour, going in and out of different stores. Forever 21, Bath & Body Works, Aldo.

Eventually I lose my enthusiasm and end up chilling at a table in the food court, people watching. I guess it's lunch because the place is super crowded. Maybe I should get something to eat.

SLOP!

Something smacks the back of my head. I reach my hand up and feel cold, wet, and mushy. Something falls from my hair and clatters on the tabletop. An M&M. I twist around and see Ashley Masters standing behind me, flanked by Brittany Price and Monica Webb. All three of them hold Fro-Yo cups.

"Did I give you brain freeze, Slutbright?" Ashley twinkles, holding her empty Fro-Yo cup.

I scowl up at her from my seat, "How's your face?" Meaning: my slap.

Ashley's twinkle tarnishes into a snarl. She snatches Brittany's Fro-Yo cup out of the girl's hand and jerks it in my face. Ironically, the yogurt doesn't fly. It just sort of plops out and splats on the tiled floor at her feet.

SPLASH!!

From off to the side, an entire cup's worth of soda flies in Ashley's face. Cola drenches her head and shoulders, dribbling down her fancy embroidered white cami in brown streaks. The blonde hair at the front of her face clings to her cheeks in sticky streaks.

"Take a hike, Ashhole," Rox says victoriously, holding a large empty cup in hand.

"Did you just call her *Ash*-hole?" I marvel.

"I did. And I'll kick her asshole if she even thinks about doing anything with Monica's Fro-Yo. Other than shoving it up her own *ash*, that is." Rox smirks confidently.

Ashley scowls, "I need napkins. Get me some napkins!" She glares at Brittany and Monica. "You two are useless!" She storms off without them.

Monica and Brittany glance at each other nervously.

"Brittany! Get over here!" Ashley yells from where she's stealing napkins from Panda Express. "You too, Monica!"

"Your master is calling," Rox says. "Oh, wait! Her name is Ashley *Masters*! No wonder you guys do everything she tells you."

Brittany and Monica exchange a disgusted look and walk off in the opposite direction of Ashley.

"You're gonna regret this!" Ashley yells, but they ignore her.

Rox turns to me like it's business as usual, "Such bitches."

"Thanks," I say reluctantly. We haven't spoken in over a month. It's the longest we've gone without speaking. Ever.

"Mind if I join you?"

"Where are Nicole and Kayla?"

She shrugs, "They were annoying me today. It's not as fun hanging with them when you're not around."

"Aren't you still mad at me?"

She shrugs again, "No. I miss you too much."

I hide a smile.

"You have yogurt in your hair."

"And M&Ms." I claw one out and toss it onto the table. The red M&M skids across toward Rox.

"Get that away from me! It has Ashley cooties!" She giggles and flicks it off the table with her finger.

The M&M bounces right onto the table next to ours and hops onto someone's plate of spaghetti. The guy whose food it is is turned away at the moment, looking at who knows what while he chews. Unaware of the M&M, he turns back to his food and jabs his plastic fork into his spaghetti. The fork clicks against the hard candy shell and the guy frowns, confused. He leans his head to the side, trying to figure out what happened.

Rox represses a laugh and grabs me by the arm, pulling me out of my chair and away from the tables. I stumble after her, laughing as we exit the food court and head toward the rest of the mall.

"We need to get you cleaned up," Rox says. "Wanna go by my house before lunch is over? I'll rinse your hair out over the sink, so you don't have to use the nasty mall bathrooms."

"Sure," I smile.

And like that, we're BFSFs once again.

oOoOoOo + O+O+O+O

"You're getting yogurt jizz in my eye!" I squeal with my head over Rox's kitchen sink. Water from the faucet rains down on the back of my head.

She laughs, "I think yogurt jizz is supposed to be good for your eyes. All the lipids or vitamin E or whatever."

"You're making that up."

"Probably," she chuckles, hosing my hair down with the spray gun. She adds shampoo and lathers it up with her fingers.

"I feel like I'm in a hair salon."

"Then you better tip good," she chuckles. "Hey, I found a green M&M. You want it?"

"Ew!"

"Okay. I'll eat it," she quips.

"Gross, Rox! Throw it out!"

"Too late," she laughs. After massaging the suds for awhile, she rinses me again. "All done." She pulls my hair back and blots it with a towel.

When she finishes, I stand up and pat my hair dry. Good thing I don't have a jungle growing from my head like she does, otherwise we would've made a mess all over the kitchen. I mop up what little water splashed on the floor with my towel, then we go into her bathroom and she gives me a light blow-dry and style. She insists on doing everything while I stand in front of the mirror. She spritzes some product in it and artfully arranges my bangs.

"There," she smiles. "Perfect."

"Wow, Rox, I can never get my bangs to do that without them looking stringy."

"It's probably the yogurt," she snorts. "Or my conditioner. You need to stop buying yours at Walgreens."

"I don't! I buy it at Ulta! You know that."

"Oh yeah. Then you need to let me pick it out for you," she winks. "We should probably head back to school. We're way past late for fifth period."

I grimace. "I was planning on cutting the rest of the day."

"Okay," she grins. "What are we gonna do?"

I can't decide if she's trying to be extra friendly to make up for the last month or not. I sigh heavily. I've been avoiding the elephant in the room since the mall just like she has. "Rox, Dante left." Okay, now it's out. Either she's gonna be pissed all over again, or we're gonna get past this thing.

She purses her lips and her brows knit, then she takes a deep breath and her face softens. "Does it hurt?"

That wasn't what I was expecting, but it was exactly what I needed to hear. "Yeah," I mutter.

"What happened?"

"He got in a fight with my dad."

"I knew that would happen sooner or later. Your dad is like that. Was it a *fight* fight with fists and stuff?"

"Sort of. Not really. Dante pushed Dad and Dad tripped and knocked himself out on a vase."

"Oh. Is he okay?" Her concern is genuine.

"Yeah, he's fine. But Dante got all pissed afterward and he left." Now I'm crying. Tears drip onto the bathroom floor.

Rox wraps her arms around me and hugs me hard. The flood gates open and I sob against her chest. She rubs my back and hugs me and holds on like she never let go in the first place.

I hug back limply because all the strength left my body the moment I let out my pain. "I loved him, Rox," I sob.

"I know," she whispers.

"He was so mean," I wail. "He said all he wanted was a three way with the two of us, but you were only 17. So he went after me."

"What an asshole!" she hisses. "I should've known he was a total prick. I'm so sorry, Skye. I can't begin to apologize for how mean I've been to you.

That makes me cry even harder. "I had sex with him, Rox," I sob, snot running down my nose.

"It's okay, Skye," she soothes. "It's okay."

That she isn't mad or jealous allows me to feel the full pain of it without defending myself or holding anything back. My wails overwhelm me and I sink to the floor. Rox kneels down with me, cradling me in her arms.

I cry harder than I've ever cried before.

My best friend since forever holds me the whole time.

oOoOoOo + O+O+O+O

Eventually, I stop crying, but only because I run out of energy and tears. I lie on the bathroom floor on my side, staring at the wall.

"We missed fifth period," Rox says. "And half of sixth. I say we bail on the rest of the day."

"Oh shit," I mumble. "I forgot I have detention today."

"Why?"

"Because Ashley turned me in to Principal Brown for posting my slap photo on ChatBrat."

"I saw that!" Rox laughs. "Total girl power post! You go, bitch slapper!"

"Bitch slapper?"

"What?" she chuckles. "That's what you are, isn't it?"

"I guess." I half smile, much to my surprise. A half hour ago, I thought I might never smile again.

"Hold on a sec." She stands up and dashes out of the bathroom. She returns a moment later with her phone. "Holy shit! That photo is at the top of ChatBrat! It's already got almost 900 kisses!"

"Kisses? Not Disses?"

"Yup," she grins. "And the comments are all positive." She scrolls through them. "People love that you showed up Ashley. They're calling you some kind of hero for dethroning the queen of North Valley."

"People are stupid. They thought I was a slut the day before yesterday."

"I never did," she says somberly. "I was just jealous you got the hottest guy we've ever seen."

"Are you still jealous?" I ask carefully.

She wrinkles her nose, "Was the sex any good?"

"What kind of question is that?" I frown.

"An honest one."

"Yes," I groan.

"Sorry."

"Why are you sorry?"

"Duh! Because I feel bad for you!"

I shake my head, grinning, "You are so lame."

She huffs. "I know. I've been a total bitch. I don't know what I was thinking. Dante picked you. We agreed we'd let him decide."

"In the end, he didn't pick me either."

"I can't believe he said he wanted a three way with both of us."

"Why not? That's what every guy wants."

She shakes her head, mystified. "Skye, I've never seen a guy *less* into me than Dante. He wouldn't even look at my boobs at Blazing Waters. That is scientifically impossible."

"That's a laugh. Guys always stare at your chest."

"He didn't. I'm telling you, Skye, I always know when guys look at my ladies," she grins and glances at her chest.

"Yeah, yeah," I groan. I know she knows. Whenever we go out, she always tells me when she catches guys staring at her chest. From the way she tells me, you'd think she was as happy about it as she was mad. I never quite understand it because guys rarely look at my non-chest. When they do, it's by accident. I suddenly remember Dante's reaction to seeing my naked breasts. A wave a sadness washes over me. I ride it out until it passes.

"What?" Rox asks.

"Nothing," I lie. "What were you saying about Dante?"

"He wouldn't stare at my chest. It was the weirdest thing. It made me crazy jealous."

"Why?"

"I don't know. Maybe because guys *always* look. It was like there was suddenly something wrong with me. It drove me nuts. It was weird. I can't explain it."

"Why? You get tons of guys."

"Not like Dante," she scoffs.

"You're not missing out. Trust me. He's a prick. Just like all the rest."

"Now I feel awful," she groans.

"Don't."

"But I do. I let a hot douche come between you and me."

"Hot douche?" I chuckle. "Is that like a hot wax, but on the inside?"

She cringes. "Who would do such a thing?"

"I don't know, a plumber?"

"No, I meant who would *get* one, not who would do it."

"Oh," I snicker. "I thought you meant the pubic stylist, or feminine landscapers—" I shake my head, searching for the right word, "—or... *whatever* they're called."

Rox stares at me like I'm the crazy one.

"Pubic plumber?" I offer.

She laughs, "Okay, now I'm picturing going in to get a Brazilian and the guy behind the counter is hairy and smoking a cigar and he's like, 'Lady, the Brazilian is $29.95, but the hot douche injection is 15 bucks extra.'" She says it in a mannish voice.

"Have you ever even had a Brazilian?" I snicker.

"Just the one I gave myself, remember?"

"Oh yeah," I laugh. "You said it itched to sit for three days!"

"More like burned for three days!"

"That's right! Why did you do that?!"

"To impress some guy whose name I've forgotten."

Still grinning, I snort, "You can add Dante's name to the list of forgettables."

"Dante who?"

"Exactly," I grin.

For the first time since Dante left, I feel vaguely close to normal.

I hope this feeling lasts all day. I don't want to go back to being miserable any sooner than tomorrow.

oOoOoOo + O+O+O+O

Rox drives me to detention. I want to see if Ashley shows up. She doesn't.

Since I'll have to sit through detention sooner or later, I decide to get it out of the way now. Besides, staring at my fingernails for over an hour is about all I'm good for this afternoon.

Rox is waiting for me outside when I finish and she drives me home.

"Thanks for the ride," I say when she stops outside my house. "You want to hang out?"

"Sure."

We end up kicking it in my room. Rox sits against the headboard and I'm draped over the foot of the bed on my back, staring at the ceiling with my feet hanging over the side. I already changed out of my SLUT shirt and into a clean T. The SLUT shirt sits folded on top of my hamper so the stain won't get on anything else. We'll see if the lipstick comes out. Not that I care. I kind of like it. Maybe I'll wear it again before I wash it.

"Have you started filling out your college craplications yet?" Rox asks.

"Did you just say *crap*-lications?" I giggle.

"Yup," she grins.

"Yeah. I've been looking at them."

"Have you picked a major yet?"

"No. But it won't be Business. Don't tell my dad. He'd totally blow a gasket."

"Yeah," Rox grins, "I can picture him with steam coming out of his ears."

"In other words, the usual," I laugh.

"Yup. Have you started working on your college essay yet?"

"You mean my personal statement?" I say sarcastically.

"Yeah."

"I've been thinking about it. But that's it."

"Me too," Rox sighs. "I have no idea what to write."

I roll onto my stomach and grin at her, "Just write about the time you gave yourself a Brazilian wax job and how you don't want other women to suffer through the same PBWJSD you did."

She shakes her head, "The PB and J *what*?!"

"No, PBWJSD. Post Brazilian Wax Job Stress Disorder. Duh."

She frowns, "That's El Oh Lame-O."

I frown back. "Hand me my pillow."

"Why?"

"Just hand it to me."

She reaches behind her head and tosses it to me.

I catch it and throw it back at her face.

She catches it. "Oh, this is *so* on! Pillow fight!" She swings it two-fisted like a baseball bat.

A giggle-infused pillow fight follows. It feels so good to have Rox back. When we run out of steam, Rox grabs her phone and checks it.

"Did someone text you?" I ask.

"No. I wanna see how your 'Take Back The Slut' photo is doing in ChatBrat."

I roll my eyes, "Why?"

"Because you're a role model, Skye! Don't you get it? That photo literally says 'fuck you' to slut shamers everywhere."

"I guess."

Rox leans over her phone. "Wait, what the F is this?"

"What?"

She holds up the phone, showing me a picture of a fully nude woman getting banged from behind by a hairy chested guy. It's some random porn photo from the 1970s of two people doin' it doggy style, but my head has been Photoshopped onto the woman's. Rox's face has been pasted over the man's, but just her face, keeping the guy's 70s perm intact. The caption reads:

Skye Albright, the local Slut Sore, is at it again! She needs to upgrade her Scarlet I to a Scarlet S! This girl is a super slut! Everybody grab a pitch fork and lets get this slunt hunt started!

I roll my eyes and flop back on the bed. "Ashley Masters is at it again. Doesn't she realize that a Scarlet S on my chest would look like Superman's logo?"

"That's my face!" Rox groans, ignoring my comment.

"And mine. So?"

"So? We have to put a stop to this!!"

I take the phone from her and examine the photo, grinning. "I don't know, Rox. You look pretty good with a hairy chest and a gold chain around your neck. I love the permed hair. Curls on guys are super sexy.

The only thing missing is a thick 70s mustache."

She throws another pillow at me.

I laugh.

She huffs, "I'm serious, Skye. We need to shut the bitch down."

"You mean Ashley?"

"Of course."

"You wanna start a slut fight?"

Her eyes flash, "Yeah!"

"No."

She deflates. "Well, we should do something."

"I'm open to suggestions."

"We need to hack ChatBrat and delete these posts or figure out who's posting them so we can get them in trouble or something. Anything."

"Wait, what did you just say?"

"We need to get whoever's doing this in trouble."

"No, before that."

"Uh, we need to hack ChatBrat?"

"O. M. Genius!" My eyes light up. "You just gave me an idea."

"What do you know about hacking, Bill Gates?"

"Nothing. But I can get us Bill Gates," I say dramatically.

"Huh? How?"

"I'll tell you tomorrow."

She frowns, "Isn't that the punchline to that old joke, 'How do you keep a moron in suspense?'"

"Yeah," I laugh.

"Slut fight!!" she squeals and hits me with yet another pillow.

My world is nearly perfect. Except for the hole Dante left in my heart. I just need to work on getting over it.

Chapter 19

That night when I go to bed, I'm actually in an okay mood.

Having Rox back in my life has reset my world. She stayed for dinner, which lightened Dad and Catarina's mood too. It's like they missed Rox as much as I did. After Rox left, I even managed to do some homework before bed.

With clean teeth and a freshly scrubbed face, I climb into bed. I don't fall asleep right away. I'm too excited about my master plan.

Tack tack tack...

It all starts tomorrow. I'm gonna teach Ashley Masters a lesson about being a bullying bitch. I've had it with her. I'm not gonna take her bad behavior lying down. I smirk to myself. Sure, I'm lying in bed at the moment, but it's just a figure of speech.

Tack tack tack...

First thing tomorrow, I'll be on both feet fighting.

Tack tack tack...

What the hell is that noise?

I sit up in bed and listen. All I hear is water running in the master bedroom. Other than that, the house is silent.

Tack tack tack...

Where is it coming from? Is it the heating vent? No, the heat is off. It's still October so it's still warm at night. I climb out of bed and lift the comforter, looking for Leprechauns digging for gold under my bed. Don't dismiss. You never know where those little guys bury their pots. I kneel down to get a better view under the mattress. No Leprechauns.

Tack tack tack...

What the? I sit bolt upright.

Tack tack tack...

I spin around and whip my drapes open.

Dante.

Damn it.

A mixture of feelings overwhelms me. Anger. Joy. Hate. Love. Fear. Hope. Irritation. Relief.

"Get out of here!" I whisper harshly. "Dad will kill you if he knows you're here!"

Dante squats on the roof outside my window. He raises a forlorn eyebrow. His blond bangs fall and drift over one emerald eye. The other shines like a green beacon.

Why does he have to be so damn handsome?

"You look like a vampire out there!" I hiss, placing one hand against the glass.

He smirks a grin. He places his palm against mine on the glass. He says something, but the words are muffled by the glass. His deep voice vibrates the window pane ever so slightly.

I crack my window open an inch. "What did you say?" I whisper.

"I said: then let me in and I'll make you immortal," he says quietly.

"No! You're not turning me immortal! And I didn't give you permission to come in when I opened the window. No vampires!"

"Please let me in."

"That's what vampires always say! Go suck Phoebe's blood or something."

"Please, *Cielo*. Let me in."

My heart skips when he calls me *Cielo*. I grimace, "I thought that name didn't mean anything to you."

"It means everything to me."

"Liar." I scowl.

"I'm sorry, *Cielo*. I made a mistake. Let me in so I can explain."

I slump my shoulders and my head tips back. "Fine," I groan. "But don't try anything… *vampiric*." I slide the window open all the way and make a cross using both my index fingers, warding him off.

He rattles something around outside.

"What are you doing?"

"The window screen? I can't get it off."

"Oh."

"You have to undo it from the inside."

Having never done it before, it takes me a minute to figure out the little spring tabs on each side. I set the screen on the floor and back away as Dante climbs through. I make the finger cross again.

"I'm not going to bite your neck," he chuckles quietly.

"Or anything else." I sit on the foot of my bed and look up at him. "Well?"

He's so damn tall it's ridiculous. As always, stubble dusts his strong jaw and he wears his leather jacket and jeans. "I shouldn't have said what I said to you the other night."

"Duh. You could've just said you were moving on and left it at that." I wrinkle my brow. "Why did you have to be so mean?"

"Because I wanted you to let go."

"Let go of what?"

"My heart."

"Oh." I cock my head. "Wait, what does that mean?"

"I tried to leave, *mi Cielo*. But I couldn't. When I got on my bike and rode off, my heart hurt. The farther I went, the more it hurt. It's like my heart is tied to yours and I was stretching the connection to the breaking point. I couldn't do it."

Awww...

Okay, I'm melting. But I don't let it show. And maybe I'm a little wet. I squirm ever so slightly on the top of the comforter in my cotton shorts. I'm not wearing any panties at the moment. If this continues, I won't be able to stand up without leaving a wet spot. My comforter might be patterned, but my shorts aren't.

The glacier around my heart also starts to melt, which scares me to death.

He sits down beside me, but leaves a foot of space between us. Some would call that 30 centimeters, but I don't want to think about metric conversions or anything else vaguely related to the SATs or College or Chemistry class right now. I sigh with frustration. My mind is a jumble. I think I'm trying to avoid feeling anything by making jokes in my head. I smirk dumbly and put my hand on his knee, "Tell me about your heart again?"

A flicker of amusement twitches his cheeks. "Yeah, sure. Where was I?"

"Our hearts are tied together?"

He nods. "Yeah. Uh..."

"I'm sorry," I grimace. "I'm ruining your moment."

"It's okay," he grins. "But I like to think of this as our moment, *mi Cielo*."

I heave a sigh. As much as I'd like to fall into his arms, the half-melted glacier around my heart reminds me there's much left to resolve. I pick at my fingernail and mutter, "You said some really hurtful things to me, Dante."

He hangs his head. "I know. And I'm so *so* sorry I did. I didn't mean any of it."

"Then why did you say it?"

"Because I thought it would hurt you less if you hated me. I thought it would make it easier for you to let go."

"I never wanted to let go, Dante."

"But you have to let go."

"Why?"

"Because I don't want to ruin what you have."

"Huh? I had you. Or at least I thought I did. I don't, I mean, I *didn't* want to ruin that."

He shakes his head. "No, I mean this." He motions around the room. "This world of yours. This house. Your dad. Catarina. Your family. This... *home*." He starts to choke up. "I haven't had a home in a long time, and I know how important it is. I didn't want to destroy yours."

"You didn't," I plead.

"That's not how your dad sees things."

I groan. "Yeah. You're right."

"He doesn't want me in your life. I didn't want to force you to chose between your home and me."

"But it's your home too, Dante."

"No it's not. The only thing here that could maybe be called mine is my mom. But she's your mom now. I see that. And I want you to have a mom."

"She's your mom too."

"Yeah, but I don't want to make her choose between me and your dad. That's not fair to her. They love each other. Your dad's not such a bad guy. He just has a bug up his ass about me. For whatever reason."

I've never told Dante anything about my real mom. "My real mom was a bit of a ho," I sigh. "She slept around on Dad. A lot of her boyfriends rode motorcycles or had tattoos." I cringe as the memories prod at my heart. "I hate talking about her. Anyway, Dad thinks I'm going to turn out like her. You know, because you're like mom's boyfriends. Well, maybe on the surface, but I don't think you're anything like them."

Dante nods thoughtfully. "Now it makes sense. Your dad doesn't read a lot of books, does he?"

"Huh?"

He grins, "He was judging this one by it's cover since day one." He cocks a thumb at himself and flashes his dimples.

"Right," I snicker.

"But I'm not here to prove anything to your Dad." His tone returns to more serious. "I'm here to apologize to you, *mi Cielo*. No matter what happens, I need you to know that I never wanted a three-way with you and Rox, and it wasn't just sex. Being with you was..." he stares at his hands. "It was everything, *Cielo*." He reaches over and squeezes my hand.

My heart thrums. I lock eyes with him.

His emerald gems speak the truth. They flicker in the pink glow of my nightlight. He whispers, "I've always run away from my problems in the past, *Cielo*. But I can't run away from you. It would kill me. I can't go, I just can't. But I won't be the guy who tears apart your family." He sounds desperate, torn between the horns of his dilemma. "I won't do that to you, and I won't do it to my Mom."

"Oh, *Tierra*," I moan and throw my arms around his shoulders. Hope floods my veins. My entire body sizzles with optimism. "They're *our* family Dante! We can work through this. We can figure this out together. We can convince my dad that you're not turning me into my mom. We'll prove you're a good person. Catarina will back us up. We'll wear Dad down. We can do it, Dante. Together."

"But my mom..." he mutters. "She loves your dad. He's a decent guy. They need to be together."

"*We* need to be together Dante." I skooch over next to him on the bed until our thighs are touching.

His hand lifts and brushes one of my long bangs out of my eyes. He licks his lips and they glisten.

So do mine. Both pairs.

"*No puedo vivir sin ti, mi Cielo*," he sighs. *I can't live without you, my Heaven.* He leans toward me.

The scent of his dusty leather jacket and tanned skin overwhelms me, hypnotizing me. The entire universe outside my bedroom ceases to exist...

Knock, knock, knock.

"Skye?"

"Dad!" I hiss.

"Are you awake? I thought I heard something."

My eyes goggle at Dante. "Closet!" I squeak.

"What's going on, Skye? Is someone in there?"

Dante stumbles over me, trying to get to the mirrored closet doors at the foot of my bed. His boot thuds on the floor as he stops long to avoid crushing my bare toes.

"Skye!" Dad calls. "I'm coming in!"

Dante spins back around and dives between the bed and the wall, landing below the open window. Amazingly, he avoids crushing the window screen leaning against the wall.

My door opens and Dad leans into the room. "What's going on in here?" he asks, eyes darting around suspiciously.

"Nothing!" I spin around on the bed, crossing my legs and leaning back on my arms. I'm trying to cover as much space behind me as possible, sort of like a goalie, only instead of protecting the goal, I'm trying to hide Dante. Well, he's totally my goal, but you know what I mean.

Dad narrows his eyes. "What was all that noise?"

"What noise?"

"I thought I heard you talking in here."

"Just talking to myself," I cackle. Wow, I sound insane.

"Why were you talking to yourself?"

"Reciting poetry?"

"Poetry?" He's not believing me.

"For English class? We had to memorize poems and recite them in class?" I may have done that in 7th grade, and it sounds a bit unlikely for a senior, but it's all I had.

"*Oooookay.* Why is your window open? And why is the screen out?

"I thought I heard a raccoon outside!"

"A raccoon?"

"Yeah! It sounded rabid! I wanted to make sure!" *Lies, lies, lies!!*

"Rabid? It *sounded* rabid?"

"No! It was, uh, foaming at the mouth!" *Guilt, guilt, guilt!!*

Dad frowns, "Then why did you pull out the screen? Did you plan on petting it?"

"Uhhh…"

"Dante!" Dad shouts.

I spin around and see Dante standing up. "Lie down!" I bark. "He can see you!" I don't know how that's going to help now, but it seemed like the right thing to say a second ago.

Dad takes a step into the room. "Get out of here, Dante! Who let you in?!"

"I did!" I shout, standing up.

"Why?" Dad growls.

"Hello! Haven't you figured that out yet, Dad?!"

"What's going on in here?" Catarina gasps. "Dante! You came back!" Her excitement is obvious.

"God damn it, Catarina!" Dad yells. "He can't be here! Get out of my house, Dante! Right now!"

"No!" Dante shouts in his booming baritone.

The room goes silent.

Everyone stares at Dante.

He runs his hand through his hair, sweeping the blond spray off his brow. He gives Dad a pleading look.

Dad scowls.

In a frustrated and strained voice, Dante hollers, "Don't you get it, Gordon?! I love your daughter!! She's not my sister!! I'm not your son!

And Skye is not like her mom! So quit fucking ruining everything for everybody else!!"

Not only does my heart melt completely, so does every other part of my body. Lungs, spleen, liver, bones, and yes, the yummy bits between my legs. I should sit down. Or put on some yoga pants or something. I think I'm dripping.

Flustered, my dad makes a bunch of weird noises that are half-words. "I, flab, dyou, koosh, whaz?"

"I love her, Gordon." Dante turns to look at me. "I love her. She's my sky, my world. She's my everything." He chews his lower lip. "She's *mi Cielo*."

I knew it! He meant it the first time he said it! Even if it was in Spanish!

"*Te amo también, mi Tierra.* I love you too," I mutter foggily. I'm about to swoon. I start to weep softly.

Dante steps around the bed and wraps his arms around me, hugging me tight. In my ear he whispers, "I'm so sorry, *mi Cielo*. I love you. I love you so much." His voice cracks with emotion.

"Oh my goodness," Catarina sniffles, wiping her eyes with her fingers. "Look at them, Gordon. They're perfect for each other."

Everyone turns to face my dad.

His scowly face softens for the first time since he laid eyes on Dante. A surge of emotion spirals across his face. He shakes his head slowly, as if dumbfounded. "I... am *such*... an ass."

I repress a blurt of laughter.

Catarina grins at Dad. Then she wraps her arms around him and coos, "It's okay, Gordon. I still love you."

Dad leans into her and puts an arm around her shoulder. Then he kisses her cheek. "I love you too, *mi Gatita hermosa.*" *My beautiful kitten.* Or *beautiful pussy*, depending on who does the translation.

Surprised looks lighten all our faces.

"What?" Dad chuckles, "I know some Spanish too. I'm not *that* bland and boring."

oOoOoOo + O+O+O+O

"Can we have a moment, Dad?" I ask.

"Oh, sure." He remains standing in place.

"In private?"

"Come on, Gordito, let's go." Catarina chuckles.

"Hey! I'm not fat," Dad whines. He really isn't. He almost has a six pack.

"Only where it counts," Catarina purrs, tugging on the waistband of his sweats.

"Oh, gross!" I guffaw.

Dante winces, "I think that qualifies as TMI."

"Obvi," I groan.

Catarina drags Dad out of the room and closes my door behind them.

"Don't make too much noise!" I yell, hands cupped around my mouth.

Dante snickers. "Don't get me thinking about it." He grimaces and shakes his head.

A second later my door whips open and Dad leans in. "No fooling around in here, you two."

I roll my eyes at him, "18, remember?"

"Still my house, remember?" he mocks.

"Whatevs," I groan.

Dad pulls the door closed, but stops a few inches short of latching it. "Leave this open. I'll be checking back every five minutes."

"Five minutes?" Catarina blurts in the hallway. "You've gotta be good for more than that!"

Dad smiles gleefully and chases her down the hall.

I shake my head, "I think we're a bad influence on those two."

"I disagree."

"How?" I challenge.

"Maybe we inspired them with our own love."

I roll my eyes and chuckle. "That's not just a line, is it?"

"No, *mi Cielo*. It's the truth."

"I hope so, because it sounds too good to be true."

"That's the thing about love," he smiles, "true love always is."

"Is what? Too good? Or true?"

"Both." His eyes sparkle as he leans down to kiss me.

oOoOoOo + O+O+O+O

I wake the next morning in Dante's arms.

"*Buenos días, mi Cielo*," Dante whispers. *Good morning, my Heaven.*

"*Buenos días, mi Tierra*," I sigh. *Good morning, my Earth.*

We slept in the guest bedroom. My bed was way too small for both of us. Heck, Dante could barely fit by himself. So we snuck in and used the queen sized guest bed. I was paranoid Dad would check on us at some point, but he never came out of the master bedroom all night. He and Catarina must have used a sex silencer, because we didn't hear them once. Yes, I closed the heating vent and put a stack of books over it, just in case, but the house didn't rumble, there was no headboard banging, etc., etc.

I stretch my arms over my head and yawn. Then I resume gazing into Dante's eyes. It's the awesomest thing ever.

He cups my cheek gently and smiles sleepily. "*Esto es el cielo, mi Cielo*," he mutters. *This is heaven, my Heaven.*

"*Sí, para mi también, mi Tierra.*" *Yes, for me too, my Earth.*

We kiss softly for a few minutes.

When we finish, I lazily stroke his blond hair, brushing locks of gold out of his emerald eyes.

"I'm so lucky you stumbled into my life, Dante."

"Me too," he whispers.

"How did that happen, anyway?"

"Pure luck, I guess. We can thank our parents for that," he winks at me. "If they hadn't met, we never would have."

"I know, right?" I think about that for a second. "But if you hadn't decided to come looking for your mom, we *still* wouldn't have met."

"True."

"So why did you come looking for her? And why did you ever leave? Catarina is awesome. I love her. I can't imagine a better mom."

He turns his head away to stare at the ceiling and sighs. "It's a long story."

"I've got time," I grin.

He smirks but doesn't look at me. "Don't you have school?"

"At some point," I joke.

He smiles at me but his face starts to flicker uncertainly.

Maybe I shouldn't have asked. "I'm sorry. You don't have to talk about it. Some other time."

"No, it's okay. As you probably noticed," he quips, "I have a tendency to run away from my problems."

I shrug. "I guess. But you always come back."

"Yeah, but only for people I love." He turns to me with a huge grin on his face. "And I love you very much, *mi Cielo*." He squeezes me briefly against his side.

I fold into him. "Me too."

"I really need to do something about this running away habit of mine," he muses thoughtfully.

A twinge of fear pinches my heart. I hope he doesn't plan on running away from me again. It would break my heart all over again.

He says, "When you're young, sometimes that's all you know how to do." He pauses and closes his eyes.

I watch his brow tighten and bunch as pain plays across it.

His eyes remain closed as he begins to talk. "After my dad left us when I was 12, things were tough. Back then, Mom didn't have much money. She was a housewife, not a successful real estate agent. So she took the first waitressing job she could find. Things were really hard for us. We were broke all the time. I got in fights at school and I fought with Mom at home. I blamed her for making Dad leave and ruining our lives. I was such a dick to her. The only time I ever felt normal was when I talked to my dad on the phone. Talking to him made me feel like life wasn't coming apart at the seams. I would hear his voice and instantly feel better." A complex dance of emotions is flashing across Dante's face as he tells the story. "Eventually my dad convinced me I'd be happier living with him. He was always telling me what a pain in the ass my mom was and how easy things would be with him. At the time, I completely believed him. He sent me a plane ticket to La Paz, so I could join him in Baja. I wanted to go bad. Mom was pissed and said no, but I wouldn't back down. Finally she gave in and took me to the airport herself. When I touched down in La Paz, my dad picked me up and drove me to his place in San Carlos. His house was right on the ocean. At first it was incredible. Me and my dad, kickin' it Baja style. Surfing every day, kite boarding, fishing for dinner right out of the ocean, my dad grilling up our catch of the day and the two of us eating the freshest homemade fish burritos you've ever had. So good. It was hella kick back. I didn't even have to go to school!" He chuckles. "I just surfed every day. The bad news was, the truth about my dad came out piece by piece. It took me a while to see him for who he was, but eventually, I did. Nothing but empty promises," he smirks with disgust. "*He* was the big asshole, not my mom. Going to live with him was a huge mistake. Huge. Being in a foreign country made it worse. Mom couldn't just hop in a car and drive two cities over to come pick me up. I was stranded." Dante's eyes are haunted. He smears a hand over his face. I can't tell if he's wiping away a tear, or just wiping away painful emotions. It amounts to the same thing.

"What happened?" I ask with rising dread.

He stares at me for a long time, his eyes shimmering. He shakes his head. "You don't want to know." His tone is ominous and frightening.

Based on his strained face, I think he's right. Maybe some other time.

"Anyway," he sniffs, "what a disappointment. I was decimated. When things got way too crazy, I took off."

I'm afraid to ask what "too crazy" means, so I don't.

"For a while," he sighs, "I lived with some friends I'd made in San Carlos. But it only takes so long before you wear out your welcome. You piss off someone's parents or your buddy thinks you're trying to steal his girlfriend, and out you go. Same old shit every place I went. So I ran away from those problems too, and ended up on the streets."

"That's terrible."

He shrugs, "Baja is warm. I didn't mind. And the streets were the only place I felt like my dad wouldn't find me..." he trails off and swallows hard.

Now I'm really afraid to ask about his dad. Something bad happened. I can feel it.

"Why didn't you call your mom? I'm sure she would've hopped on a plane to come rescue you. She missed you like crazy, Dante. I saw it in her eyes whenever the topic of you came up."

He stares at me for a long time. "I guess I'm fucking stupid sometimes," he laughs with painful irony. "I have an ego, if you hadn't noticed."

I grin at him.

He heaves a sad sigh. "When I first moved to Baja, I was just a kid. I didn't really understand what a dick I had been to my mom. When I bailed on my dad, because I finally knew how fucked up he was, I realized what a dick I'd been to my mom. I think I was probably too embarrassed to call her. I didn't want to admit to her face that she was right and I was wrong." His face flounders with awkward regret. "But I also wanted to see if I could make it on my own. I wasn't a kid anymore. People didn't treat me like one either. Not adults, not girls, nobody. I was becoming a man. And men solve their own problems, you know?"

"I'm not a man," I joke, "so only kinda sorta."

"No, you're not," he grins lustily. "Anyway, when I got sick of street life in San Carlos, I hitchhiked to La Paz and talked my way onto a ferry to Mazatlán. The boat took forever to get to the mainland, but once I landed in Mazatlán, I felt a huge weight lift off my shoulders, like I'd left all my problems behind. A week later, I found a job working at a resort hotel. That turned into working on a cruise ship a few months later. Everybody liked me. I always knew what to say to make friends. I met a ton of cool people on the boat that way. Crew and passengers. Every one of them had amazing stories to tell, and they were from all over the world. That's when I really started traveling. Either working a different ship or jumping on a plane to wherever the wind blew me. Every time I went someplace new, I was happy. I'd work for a while if I had to, then move on when I got bored. Or got into too much trouble," he chuckles.

"You? Trouble?" I quip.

"Exactly," he grins. "The adventure of discovery was the ultimate drug for me. It fixed my problems and filled the empty holes in my heart. The next thing I knew, I had been all over the world, and I'd made friends everywhere I went." The way he says it makes his life sound like a non-stop vacation.

"That's amazing," I sigh. "I'm super jealous. I wish I could've gone with you..."

"You still can. There's lots of the world left to explore."

"Will you take me with you?"

"Of course I will, *mi Cielo*." He smiles lovingly.

"So, why did you decide to come looking for Catarina now? I mean, your life was full of adventure. What was missing?"

"This," he says, gazing into my eyes.

I feel warm and fuzzy all over.

"Love," he sighs. "You make incredible friends when you jump into chaos and travel. People somehow show up and help out. It's insane when I count all the times some random person opened their home to me and gave me a place to sleep and food to eat. People in this world are crazy generous if you treat them with respect. But for all that, it's not the same thing as family. *Real* family." He hugs me and I hug back.

He sighs, "I decided it was finally time for me to look up my mom and apologize for all the nasty shit I said and did when I was a kid. I needed to un-burn that bridge. It's one thing to run away from your problems. It's another to come back and face them. Running away never fixes anything." He smirks at himself. "I needed to fix things between me and Mom. And look what happened? I found my family, and I found you."

"Awww," I snuggle into him. I could lie in his arms forever. I surrender to his warm embrace and instantly start to drift into slumberland.

"Don't you have school today," he offers, jolting me awake.

"Way to ruin my moment!" I giggle softly. "What time is it anyway?" I tilt my head up, but the guest bedroom doesn't have a clock.

"I have no idea. Six?"

"If you don't know the time," I quip, "how do you know it's six?"

"From living without clocks for years, that's how. It feels like six."

I sneer, "I'm not buying it. I want to see a clock. Where's your phone?"

"In my backpack. Right side pouch."

I slide out of the warm bed. The room is cool, but not cold. Even so, I'd rather stay cuddled up with Dante all morning. But duty, and my master plan, calls. I unzip his backpack and dig for his phone. I grab something velvety. My eyes pop. "Dante…"

"Did you find something?" he asks, amused.

I pull out a velvet box. The kind of box rings come in. "What's this?" I gasp.

"It's not an engagement ring. If that's what you're worried about."

Slightly disappointed, I unhinge the box, revealing two silver pendants attached to a silver chain. One pendant is a silver circle attached to two smaller circles, one on each side. The other is a circle with a plus sign in the middle of it. "What are these pendants? Do they mean something?" I pull the necklace out of the box and hold it up.

"The three connected circles symbolize air. I think they're supposed to look like clouds. The circle with the cross is the astrological symbol for Earth."

"*Cielo y Tierra…*" I mutter. *Heaven and Earth.*

"*Sí, mi Amor.*" *Yes, my love.* "When you think about it, the circle is the perfect symbol."

"Oh. How?"

"The circle is eternal. Clouds are eternal. There will always be clouds, as long as the Earth has a Sky. The Earth is also eternal. And inside the infinite loop of the Earth, the plus sign symbolizes two lines, two distinct entities, joining together in the middle, at their *hearts…*"

I totally melt when he says that. Could he be any more romantic? Nope. Shaking with emotion, I unclasp the necklace and fasten it around my neck. The pendants rests just below the hollow of my neck, close to my heart. "When did you get this?" My eyes are getting wet.

"Yesterday. I thought I might need proof I was serious. For when I knocked on your window. And since it's silver," he grins, "it's proof I'm not a vampire. I think they hate silver, right?"

"That's werewolves," I giggle, weeping softly.

He chuckles, "Either way, it's proof I love you, *mi Cielo.*"

I dive into his arms. "*Mi Tierra…yo también te quiero.*" *I love you too.*

"I'll never run away from you again, *mi Cielo…*" His voice chokes up with powerful emotion. "*Te quiero MUCHO mucho…*" *I love you too much…*

We start to kiss.

"Skye?" Dad calls through the door. "Are you in there? You're going to be late for school."

"Yeah!" I holler, rolling my eyes. I wait for him to bust down the door with a pickax and give me and Dante another lecture.

"You better shower," Dad suggests calmly. "Catarina made everyone breakfast."

She never makes breakfast during the week. I guess we're celebrating?

"Hurry up, or the food will get cold." Dad sounds way happier than I've ever heard him. I guess he had a great night with Catarina last night.

"Okay!" I holler through the door.

"Go shower!"

"Okay, Dad!" I wait for him to say more, but he doesn't. His footsteps fade down the hall. I shrug at Dante. "We'll have to pick this up later?" I wait for a response.

"I'll be here, *Cielo*. I'll always be here."

oOoOoOo + O+O+O+O

The shower runs, warming up the water. The overhead fan hums as well.

I stand in front of the mirror naked, putting my hair back in a short ponytail. Rox washed it plenty yesterday afternoon, and I don't have time to deal with hair right now. I'm late enough already.

The bathroom door suddenly opens and I jump, my chest seizing. I instinctively grab for the nearest towel, which is on the rack behind me.

Dante walks in completely naked. He tosses a small box of condoms on the bathroom countertop and closes the door behind him, locking it.

"Dante!" I gasp.

He is muscled from head to toe. He is gorgeous, and he is mine. His cock is hard and proud. He grins at me, "You didn't think I was letting you get away that easy, did you?"

I flash my eyes at him, speechless.

He stalks toward me, all big and manly and tan, an earthy contrast against the white of the bathroom. Is he on fire, or is it just me? Because it's *really* hot in here right now. And not because of the shower. Although, the shower is making plenty of steam...

Dante backs me against the counter, pressing his cock up against my stomach. He sure likes to do that.

I can't help but stare down at it.

It's huge.

It throbs.

Pre cum glistens on the tip.

"Oh my gosh…" I sigh. I tilt my head up and gaze at his gorgeously rugged face.

He leans down and our lips weld together in a tangle of hot flesh. His tongue lashes against mine. His hands grasp my ass, squeezing hard.

I yelp into his mouth and claw his back with my fingers. I have barely any nails, so I really dig in.

He grunts into my mouth and surges his hips into me.

Damn it, he is huge and hot and forcing himself on me.

I wouldn't have it any other way.

He pulls me away from the counter and digs his own hands into my ass. He grunts, "Mmmm. That ass." He looks over my shoulder at the mirror.

My small naked body stands in front of his.

"There is no other ass on the planet this nice," he growls.

"Yeah there is," I squeeze his. "Right here."

He grins at me with ferocious hunger and we kiss again.

As my excitement builds, I feel myself getting very wet. Far wetter than the shower is at the moment. I break our kiss and glare at him. "Fuck me, Dante. Fuck me hard."

"I don't think you can take it as hard as I can give it."

I slap him right across the face. Not as hard as I slapped Ashley, but close. My eyes goggle at him. "Oh, sorry!" I cover my mouth with my hand, shocked by my own behavior. "I don't know why I did that! Sorry!"

His eyes flash with amusement. "What the fuck was that?" he snorts.

"I don't know!"

He leans over and grabs the box of condoms and tears it open. He rips open one of the packets and rolls the condom on. "You're gonna pay for that." His face is a blend of anger and hunger.

"*Okaaaaay…*" I chuckle.

He reaches under my ass, lifts me up, and sits me on the counter. I grip the edge of it with my hands, shaking with anticipation. He places a big hand on the small of my back and jams one of my knees high. He pushes my other knee out to the side, opening me. Then he fists his cock and jams it against my wet lips. I'm drenched and ready for him. He slides right in, groaning as he sinks in to the hilt.

"Oh, god," I moan, my entire body sizzling. I lean back on my arms, feeling him fill me perfectly. I hook my free leg around his waist as he starts to thrust.

He reaches down with his hand and circles my clit with his thumb.

Pleasure whirlpools through me, in synch with the motion of his thumb, magnifying and spiraling inside my body. My head bounces lazily as he thrusts in and out, grunting and groaning.

"*Cielo*, fuck, *Cielo*..."

The building orgasm swirls in my pelvis. It's going to be big. I can already tell. It surges in building waves. I can't believe it's happening so fast. It's like all the pent up desire and emotion of the last several days is ready to blow me apart. It's been forever since we've had sex. For a while there, I didn't think we'd ever have sex again. That desperation feeds my need. I throw my arms around his neck and shoulders as he pushes deeper. He stands up, lifting me with his powerful arms. I try to time our thrusts by lifting and falling in a matching rhythm. Something about the way I'm using my thighs to lift myself causes my core to clench deliciously each time I squeeze. "*Ay, dios mio, mi Tierra...*"

"*Cielo...*"

My orgasm starts to eclipse all other awareness. I feel him swell inside me like a rumbling volcano ready to erupt, forcing me open while I clamp down on him with every thrust.

"So fucking tight," he hisses. "Oh, fuck, *Cielo*, I can't stop, I can't, I'm going to... I'm going to..., oh, fuck! *Cielo!*" He blasts deep inside me, drilling into my core one final time, forcing himself all the way in, pressing hips against my clitoris in one final earth shaking thrust.

"*Tierra!!*" I cry. Orgasm quakes through me, rocking my world.

Water rains down from the shower head as I rain down on Dante.

Steam fills the room.

The fan overhead blows all of the energy in the room skyward.

I sag against Dante, coming to rest against him, supported by the granite of his hands.

Once again, I float in his arms.

oOoOoOo + O+O+O+O

"How was your shower?" Catarina asks when Dante and I come downstairs together, fully dressed.

I stumble to a stop. My eyes headlight.

Dante stifles a snort.

Catarina grins at us knowingly. She is definitely the coolest.

I glance at Dad, who sits on a stool at the end of the granite island. There's a huge bratwurst sausage on his breakfast plate. He glares at me and saws through the sausage with his knife and fork. Symbolic?

You decide. "I don't want to know about it," he growls.

"*Oooookaaaaay*," I sing.

Catarina sets plates down on the island in front of us. "Eat it before it gets too cold." She glances at the clock on the microwave. "You've got school in twenty minutes. Hurry up!"

Fortunately, there are four bar stools so neither Dante nor I have to sit directly next to Dad. Why is it so embarrassing to sit in the same room as your parents right after you've had sex with your boyfriend? And they know about it? That's a rhetorical question. Everyone knows the answer.

"I'm running late too," Dad smiles at Catarina. "That was a wonderful breakfast. Too bad we can't do it more often."

"I'll cook this weekend," she reassures.

Dad stands and rinses his plate in the sink. "Will you two be joining us?" He looks right at me. "Or will you be on a road trip of some sort?"

"Oh, uh... yeah! I mean, no, we'll totes be here."

"Totes?" Dad smirks. "Can't you use the other two syllables? Words are free, you know," he says sarcastically.

"Obvi," I quip.

He shakes his head with infinite frustration. "I have to go." He kisses Catarina on the mouth and it turns romantic in like one second.

"Dad!" I whine.

"Mom!" Dante chuckles.

"Shut up, you two," Catarina barks. "Neither of you are in any position to make any comments."

Chapter 20

"I can't believe this!" I groan to Rox as she drives us to school.

"What?!"

"There's like fifty nasty posts about me on ChatBrat."

"Ashley?"

"Who else? Listen to this: Skye All-Slut is now the number one slut at North Valley."

"According to who?" Rox scowls.

"According to *Ash*-hole Masters, I'm sure."

Rox grins when I say it.

"And it goes on. How many guys has Skye slept with? All of them. Nicknames: The Original Girl Gone Wild. Slutmuffin. Slunt Truck. Putrid Gash. The Town Pump Dump. Jism Schism. What the hell is that?" I shake my head. "Semen Queen. Oh, geez, there's a bunch more. Skye's Favorite Sexual Position: Doggy, as in, with dogs. Sometimes horses, but only to give them blowies. The doggies give her anal. Skye's Greatest Sexual Accomplishment: Once sucked off Katie Chang's Saint Bernard named Sasha."

"Does Katie Chang even have a Saint Bernard?"

"Who knows." I scroll through more posts on ChatBrat. "More 70s porn photos."

"Am I in them?"

"No. But there's a guy wearing a space suit in one."

"What? I have to see that," she laughs.

"Wait till we hit a red light. It's not worth dying over."

"When I see it, I bet I'll die laughing," She chuckles.

When we stop at a light, I show her the photo.

She laughs, "Oh my god! The space suit is all sparkly silver satin! And he has a plastic globe helmet! You should save this one!"

I frown at her. "Nokay."

"Don't 'nokay' me! Look at that sweet Jetsons dress you're wearing! The hem looks like a silver hula hoop!"

"But it's not me."

"It's not *you* you, or the dress is not you?"

I frown at her, "Neither."

"Save it anyway. You'll laugh at it in thirty years."

"As if," I smirk at her. "Hey, can I ask you something?"

"Anything."

Reluctantly, I say, "When Ashley posted that very first post, the pic with me and Dante, the one calling me the town pump, were you one of the two people other than me who dissed it?"

She instantly glares at me. "Are you kidding? I dissed the shit out of that noise, galpal!"

"Yeah, but did you diss it because you were mad at me or because of Ashley's nasty comment?"

She slumps, "Do you seriously have to ask that? I would *never* do that to my BFSF." She's totally telling the truth.

I grin, "Thanks, Rox. You're the BBFSFFF ever."

"Bee *bee* Eff Ess Eff *Eff Eff?*"

"Bestest Best Friend Since Forever *FOR* Forever," I giggle.

"Awww, Skye, I would never throw you under the bus like that. Ever. Got it?" She glares again, awaiting my response.

"Got it," I grin.

Satisfied, she smiles.

The light turns green and we start moving again.

Feeling better, I go back to scrolling through posts on my phone. I groan, "Someone made an animated gif with my face in it!"

"What's the gif?" Rox concentrates on the road.

"Some nature video of two frogs humping. My smiling face is on the bottom frog. The frog on top keeps making this cartoon speech bubble that says 'Rippit'."

"Rippit? With two Ps?"

"Yup."

"How many kisses are all these posts getting?"

I scroll through them, glancing at the numbers. "Not many. People must be getting bored with all the slut hate focused on me."

"Yeah," Rox snorts, "They'll probably start accusing you of posting all this stuff yourself and out you as an attention whore."

"I know, right?"

"But you know it was Ashley."

"Of course it was. But she'll deny it."

She groans, "This needs to stop. What happened to you talking to Bill Gates?"

"I'm talking to him today," I grin mischievously.

oOoOoOo + O+O+O+O

"So, where's Bill Gates?" Rox asks me at the beginning of lunch.

"Here he comes now," I say, looking over her shoulder.

We stand beside my locker, which no longer says SLUT in red lipstick. I'm sure the janitor had to clean it yesterday.

Rox spins around. "Where? I don't see Bill."

A bunch of freshman guys and girls walk to and from their lockers, opening them or closing them as they drop off books and binders and head out to eat.

"Hey, Skye," Jason Carpenter says as he walks up to his locker. He wears a Marvel Avengers sweatshirt with Captain America, Iron Man, and whoever the other guys are on the front.

"Hey, Jason," I smile.

"You're Rox, right?" Jason says to her.

"Yeah. What was your name again?"

"Bill," I say.

Jason's confused, "My name's not—"

"Inside joke," I smile at him.

Rox goggles, "Oh! You're good at computers, right?"

"I guess," Jason says. "Not like Trevor and Stuart and Brian."

"Who are they?" Rox asks.

"Let's go meet them!" I smile.

At the entrance to the library, Rox says, "I'm not spending lunch in the library, Skye."

"You don't have to," I smile.

"Oh, good."

"Wait right here." I lead Jason into the library. We emerge with Trevor, Stuart, and Brian a minute later. They all wear the same outfit: nerd default. Jeans, tennis shoes, and some sort of colored T-shirt with a video game logo on it. Xbox. DragonAge. Oh wait, Trevor is wearing a My Little Pony shirt with four different horses on it. I guess Trevor is a Brony? Who knew.

"This is Rox," I say to them.

The three freshman boys stare at Rox like she's a Playboy centerfold, which she basically is.

"Rox," I say, "This is Trevor, Stuart, and Brian. We're taking them to lunch."

"We're what?" she scowls.

"Let's go, guys." I lead everyone out to the parking lot.

"You so owe me," Rox hisses in my ear.

We all pile into her Toyota. The four boys are so small and lanky, they easily squeeze into the back seat. On my suggestion, she drives us to Del Taco for lunch. It's cheap and quick. We park and everyone piles out of the car.

"Wow!" Jason says. "I've never been off campus for lunch!"

"With senior girls!" Trevor giggles nervously.

Stuart and Brian just stare at Rox and giggle like Beavis and Butt-head.

I hold the door for everyone and we file inside Del Taco.

The line of customers is long, but the kitchen staff is working double time. After a few minutes in line, I order for everyone and pay for all of it. Jason grabs a booth for us and we all sit down. Jason sits next to me and Rox (I think he made that happen on purpose), and the other three sit across from us. It's a tight fit in the booth, but we're all small, so it works. Jason and Trevor fetch our trays when the food comes out all at once. Everyone unwraps tacos and burritos and starts eating.

"I never pegged you for a Brony," I say to Trevor.

He pauses his taco halfway to his mouth and glances at his shirt. "Oh, it's not a Brony thing. It's the Four Ponies Of The Apocalypse. It's from Robot Chicken."

"I love that!" Brian says.

"Yeah, yeah!" Stuart grunts like a gremlin.

"What's Robot Chicken?" Rox asks innocently.

What follows is a fifteen minute lecture from the Four Freshman Of The Apocalypse about the genius of stop motion puppet comedy using action figures. Highlights from the show include: Voltron Got Served! The Emperor's Phone Call. Golden Girls In The City. Mario Meets The Parents (as in, the Mario from Mario Brothers). Law & Order: KFC. And most confusing of all, Sailor Moon Is Hot. After mentioning that one, the four boys stare at Rox and titter like guilty mice. Most of the Robot Chicken lecture goes over Rox and my head. At one point, I lean into her and mumble, "You shouldn't have asked." Eventually, the Robot Chicken chatter fades into reminiscent chuckling from the boys.

"So, guys," I smile at them, "I need your help."

"Anything," Jason says earnestly.

"Sure, Skye," Trevor adds.

"Okay," Brian says.

"Yeah, yeah!" Stuart grunts.

"I know you all are good with computers."

The four of them spend the next five minutes debating who's better at computers. You'd think they were comparing dick sizes based on their bravado and trash talking.

"Okay!" I interrupt. "You guys are all awesome with computers. Way better than me and Rox. But can you hack ChatBrat?"

Their eyes all glow with evil glee as they glance between themselves with jittery agitation. They seem to have an entire discussion solely by eye movement, almost like a hive of bees communicating through a complex series of body movements. Then as one, like possessed horror movie children, they all slowly swivel their heads to stare at me and Rox. I half expect the boys to begin cackling wickedly as their lips peel over needle sharp teeth the moment before they attack like a pack of piranhas and eat the two of us.

Jason mutters malevolently, "We've got this."

Just when I've reached maximum creep out, Stuart grunts his gremlin grunt:

"Yeah, yeah!"

Chapter 21

Ashley Masters is expelled from North Valley High two weeks later. The reason?

Cyber bullying. Real Bullying. Slut Shaming. Unethical Conduct. Violation of School Cell Phone Policy. The list goes on and on.

Jason, Trevor, Stuart, and Brian were able to crack through ChatBrat's security after only two hours of trying. They traced every last post to the IP address and phone of Ashley Masters. Every last post. They took screenshots of everything and emailed it all anonymously to Principal Brown. The police got involved. There was a rumor that Ashley would go to jail, but I think someone made that up.

Like I predicted, the owners of ChatBrat never responded to any communications sent to them by the school. They're in Latveria. Why would they bother?

Shortly afterward, Principal Brown announces that usage of ChatBrat is now banned from North Valley, and anyone caught using it will have their phone confiscated for the remainder of the school year.

Do I emerge as some heroic figure in all this?

No.

People call me a rat and a snitch and a do-gooder. Who knew being a do-gooder was a bad thing?

At least they stop calling me slut.

Eventually they stop calling me anything.

I succeed in fading from the limelight, which is all I wanted.

The only person who calls me names anymore is Dante Lord.

He calls me *Cielo* every single day. First thing in the morning, when he texts me randomly during the day, when I come home from school, and when he says goodnight. And during sex, duh.

Dante continues to live with us throughout the school year. Dad completely accepts him. He doesn't call him 'son', but I don't blame him. It would sound kind of weird if he did. And it's not like Catarina calls me 'daughter'. Dante and I don't flaunt our relationship in front of our parents because, well, *that* would be too weird. But we're more in love today than the first time we called each other *mi Amor*.

With Dante's help, I study diligently for the December SAT. I make sure to get good sleep the entire week beforehand. It's hard at first because stressing about the upcoming StressAT keeps me up at night, but Dante helps with that. There's nothing like regular lovemaking to help release tension. We do it in the afternoons, in my bedroom, before our parents come home. Sometimes we use the guest bedroom. Sometimes we use the kitchen. Sometimes the living room. Sometimes the garage. You gotta try every room, right?

Anyway, I take the SAT in December and do good on it. Do I score over a 2,000? Heck no! But I come close. And I do way better on the math than last time, thanks to Dante. Well, and maybe a little to Marvin the math genius, and poor Luke, who I've made peace with.

Oh yeah, I also fill out my college craplication to SDU and submit it well before the deadline. My personal statement is titled Why I'm Ready To Soar. I'm really happy with how it turns out.

The only thing left hanging over my head is whether or not I get accepted to SDU. SDU is a competitive school. With my decent grades and decent SAT score, it will be close. Fingers crossed!

If I don't get accepted into SDU, I can always travel the world with Dante.

My pink on black motorcycle helmet resides in a place of honor on the corner of my desk. The pink studded Vixen leather jacket hangs on the back of my bedroom door where I'll always see it. Both are a constant reminder of the new adventures that await me and the man I'll share them with.

Dante Lord.

Epilogue

The misty morning clouds part overhead, revealing an endless blue sky.

A rocky alien world surrounds me. Strange upside down rock formations carved by the wind defy gravity. Ancient vegetation that looks like it's from dinosaur times. Puddles of fresh rainwater everywhere in all the pocked and gouged stone. Some of the pools are big enough for several people to bathe in.

Mount Roraima, Venezuela.

The roof of the world, and we're on top of it.

Off to my left, a rainbow falls below the horizon, pouring color onto the jungle below.

"Isn't it beautiful?" Dante asks.

"Incredible," I gasp.

Ten hours in the air from LAX to Caracas, Venezuela. Fifteen hours by bus to San Francisco de Yuruaní, which included a stop to register at a military checkpoint. Another hour by hired car to the trailhead in Paraitepui. A day and a half of hiking through steamy jungle to reach the base of the peak. The whole time I'm waiting for the Jurassic Park dinosaurs to jump from the bushes and eat us, but they never do. Another half day to reach the flat summit roof.

Then we're on top of the world.

Dante leads the entire way. He's been here before.

"This place is magical," I say as we hike across the rugged sky-high terrain.

We've already passed a pair of backpackers on the summit. Yesterday, on the hike to the base, we passed several other groups. It's the dry season, which means not *as much* rain, but also tourists. Well, the hardcore outdoor adventure kind. One group hiking out greeted us with friendly smiles. They were French, and spoke little English, so we stumbled through conversation. But we all sat and talked while we shared trail mix and energy bars. When we realized that one of the French women spoke Spanish, we switched to that and she chattered away about how amazing the top of the mountain was and how they spent the night on it and they heard something stalking around in the dark. I asked if it was *dinosaurios*, but she laughed and said she didn't think so.

Despite the slight presence of people up here on the summit today, it still feels like we're on another planet. Totally alone.

"You know," Dante says as we hike, "for a long time people thought that Arthur Conan Doyle based his story The Lost World on Mount Roraima."

"I thought that was a Spielberg movie."

He grins, "I've actually seen that one."

"Oh," I giggle. "So, does that mean there are dinosaurs living up here?"

"Not that I know of." He looks around nervously, "But you never know…"

"Stop!" I whine.

He chuckles, "Kidding."

After hiking across the summit for over an hour, we stop at one of the rock pools, take our packs and hiking boots off, and soak our feet.

"Wow," I moan. "That feels good. I haven't done this much hiking all in one shot."

"Good thing we worked you up to it with all that hiking back in L.A."

"Yeah." I lean back on my arms. "You know what?"

"What?"

"You never shared any of your poems with me." I kick my foot in the water and gently splash him.

"I've never taken any women up here either."

"Oh. Wait, you haven't?"

"You hiked here," he chuckles. "How many women do you think want to go all this way?"

"I don't know! I thought maybe one of your adventurer women that you know came here with you."

"You're the only adventurer woman I know," he winks. He leans over to his backpack and unzips one of the pockets.

For a second, my heart races. I hold my hand to the silver pendant necklace resting against the hollow of my neck. I've worn it every day since he gave it to me. The cloud and earth symbol. Heaven and Earth. *Cielo y Tierra.*

He sits up with his tattered notebook in hand and opens it. He flips through several pages. He clears his throat and turns to face me. His eyes are watering, sparkling emeralds that dance between my eyes and his notebook.

"I wrote this for you," he says. "I've never written a poem for anyone. I always wrote them for myself." He clears his throat a second time, head now hanging as he stares at the page. "Heaven and Earth." He opens his mouth to continue reading, but he has to stop and clear his throat a third time.

It's impossibly sweet. My eyes are already tearing, and I haven't even heard his poem yet.

He begins again:

"Heaven and Earth

One heart wanders,
weary head, weary breast
Lonely traveller,
never rest
Scour the earth
it was a test

Young heart floats,
isolated, all alone
Hummingbird,
heaven sent
Still at home,
not left the nest

Earth below, Sky above
Joined in water
They fall in love…

One heart alone
Two hearts a home
Wind and Drifter,
together… *roam*."

I'm speechless. It's the most beautiful poem I've ever heard. I lean over and we fall into each other's arms.

That evening, we set up camp in a remote corner of the flat summit. Clouds roll in as the sun goes down, blanketing every inch of the jungle floor far below in a puffy white blanket of mist. It reminds me of when you're flying over nothing but cottony clouds in an airplane. But we're on a huge hunk of mountain, high above everything.

It is so quiet up here. We are truly floating in paradise. We eat dinner and relax afterward, lying on our sleeping bags and staring up at the heavens. The twilight sky glows deep blue. Swept away by the moment, we kiss passionately. Eventually, all of our clothes come off and we're completely naked on top of our sleeping bags and foam pads, surrounded by the tranquility of endless unadulterated nature.

We make love on the top of the world, where heaven and earth meet, his back touched by the sky, mine firm against the earth.

After we climax together, we kiss softly and tenderly, our naked bodies tied in warm embrace.

He whispers into my ear:

"I don't know what the future holds, *mi Cielo*, but I know I'll be holding you every step of the way..."

"And I'll be holding you, *mi Tierra*..."

oOoOoOo + O+O+O+O

Heaven + Earth

Want to get an email when Devon's next book is released and receive a FREE Bonus Story by email?

Sign up here: **http://eepurl.com/B7crf**

or go to **devonhartford.com**

and **click** the **blue SIGN UP button**

Personal thanks from Devon Hartford:

Thank you, dear reader, for taking the time to live with Skye and Dante for a while! If you enjoyed Stepbrother Obsessed, please leave a review wherever you purchased this ebook, on Goodreads, or any book blogs you frequent. Be sure to tell your friends about it!

Contact me and let me know if you want to read more about Skye and Dante!!

Like me on Facebook

Friend me on Facebook

Follow me on Twitter @DevonHartford

Follow me on WordPress at devonhartford.com

ABOUT THE AUTHOR

Devon Hartford spent most of his life in Southern California frequenting many of the locations in One Year Love. Devon drew upon his passion for foreign languages while writing One Year Love. He is also an artist and musician, and drew upon his experiences with both while writing his previous romance series The Story of Samantha Smith and The Story of Victory Payne.

OTHER BOOKS BY DEVON HARTFORD:

ROMANTIC COLLEGE COMEDY:
Fearless (The Story of Samantha Smith #1)
Reckless (The Story of Samantha Smith #2)
Painless (The Story of Samantha Smith #3)

ROMANTIC HIGH SCHOOL COMEDY
Stepbrother Obsessed

BILLIONAIRE ROMANCE:
ONE YEAR LOVE - Part One
ONE YEAR LOVE - Part Two
ONE YEAR LOVE - Part Three
ONE YEAR LOVE - Part Four

ROCKER ROMANCE:
Victory RUN 1 (The Story of Victory Payne)
Victory RUN 2 (The Story of Victory Payne)
Victory RUN 3 (The Story of Victory Payne)

ACKNOWLEDGMENTS

A HUGE thanks to all my passionate and fantastic beta readers: Emaleth Morrigan (mermaid), Neicy Cassidy, The REAL Julie England, Hayley Picknell, Sandye, Tamara Clark, Renee Julian, Kimber, Mandy Jamerson, Michele McKenzie, Maria Combee, Jordan Bault, Crystal, Mylinda Abraham-Powell, Natasha Slater, Michelle Crane, Wendy Boyer, Rosanne Triegaardt, Muriel Garcia, Stephanie Svajgl, Steffini Walker Texas Ranger, Tania Clark, Sarah Patton (Yak enthusiast), Jini Perez, Her Highness Samantha Sheeley (Queen of All Typos), Bethanie Melander, Mandy Karsa, Nicki Hewitt-Hart, Megan C Christmas, Anna Lamonica, Julez, Jackie (Nikki), Gloria Herrera, Elizabeth P., Saakje, and The Ever Special Mel Bushell for invaluable feedback and encouragement! You guys rock the typo sauce!

Miss Constanza from Puerto Vallarta for help with the steamy Spanish dialogue!

Becs Glass for dedicated book pimping love!

Chrissy Zent Sharp for awesome book pimpery via The Book Whore-der's Delights. Be sure to check them out if you're a Romance reader.

Hayley Picknell for awesome reviews everywhere!

Everybody's ever luvin' cowbag, Lindsey Melia for ghetto ghood pimpin'.

And last but not least, for last minute typo-snyping of the highest order and in the face of great personal danger, I award a Typo Heart to **Colonel Melanie Starr**, the one and only **Comma Bomber**, who saved this mission from certain disaster at the 11th hour, but not without significant personal sacrifice on her part. Colonel, I salute you!

Thanks to everybody else who has helped make this book a reality!

Made in the USA
San Bernardino, CA
29 December 2015